# TRACE THE STARS

# LTUE Benefit Anthologies

*Trace the Stars*

*A Dragon and Her Girl*

*Twilight Tales*

*Parliament of Wizards*

*A Hero of a Different Stripe*

*Troubadours and Space Princesses* (forthcoming, 2024)

*Dog Save the King* (forthcoming, 2025)

# Other Works Edited by Joe Monson

# Other Works by Jaleta Clegg

*Dark Dancer*

*Autumn Visions* (collection)

*Brain Candy* (collection)

*Llama Tell You a Story . . .* (collection)

*Soul Windows* (with Frances Pauli)

## Altairan Empire series

Nexus Point

Priestess of the Eggstone

Poisoned Pawn

Kumadai Run

Cold Revenge

Jericho Falling

Obsidian Tears

Chain of Secrets

An Indecent Proposal

Phoenix in Flames

Redemption

## As Editor

*Wandering Weeds: Tales of Rabid Vegetation* (with Frances Pauli)

# TRACE the STARS

edited by
## Joe Monson and Jaleta Clegg

HEMELEIN PUBLICATIONS

*Trace the Stars*
LTUE Benefit Anthologies, volume 1
Second Edition

Cover artist: Kevin Wasden, kevinwasden.com
Cover art, *Tech Master,* copyright © 2003 Kevin Wasden. Used by permission of the artist.
Originally published on the cover of *Spacemaster: Future Law* (3rd Edition) from Iron Crown
Enterprises, May 2003.

Edited by Joe Monson and Jaleta Clegg
Cover Designer: Jaleta Clegg
Assistant Cover Designer: Joe Monson
Interior layout and design: Joe Monson
Proofreaders, for whom we are eternally grateful: Jeffrey Creer, Heather B. Monson

Managing Editor: Joe Monson
Publisher: Heather B. Monson

Published by Hemelein Publications, LLC., hemelein.com

Second Edition
First Hemelein printing, July 2023
10 9 8 7 6 5 4 3 2 1

ISBNs:
978-1-64278-039-0 (trade paperback)
978-1-64278-040-6 (ebook)

First Edition information:
    First Hemelein Printing. February 2019
    978-1-64278-000-0 (trade paperback)
    978-1-64278-001-7 (ebook)
    Library of Congress Control Number : 2019900003

*To Marion K. "Doc" Smith.*

*For inspiring so many of us
to become
more than we are.
You are remembered.*

# Foreword:
## Our Very Own Doc Smith

The idea for *Life, the Universe, & Everything* was formed in 1982, when Ben Bova was invited to Brigham Young University by the English Department. English professor Marion K. "Doc" Smith was assigned to be Bova's guest liaison in between official university events. He invited some of his students to hold what was later called a kaffeeklatsch with Bova, and this inspired those students to organize their own event in 1983. A tradition was born.

Since that time, thousands of students have attended and helped run the annual symposium. Many of them also worked on the *Leading Edge*, a semi-pro science fiction magazine created by many of those same students. Through the years, the annual symposium attendance has grown from a couple dozen to over 1700 in 2018. During this growth, it has expanded from focusing only on writing and editing to include art, creating new worlds, academic papers on genre topics, creation of games of all sorts, short film festivals, and more.

*LTUE* has resisted changing into just another fan convention. In order to differentiate itself, it remained focused on the academic and professional side, and it is now one of the largest (if not *the* largest) academic science fiction and fantasy symposiums in North America. Many people at BYU (and outside of it) have helped the symposium over the years: Linda Hunter Adams, Zinah Peterson, Betty Pope, Sue Ream, Sally Taylor,

Marge Wight, and the list goes on. I became involved around the eighth year, chaired the event two weeks before getting married, and have maintained a strong connection to it ever since.

However, if you ask those who were around before *LTUE* began—and for the first several years—every one of them will tell you that Doc Smith was the main reason the symposium is still around. He helped get the initial funding. He helped keep funding (from different sources) through the years. He defended the symposium before unsympathetic faculty and administrators multiple times (ask me about the "gambling" incident sometime). He mentored everyone who worked on the symposium until his death in 2002. He always had a smile, a word of encouragement, and a helping hand anytime we needed it.

Therefore, I thought it only appropriate that the first of the *LTUE* Benefit Anthologies be dedicated to him. We will always appreciate his legacy, we still miss him, and we will do our best to make sure *LTUE* is always something he can be proud of.

Here's to you, Doc! I hope you enjoy these stories as much as I did.

Joe Monson
February 2019

# Angles of Incidence

Nancy Fulda

"What are they?" Kitty asked.

The crystalline sculptures looked like gobs of lava halted mid-flow. There were thirty-five of them, spread about the room in a roughly circular pattern, each floating above a marble base and each about two meters tall.

"We don't know," said the refined, but annoying, man whose summons had destroyed a full afternoon's opportunity to work. Two hours trapped in a stuffy gravrail compartment, shooting across the blank desert of Kokkal IV, unable even to link with the computer aboard her docilely orbiting jumpship. Agony, at least from Kitty's perspective. If the urgently blinking message had come from anyone except the ruling eighth-minister of the planet's human contingent, she would have conveniently pretended she hadn't received it.

The elaborately dressed eighth-minister—his surname was Kahihatan—paused to finger the smoky amber glow of the nearest statue. Irritation colored his voice. "We were told only that the natives will not allow us to speak with the Evermother until we have 'assimilated the shadows'. Their words, not mine. And without the Blind Queen's authorization, there will be no joint habitation on the northern continent and no subsequent export of Kokkal IV's biological crystals to offworld investors. Miss Kittyhawk—"

"Please, just call me Kitty."

"Kitty." The word sounded distasteful in his mouth. "I cannot emphasize how important this export deal is to the cultural development of our society."

*Translation: I'm several trillion credits in debt and the voters will eviscerate me if I don't fix this.* Kitty resisted the urge to roll her eyes.

"You do realize," she said, slowly parading along the row of sculptures, "that I'm a xenoarchaeologist, not a galactic linguist or an astroanthropologist?"

"I fail to see the distinction."

"Well, the biggest one is that I work with dead things." Beautiful, intriguing dead things, like the elusive remains of Kokkal's extinct third species. To the excavation of which Kitty was aching to return. "Don't you have cultural experts for this sort of thing? These statues clearly contain a message of some kind. Decode the message, and the problem is solved."

Kahihatan waved a dismissive hand. "Our analysts have exhausted all possibilities. Sound shadows. Light beams projected through the sculptures. Magnetic resonance imaging."

"Well, if they've exhausted *all* of the possibilities, then there's really no reason for me to be here."

The eighth-minister conveniently ignored this observation. "As far as we can tell," he said briskly, "the sculptures are cheap hunks of polymer suspended in antigrav fields. They contain no hidden compartments and no subtle molecular encodings. They're not even difficult to manufacture."

"So it's a test."

"Or a linguistic barrier." Kahihatan sounded exasperated. "We get those all the time. Communication with the Kokkalns works pretty well on mundane topics, but it falls apart at the abstract level. During the inauguration of my predecessor, the Blind Queen's staff kept insisting that the seventh-minister's clothes were too bright. We tried everything: black robes, white on beige, neutral brown. We nearly suggested that he appear naked."

Now there was an appalling thought. "And?" Kitty prompted, hoping to move past the topic quickly.

"As it turned out, their objection had nothing to do with fabric color." The eighth-minister shook his head in deprecation. "It was his chain of office. We'd commissioned a new design, you see, and our out-of-system manufacturer included a communications relay for security purposes. We didn't realize it was active."

Kitty winced. Ah, yes, that would do it. The Kokkalns were infamously sensitive to radio and other low-frequency wavelengths, which was why Kitty had been denied contact with her ship while riding the shared-species gravtrain. To Kokkaln senses, the broad-spectrum pings emitted by a communications relay must have been garishly painful.

"Be that as it may," Kahihatan continued, "we've run out of ideas. So when we heard you were working on the Ll'tanii rehydration chambers along the wastelands... Well. They say you're the best."

"Yeah, well, they say a lot of things." Kitty strolled again along the sculptures. Thirty-five of them, arrayed in a circle. No two alike. She sighed and admitted, "In this case, however, they're probably right."

"We'll pay you for your time, of course."

"I doubt you could afford it." *I don't want money. I don't want this job at all.* Kitty would have walked out, if Kahihatan hadn't held authority to revoke her excavation license.

Blasted politicians.

The eighth-minister said primly: "If we set up an export chain for biological crystal, we can afford almost anything." Kitty waved a hand to shut him up.

"Fine. Have your goons find me a hotel or something. I'll see what I can do."

"You honor the Ministerial Government, Miss Kittyhawk."

Kitty doubted the eighth-minister would appreciate a detailed account of what she would have *liked* to do with said government, so she prudently remained silent. She'd been on a lot of planets, some of them exceptionally well-run. Kokkal IV showed no signs of ever having belonged to that group.

She walked another circuit along the floating statues. No two had the same shape, and yet there was a nagging uniformity about them, as though they'd all been generated by the same algorithm. No, Kitty decided, it was more than that. It was as though they were all parts of the same whole.

*Assimilate the shadows.* The Kokkalns' mysterious directive made no more sense to her than it did to Kahihatan. Although, the statues *were* casting shadows. Several each, due to the half-dozen unidirectional lights set into the ceiling. But why those shadows should be important, and how one should assimilate them, remained elusive.

"I'll need to speak with the Evermother's executives," Kitty said, cringing inwardly. Live aliens were neither her passion nor her specialty. She had a habit of offending them, and they had a habit of, subsequently, attempting to consume her. Either that, or they tried to vaporize the human settlements with which she was associated.

Kitty sighed and consciously refrained from banging her head against one of the statues.

Really, she got along so much better with dead things.

KOKKAL IV'S GRAVTRAINS RESEMBLED GIANT SEGMENTED WORMS MADE OF overlapping metal plates. The Kokkalns had been using them, or similar designs, for centuries, and very happily so, before the human settlers arrived and began complaining about earthquakes. There had been a seventy-year squabble, Kitty was given to understand, resulting in a 500-page handbook on seismically responsible gravitic manipulation, which the Kokkalns had proceeded to ignore. Fortunately, surface architecture had by then become optimized for shock absorption.

"How is it," Kitty asked as the gravtrain doors hissed closed, "that humans have been living on Kokkal IV for almost two hundred years, and yet no one's ever spoken with the Evermother?"

"It hasn't come up before," Kahihatan said in a faintly peeved tone. He crammed into the transportation compartment along with his considerable entourage of aides, secretaries, political hangers-on and security personnel, who alternately jostled for seats and eyed the pungent Kokkaln passengers with distaste. Kitty, crammed between an iron support rail and the rough outer wall, couldn't help thinking that the Kokkalns, lounging atop one another on the other side of the compartment, appeared far more comfortable than the stiffly-perpendicular humans. They also resembled a platter of oversized seafood, but Kitty hoped no one had ever mentioned that aloud.

"It *hasn't come up?*" Kitty asked pointedly.

Kahihatan cleared his throat uncomfortably. "When we built the first geothermic shafts, the Blind Queen's aides simply asked for a copy of our architectural schematics. When we requested rescue crews after the fourth-ministerial subterranean calamity, her aides didn't even consult her. And back when humans first landed on Kokkal IV, nobody thought to ask permission. The Kokkalns were pretty miffed about that, for a few decades."

Kitty, who'd been gulping a swig from her water bottle, nearly sputtered.

*Miffed.* Now there was the euphemism of the century. Humans and Kokkalns had, in fact, slaughtered each other on sight until second-minister Shallans managed to hammer out a linguistic common ground. Such as it was.

Kokkal IV, Kitty decided as the gravtrain pulled out of the station, was not so much a world at peace as it was a stunningly disjointed ecology. The russet-plated, vaguely crustacean Kokkalns resided in a vast network of subterranean water pockets that riddled the planet's upper mantle. They had little interest in surface ecology beyond scientific research and the occasional spawning expedition. The planet's human occupants were likewise unimpressed by the aqueous mantle pockets.

The result was a fragile equilibrium: Two cohabiting species, biologically disparate to the point of mutual incomprehensibility, who got along primarily by ignoring each other. A match made in heaven. Or thereabouts.

Kitty's head was beginning to hurt. "Explain to me again," she said to Kahihatan, "why you want to establish a settlement on the northern continent? You're only occupying 15% of *this* one."

"Because," Kahihatan said with the air of an exasperated parent, "Kokkal IV's native biological crystals do not grow well in arid southern environments. We've tried transplanting them. Believe me, we've tried! Specialized greenhouses, localized weather manipulation. Nothing works."

"So," Kitty said, following the thread to its conclusion, "if you want to establish the crystals as a major export product, you will need to cultivate and harvest them in the northern hemisphere."

"Exactly. Which would require local scientists. Support staff. Basically, an independently functioning colony."

"I don't understand. Kokkalns are utterly indifferent to surface politics. They hardly even venture above the third or fourth sublevel. Why would a second human colony be a problem?"

"Because it's a spawning expedition. By Kokkaln terms, anyway. Spawning is very important to them, you see, and falls directly within the Blind Queen's jurisdiction."

Kitty tried to wrap her head around this, failed, and filed it away in the mental box labeled *weird alien customs*. "Ah," she said sagely.

The train clattered downward, twisting and dipping in ways thought to be artistic to a Kokkaln's spatial sensitivities. Kitty, long accustomed to hyperspace distortions, found the ensuing sensations rather prosaic.

Judging from the insufficiently muffled moans, Kahihatan and his aides were less fortunate.

"So," Kitty prompted once the train hit a steady patch, "You require the Blind Queen's approval for your 'spawning expedition', but the Blind Queen refuses to speak to you until after you've, um, assimilated the shadows."

"That's right." Kahihatan gulped an anti-nausea pill. "It's a nightmare! Do you know how much funding we have tied up in preparations for the new colony?"

"Honestly? I don't care."

"Or how many jobs it will create?"

"I don't quite see—" Kitty was going to say *how that's relevant*, but was cut off as the train dropped into another spiral descent. She tried to map the pathways in her mind, corkscrews followed by staggered ramps, but quickly lost track. For Kokkaln parietal cortexes, which reputedly were capable of visualizing fourteen dimensions at once, it was probably the equivalent of pleasant elevator music.

Kahihatan moaned and gripped the support rails.

The gravtrain screeched, decelerated, and jerked to a halt at the first transfer station. Kahihatan and his aides gasped for breath, grumbling loudly about Kokkaln aesthetics. Kitty refrained from mentioning that the planet's human contingent was welcome to build its own tunnel network. Not only would it send Kahihatan into another soliloquy on finances, but she wasn't sure human tech could even penetrate to these depths. They were at the second sublevel now; the air was sticky and Kahihatan's aides were already fastening respirators over their faces.

The Kokkalns on the far side of the compartment began to disembark, clambering over each other with dozens of segmented legs. Incoming Kokkalns swarmed through the doors at the same time, clinging to walls and ceiling. These new arrivals were larger than those who'd boarded at the surface, with darker chitin and pronounced dorsal ridges. Kahihatan's security detail watched them suspiciously.

"Do not move suddenly," one of Kahihatan's aides said to Kitty. "Kokkalns in this size range are bull-headed and aggressive, and native laws do not prohibit brawling."

Kitty nodded and affixed her own respirator, blocking the wafting scents. Hot, humid mist sprayed into the compartment.

The nearest Kokkaln compressed and distended in languid rhythm, mouthparts undulating. Kitty watched from the corner of her eye, surreptitiously studying its anatomy.

*Assimilate the shadows...*

Kitty flipped open her datapad, checking to be sure the transmitter was disabled. She called up an image of the mysterious amber sculptures. They shimmered as she rotated the view, shadows springing to life against the pale grid of the background.

"What are you doing?" Kahihatan had leaned to peer over Kitty's shoulder. Kitty pulled the pad instinctively toward her chest.

"Searching," she said curtly. "Exploring. Trying to understand." When Kahihatan failed to take the hint and go away, she sighed and explained: "A shadow is essentially a mathematical projection. Compress a three-dimensional object, and you get a silhouette. Compress it along a different axis, and you get a different silhouette. I'm searching for patterns in the silhouettes."

"There aren't any. Our cultural analysts already tried that."

"I doubt I'm looking for the same kinds of patterns as your analysts." Kitty shifted the simulated light source, watching the shadows deform. Many species were fond of luminal art, but Kitty didn't expect to find any shadow puppets here. The Kokkalns were not a visual species.

"How long will it take you to decipher the pattern?"

Kitty shrugged. "That depends on what I learn from the Blind Queen's executives. It would help if I could view more of their architecture. Archaeologists learn a lot from architecture."

"And from junkyards," Kahihatan pointed out.

"Junkyards are overrated. They can teach you how a species lived, but not what they dreamed. Graveyards and spawning chambers are your best bet." Kitty continued tapping keys on her datapad. "Your analysts were looking for messages in the shadows, data, images, sequences of prime numbers, that sort of thing. Me? I'm looking for insight into the Kokkaln view of reality."

Kahihatan gripped the handrails as the gravtrain swung into motion. "I don't see how one set of sculptures will give you that kind of insight."

"By itself? It won't."

"Then how do you expect to—"

The train dipped sideways and swung into a noisy spiral, sparing Kitty from further conversation. She sighed, yearned wistfully for her abandoned excavation site, and continued examining the diagrams on her datapad.

Two hours and three transfers later, they reached the outer caverns of the Everqueen's bubble complex. Fourth-molt Kokkalns scanned them officiously as they exited the train.

The cavern seemed to vanish beyond the running lights of the grav-train, nothing but inky blackness punctuated by reddish blobs at the perimeter. Sweltering humidity crept past the edge of Kitty's respirator, mixed with the stench of Kokkaln biology.

"Adjust your translator several centuries back," one of Kahihatan's aides advised Kitty in a low voice. "Her Majesty's representatives are quite old."

"I wasn't aware that it mattered."

"Kokkaln neural pathways calcify during their first years of life. Young Kokkalns can learn the dialects of the past, but subsequent linguistic shifts become opaque to them."

"You're saying that teenage Kokkalns literally do not speak the same language as their parents?"

Was that a smile behind his respirator? In the darkness it was hard to tell. "It's not common knowledge. Most humans never venture beneath the first sub-level, and Kokkalns don't tolerate surface conditions well once they've passed their third molt. There's enough linguistic overlap between generations that most offworlders never even notice the variations."

"But given enough time, the dialects mutate beyond recognition?"

The aided nodded. "The language spoken by modern Kokkalns varies greatly from the language originally spoken by second-minister Shallans. We have to recalibrate the translators every decade or so. Not that we always get everything right," he hastened to add. "Speaking to a Kokkaln is a bit like trying to read old Earth Standard without a dictionary."

"I've done worse." Kitty examined her control box, found the dial for historical conformity, and set it back a few centuries. "How will I know I've got the right age for the Kokkaln I'm speaking to?"

"It's a bit like tuning a radio. Just wiggle the dial until something intelligible comes out."

"Great." Fortunately, the process turned out to be almost as simple as Kahihatan's aide made it sound. By the time they'd felt their way across the dim cavern, she'd keyed in to the conversation of the Kokkalns who'd exited the gravtrain along with Kitty's party. They were complaining about having to share a compartment with a crowd of ill-mannered humans.

Kokkaln public lighting did not extend much beyond the infrared range, but Kitty's eyes gradually adjusted. Soon she could see the massive Kokkaln blocking the tunnel to the inner caverns. It was old, well past the twelfth or thirteenth molting, with mottled calcifications along its dorsal plates.

"You have changed since your last molting, Minister," it said formally. "You have become quite tall."

Kahihatan bowed and spread his arms wide. "I am eighth-minister Kahihatan, newly elected in the place of my predecessor. I am honored to make your acquaintance." The translation unit at his waist emitted a series of Kokkaln clicks and whistles, accompanied by the occasional moist growl.

The Kokkaln seemed to grow larger. "I liked you better the last time you visited. Be greeted in the domes of the Evermother, eighth molt-child of the human called 'Minister'."

Kahihatan's aide leaned toward Kitty. "The Kokkalns believe all of the planet's human ministers are the same entity. Whenever we have a change of office, they insist on calling it a molting." He shook his head in puzzlement. "For an advanced technological species, they can be pretty dense."

Kitty glanced at the aide, a gangly fellow, barely more than a teenager, with precision grooming and a spine that never varied more than a few degrees from ramrod straight. "I don't think they're being dense," she said.

"Well, ignorant, then. They certainly don't seem to understand human biology."

"Perhaps they're just being polite. I doubt that a first-molt of any species would be allowed to speak with the Everqueen. So they courteously overlook our deficiencies."

The aide looked angry, then thoughtful. He glanced at the Kokkaln guarding the tunnel entrance, noting the biotech along its carapace. "You're very good at what you do," he said to Kitty after a while. "Aren't you?"

Kitty smiled and turned to observe the convoluted process of acquiring access to the deeper tunnels, which seemed to involve Kahihatan personally vouching for the parentage and accomplishments of each member of his entourage. When he reached Kitty's name, the Kokkaln raised its head.

"You are the human who will assimilate the shadows?"

Kitty nodded.

"It is fitting that you are so young. Perhaps the eighth-minister has not become completely decrepit in his latest molt." Kahihatan ruffled, and Kitty stifled a smile. She was beginning to like this Kokkaln. "Eighth-minister states that you desire speech prior to assimilation. Is it so?"

"If it is permitted, yes. I wish to speak with an executive of the Blind Queen."

"This will not help with the assimilation. The Evermother is older than caverns, older than water pockets. Her executives are but eggs without shell in the ripples of her glory."

"Nevertheless, I desire speech."

The Kokkaln hesitated. Kahihatan and his aides shifted uncomfortably. Kitty remained perfectly still, waiting for the alien's response.

"It shall be so," the Kokkaln said finally. It turned and issued a series of clicks which her translator was unable to decipher. Several smaller Kokkalns scurried away into the blackness. "I will guide you through the deeper tunnels. Inform me if you become distressed."

"Thank you," Kitty said. "May I know your name?"

The Kokkaln turned sharply and rose on its hind-segments. Kitty backed away, wondering whether she'd committed a social blunder.

"My name?" The Kokkaln arched its dorsal plates and seemed to sniff in disdain. "Your translation boxes mangle it badly. I will not sully my reputation by releasing it. You may call me by my function: Guardian."

Guardian turned and vanished into the tunnel. Kitty followed, trailed closely by Kahihatan and his entourage. The air grew thicker as they descended. Heat wafted upward. Soon Kitty's clothing was clammy and her hair stuck in wet clumps to her neck.

Kokkalns lined the tunnel, watching the trespassers with glittering eyes. There were only a few at first, but within a few minutes Kitty was pressing between russet-colored segments, ducking to avoid dangling appendages of aliens clustered two and three deep along the tunnel's ceiling. In the dim reddish light, they seemed like a single, massive creature, bristling with claws.

"Something's wrong," Kahihatan's aide murmured. "There shouldn't be so many." He glanced toward the guard detail. Their hands hovered above their weapons, heads swiveling in all directions.

"I have sent messengers ahead," Guardian said from his position at the head of the group. "The Evermother's executives await us in the Bubble of Assimilation."

"Bubble?" Eighth-minister Kahihatan pushed his way forward, voice rising several pitches. "Guardian, forgive me, but humans are not equipped to inhabit aqueous mantle pockets. Our bodies require oxygen, you see, and—"

"We have compensated for your inadequacies," Guardian said, unperturbed. "Proceed at your usual tempo."

Something rippled in the darkness. Guardian moved forward and the lower half of his body melted into the floor. No— not the floor. The tunnel sloped downward into steaming water. Guardian's body, mostly submerged, vanished with a moist flip of his tail.

"Wait!" Kahihatan objected. "You don't understand. We'll die in there!"

He tried to squirm backward, but the press of Kokkalns from behind was too powerful. Bodyguards pulled into formation, surrounding the eighth-minister with pistols drawn.

"Oh, for the love of—don't shoot!" Kitty said sharply. "Keep your weapons low. I'll try it first."

She stepped to the edge of the water, moisture beading on her face. Kokkalns watched her from the ceiling. The air was sweltering, and rancid scents crept past the edge of her respirator. Kitty took a breath and stepped forward.

Something pressed against her, flickering. The water parted in front of her foot. She took another step. And another. Water bulged outward, leaving a cushion of air around her body.

To either side, a pair of Kokkalns chittered, waving appendages as if to motion her forward. Something rippled at the edge of her vision, like a gossamer fabric that could only be seen in periphery. She turned her head, trying to catch sight of it. There, a fragile membrane of graviti-cally-charged particles pushing away the water. Clever.

Kokkalns moved behind her, manipulating devices she could not see. The water was as high as her waist, now. As high as her chest. Kitty stepped beneath the surface, and the overlapping voices of Kahihatan and his entourage faded away. Light gleamed from the membrane, soft and shadowless.

The world beneath the water was far more entrancing than the surface tunnels. Kokkalns swam in graceful arcs, ducking through caverns filled with coral lattices and sheets of luminous algae. Clicks and trills reverberated through the water, sounding far more melodious than the aliens' airborne speech. Kitty removed her respirator and found that she could breathe freely. She reached a hand toward the rim of her bubble, but quickly drew it back. The water was scalding.

"...highly unconventional," eighth-minister Kahihatan said, moving into Kitty's vicinity. Their bubbles merged as he approached, becoming a single unit. "We've negotiated with the Kokkalns dozens of times. They never brought anyone below the water's surface."

"You've never prepared to speak with their queen before, either. Perhaps the protocol is different."

"Miss Kittyhawk, I have a *lot* of experience with these creatures. They've never acted like this before. It's almost like..."

Dozens of Kokkalns had followed the procession into the water. No, hundreds. They crowded overhead, swimming in intricate clusters, with more still arriving. Guardian swished past, distinctive due to his dorsal calcifications. Cybernetics gleamed along his carapace, and an amplified version of his whistles penetrated the oxygen bubble. "You bring great excitement to our people, Assimilator. It has been many decades since the Evermother last surfaced."

"...like they expect you to speak with her *today*." Kahihatan concluded in a tone of rising panic. "I don't understand. We merely asked to speak with the executives, we never said you were ready to speak with the Evermother!"

Guardian circled their bubble, his movements somehow indignant. "You said you wished to speak with the executives prior to assimilation. All is in readiness. The Evermother stirs from her slumber."

"But we didn't mean to complete the assimilation *right now*. Miss Kittyhawk requires—"

"Miss Kittyhawk is the human who will assimilate the shadows. I do not see why this is so difficult."

"Because... Because—"

Kahihatan gestured incoherently. Kittyhawk laid a hand on his arm. "Guardian, is it possible to delay the assimilation?"

"The announcement is made. The Everqueen rises." The ancient Kokkaln swam in a tight circle. "Death and dismemberment await those who summon her frivolously."

"If we don't assimilate the shadows before she arrives, then we'll die?"

"You are young. It will not be difficult."

Guardian turned with a flick of his tail, leading the way to the deeper tunnels. He did not respond to Kahihatan's calls.

The humans continued down the tunnel in tight clusters. The conversation with Guardian must have been broadcast to all of the oxygen bubbles, because Kahihatan's entourage had pulled into agitated groups.

The security guards had their weapons out, clearly eager to retreat and regroup in the surface tunnels, but also clearly unwilling to start a firefight in the middle of a pocket of super-heated water. Kitty flipped through her datapad, searching for records on Kokkaln biology.

"This is all your fault!" Kahihatan hissed. "If you hadn't—"

"Quiet. I'm thinking."

"But you allowed the Guardian to presume that you were ready to begin the assimilation!"

"I told you, I don't have a lot of experience with live aliens. Mostly I specialize in dead ones."

"Pretend they're dead, then! Shall I have my security detail shoot a couple?"

"Please no!" Kitty lowered her forehead to the datapad. "Look. I appreciate that you're under a bit of stress right now, but I really need to concentrate."

Kitty increased her pace, pulling her oxygen bubble away from Kahihatan's. How did she always end up in these messes? She just wanted to dig up skeletons and reconstruct alien ruins.

*Assimilate the shadows...*

She didn't even know what assimilation meant to a Kokkaln, or whether the "shadows" were literal or metaphorical in nature. She was making progress in other directions, though. She was fairly certain that this shadow business was more than just a rite of passage or glorified IQ test. The Kokkalns were an eminently pragmatic species, and not prone to artificial barriers. If they claimed that assimilation was necessary in order to speak with the Evermother, then there was a legitimate, inescapable reason for it. Perhaps the queen's body emitted airborne toxins, and the sculptures contained an antidote? Kitty checked the materials analysis, but came up empty-handed. As far as she could tell, the stuff comprising the statues was chemically inert.

"Don't worry," said a voice at her elbow. She glanced up to find that Kahihatan's aide had approached, merging his oxygen bubble with hers. "We have a plan. If they become aggressive, we'll take the queen hostage!"

"How is that a plan for anything but suicide?"

"They're not going to risk their queen, are they?"

Kitty glanced at his name tag. "Mr. Johansen, your weapons will barely pierce the shell of a twelfth-molt Kokkaln like Guardian. The queen is centuries older than him. She must be huge."

"Um." Johansen drew his brows down, clearly discomfited. "Well, don't worry. We'll think of something."

They passed beneath a mountainous archway into a twining under-water cavern. "This is the Bubble of Assimilation," Guardian proclaimed, circling back toward the humans. "We now enter the Corridor of The Shadows."

Kitty rounded the curve and stood rooted, breath caught in her throat. The passageway was gigantic, so large that the upper regions faded into darkness. Kokkalns drifted in every available space, motionless as driftwood. Amorphous blobs hung in the water, huge enough to dwarf even Guardian. They glowed with a faint amber light, and after a moment Kitty jolted in recognition.

"The sculptures," she murmured, more to herself than to the other humans. "These are the originals. The ones given to Kahihatan were just replicas."

"It is so," Guardian affirmed, swimming placidly alongside Kitty's bubble. "These are constructed from the saliva of our artisans. The glow comes from a species of microorganisms that reside within the excretions."

"That's... interesting," Kitty said, moving toward the sculptures. "Are those the Evermother's executives?" A group of ancient Kokkalns, even larger and more encrusted than Guardian, lounged beneath the nearest sculpture.

"Yes. They await your approach."

As if by unspoken signal, Kitty's oxygen bubble flashed and expanded outward. The other bubbles followed suit, merging into a dome nearly thirty meters wide: large enough for Kahihatan's entire entourage as well as for the Blind Queen's executives.

"Speak in the language of the eldest," Guardian advised. "Among our people, the younger speak always after the manner of the elder."

Kitty took a breath and stepped toward the executives, adjusting the dials on her translator to the oldest possible setting. "I thank you for your courtesy," she said, hoping she was using the right phrasing. "My name is—"

"The Evermother will hear your petition for spawning," the largest of the Kokkalns said briskly. The clicks emanating from his carapace were so breathy that the translator clearly had trouble deciphering them. "Be warned. She has never received an offworld petitioner before. She will likely deny your request."

"If she does, would we be permitted to try again later?"

"If she denies your request, you will be dead. The Evermother devours the head and central organs of any who summon her unnecessarily. You should have known this."

Kitty cast a sour glance at Kahihatan. "Apparently *someone* forgot to do adequate research before beginning this project."

Kahihatan opened his mouth to object, but the Blind Queen's executive was still speaking. "We understand that you desire speech prior to assimilation. The Everqueen rises. Voice your questions."

"Right. Well, mostly, we require information as to the nature of assimilation."

"You must assimilate the shadows before you may speak with the Evermother."

"Can you explain the function of the shadows?"

"Speech with the Evermother is impossible until the shadows have been assimilated."

Kitty rubbed her forehead. "Right. Okay, let's try a different tack. Who created these sculptures?"

"Our artisans built them when the Evermother devoured the last of her molt-mates. Your inquiries are senseless. The Everqueen rises. Assimilate the shadows."

"One more question!" The dispersing Kokkalns paused. Kitty looked around desperately. Surely there was a clue somewhere. There was always a clue. "What are those first-molts doing?" She pointed. Immature Kokkalns crawled along the surface of each statue, brushing abstract contours with their mouths.

"They are artisans. They adjust the shadows each generation, so that our connection with the Blind Queen may continue. It is a task only the young may perform."

"Only the young." Kitty trailed off thoughtfully. Guardian had said something similar when they'd met in the upper tunnels. He'd claimed that Kitty's youth made her well-suited to assimilation.

What did she know about first-molt Kokkalns? They were smaller than their seniors. They were better able to tolerate surface conditions. They had sophisticated mathematical skills and excellent spatial perceptions, and—

Their linguistic pathways hadn't calcified.

Kitty's heart skipped a beat.

"It's a language map!" she shouted, far more loudly than she'd intended. She whirled to face Kahihatan's entourage. "The Kokkaln language permutes with each generation. Typically young Kokkalns learn the language from their elders, but the Blind Queen is older than any other Kokkaln alive, and she almost never interacts with her subjects. So how would the younger generations learn her language?"

"By speaking with older Kokkalns who already understand it?" Johansen hazarded.

"That might work for a generation or two, but over time the phonetics would degrade. A non-native speaker tends to pronounce sounds differently. If you learn a language from a non-native, then teach it to someone else, who in turn tries to pass it on to a fourth student—"

"It all ends up garbled."

"Exactly." Kitty's eyes flitted to the sculptures, jumping from contour to contour. "These statues contain a mathematical map describing exactly how the phonemes have shifted over time."

"But that makes no sense," Johnson objected. "Phonemes don't always morph in the same direction, and new words are being added all the time."

"That might be true for human languages. But I'd bet my next three dig sites that Kokkaln speech evolves differently. Check your translation algorithms. I expect you'll find direct polynomial functions describing the progression of the language from each generation to the next."

Johansen frowned and dug into the records on his wrist-com.

Eighth-minister Kahihatan drew near. "So when the Kokkalns said we could not speak with the Blind Queen until we'd assimilated the shadows—"

"They *literally* meant that speech was impossible. If you don't understand the permutations in the language map, there's no way to communicate with a Kokkaln that old." Kitty's heart was racing. She felt like an archeologist on the verge of a giant discovery, almost as though she was back at the dig. All of the pieces were here. She just had to put them in the right order.

"Well?" Kahihatan demanded, brushing a speck of dust from his sleeve. "What are you waiting for? Run the permutations and recode the translators to speak the Blind Queen's language."

"It's not that easy. The algorithms are encoded within the statues, I'm sure of it. But there are hundreds of phonemes in the Kokkaln language, and only three dimensions in each statue. The answer must have something to do with the shadows, but I can't—"

"Miss Kittyhawk, we're in a rather urgent situation."

"I'm thinking, I'm thinking!"

"The Everqueen has risen," the executive said. The Blind Queen's aides dispersed, passing through the edge of the oxygen bubble. They joined the eerie mass of aliens drifting overhead, utterly motionless. Silence fell across the water. The entire world seemed to hold its breath. Kitty moved toward edge of the oxygen bubble, peering toward the depths.

Something massive moved in the darkness. Currents struck the oxygen bubble, rippling the boundary. Mud rose in swirling clouds. One segment at a time, a gargantuan Kokkaln lifted itself from the deeper caverns. Truck-sized foreclaws pulled the creature forward. Eyes larger than space shuttles gleamed through the murk – scarred and pitted, obviously sightless. The creature struggled upward, filling the cavern. Several of the giant glowing sculptures were displaced by its bulk.

Sonorous clicks vibrated the stone, but of course Kitty's translator was unable to decipher them. Kitty sighed and wished for her quiet excavation dig. Mentally, she reviewed the list of things dead aliens did not do. Dead aliens did not misinterpret your intentions. Dead aliens did not bite your head off if you woke them unnecessarily. Dead aliens did not—

"Miss Kittyhawk!"

Eighth-minister Kahihatan was clutching her sleeve. She shook him off and concentrated on the sculptures.

*Assimilate the shadows...*

She understood the purpose of assimilation now. She was supposed to internalize the message of the sculptures and use it to communicate with the Blind Queen. But what about the shadows? *Which* shadows? In this murky dimness, lit by their own internal glow, the sculptures cast no shadows.

"Watch out!" Kahihatan's aide darted forward, trying to impose himself between Kitty and the creature now looming over them. The antennules near its mouth rippled, testing the water. The beast arced its spine and, almost casually, snatched one of the drifting Kokkalns out of the water. Its head and upper thorax vanished with a *crunch*.

Kitty gripped Johansen's shoulders and moved him to the side so that he was no longer blocking her view.

Thirty-five statues. But what did they mean? How would the Kokkalns, a species with excellent spatial cognition, encode phonetic drift? She ran a couple of trial calculations, but came up empty. The phonetic landscape was too complex.

The Blind Queen snatched another of her subjects from the water. Her body, like the statues, was a three-dimensional structure, but it contours were determined by dozens of variables: the arch of her spine, the angle of her joints, even the amount of food in her stomach.

*Assimilate the shadows...*

Of course.

"The sculptures don't *cast* shadows," Kitty said, glancing at Kahihatan. "The sculptures *are* shadows. They're three-dimensional projections of a multi-dimensional space."

Kahihatan's response was neither coherent nor, Kitty suspected, appropriate for polite company.

Johansen was more concise. "Mother of demons. You mean the Kokkalns exist in multiple dimensions?"

"Of course not. I'm talking about a *mathematical* space. Each sculpture is a compression along a different axis. That's why they all seem like pieces of the same whole."

Kitty pulled up the models on her datapad, briskly tapping at keys. "Kokkalns can envision up to fourteen dimensions, right? But of course they can't build a fourteen-dimensional statue. They have to use lower-order representations."

"But that makes no sense!" Kahihatan said, cringing as the Blind Queen drew nearer.

"Doesn't it? Humans use the technique all the time. Paintings, road signage, data screens, you name it. We create a 2D image to convey a three-dimensional concept."

The Blind Queen lurched forward, feelers piercing the oxygen bubble. Kitty dropped to one knee, hardly aware of the chaos around her. Humans screamed and scrambled backward. One of Kahihatan's aides backed straight through the edge of the bubble and had to be retrieved from the scalding water.

The models on Kitty's datapad came to life, converging into a tangle of lines and cross-sections, a multi-dimensional structure her mind had no chance of comprehending. She opened a database of Kokkaln dialects, keying commands that would map recent phoneme shifts onto the contours of the wireframe structure. In moments, the pad's AI found a pattern match.

"Dr. Kittyhawk!"

The Everqueen loomed overhead, forelegs extended. Kitty synced the datapad to her translation unit, hijacking its input/output streams. It was almost like rerouting the communications relay on her jumpship. Except without the giant head-crushing alien.

"Evermother!" Kitty cried, waving to draw the beast's attention. "Evermother, can you hear me?"

She waited, heart pounding, while the pad converted her translator's output into a series of resonant whistles. The humongous creature paused. The head lowered. Kitty tensed, ready to leap aside to avoid decapitation, but the outer mandibles did not extend.

Deafening clicks ensued, quaking the stone beneath Kitty's boots. Echoes bounced off the edge the cavern. "Who speaks? You are not one of my executives."

"I am a visitor to your world. I've come to petition for spawning rights."

"Why should a visitor wish to spawn?"

"Ah..." Kitty floundered. Should she explain Kahihatan's financial motivations? She doubted that projected fiscal returns would matter to a creature that ate its subjects and lived in underground caverns. "Perhaps it is best if you speak with eighth-minister Kahihatan. He is the leader of this group, and the initiator of the petition."

Kitty grabbed the eighth-minister's shirt, ignoring his frantic objections, and dragged him into position beneath the Evermother's gaping maw. He glared at her, but wet his lips and began speaking.

"Oh, wise and glorious Evermother, I come to you with a request which shall benefit both our peoples. The surface of this planet, as you most surely know, is a barren wasteland. But for creatures such as myself, there is much of value to be gleaned there. I wish to propose a joint-habitation arrangement of mutual benefit to..."

The speech droned on, and eventually Kitty stopped listening. She opened a side-screen on her datapad and flipped to the latest data dump from the Ll'tanii rehydration chambers.

"I hope you're satisfied," Kahihatan said several hours later, as they walked toward the surface tunnels.

"Why?" Kitty asked, barely looking up from her datapad.

"Weren't you paying attention? I'll have to resign as part of the colonization agreement. The Everqueen expects me to direct the colonization efforts personally."

"Ah. Well, at least you'll have your crystal exports."

Kahihatan huffed. *Translation: the whole point of those exports was to secure my re-election next quarter. Now I've exiled myself to a rustic colony site. This is not the way I planned things at all.*

Kitty smiled and kept walking.

"He'll get over it," a voice said at her elbow. Ministerial Aide Johansen was walking beside her, voice lowered to a conspiratorial tone. "To be honest, I think he'll do better as a colonial supervisor than as a planetary minister."

"Hm."

"So... would you like to grab a cup of coffee once this is all over?"

Kitty thought of her rehydration chambers. The energy outputs would be spiking soon. If she hurried, she might catch the final readouts in real time. "I really ought to get back to the dig."

"Some other time, then? When you... come into town for supplies? Or something?"

"I doubt I'll be on the planet for much longer." Kitty tapped the screen, noticing a couple of unusual readings. Now that was odd.

"Oh. Sure, ok. No problem."

Kahihatan's aide wandered away. Kitty glanced up as he left, noting for the first time the slump of his shoulders, the obvious disappointment in his expression. Blast. She probably ought to have phrased her rejection more diplomatically. Although, to be honest, she wasn't entirely sure what she could have changed. She sighed and thumped her head against the datapad.

Dead things. She was always so much better with dead things.

# The Road Not Taken

## Sandra Tayler

C araline sat at the spaceport cafe table and watched herself walk in. As always, it was a strange experience. The woman paused in the doorway until she spotted Caraline. Then she wove through the tables toward her. The other woman had gained some weight, softened. Caraline straightened in her seat, suddenly conscious of her slender frame and stylish pantsuit. Perhaps she should have dressed down more, to match the other woman's comfortable jeans and sweater.

"Hello Caraline."

"Hello Cara."

Prior to the accident she had been both Cara and Caraline depending on the situation. Now she was just Caraline. It was a simple way to distinguish, to declare some semblance of separateness.

A waitress appeared to take drink orders, then left them alone. Caraline flinched away from the eerily familiar eyes. Instead she studied their hands on the table. Her own were smooth with painted fingernails. Cara's were chapped with blunt tips. Cara's hands curled up as if they noticed the scrutiny and wished to hide. Caraline slid her own hands into her lap.

"So, I saw that you're having a showing next month," Cara ventured.

Caraline seized the proposed topic for conversation: "Yes. It's very exciting. I've lined up all the girls and the runway. Now I'm frantically finishing the clothing. The designs are all done, of course, but I keep seeing small things I want to change. This could really be my big break."

Cara smiled, encouraging and yet wistful. "Are you going to use that swirling dress I doodled during history?" Cara blushed, "We doodled."

Caraline remembered the dress. She remembered drawing it out of boredom. That had been back when she was singular instead of plural. Now two women remembered drawing the dress.

"Yes, I'm using the dress. I found the most heavenly blue Rigelian Spidersilk. It looks like the ocean."

Cara's sigh was full of longing. "I wish I could come to the show."

Caraline did not respond. She did not want Cara at the show. It would be . . . awkward. It would also violate their agreement to stay out of each other's lives. Cara knew this. Cara would not come even if the show had been on the planet where Cara lived rather than half a galaxy away.

The waitress returned with two identical drinks. "Here you go sweetie." The waitress set the drink on the table and paused a moment when identical faces looked up at her. "Are you two twins?"

Cara opened her mouth, but no words came out. They were not twins; they were a person divided. Caraline still remembered the nauseating lurch of the wormhole jump unlike any other she'd taken before. Only later had she learned it was caused by a bizarre accident which no one could yet explain. Instead of a single ship emerging from the wormhole, there had been two identical ones.

Caraline smiled her polite-but-busy smile and firmly said "Yes we're twins." She really didn't want to go through all the questions the waitress would have. The accident had been net-wide news. The whole galaxy was fascinated by the resultant pairs of duplicated people. Most of the duplicates continued to live in a swirl of media attention. She and a few others had chosen differently. The waitress smiled and went away.

Caraline turned back to Cara, studying her face openly now. That could be me. She faced the thought. Cara was thinking it too.

Caraline sipped her drink. "How is Ryan?" Ryan of the deep brown eyes and curly hair that her fingers itched to touch. The three years since the accident had surely not changed his broad smile and cheerful laugh. Caraline's eyes stung and she blinked a couple of times to prevent tearing. She could not cry here.

Cara's expression softened, "Ryan's doing well. He's a partner in Baxter Woodworks now. That means he doesn't have as much time for carving as he used to."

That was a shame. Caraline had always loved to watch Ryan's hands as he worked with wood. But owning the company was his dream.

"I'm glad." Caraline was glad. A tear rolled down her cheek. She met Cara's sympathetic gaze.

"I still miss him."

Cara nodded. "I can't imagine being without him. I've even started helping out in the workshop." Cara traced a droplet down the side of her glass with a single finger. "I never thought I'd enjoy woodwork, but I do."

Caraline wiped away the tear. She could not imagine enjoying woodwork. The dust got everywhere and the work roughened hands so that they snagged on fine fabrics. Caraline drifted her smooth hand across the sleeve of her silk jacket.

Cara's hand's twitched as if she too longed to touch the smooth sleeve.

Caraline took a big gulp of her drink. It was best if she didn't think too much of Ryan. He knew she existed, but did not need her. He had Cara who had given up her career to live with him on his rural world and help in his workshop. He did not want or love Caraline the up-and-coming fashion designer.

Caraline stared at the surface of the table, noting every dent in the surface. She wanted to talk to this other version of herself, to hear about her life, but she did not know what to say. At the time of the accident it had seemed almost a boon. She no longer had to choose between the man she loved and the career she longed for. The two of her had drawn straws.

But she did choose. She did not get to be both. Everyone made choices, but only a very few had an annual meeting with their might-have-been self.

"Perhaps these meetings are a bad idea," Cara spoke Caraline's thought aloud.

Caraline looked up and studied Cara's face. "They probably are," Caraline agreed. "But could you stand not knowing?"

Cara shook her head.

Each woman took a drink and studied the other.

# Log Entry

## Kevin J. Anderson

According to his brief service record, Cadet Connor Pardee was a good, if unremarkable, recruit. One of his spaceflight instructors made a notation that he possessed "a reasonable amount of potential."

Connor's actions after his death, however, made him a hero lauded in all the Corps historical archives.

IN THE DOGFIGHT OVER A SUN-GRAZER ASTEROID, THE CORPS SCOUT SHIP was woefully outnumbered. Four unmarked smuggler vessels closed in to intercept the cadet before he could transmit a signal back to base. The smuggler ships had been stripped of all insignia and equipped with three times their original complement of armaments. They opened fire. The cadet's ship spun through a wild course, launching potshots as it tried to evade the pursuers.

From their heat tunnels in the cracked surface, the ffrall watched with interest. In the black vacuum sky above the asteroid, the battling spacecraft were merely flashes of light, hot maneuvering rockets, and blazing energy bolts.

The ffrall were a race of liquid energy beings, interconnected nodes of sentient power. For the last half cycle—as the asteroid soared away from the sun, cooling in the chill of space during its long, lonely year—the ffrall had observed the activities of humans. Ships streaked overhead, bright lines against the backdrop of stars. A few had landed on the asteroid and erected structures, a base from which they launched more ships. The ffrall did not understand.

They inhabited catacomb cracks leading to the asteroid's warm radioactive core, from which they drew energy. Each cycle, as their rocky home passed through the star's blazing corona, the asteroid flexed and heated, charging like a battery. The ffrall would commune during the long cooling journey up to aphelion, the asteroid's farthest and coldest point from the sun, then hibernate to hoard their reserves. The creatures would awaken only when the asteroid plunged again to a warmer part of its orbit.

Soon they would hibernate, but before their long dreaming began, the ffrall wanted to understand these odd strangers.

The dogfight overhead continued, the unmarked ships launching a concerted barrage against the now-damaged Corps scout. With a direct hit on its lower hull, the scout careened out of control. An electromagnetic signal burst out, which the ffrall heard through their extended senses.

"Emergency! This is Cadet Connor Pardee. I'm in trouble. I've stumbled upon a nest of asteroid pirates. They've got me in their sights. Please, anyone in range—I need immediate assistance. I know this signal won't reach base for days, but if there's anybody out there, my coordinates are—"

Another shot from the asteroid pirates knocked out his transmitter. Leaking fuel and out of control, the scout ship crashed into the rocks, rebounded in the low gravity, then tumbled before grinding to a halt. Atmosphere gushed out from hull breaches like arterial blood. The ship lay motionless, systems already cooling.

The four unmarked smuggler vessels circled slowly. One swooped low to confirm the kill. After conferring for a few moments on a coded channel, the raiders sped back to their base on the far side of the asteroid.

Oozing out of their cracks and glowing with internal energy, the ffrall went to investigate.

CADET CONNOR PARDEE'S LOG ENTRY

The Academy is everything I thought it would be, as hard and as joyful, as challenging and as rewarding. The training is relentless, and the instructional classes are harder than anything I ever crammed for in civilian university. No matter how much you read ahead of time, no matter how much you exercise and mentally prepare yourself, you just plain can't be ready for this.

I was talking with one of my fellow cadets, Daniel Jones, and he nailed it. He said, "I never knew how much I could sweat before the sun came up. I never knew how hard I could run in the pouring rain. I never knew how much sleep I could go without. I never knew how much I weighed until I carried my weight in a pack on my back. I never knew how much I could miss everyone until they were so far away. I never knew what my limits were until I looked behind me and watched them disappear in the distance."

The food is terrible, but after a hard day nothing could taste more delicious. The beds are uncomfortable, but I've never slept so well in my life.

The people here are the same mix you'd encounter on the outside. Sure, some I like better than others, but there's a difference: Here, even if I don't see eye-to-eye with someone, even if I actively dislike one of my fellow cadets, each of us knows we can depend upon the other with our lives. Really. Comrades in arms, and all that. It's a tangible thing.

We do speed-timed suitup exercises, explosive decompression drills, and simulated combat runs modeled after actual splats from the First Pacification Wars. I've nailed flight tests on seven different models of spacecraft, and I'm cramming how to repair every one of them. The Corps won't let you fly a ship solo until you know every circuit, every cog and linkage, every rivet on every hull plate. It's a lot to remember.

Funny how you start to realize obvious things. I've never loved my mom and my sister more. I look forward to their transmissions as much as any kid ever anticipated a Christmas morning. Even when they don't say much of anything at all, the sound of their voices and the expressions on their faces warms my heart. "How are you? I am fine" never sounded so good.

Last week my mother shipped a package of home-baked cookies —my favorite, butterscotch oatmeal. Even with military subsidies, sending the package probably cost her a month's rent. I shared them with my buddies, and we licked every last crumb from the wrapping.

I know my father would be proud of me. Maybe he's watching up there from somewhere between the stars. He talked about the Academy ever since I was eight years old, and he counted on me entering the Space Corps, just like him. He had the good fortune of serving during the Long Peace. Never once saw combat, not even a police action to quell a minor revolt on an unruly colony planet. When telling stories, he called the timing "bad luck," but I think Mom was relieved. He died at the age of forty-nine in a stupid loading-bay accident. The power source on a gravlifter failed, and a cargo pallet of terraforming dozers dumped onto the workers below. Because he'd been killed in the line of service, my father received a posthumous medal, and Mom got an extended pension.

Times are a lot rougher now. Since the defense corps is spread so thin, asteroid pirates, smugglers, and other unsavories have become more than a nuisance. They hit civilian cargo ships, passenger liners, even colony transports full of wide-eyed settlers. Pirates blast holes through the hull, decompress the whole ship and let their victims suck vacuum. Then they go aboard, ransack the hold, even pick the pockets of the floating corpses. Not very nice people.

Once I graduate, I'll keep those scumbags in line. If I nail my next set of trial runs, I'll get my scout pilot cert, and I might even grab command of my own ship.

Then those asteroid pirates better watch their butts!

WITH SMALL DISCHARGES OF ELECTRICITY, THE FFRALL CREPT ACROSS THE uneven ground, envelopes of crackling static moving of their own volition. The ffrall surrounded the crashed ship and studied its exterior by flowing over the conductive metal hull plates. They tasted the shape of the craft, found where the hull had been broken open, where the engines had been burned.

The ffrall oozed through gaping holes to the interior. The crashed ship was interlaced with circuits, power conduits, and a diagnostic sensor array. The energy creatures easily followed these pathways, sniffing information, gleaning residual power traces.

All of the ship's primary circuitry was gathered into a single computer center in the smashed cockpit. Once the ffrall realized that the memory records were a form of communication, they began investigating further. They consumed and downloaded the information. Seeking clues and cross-references, they began to digest the log entries, conferring amongst themselves and comparing their insights. Gradually they incorporated enough knowledge to understand this ship, its alliances and enemies—and its pilot.

The ffrall discovered that the spacesuited form, with its smashed faceplate and a jagged chunk of shrapnel punched through the body core, was a cadet named Connor Pardee.

CADET CONNOR PARDEE'S LOG ENTRY

The day I was accepted into the Academy was the happiest day of my life. And then it got better. I aced every class in basic training, and I'm totally ready to be deployed as a rep for the Corps. A genuine space cadet.

Most cadets consider the course on ethics and galactic law to be the dullest part of the curriculum. As fully empowered reps of the Unified Civilizations of Earth, we have to know the nuances of the various articles of independence, the code of unification, and interstellar commercial treaties.

They say new cadets are the most vigorous enforcers. Is that something to complain about? I intend to be one of them. As soldiers grow older, they let more slide, give a little more leeway, but I hope I can stick to the truth. It's a slippery slope—once you make a minor exception and let somebody overstep the bounds, the next time it gets easier.

Before the Pacification Wars, we all saw the price of lawlessness. Fanatics everywhere. The chaos got so bad that all the colonies, even with their fundamentally opposed religious and governmental philosophies, found common ground and came together under the banner of the Corps. My father instilled that pride in me, the reverence for law and order.

Smugglers and asteroid pirates are the scum of space, the dregs of any society. They twirl and dodge and sidestep with technicalities, as if the law were some sort of old-fashioned dance. And they leave way too many bodies and drifting ghost ships in their wake.

I don't intend to let them get away with it. Not me.

When I finally got my cert as a scout pilot, I landed an assignment to patrol the outer asteroid fields. And my own ship, my beautiful scout ship. I could go on and on citing her engine specs, fuel capacity, cargo and passenger load, max accel, firepower, docking requirements, air reserves, even the full food menu programmed into the dietary synthesizer. But that would be just repeating rote statistics (and it would make my personal log unspeakably boring). Having learned them all for my final exam, the stats are forever burned into my memory.

Right now my ship has nothing more than a call sign, XFE0017, a designation that nobody's brain can wrap around. By tradition, cadets don't christen their ships with a real name until after they've flown their first mission. I've already got my name picked out, and I'll take great pride in stenciling it on as soon as I land after my first patrol.

"Mongoose"—my father's call sign, the one he never got to use.

From the information in the scout ship's database, the ffrall gleaned knowledge of the vessel, absorbed how the engines functioned and how the weaponry worked. The energy creatures spread throughout the crashed ship, suffusing the systems and manipulating the atoms of the metal alloy hull and the polymer molecules in the circuitry.

With the care of artists working on an extravagant new project, the ffrall began to reassemble the ship back to its optimal state. The creatures had every instruction manual and every repair blueprint they could possibly need.

When they investigated closely, the figure inside the spacesuit displayed no life energy whatsoever. Its bodily functions had ceased, and cellular chemistry had begun to break down. The only residue was a bit of thermal energy, body heat, trapped within the suit but leaking out into the cold vacuum through the shattered faceplate and the massive chest wound.

Now that they understood and shared the ship's log entries, the ffrall knew the identity of the cadet, his life, and intricate details of his biology from the library database. After evolving, communing, and hibernating alone for so many cycles, they were intrigued to learn the passions and the scope of these humans.

One of the individual ffrall remained by the motionless body of the cadet. Because the spacesuit was insulated, the creature could not penetrate it electrically. Forming itself into a liquefied, shapeless mass, the blob of crackling energy poured through the crack in the faceplate, oozing into the gap and into the tissues of Cadet Connor Pardee.

This was another vital part of the learning process.

CADET CONNOR PARDEE'S FINAL LOG ENTRY

I'm not complaining, but this is really boring. Like watching sealant dry.

I couldn't wait until I got my assignment and flew away from the base in my scout ship. I had checked and triple-checked all the systems, by the book and then some. Even though one of the other cadets razzed me for being a mother hen, I wanted everything to go right for my first mission.

But now that I've been on patrol for four days, in and out of the asteroid belt two systems away from the main Corps base, I never thought it would be so . . . well, dull. After the first few hours, the asteroids all start to look the same. Space junk, planetary leftovers.

I'm amusing myself by imagining that one looks like a potato, another like a fish, one like a beehive. They're all pock-marked with craters, ridged from melting and reforming. They tumble along in random orbits, nudging each other, jockeying for position around the sun. I haven't found any excitement yet, but I'll keep patrolling.

The asteroid I'm currently scanning is a sun-grazer in an elliptical orbit, cooling off now that it's heading back out from the star. The most interesting thing so far is a set of anomalous energy readings. At first I was excited, thinking it might be a secret outpost of asteroid pirates, who are known to have major activity in this system. But the readings are off-scope, out of parameters. Wouldn't be the first time the Corps textbooks were missing a key appendix or two. The readings look almost like life signs, but this scout isn't equipped with scientific sensors to get the data we'd need.

I'll log it, and maybe somebody will come out to investigate. (Although these days the constant threat of pirates has put a crimp in most scientific work. A research base would just be too vulnerable to raiders, and the Corps doesn't have enough extra personnel to send troops for security.) Nevertheless, this is intriguing enough that I'm going to do a full mapping of this asteroid, cruise over the craters just in case somebody might be hiding down there.

Wait—something's wrong with the comm systems. I'm being jammed. What the hell?

I see domes, reactors, life-support shacks—and ships. Asteroid pirates, a full-blown base! Damn, I'm still being jammed! Uh-oh, they've spotted me. Marauder ships are launching, four of them. Even this sweet little scout can't outrun four souped-up raider ships. I'll try evasive action. I've got weapons, and I'm not going to go down without a fight.

They're shooting at me. That was close! I've got to get out of here and concentrate on my flying and fighting.

Log entry, signing off. When this is all over I have one of those great stories, just like my Dad always wanted to tell.

When the ffrall completed their repairs to the scout ship and sacrificed some of their power to reenergize the mechanical systems, the crashed vessel lifted gently.

The single ffrall that had infused the cadet's dead biological body repaired the crack in the faceplate and sealed the grievous injury where shrapnel had punctured the chest. Even after rectifying the physical damage, the ffrall could not bring back Cadet Pardee; however, it could animate the form inside the suit so that it was able to operate the scout ship's controls—and complete the mission.

The energy creatures had learned everything about the young man, his sense of honor, and his allegiance to the Corps. They had scoured all the details of galactic law. Now, the ffrall knew what they must do. The creatures would take it upon themselves to finish the cadet's obligations before they went into their hibernation state. Perhaps by the next cycle, when the asteroid heated up again, the ffrall might emerge as emissaries and contact the humans in the Corps.

Discharging themselves through the hull, the other ffrall left the ship, returning to their energy sockets where they would soak up the ebbing heat of the asteroid's core. Only the one ffrall remained inside the suited form.

The repaired scout ship set off to where Cadet Pardee had discovered the pirate base. From here, the smugglers would launch their raids on helpless civilian ships passing through the isolated system. The ffrall had long been aware of the strange settlement on the far side of their asteroid, but had avoided any contact.

Now Pardee's ship skimmed low over the surface, beneath the enemy's sensor net. The ffrall worked the cadet's body, lifting gloved fingers to activate precise targeting controls and prepare the weapons systems. As soon as the scout ship soared over the upraised lip of a large crater, the ffrall reacted. It was just like one of the simulated exercises stored in the computer database.

The four pirate ships were there, now refueled and ready to fly. The scout fired precise blasts, each one destroying an engine pod and leaving the enemy ships grounded. As the scout circled again, the ffrall carefully targeted the base's life-support sheds and eliminated them. Every step went like clockwork, by the Corps Manual.

Now the pirates had no way to get off the asteroid, and their air and power would fail within a few days. They would have to send out a distress call and surrender to the Corps.

Within the cadet's body, the ffrall did not respond to the pirates' shouted curses over the comm lines. Instead, it calculated how much longer its energy would last and decided it had just enough strength left to animate this body and take the scout ship to the nearest Corps base. Back home.

Coursing through the young man's nervous and circulatory systems, the ffrall was too much for the fragile human body, close to igniting cells on fire. Its own life energy was dwindling swiftly, but even as it faded, its memories and thoughts were linked to the other ffrall. It could still operate the ship's controls. It could complete the mission.

Because the gathered ffrall had repaired the ship's engines perfectly, and because the animated body in the suit was no longer alive (and therefore no longer vulnerable to extreme acceleration), the ffrall was able to fly much faster than any human could have endured.

By the time the scout ship reached the Corps base, the lone ffrall had dwindled to little more than a spark. As Cadet Pardee's ship delivered its appropriate ID signal and landed inside the main dock, the ffrall transmitted a synthesized recording. During the journey, it had patched together voice records from the log entries so that the words sounded as if they were spoken by the young man.

"This is Cadet Connor Pardee, delivering my report. I located a secret base of asteroid pirates and surprised them before they could launch their ships after me. I destroyed their ships and took out their life-support capabilities. They'll need somebody to pick them up. By the time a mopup squadron gets there, I don't expect they're likely to put up much resistance. Transmitting the coordinates now."

With the last flicker of its energy, the ffrall ended the report, "This is scout ship XFE0017, christened *Mongoose*—signing off."

INVESTIGATION SUMMARY—CLASSIFIED: RESTRICTED ACCESS

This report has many questions and few conclusions. Because no logical answers fit the recorded facts, I will simply state the data.

Cadet Pardee's information was valid. We dispatched a Corps squadron to the location of the suspected enemy base, where we easily rounded up thirty-seven prisoners, all of whom will be prosecuted to the fullest extent of galactic law. We have reason to believe this was an extremely important base, housing several of the most-wanted asteroid pirates. The information we gleaned from this operation could well shut down their whole network in the sector. This one victory probably saved thousands of lives.

However, we cannot figure out what Pardee did, or how he did it.

Our engineers and technicians have combed his scout ship and found many anomalies. The craft appears to have been severely damaged and then repaired. *Perfectly* repaired. Onboard diagnostics show that it was flown back to base at extreme acceleration, which would certainly have been lethal to any pilot.

Cadet Pardee was found dead in the cockpit, though his suit was intact. The autopsy found severe cellular damage, as if from extreme energy exposure. However, the actual cause of death appears to have been explosive decompression and deep trauma from a foreign object, presumably shrapnel, which was found still deeply embedded in his chest, though his skin was perfectly healed over it. His last transmission was made immediately prior to his arrival at the base, but our doctors insist that Cadet Pardee had been dead for several days before he landed in our docking bay.

I had the sad duty of informing Cadet Pardee's mother and sister of his death. Unfortunately, I was forced to be vague, because the details make no sense. I informed them that Cadet Pardee died in the line of duty and that he was a genuine hero. I recommend awarding him a posthumous medal of honor.

I do not wish for the mystery to diminish or taint in any way the service our brave cadet performed for the Corps. In some exceptional people, dedication to duty is so strong it survives even their physical death. We do not need to understand our dead to honor them.

I recommend that these records be sealed. Permanently.

# The Ghost Conductor of the Interstellar Express

### Brad R. Torgersen

A s planets went, New Olympia was a hopeful disappointment. The right size and mass—to roughly match Earth—it even orbited within the theoretical green zone of its yellow dwarf home star. Alas, similar to Venus, the atmosphere of New Olympia was choking and toxic. A problem that was not wholly insurmountable, given current bioengineering and atmosphere conversion science. But if there ever was to be a truly blue sky on New Olympia—and seas of water to match—these things were very far in the future. Humans had only been working on the problem for a scant handful of years, since the colony boat *Mainfront* arrived—following its two century journey from Sol System.

Caddy Brenton barely remembered the cities of Earth. She'd been single-digit-old when her parents put her into the stasis bed before the flight, and she'd emerged more or less in the same state on the other side —just she and her older brother, Peter. Mom and dad hadn't been qualified for the flight. Too old, according to the surgeons doing the colony screening. Caddy had begged mom and dad not to make her go. But Old Earth had been dying. Too dirty. Too crowded. Too used-up. Or so she'd been told. The accessions officials for the Emergency Resettlement Project had been taking children—and children only—for their bulk colonist manifests. So, Caddy and Peter were consigned to one of the big boats being built. And launched on a very long, one-way trip.

Strange, Caddy often thought, that twenty decades could pass, without her mind being wise to the fact. Life in the stasis bed had been virtually dreamless. Sometimes, she wished she could get back into the stasis bed, and let twenty more decades pass. Maybe by then New Olympia would be ready for habitation. What good was a new life, if all it meant was being confined to the habitat modules slowly spreading across the surface of the asteroid *Mainfront* had towed into New Olympia orbit? Perhaps her great-great grandchildren would get to rub their toes in the New Olympian sand. But Caddy would not. And this filled her with an almost unutterable bitterness.

That, and the fact that Peter had left.

"Uh oh, I know that look," said a voice over Caddy's shoulder.

She turned away from the observation bubble—aimed perpetually down at New Olympia's rocky, dangerous, altogether inhospitable surface —and greeted her friend Troy.

"Yo, man," she said, waving a hand half-heartedly.

"Blues got you down again?" Troy said, floating up beside her. The asteroid had a tiny bit of gravity, enough to eventually bring everything to rest on the floor, if you stood still. But not enough to make walking possible. Every module and connecting tube was therefore lined with railings and handholds—a person pulled herself through the world, as much as pushed off.

"You might say that," Caddy said, turning her eyes planetward. Even she wasn't sure why she spent so much time here. It wasn't like staring at New Olympia was going to transform the surface any faster. There wasn't even a guarantee that the aerosol pods being dumped into the atmosphere every month—containing hundreds of kilograms of genetically-modified one-celled plants—were going to work. There was only the *theory* of them working. Just as the *Mainfront* had come all this way on the *theory* that a roughly-Earth-sized world at roughly the right distance from its roughly-Sol-like star, would have liquid water, and the potential to support an oxygen-nitrogen atmosphere. And Caddy knew damned well how *that* particular gamble had turned out. Much to her dissatisfaction.

"Just think," Troy said, "We could still be stuck—"

"—on Earth," Caddy said, finishing his sentence for him. "Spare me, please. I see the broadcasts that the *Mainfront* mayor disseminates into the school files. How the skies on Earth are always gloomy. How they're rushing to do for the Earth's atmosphere what we're trying to do here; before Earth goes like Venus. Everyone walking around wearing masks. Barely any elbow room. It looks awful. But Troy, did you ever stop to wonder how *accurate* that all is?"

"What do you mean?" the teenaged boy—young man, really, with arms and shoulders thickening and broadening handsomely—said, looking at her sideways.

"I mean," Caddy said, "What if they just *tell* us that Earth's terrible, because they don't want us to get homesick?"

"How can we get homesick for a place we barely remember?" Troy asked.

"Well *I* remember," Caddy said defensively, still glaring down at New Olympia's surface. "It wasn't that bad when we left. It wasn't like they show it now."

"The way they show it now," Troy said, "is the way it looked two hundred years ago. Two hundred years for the broadcasts to reach us. I bet it's *worse*, at this very moment, than either of us can imagine. Only we won't see it for two hundred years. Do you really think we'd be better off if we never came?"

"I . . ." Caddy said, then shut her mouth.

Troy maneuvered up close to her and put a hand on her shoulder.

"I don't know what to think," Caddy finally said, rubbing her eyes with her fists.

"Peter believed in this place," Troy said, sweeping his arm out toward the planet below. "That's why he volunteered to be part of the first wave of comet-catchers."

"And vanished into thin air," Caddy said.

"Yeah, well . . ." now it was Troy who shut his mouth.

"Sorry," he said, after a long pause. "I know you don't like to talk about it."

"No, I don't," Caddy said.

"But you for sure will want to talk about *this,*" Troy said, fishing a small phone out of his jumper's zippered breast pocket, and using his fingertips to pull something up on the small screen.

Caddy peered at what the screen said.

"Scores have been released?" she asked.

"Not officially," Troy said. "But I know the girl in the office who runs the workstation for the testing administrator, and she slipped me the data a day early." He winked at her.

"Dance your way around too many flames," Caddy chided him, "and you may eventually get burned."

She followed up the comment with a fist slugging playfully into Troy's shoulder. He went flying across the module, laughing and rubbing his arm. His phone remained in Caddy's hand, as she looked more closely at what he'd come to show her.

"I've passed," she said, suddenly turning serious.

"Not *just* passed," Troy said. "The same girl who gave me the scores, told me that they've already been picking names for the next class being trained to run the comet-catchers. Your name is on that list. And a year earlier than you expected it to be, too."

Caddy clutched the little phone to her chest.

"I'd hoped," she said, then allowed herself a small giggle, and a grin. "I mean, I worked hard and I pestered them endlessly to let me try for the next group. So what if I am only seventeen."

"I think the fact you're following in Peter's shoes . . ."

But Troy never finished the thought.

Caddy's brother was like a friendly ghost, forever flitting about in the periphery of their vision. Not dead. Not here. Just . . . *missing.* One of the other comet-catchers had found Peter's ship slowly drifting back into the inner system, gently shoving its captured comet; on pure autopilot. No Peter. No sign of an accident. No evidence at all that there had been any problem. And a log that had been wiped blank, so no records or telemetry to tell what had become of him.

After that, solo missions were off-limits. All comet-catcher ships went out with two and even three people aboard. At minimum. Whatever had happened to Peter, the *Mainfront* executive council determined that they didn't want it to happen again.

Caddy?

Part of her still felt that Peter was out there, somewhere.

"Hey," Troy said, "remember what I said when I came in here? About knowing that look on your face? Now you've got a different one. I am sorry I brought your brother up."

"No, this is great news," Caddy said. "Peter would be proud of me, I am sure. This is my big chance to get out of here, too. To see the far edge of the system. Being stuck here? It's like living on the front porch of a house I can never enter. I don't want to spend my life doing that. So, if I can't go down there—"

She pointed at the planet.

"—I want to be out *there.*"

Her finger moved off the limb of the world, and aimed for deep space.

"Well, I hope you make it through training," Troy said. "I am sure you'll be the best comet-catcher of them all."

PILOTING IN THE NEW SCHOOL WAS AN EXERCISE IN LEARNING TO THINK big. Technically, every single person who'd come with the *Mainfront*—both young and old alike—knew how to operate the little shuttles and other vehicles that serviced their budding, single-asteroid civilization. If you understood thrust vectoring in a microgravity environment, and could manage a finite fuel source, there was very little chance to screw it up. The comet-catchers merely amped the equations, because instead of pushing ore cargo or container boxes about, a comet-catcher literally herded an entire cometary body out of its long-period orbit at the edge of the star system, into a short-period orbit which would eventually line it up for an insertion around New Olympia proper—before eventually being de-orbited at a velocity that wouldn't send the comet smacking into the planet's crust at speeds guaranteed to cause tectonic turmoil.

To that end, each comet-catcher was almost like a miniature version of the *Mainfront* itself: big fuel tanks—both for reactor consumption, and for working mass—and a big, high-efficiency, low-thrust fusion engine. The life module and pilot's globe were small in comparison to the rest of the ship. It was made of as few parts as possible, all machined in the colony's ever-expanding nano-augmented fleet yard. And each prospective pilot—as well as her onboard backup assignee—was trained to make fixes to potential problems en route.

Losing comet-catchers was not unheard of. The risk merely added to the job's glamour. But the executive council didn't want to sacrifice any more ships or lives than were absolutely necessary. The objective was to bring back water—as much as could be had—for the terraforming effort. Not fill the comet-catcher academy memorial board with names.

"Your objective is the snowball," Caddy's instructor said to them all as they floated in a loose formation around the scale model of the comet-catcher the academy had constructed at the center of its bubble-domed, one-room schoolhouse. There were two dozen in Caddy's class—the biggest yet. With the fleet yard able to build more ships with greater efficiency each year, the comet-catcher arm of the terraforming effort was picking up steam.

The instructor—Chief Pilot Okatsu—pointed a thin stick at the bow of the model.

"Your most delicate piece of equipment is also your most important. The pusher web is stored in its protective cocoon until you need to deploy it. Once it is deployed, it cannot be quickly stowed. The web itself expands until it forms a semi-flexible glove or bowl, roughly one kilometer in diameter. Far, far bigger than your craft itself, but more than big enough to serve as a . . . as a *snow shoe* for you, when you have to begin 'kicking' your target back home."

Caddy raised her hand.

"Candidate Brenton," the Chief said, pointing at her with the stick.

"Why doesn't the web collapse as soon as it touches the comet's surface?" she asked.

"Good question," Chief said. "I was just getting to that part. The web itself is actually a nanofiber filament that can be electrically charged. When it's left idle, it's like a draw string on your jumper. It hangs loose. When you activate the charge, the filaments in the fiber compress and align in one direction. The web is woven such that the compression and straightening forces the web to assume the shape we want. But it's still flexible—and large—enough, so that when you touch down on a comet's surface, the web should bend without breaking. We want both you, and the comet, to come home in one piece."

Chief pulled up a holo-video above the scale model, showing a sped-up animation that demonstrated what he'd just described. Like a flower blooming, the web unfurled out of the front of the comet catcher, until it was like a wide, shallow cup.

"Now, ordinarily, that web wouldn't stand up to you or I pushing against a single strand with so much as a finger's strength. But taken as a whole, the web will disperse the force of your ship's thrust across the surface of the cometary body, allowing you to manipulate the comet without sinking *into* it."

As if on cue, the computer animation showed the little ship maneuvering to place the near side of an amorphous comet—lumpy, somewhat rounded in shape—into the business end of its web. When the ship began making sudden movements, the web eventually shattered, and the little ship tunneled its way into the comet.

"Bury yourself like this," the Chief warned, "and you might be digging yourself a grave. I've been on this operation from the get-go—when most of you were still young, and fresh out of your stasis beds. I've lost friends to carelessness. Please don't join their ranks."

*Which is not,* Caddy thought, *how Peter was lost.* His ship had come back fine—just missing the pilot, was all.

A tiny prickling sensation went up Caddy's spine.

"Now," Chief continued. "You've all been spending a lot of time in the simulators, and I know it's not much fun. But really, you're going to have to get used to it. You need to be prepared for every possibility, including sudden instrumentation or mechanical error, during your approach. You get one chance to snag a comet the right way. Screw it up, and wreck your web, and it's a long trip back home to get your ship fixed —and we might decide to let somebody else go out in your place. We're too young—as a colony—to be able to afford careless mistakes. The number of comets that need to be harvested for the transformation of New Olympia is immense. But every single one counts. Which means *you* count. Understand?"

A chorus of *yessirs* echoed around the schoolhouse.

"Good," Chief said. "Now, let's break for fifteen, and then we can start talking about how to work your fuel replenishment electrolyzers. Your comet is not just your target object, it's also your source of working mass for getting yourself back home."

The various candidates split off or split up, veering around Caddy as she remained and stared at the scale model. When the room had emptied, leaving just herself and Okatsu, he stepped closer to her— staring at the little empty pilot's globe.

"I knew Peter," he said quietly. "He had a gift for this work. One of our most productive pilots. Seventeen lifetime catches without a single accident. I am sure he'd have tried for hundreds more."

Caddy wrapped her arms around herself, and rubbed her palms along her triceps.

"It's going to be lonely out there," she said.

"It is," Chief said. "But then, that's part of how we pick you all for this job. Each pairing works in twelve-hour shifts. One of you is resting in the living module, while the other is in the pilot's globe. You will have as much or as little contact with each other as you want. Your file says you like to spend a lot of solo time looking at the stars. And down at New Olympia. Your brother's file said the same."

"I hope I can fill his shoes," Caddy said. "I'm just a little scared, is all."

"You should be," Chief said. "These missions are going to be long, and a lot can go wrong on the way out, and on the way back. You won't follow your comets in—your job is to nudge them in the right direction, then let gravity do the rest—but between the time you leave here, and the time you return for refurbishment and resupply, it might be a year or more."

Caddy nodded her head, absorbing the older, more experienced man's wisdom.

"Sir," she said, "can I ask a question—not related to class?"

"Okay," Okatsu said, fishing a water bottle out of a pocket and taking a drink.

"Was Earth *really* bad?" she asked. "When we left, I mean?"

The man's eyes lost focus for a second, and he slowly swallowed several mouthfuls of water, before putting the bottle back in its pocket.

"Yup," he said.

"I just can't remember that well," Caddy admitted.

"You wouldn't. You were . . . six years old? When your parents signed you over to us? I was twenty five. Spent my whole life in Japan. If you think things are cramped now—the way we live on this asteroid—try living in a country where people hot-bunked in shoe-box style dormitory structures that make our present living quarters look palatial by comparison. Once the geriatric medicine boom of the late twenty-first century took hold, suddenly people were living far healthier lives for far longer. Global population tripled inside of a generation. They eventually locked the clamps on with mandatory birth control, but by then all the old, chronic problems had come roaring back to bite us. Trust me, Earth is not somewhere you'd choose to live. They're banking on us making these colonies work, so that maybe in another five hundred or a thousand years —however long it takes to crack the bulk transit barrier, or the light-speed barrier; whichever falls first—we can be a safety valve."

Okatsu suddenly began to chuckle. It was a harsh sound.

"Of course, by that time, the colonies might have ideas of their own," he said.

"What do you mean?" Caddy asked.

"Just because Earth wants to send more people, doesn't mean we necessarily want more people. Hell, for all we know, a string of sister ships—to the *Mainfront*—was launched in our wake. We won't know about it until those ships suddenly begin arriving. Do we have room for all the new people? *Will* we have room? If New Olympia has oceans and breathable air—and land aplenty to fertilize and cultivate with Earth life —that's one thing. But if we're still living on this asteroid, and tinkering with New Olympia's air—the sudden arrival of an additional thousand mouths to feed . . . anyway, this is all kind of political. I'm getting ahead of myself. Us oldsters talk about this crap. You kids don't need to worry about it. Just focus on learning to operate the comet-catchers, then get out there and do us proud. Do *Peter* proud."

"TARGET BODY IS IN THE GREEN, PLUS OR MINUS TEN," CADDY SAID. SHE was cradled in the simulator's pilot's chair, surrounded on all sides by what was—for all intents and purposes—a working version of a comet-catcher's pilot's globe. The globe itself was a solid piece of transparent, micrometeroid-proof plastic that gave her virtually unlimited visibility in every direction. The chair proper was mounted on a single pole that projected out into the globe, and allowed the chair to pivot or swivel according to the pilot's preference. Presently, the globe was surrounded by a very realistic three-dimensional projected of deep space. A shadow —representing a soon-to-be-captured comet—loomed in the "far" distance. Caddy had her comet-catcher's web fully charged and extended. She couldn't see it, except for the false-color imagery that showed the web superimposed over a different false-color image of the comet proper.

Sweat slowly formed across Caddy's skin as she used the finesse controls to gently dial up her ship's thrust. She was approaching the comet at mere meters per minute now. Any faster and she risked impacting too hard. Any slower . . . and her nerves would break. Things were taking too long as it was. She resisted the urge to rush the job.

This was the final phase of simulator testing. Once they passed this, they'd graduate to live ship exercises. Beyond which lay graduation, and promotion to live flight status.

But being able to prove she could stick the catch was the biggest test to date.

*Peter, if you're out there, help me do this,* Caddy thought silently as she watched the proximity sensors. The space between herself and the simulated comet shrank, and shrank, and shrank.

Just a bit more . . .

Suddenly a *bwooping* alarm hit her ears.

The comet-catcher began to accelerate, and drift down.

"What the—" she began to swear, but her hands were already in motion. The heads-up hologram indicated that a thrust unit on the rear of the ship had gone active, and was refusing orders to switch itself off. Caddy's mind went white for an instant, as she realized she was moments from wrecking her web, and even burying the snout of her ship in the foamy, filthy ice on the comet's surface.

*Counterthrust,* she thought defiantly, and instantly pulled up a tactical display showing the numbers from the malfunctioning unit. She dialed the unit on the exact opposite side of the axes to an identical level of thrust, and watched as the ship's dangerously increasing velocity held steady . . . but did not decrease.

"Shit," Caddy said, and realize she didn't just have to combat the effects of the broken unit, she had to correct for the mistake which had already happened. She opened up her forward thruster array and dialed responses by feel. The *bwoop* from the computer continued, as the comet was now dangerously close to the web, and she was still moving forward and down at the wrong angle.

When the *bwoop* was joined by a second, angry *pang* sound, Caddy knew she was in the red zone. She opened all of the forward thrusters up to one hundred percent in a desperate attempt to reverse course. If she could back off in time, maybe she could get the broken thruster taken care of, and take another crack at it.

But then the pilot's globe lit up with warnings about stress failures along the breadth of the web. She was slamming to stern, but with such sudden force that it was not only causing her to pull into the straps of the pilot's chair, it was collapsing the web as well. She tried to dial back the action, but it was too late. The web was in pieces now, and the comet was receding. Unharmed, but also untouchable, now that she'd ruined her chance.

Caddy spat a blue streak of profanity, and slammed her arms onto the rests on either side of the chair.

"Easy," said a voice over the simulator speakers. It was Chief. "Learning how to keep cool in the face of a defeat is as important as learning how to keep cool on the brink of victory. The chances of that actual malfunction happening during a live catch are extraordinarily low. The computer is set up so that a stuck thruster unit has its fuel supply automatically cut off after five seconds. For both the thruster to fail *and* the computer cutoff to fail . . . well, it's not impossible, but it's unlikely."

"Then why'd you throw that one at me, boss?" Caddy said, slowly peeling herself out of the chair—soaked with perspiration, and very much in need of a shower.

"I've got a mean streak," was all the voice said. "Chalk it up to lesson learned, Candidate. Now get out of my simulator, and don't take it personally. Everybody's getting roasted during Finals Week. Or did you think I'd just let you cakewalk your way to the live exercises?"

Caddy was tempted to make an obscene gesture at the several cameras she knew were monitoring her as she floated toward the neck of the pilot's globe—and the door back to the rest of civilization—but decided she was too tired to make the effort.

LIVE PILOTING INVOLVED REPEATS OF EVERYTHING THEY'D PRACTICED IN the simulators, except they weren't using actual comets. They were using scaled-down, inflated balloons which represented comets, with webs scaled accordingly. Captures and other maneuvers were noticeably free of mysterious mechanical glitches—Caddy found it a much more relaxing experience than anything she'd gone through in the sim—and everybody was proceeding through class more or less according to the book.

Outside class, Caddy kept to herself much of the time. But then, so did the others. The Chief had said it: they were each chosen for their comfort in solitude, as much as for the potential aptitude with the ships. And though they all bunked dormitory style, Caddy avoided the eventual pairing off that began to occur, as people realized graduation was approaching, and it would soon be time to go out on a real mission. Nobody had been told how the crews would be selected. Everybody seemed to be assuming that whoever was their buddy now would be their buddy when they launched in their actual comet-catchers.

But Chief had never made any such promise, and Caddy suspected there might be some rude surprises when the time came for them to leave orbit.

One of their final exercises was not an exercise at all, but rather the passive observation of an in-system capture. For years, comet-catchers had been working in the cometary halo at the very edge of New Olympia's system, diverting comets onto short-period trajectories that would bring them within reach of New Olympia's expanding in-system space infrastructure. So, to complement the comet-catchers working on the edge, an almost identical team of comet catchers worked closer to home: flying out to meet comets as they came in: each of them streaming huge, bright tails of sublimated gas and dust, blown off by the solar wind from New Olympia's home star. Those comets were then slowly herded toward New Olympia itself, and prepared for an eventual de-orbit—their precious water being added to New Olympia's gradually moistening atmosphere.

Nobody knew how many comets in total it would take, before New Olympia had enough water for the atmosphere and climate to change dramatically. At present, it was much, much too hot, and composed of all the wrong gasses. With time, and the relentless addition of water, nitrogen, and whatever else the comets brought with them, New Olympia might eventually resemble a world worth growing things on.

During the observation, Caddy and each of the other students were strung out in a line—each of them commanding one of the many pint-sized trainer ships that the academy used for training hops close to home. Being able to see an actual comet—gloriously dazzling, surrounded by its coma of gas and dust—was as exhilarating as it was sobering. The comet was literally *huge*. A monster. A megaton ball of packed ice and snow, left over from the formation of the system at least a billion or more years in the past. The comet-catcher—the actual one assigned to make the snag —was like a tiny insect compared to the object it was attempting to corral. The web proper was not even visible, having been deployed in full.

"Watch how gently she does this," Chief said over the instructor net, as they waited and watched. The comet-catcher seemed to be barely moving at all as it slowly closed on the comet. Relatively speaking, they were all hurtling toward the home star at several tens of thousands of kilometers per hour. Just matching velocity had taken them over a day's worth of careful maneuvering.

Caddy's pilot's globe display showed the core of the comet, hidden behind the bright gas and dust. The comet-catcher maneuvered toward it like a tiny dust mite wielding a salad bowl on its head. Second by second, the distance shrank. Occasionally, the comet-catcher pilot muttered something into her mic: numbers, or a comment about what she was seeing on her readout. Deadpan tone of voice. Cool as cucumber, one might say.

Caddy wondered if she'd ultimately be that steady when clutch time came.

Eventually the comet-catcher disappeared into the comet's coma, but there was still a ways to go before the web made contact. Once that happened, the web itself would begin to partially conform to the unique crevices, bumps, valleys, rifts, and other features on the comet's surface. That would allow the web to get a good "grip" prior to the comet-catcher sinking in its fuel reclamation hoses, and beginning the process of tanking up on fresh working mass for the push toward home.

The most deceptive part, was the perception of the comet as a solid. Chief had drilled this fact into them over and over again. It might seem solid. It might look like one big blob of stuff on the displays. But if a comet got nudged too hard in any particular direction, the comet's constituent pieces could go flying apart. That would waste the opportunity to bring the comet back to New Olympia orbit, but also create lots of dangerous trash that would eventually need to be policed up—otherwise it could pose a threat to comet-catching and other ships in the future. Even a small, muddy clump of sand, going at the speeds comets tended to achieve, would put a lethal hole in the best craft New Olympia could build.

So, making the snag on the first try—and doing it right—was of utmost importance. Somebody had managed it out on the edge of the system. Now somebody had to manage it close to home.

Caddy was almost unable to breathe as the final few meters were closed. And then happy chimes sounded across her pilot's globe, as the comet-catcher's sensors reported good contact across the web, and the bow of the craft gently came to rest against the comet's surface proper.

Cheers rang out across the instructor net, including those of Chief, who was among the loudest.

"That's how it's done," he said proudly into their ears. "I can't emphasize it enough, Candidates. Slowness and patience win, every time. If you feel like it's not right on the approach, don't be afraid to gently back off, get your attitude and your trajectory right, and try it again. There's no shame in making a second, third, fourth, or fifth try. But you only get one time to screw it up. Then your ship is fouled, and you have to come home. Or, worse, you're too fouled to effect your own extraction, and you're signaling for rescue. And out there in the cometary halo, the distances are often too big for help to arrive in anything less than a few weeks. You don't want to be stuck with your thumbs sticking up your you-know-whats, waiting for others to come clean up your messes for you. Roger?"

Caddy and the rest sounded an immediate *roger* through the net.

"Now the long, gentle push to get this thing to New Olympia," Chief said. "Which we won't stick around for. Hey, Sarah—" Chief momentarily keyed over to the live net, to talk to the pilot who'd made the successful snag "—thanks for showing the new kids how it's done. Nice work out there. You made it look almost too easy."

"Happy to influence the new generation," said an older woman's voice, followed by the sound of her yawning and stretching. "Right now I am going to let my partner in crime take over, while I go get some sleep. One thing you newbies need to remember: even though this is not physically strenuous work, once you're dialed in and focused on making a snag, everything goes into time warp. Hours will pass in what seem like moments. Muscles will cramp. You will complete the snag, only to discover that you haven't eaten in a whole day, and suddenly you want to eat until your sides split. Don't overdo it. Just disengage, let your partner come up after you—fresh and ready—and let yourself decompress. Good luck after graduation, okay? I will see you all out here."

Caddy and the other Candidates voiced their understanding and appreciation for the comet-catcher's words of wisdom, then they busied themselves for the return voyage home. It had certainly been a day to remember.

"But . . . I *graduate* tomorrow," Caddy said hotly.

"Graduation doesn't always mean being put on the job right away," Chief Okatsu said. "Not everyone has a ship waiting for them at the end of school. Since we lost one of your classmates to a medical problem at the last minute, you're now the odd woman out. I am sorry. Look, it's not the end of the world. We'll just mate you up with one of the students from the next class."

"Which will be *months* away," Caddy said, still fuming.

"It can't be helped," Okatsu said. "Nobody flies alone. Not anymore."

Unsaid: *not since your brother disappeared.*

Caddy could feel the hot tears pushing at the corners of her eyes, but she held them back. This was not the time to vent. She'd do that later, alone. When she could throw a pillow. Maybe even kick something. And nobody would see her. She'd worked too long and too hard for this. That things were being delayed at the final moment . . . bad luck. Dumb, stupid, bad luck.

Her breathing slowed, and she momentarily closed her eyes. They were in the main school room, long after the final chime for that day's concluding briefing had sounded. Everyone else was gone to get something to eat, and to talk excitedly about the big day tomorrow. It was just Caddy and the instructor.

She gently rested a hand on the comet-catcher scale model at the room's center—to steady herself.

"Stupid Peter," she finally said, breathing the words out with a long breath. "Always leaving a shadow for me to fall into. If he never vanishes, solo missions are still on the books, and I go out as soon as there's a ship for me."

Chief folded his arms—the grip surface on his toes keeping him in place on the floor.

"There was already talk about going to double and triple crews, long before Peter's accident."

"They ruled it an *accident?*" Caddy said, laughing sarcastically.

"No other way to classify it," Chief said. "Ship returns on auto-pilot, nobody aboard. Did your brother go outside to fix something? Was he in the airlock when it accidentally got triggered? It was like he just . . . left. No indication whatsoever that there had been any problem. But also no record to tell us about the final days leading up to his ultimate vanishing. Your brother is a giant question mark in the minds of all of us dedicated to the comet-catching team. But don't think his story alone caused us to change policy. We operated solo in the early days because we had so few pilots to work with, and the executive council wanted us to begin retrieving comets immediately. But as the number of qualified pilots began to grow, we knew it was simply common sense to jump to double crews. Your brother's circumstance . . . merely solidified that decision. Since then, we've never lost a ship or a crew without knowing exactly how, and why."

Caddy chewed air for at least a minute. She wasn't sure what else could be said. Obviously Chief was the final say on the matter, and she respected the man too much to begin calling him names, for simply having prudence.

"Look," he said, putting a gentle hand on her shoulder, "getting out there now won't make it any different than if you wait for the next class to finish. I've seen the way you watch the stars, when class is taking a break. I can tell you're searching out there. With your spirit."

"For *him,*" she said. "I don't think I even want to bring him back, I just want to know what happened. What became of him, you know? Not having an answer . . . it's like I can't go out there—doing the job that he did—without trying to find the solution to the mystery. Maybe you're right, maybe it's something I have to let go of. But dammit, he's my older brother, and he was the only family who came with me from Earth. I've been like an orphan since he went away. I just want something to close the hole. Does that make sense?"

"It does," Chief said. "And I'd be lying if I told you some of the other instructors didn't want you *off* the project as a result. They think you're going to do something stupid trying to discover what became of Peter."

"So why don't *you* oppose me doing this job?" Caddy asked.

Chief ran a tongue alongside one cheek, and his eyes lost focus for a moment.

"Because it's not my right to tell you that you can't fulfill your destiny."

"My *destiny?*" Caddy said. That was a word she'd almost never heard anyone use before, outside of grand political platitudes from the executive council, regarding eventual human settlement on the surface of New Olympia.

"Yes," Chief said. "Each of us has one. And only we—ourselves—can ultimately figure out what that destiny might be. I tell you not to go out there . . . and it's likely you find a way to go out there anyway, whether I like it or not. People are funny like that. You tell them no, they just redouble their efforts to go ahead and do something anyway. Maybe, as part of the comet-catcher program, at least you're using your instincts for something practical. Besides, I think your brother would be proud of you."

"Thanks," Caddy said, standing up a little straighter. "I'd want Peter to feel proud of me."

"Wherever he is," Chief said, squeezing her shoulder, "I think he is that. Oh yes, I think that very much."

Post-graduation was like an exercise in slow-motion dentistry.

To keep herself from going stir-crazy, Caddy used all the spare simulator time the schoolhouse could give her. In this regard she became a bit of a rump student: someone the new class veered around as they went through the motions.

Everyone except Troy, that is.

How or why he'd gotten into the program, Caddy couldn't be sure. He'd never expressed the slightest interest in being on the comet-catcher missions. And if his grades actually supported his application—which they clearly had—it was surely by the smallest of margins. Troy had never actually *tried* for anything in his academic life, so far as she knew. He was one of those guys who seemed content to just sail through things, until he latched onto something that might be popular with the girls.

Which comet-catching definitely wasn't.

"Seemed like the best job of any," he said one afternoon, while they hung around the cafeteria, slurping on trays of stir-fry vat-grown beef, with veggies and noodles.

"I *know* you," she said, eyeing him across the table. "You're a people person. You thrive on attention. Where we're eventually going . . . you're going to be stuck with nobody to talk to."

"There'll be my partner," he said. "I can talk to that guy."

"Assuming 'that guy' even *feels* like talking," Caddy said. "Look, comet-catching is a lonely job. No joke. You haven't been out there to see what it's like."

"Oh, and *you* have?" Troy retorted, raising an eyebrow at her.

"I've seen more of the job than you," she responded. "Spent more time around the working pilots, too. We're a quiet lot. We prefer the silence. When have you *ever* preferred silence to a noisy gaggle of hangers-on, Troy? People you can send into hysterics with your latest joke, or cutting up in front of the teacher? Well, we're not in school anymore. This is serious."

"Hey, wait a minute, why are you throwing cold water on this with me, huh?" Troy said, sitting up straighter and putting his arms on either side of his tray—fists balled defiantly. "I've got just as much right to be here—to take my shot—as you do. The tests said I'm in, so I'm in. Every week I pass the exams and move on to the next phase, I *move on to the next phase.* Just like you did. And you've never been on a snag before. Not for real. You want to find out if you've got what it takes. And frankly . . . so do I."

"You don't think I have what it takes??" Caddy shot, her cheeks turning red.

"No, that's not what I meant," he said, relaxing his hands. "Look, Caddy, since that day we talked in the observation module—when I brought you your scores—I've been thinking. You're right. Bumming around the colony isn't exactly how I want to spend the rest of my days. I am sure I could get engrossed in the mines, or running some automated milling operation, or even learning to become a medic, or, heck, a *surgeon* if I felt like it. I think I'm smart enough to do anything I feel like. My parents used to tell me that, back on Earth. 'Young man, you're smart enough to do anything you put your mind to.' Well, this is what I've decided I want to put my mind to. At least for now. If I get bored and decide to change jobs, I am sure you will be the first to know."

They ate in silence for several moments. Caddy didn't really have a good reply to any of that. It was largely the same speech to herself she'd been rehearsing in her own mind—in various forms—over the years. Just because Troy had always seemed too unserious and freewheeling to ever make it on the *oh-so-serious* comet-catcher team . . . didn't mean she was

qualified to tell the man no. Any more than Chief Okatsu had felt qualified to tell Caddy no.

"You ever miss them?" Caddy finally asked, changing the conversa-
tional direction.

"My parents?" he asked.

"Yeah," she said.

"Sometimes. It's like, I can never be sure when that feeling is going to
hit. It gets me at the strangest moments. I mean, the adults here are all good
people and they did their best to finish the job our parents started . . . but I
can never quite get over the fact that our parents aren't just far away in
space, they're also far away in time, too. While we slept on the trip aboard
*Mainfront* they lived out the rest of their lives on Earth. Or did they emigrate
to one of the colonies in Earth's solar system? Did they have any more kids?
Do we have brothers and sisters who also had kids, and then their kids had
kids, and somewhere back on Earth right now, people our age—the descen-
dants of siblings we never met—are looking up into the sky, and wondering
about us: the relatives they will never know, other than in name?"

"I never thought about it that far," Caddy admitted.

"I did," Troy said. "Especially after you and I talked, and I could tell
how happy you were at the chance to become a Candidate in the comet-
catcher business. I realized that if ever our relatives—far, far away, on
dirty, crowded, dying Earth—are ever going to have a chance to meet *our*
children, or our children's children, we have to make sure that New
Olympia *works.* That there is an actual, living world for the people of
Earth to come to. A place for them to settle."

"Assuming we let them," Caddy said, remembering what Chief
Okatsu had once told her.

"Yeah, well, right, assuming we can *stop* them if we want to," Troy
said, correcting her. "If a dozen sister ships to *Mainfront* showed up in
orbit tomorrow, who do you think would cast the deciding votes? Which
people on the present executive council would try to overrule the decision? Naw. Our best bet is to make sure New Olympia is a huge, wide-
open, living planet. Forests. Seas. Life from pole to pole. Enough room
for twenty billion human beings, if necessary. We give them enough room
they can lose themselves in it, we won't have any problems. In fact, it will
be payback for the effort invested in launching *Mainfront* in the first
place."

"You make it sound like we owe Earth a debt," Caddy said.

"I think maybe we do," Troy said. And then he went back to eating.

*Surprise, surprise,* Caddy thought. She'd never realized that happy-go-lucky Troy could think such thoughts.

Then again, with both of them being quickly thrust into the adult world, switching gears into grown-up mode was something Caddy had been forced to grapple with, too. What *would* the future hold? Assuming she liked comet-catching, would she simply do that job . . . forever? The initial agreement—upon signing as a Candidate—was for ten years of service. But beyond that, what did she want to do? Where did she want to go? Troy had mentioned children. Caddy hadn't even considered the possibility before now. But Troy was right. Unless disaster struck, some day, New Olympia would be a destination for fresh colonists leaving Earth. Caddy herself might be gone by then, but her legacy might live on. Assuming she found someone with the right components to be a husband.

She eyed Troy over the food between them, and didn't say another word.

DEEP SPACE WAS LIKE A LITERAL COAL SACK. OTHER THAN THE BRIGHT stars glowing perfectly across the sky, no other light source was discernible. Even New Olympia's home star was just a bright, yellow-white bulb, almost small enough to disappear among the other stars.

Thrusting out this far had taken months. Time during which Caddy and Troy traded off piloting the ship. They didn't have a name for their craft. It seemed neither large enough, nor important enough, to give it a name, the way *Mainfront* had a name. They were merely a call-sign on the comet-catcher net. Assigned to rendezvous with a numbered objective which had been identified for them well in advance of their departure. It was their first designated capture. And they'd gambled to see who would be the one to make the attempt upon arrival—with Caddy coming out on top.

Troy seemed to take it in stride, much to Caddy's surprise.

"Less pressure on me," he chided during one of their mid-shift swapouts—when she would go back to the living module and begin her twelve hours of down time, while he went into the pilot's globe and spent twelve hours keeping the ship on course.

Much could have been left to automatic control, naturally. But comet-catcher doctrine was to never leave the pilot's globe empty for more than a few minutes at a stretch. And both Troy and Caddy adhered to doctrine in a by-the-book fashion.

Food was plentiful. The only real concern was making sure the electrolyzer worked correctly once they sank their web into the target comet. That electrolyzer would ensure they had fuel, air, and water for the return trip. Or at least enough air, fuel, and water, to get the target comet headed on its way—at which point they would detach, receive new instructions for a new target comet in their relative vicinity, and the process would begin all over again.

It was assumed they could divert dozens of comets before diving back into the inner system, for docking and refitting at home.

Caddy felt herself marveling at the absolute, magnificent solitude she enjoyed during her stints in the piloting globe. With gentle music—the countless millions of recordings from Earth—playing into her ears, she could turn off all the lights and feel like she was practically one with the cosmos. A disembodied personage, floating free through the ether of time and space. She wondered if this was how the very first astronauts—riding alone, aloft, aboard their primitive rockets—had felt. She also wondered if this is how Peter had felt too. Before . . . before whatever took him away.

Which was one thing Caddy had gradually become sure of: whatever had happened to Peter, it hadn't been something premeditated or planned. He'd been enticed by something. Maybe the very nakedness of space itself. Caddy wondered whether on one of those long, lonesome stretches of time, Peter had simply decided to eliminate all barriers between himself, and cosmos proper. Perhaps he'd felt so completely and absolutely in unison with the quiet blackness surrounding him, he'd stepped to the airlock, and calmly let himself outside. To make the marriage—the man, and the void—complete.

A morbid, and yet also very eerily elegant thought. Or so Caddy admitted on one of her many shifts at the comet-catcher's controls.

When at last their target comet presented itself, it was as a massive, dark shadow that blotted out the stars. No beautiful coma this far from the sun. Probably the nucleus had not felt any warmth for hundreds of thousands, or even millions, of years, depending on its actual period.

The capture proper was a thing of held-breath anxiety, yet it yielded no drama whatsoever. Caddy had practiced the maneuver how many times, back in the simulators? And this time there was no mischief-making instructor to throw her a technical curve ball right when she was making her final approach.

THE DREAMS BEGAN AFTER THE FIFTH CAPTURE.

Not vividly, at first. But gradually growing in frequency and intensity, until—by the ninth capture—Caddy was positively agitated. The dreams were too real, and they were beginning to get to her emotionally. She couldn't make them stop, and they seemed to be directly connected to the fact that they were progressing more deeply into the cometary halo than anyone else ever had in this region of space before.

Nervously, she told Troy about the dreams. The book said every pilot was responsible for keeping her partner fully appraised of any irregularities or issues which might affect the mission. And if Caddy was slowly losing her mind, Troy deserved to know about it before it got too serious for either of them to handle.

"This is where they think your brother vanished," Troy said.

Caddy raised both eyebrows. "How do you know that?" she asked, shocked. "Even I was never told that."

"I sleuthed the coordinates out of your brother's sealed case file, before we left."

"Let me guess: you're in tight with a girl who—"

"No, listen," Troy said. "It's not that. Chief Okatsu pulled me aside the day before we left dock. He asked me to keep an eye on you. I told him I would, but I also asked him if there was anything I should know— something nobody had officially been told. He let me look at the flight forensics for your brother's ship. Where he was at the time of the expected disappearance, and about how deep into the cometary halo. We're entering that general zone now. At least if all my relative calculations are correct. So tell me again, exactly, what happens in the dreams?"

"It's Peter," Caddy said, closing her eyes and picturing her brother's face. "He's in his pilot's suit. He's trying to talk to me, but he's not making any sound. It's like I'm in the pilot's globe, and he's right *outside* the globe. Only the vacuum of space isn't hurting him. I read his lips. I want to make out the words."

"Is he warning you?" Troy asked. "Is he trying to tell you not to do something?"

"No," Caddy said. "It's like . . . it's just the opposite. It's like he's *found* something, and he wants me to come see. And every time I unbuckle from the pilot's chair and float to the exterior of the pilot's globe, he vanishes. And then I wake up."

"And it's like that every time?" Troy asked?

"Yes," Caddy said. "It's been like that for at least the past few weeks. And the dreams get more vivid every night. I ignored them awhile back, just because I thought maybe I was simply beginning to feel the effects of us being gone from home for too long—they told us that extreme isolation would do strange things to our sleep cycle. But this isn't just my mind playing games with me, Troy. I think this is something else entirely."

"Except . . ." Troy said, and didn't finish his thought.

"Except what?" Caddy said, grabbing his wrist with more force than she had any right to.

He looked down at her white-knuckled hand.

"Except I've not been having the same experience, Caddy. My sleep's been fine. If there is something about this region of the cometary halo that is specifically affecting you, why isn't it affecting me too?"

"I don't know," Caddy said.

"Well, whatever it is, do you I think we should abort and go home?"

"So soon?" Caddy said. "We're due for more snags! What will they say when we return early? God, Troy, they'll take away my flight status! I'll get thrown in the psych unit for sure!"

"Hold on, hold on," Troy said, holding up his hands to placate her. "It was just an idea. But what else can we do, Caddy? What if the dreams get more intense? What if you can't rest? You're no good to us if you can't fly the ship. And the book says I can't fly this mission solo. If you're incapacitated to the point you can't function—"

"But I'm not incapacitated," Caddy said. "I'm clear as a bell when I'm awake. Dammit, Troy, I just want you to know what's going on, okay? I don't want you to be in the dark—and I can't keep this to myself forever. I had to tell somebody."

"Got it," Troy said. "Thanks for trusting me. Okay, look. Let's do this. Proceed with the mission. You start telling everything you know—everything you've told me—to a video log. We won't send the log back home. We keep the recording with us. So, if something really weird happens, there is at least some kind of file they can look at . . . when they recover the ship."

Morbid thoughts, indeed. But Peter's disappearance was utmost in their minds.

"And hey," Peter said, "if I start to notice anything funny with me? I'll be the first to say so. I promise."

"Thanks," Caddy said, and reached over the table to pull Troy into a hug. He returned the gesture for a surprisingly long time.

THE GHOST CAME LIKE A MOTH TO A FLAME. IT FLITTED ABOUT, JUST ON the periphery of Caddy's vision. Per usual, when she was piloting, she had all the lights dialed low, and a melodic piece of symphony orchestra music piping gently over the piloting globe's speaker system. The coal sack effect was on brilliant display—a million tiny jewels scattered across an endless ocean of absolute black—but a particular light seemed to be dancing crazily just off to the side. Yet every time Caddy snapped her head to look, the flickering would vanish, only to reappear, moments later, on the other side of her peripheral vision.

"Dammit," Caddy said. "I hope to hell I've just dozed off. I can't afford to begin seeing things while I'm damned awake!"

She'd practically shouted the last words, and was shocked at herself for doing so.

She was even more shocked by the words that came in reply.

"But you are awake, sis."

Caddy froze. The voice was clear and strong, just as she'd remembered in the years since Peter's final voyage.

Suddenly, he was there. Smiling slightly. So close, she felt she could reach out and touch him. Unlike in her dreams, he was clearly *inside* the piloting globe this time. Caddy's hand shook badly as she reached out for him—hoping to touch his full head of gently wavy brown hair.

"You can't touch me yet," he said—forcing Caddy to snap her hand back.

"Peter . . ." she breathed, feeling the tears flow hotly at the corners of her eyes.

"It's me, sis," he said. "But not like you remember. If you touch me now . . . you'll be transported to where I am. Before that happens, we have to talk."

"Peter, oh God, this can't be real," Caddy croaked, swiping at her face with the sleeve. Surely she'd dozed off at the controls, and the life monitor computer would pick up on the error at any moment, and begin to gently chime her back to wakefulness. But a quick glance at the life monitor told her that all was well. She was as alert as she should be. Nothing was amiss. Except . . . Peter was standing there in mid-air, having a conversation with his kid sister, like he'd just walked into her bedroom while she was doing homework.

"Peter . . . what *happened?*" Caddy asked. "Everyone has been trying to figure out what went wrong with your flight."

"Nothing went wrong," Peter said. "Everything went exactly the way it's supposed to. Except, I found something out here. Something nobody could have expected."

"What?" Caddy asked, still desperately wanting to put her hands on her brother's face—to experience the warmth and tangibleness of him.

"I can't explain all the technical details to you," he said. "That would be too time-consuming, and it wouldn't make any difference. Suffice to say that the portion of the star system you're in now, is like the platform for a subway train. Remember those from Earth? You'd go down from street level, and there would be a huge, long tube? It was empty most of the time. Except, every few minutes, a train would come through, stop, pick up people, drop others off, and move on down the track. Well, this part of space is the same thing. It's a waiting area for a galactic train system that stops through every once in awhile, picks up passengers, drops other passengers off, and then goes on its way. Except, I don't think the people who originally built the subway exist anymore. When the train came through last time—when I was out here—climbing aboard showed me nothing but an empty car. And though I've ridden the car through a thousand different star systems by now, I've never seen any sign of anyone who knows how the system was built."

"Aliens," Caddy blurted, still wiping tears from her eyes.

"Yes," Peter said.

"Then how come your whole ship didn't get taken?" Caddy demanded. "Why did your ship come back untouched, without you in it, and all the logs and memory discs erased?"

"It was a sudden thing, really," Peter said, his face making an expression Caddy remembered, from when she was much younger, and her older brother was trying to explain complex things to her—things he wasn't sure she could fully understand. She'd found the expression infuriating then, but it only made her heart break now. She wanted nothing more than to wrap her arms around his neck and pull him to her.

"Try to tell me," Caddy said. "I don't care if you think it won't make sense. Tell me *everything* that happened."

Peter rubbed a thumb along his jaw—he seemed to have not aged a day since he last left home.

"I was comet-catching," he said, "like you are now. And I started having vivid dreams. I didn't understand them at first. But eventually I interpreted them as a kind of waking dream—the ones they say you can control, if you become aware of what they are. In the dreams I was able to take a kind of time and space warp far away from this system. Far away from any systems even remotely close to Earth. I could pick and choose which stars and planets I wanted to see. It was like playing tourist. I began to see other civilizations—built by amazing creatures of all manner and description. It was exciting. I almost began to think it was real. And then, one day, while I was in the pilot's globe—like you are now —it *became* real. It was like the door to the subway car opened in my mind, and I stepped through it. Ever since then, I've been riding the system. You can't believe the places I've been. The galaxy is alive with different people, many of them far older and wiser than humans are."

"How come Earth never knew about any of this," Caddy asked. "Why doesn't the . . . Subway? . . . Why won't it run to Sol?"

"I think the original builders never got around to building a stop there," Peter confessed. "Back when they were creating the subway, humans didn't exist yet. I don't even think the dinosaurs existed. Earth hadn't gotten *interesting* yet. That seems to be the key. The subway only stops at places that have something interesting going on—development, technology, signs of intelligent industry."

"If that's true, what makes *this* system so special?" Caddy asked. "New Olympia is dead as a doornail."

"But it didn't used to be," Peter said. "Long, long ago, there was a civilization on the surface. Advanced enough to build radio telescopes, and begin launching rockets into orbit. But the climate was changing too fast. They never had enough water to sustain the plants, to sustain the biosphere. A little bit like Mars, but a little bit like Venus too. Eventually they died out, before they could ever launch a ship deep enough into space to reach the subway. But the makers left the subway stop here anyway—just in case. Which is where I came in. I happened to be in the right time at the right place, and I climbed aboard when the chance presented itself. And I'm back now. The train is coming through again. I never thought it would be you out here, sis, but I'm glad that it is. I know how much you hated life back home. How much you dreaded being stuck on that asteroid with nowhere to go and nothing to do. Come with me, and I can show you all the places I've seen—the amazing life that waits for us in the galaxy."

Just then, Troy popped the hatch to the pilot's globe. Both Peter and Caddy spun to face him as he floated in. His eyes were so wide, the whites were bright—even in the dim light. Peter seemed to shine of his own accord, like a lamp from nowhere were projected upon him at all times.

"Can . . . can . . ." Caddy whispered to Troy.

"Can I see him?" Troy said. "Yes. Sorry, Caddy, but I've been running a monitor on your piloting sessions ever since you told me about your dreams. I programmed the monitor to wake me up if ever it caught you talking to yourself. I never guessed you'd actually be talking to—"

"A ghost?" Peter said, smiling.

"If that's what you are, then yes," Troy said, clasping the handholds on the side of the pilot's chair. He regarded Peter's avatar warily.

"Peter," Caddy said, composing herself, "if this 'subway' is real, and you could get on, can you not also get *off?* Stay with us. Come back to the colony. Everyone will be amazed by what you've discovered! You have to tell them! You'll be famous! They'll broadcast the news to Earth!"

Peter's face darkened.

"It's not that simple," Peter said.

"Why not?" Caddy demanded. "Damn you, do you have any idea what you've *done* to those of us you left behind?"

Suddenly Peter became aware of Caddy's red, damp face—as if for the first time.

"I'm sorry, sis. I didn't . . . I didn't mean to *hurt* you."

"No, of course you didn't," she said, sniffling. "But why did you have to vanish without a trace?"

"There are certain side effects to how the subway works," Peter said. "Our technology is too primitive. Our data storage is too vulnerable to the wave effect the subway leaves when it passes.

"You couldn't have written a stupid note on a stupid piece of paper?" Caddy practically shouted.

"Who uses hardcopy anymore?" Peter said. "Look, I'm sorry, and I mean it. Sis . . . I've come *back*. Isn't that all that matters now? You can come with me this time!"

"What about Troy?" Caddy said.

Peter considered the other young man in the globe.

"He can come too, if he wants."

"And back home, nobody knows anything about what happened to any of us," Troy said.

"If it's like last time? No, probably not," Peter admitted.

Caddy could see the sparkle in Troy's eyes—he was considering it. Just as Caddy herself was considering it.

"You said it's not that simple, when I asked you why you can't come back with us," Caddy said. "Explain what that means. Why can't you come back?"

"It's like . . . sis . . . I've seen *too much*. If you'd been some of the places I've been . . . the subway is an instant transport. It takes mere seconds to jump me *tens of light-years* in actual space. And each step of the way, I get to meet the other people who are waiting. They know about the subway. They even use it from time to time. They tell me about their worlds. I get to see images, listen to music, hear their speech—did you know there is a universal language that dates all the way back to the builders? The subway itself teaches you the language, if you're patient enough to sit and learn."

"So how come we can't see it?" Troy asked. "Why can we only see you?"

"The subway functions apart from our ordinary concept of space-time," Peter said. "I can use the subway controls to project myself into our space-time for a short while—just as long as the car is at the platform in this system. As soon as the train leaves again—as soon as the particular car I inhabit, goes away—the *me* that you see, will vanish. But if you take my hands—both of you—I can use the car to *jump* you to where I am now. You'll leave the comet-catcher behind. No help for it. But once you're here, seeing what I've been seeing, I think everything will make a lot more sense."

Caddy was breathing rabidly, her heart pounding. This was too much for her to accept at face value. Her brain demanded hard evidence, before she'd accept the hallucination that she—and now, Troy —had been thrust into. Still, it was also an answer to her most fervent wish: to be offered a free ticket out of the purgatory of her colonist exis-tence. Away from New Olympia. Away from human beings altogether. Pure adventure. If Peter was right, the potential was practically limitless.

Still, something nagged at her conscience.

"People have been working too hard," she said, her brown knit.

"At what?" Peter asked.

"New Olympia," Caddy said. "The colony. Troy and me, we spent months and months in simulators and exercises, preparing to come out here and do a job."

"It's a *boring* job," Peter said. "I can tell you that better than anybody."

"But Peter," Caddy said, "sometimes the things which are most worth doing, *are* boring. Troy and I talked about this, and I've decided that he's right. Earth is depending on us to make New Olympia into a planet worth settling some day. Those old aliens—the ones who lost this world in the first place—they never had the technology to save themselves. But we *do*, and though it might take a long time, *somebody's* got to try."

"There are plenty of people to run the comet-catchers," Peter said, dismissing her words with the wave of his hand. "What I'm offering you is the voyage of *eternity.*"

"I don't doubt it," Caddy said, considering her thoughts as she formed them into words. "And maybe, some day, when I'm old, and I've given my life to making New Olympia a better place than how I first found it, I will want to retire—come out here, climb aboard your train, and take a trip. But now? Now . . . I'm *dug in*, big brother. Going through Candidate school? Our first snags? Sending those comets back to the inner system? I feel like the things I am doing finally *count* for something. I've never felt that before. And I don't feel like I'm done yet."

"I don't think I am either," Troy said, nodding his head along with Caddy's words. "You know, you've become a legend, Peter. And I'm sure after we get back and tell everybody about this, you'll become an even bigger legend still. Assuming anyone believes us. I am assuming when you . . . *warp* out of here, that our computers are going to get wiped?"

"Probably, yes," Peter said, nodding.

"No worries," Caddy said. "We have protected backups for all the programs to continue the mission. But what about our *minds?*"

"The subway won't do anything to those," Peter said. "I can assure you."

"Well, then," Caddy said, suddenly feeling warmth building in the center of her chest, "I respectfully decline your offer, big brother. Not easily, mind you. I am sure there will be many nights when I will regret not taking you up on this . . . thing you've embarked upon. But there's comets that need catching, and Troy and me, we're comet-*catchers*. New Olympia needs the air and the water. It won't be fit for man or beast next year, nor in ten years, nor maybe even in a hundred years. But if you're right—and this subway comes through again—I think there will plenty of time for me to make my mark in this little corner of the galaxy. Before running off to see all the rest."

Peter was actually smiling at this point. "I always thought your heart was in the right place, sis."

"And I never stopped loving you, big brother," Caddy said.

Peter turned his attention to Troy.

"You," Peter said sternly, aiming a finger at Troy's nose.

"Yessir?" Troy said reflexively.

"You be good to her," he said. "And be a good dad to my nieces and nephews, understand?"

"But I—" Troy began to sputter.

"Understand?" Peter said again, his finger waving sternly.

"Got it," Troy said, and swallowed thickly. "I promise."

"Right," Peter said. Then he turned his attention back to Caddy.

"I have to go now," he said, his tone turning soft. "The window for me to be here is almost shut. If I had more time, we could talk more. I mean it when I say you can't believe the places I've been."

"I'll get my chance!" Caddy said, tears forming anew. "But first, there's work to be done. Just make sure the damned subway never misses this stop, okay? I have a feeling whole boatloads of people will be coming out here eventually, to take you up on your offer. You'll become known as the ghost conductor of the interstellar express!"

Peter laughed, and ran a finger along his jaw.

"I like the sound of that."

And instantly, he popped out of existence. No sound. He just . . . wasn't there anymore.

For many minutes, Caddy and Troy simply stared in silence. Nothing was said. The soft orchestra music continued to play. The sparkling vastness of the coal sack night was everywhere at once. Magnificent, chilling, and larger than any single human mind could grasp.

"Do you think anyone will buy it?" Troy said. "When we tell them?"

"Does it matter?" Caddy responded. "Just us telling the story is going to get explorers scrambling out here to check it out. At first they'll say we're nuts—and maybe they will be right. But if what just happened, happened, sooner or later somebody other than us is going to be around when Peter's train pulls through, and that's when it's gonna get *real* interesting."

Troy laughed, then swung his way back toward the hatch that led out of the pilot's globe, and back to the living module.

"Leaving so soon?" she said.

"I've still got a few hours sleep to get, before my shift!" he shouted.

"And what about when—"

Suddenly all of the electronics onboard fluttered, and died. Only to come back to life ten seconds later.

"—all the equipment kicks over?" Caddy finished, realizing that the so-called "warp" had done precisely what was expected.

"As if you don't know the system restore drill by heart?" Troy scoffed. "Phone me when a *real* problem develops! You've got this. I am going to bed."

Caddy actually laughed out loud, her fingers automatically beginning to press the key sequences which would boot the ship's software from the hardened disc in the "storm cellar" where radiation couldn't reach. Meanwhile, she made a silent promise to return to this place, and see her brother again. Maybe when she could bring her grandchildren, and make a holiday of it?

# A Veil of Leaves

## M.K. Hutchins

My heart thrilled as the skyman streaked toward the ground, like a single raindrop on a sunny day. What a lucky omen, to have a skyman return on my wedding day.

Grandma smacked her gums. "Last time they came, they stole. Thieves. No good, no good."

The other women shushed her and I spoke gentle. "Skypeople didn't steal anything."

"They built the lightfence between us and the ravencattle. Just as good as stealing." Grandma had been a girl when that happened.

But the Skypeople gave us lights and hotplates, too—they weren't evil. "Ravencattle must've been sick."

Grandma opened her mouth, but the women told her to hush and paint her broadleaf. Most could barely follow their own advice, eyes flitting off into the distance where the skyman's ship was landing. Each took a turn showing me what they'd painted in honey water, anyway. Sister painted a rock for a strong marriage. My cousin painted freshrain for strong broadleaf trees. My aunt painted something I didn't understand, but she winked and giggled until Mother scolded her away.

Soon enough the skyman strode up. He looked like a normal man, except he wore clothes just as silver as the hotplates the skypeople gave us. Red dust clung to it.

He looked over us, face smooth as baby skin. He peered at the wreath on my head. "You're in charge? I'd like a meal—the best you have."

Something silver sat inside his mouth. When he talked, it looked like he was chewing a grub.

The woman nudged me forward and I swallowed my nervousness. A skyman, talking to me! "I'll feed you at my home."

The women jabbered as he passed, trailing their fingers over his silver clothes. Except Grandma. She crossed her wrinkled arms and muttered. Every day of my life, I've seen those feral ravencattle through the light-fence, and I'm glad it's between us—even if Grandma said they used to be tame. The sleek beasts snort and stomp, then stretch their twisty necks and bare their long teeth, so good at shearing leaves and grubs.

The skyman ducked as we entered my hut. The women helped me build it for when my husband comes: straight lashed poles topped with a thick layer of thatch.

"What do you eat now, without the ravencattle?"

"I'll show you." I grinned. I'm the best cook for days all around. Papa says that's why he could bargain for such a good husband for me. It will be lucky, to have a skyman smile on my wedding day.

I waved my hand over the silvery hotplate and it glowed red. I pulled a handful of grubs from a basket—we'd just killed these yesterday. I slit them in two and squeezed their guts into a mortar before tossing them onto the hotplate. They sizzled and jumped.

I added oniongrass to the guts and ground it, tossing it over the hotplate when the grubs were nearly done. I scooped it all into my best bowl, the one my brother made down by the river. Smiling wide enough to sprain my cheeks, I handed it to the skyman. It smelled like freshrain and celebration. "Here's our best."

He was lucky I had a wedding tonight, or there wouldn't have been oniongrass.

The skyman's skin greened. "Bugs? You eat *bugs?*"

"They're *grubs*. Can't you see how big they are?" I frowned. Maybe his long fall did something strange to his brain.

The metal thing in his mouth bobbed like a second tongue. "You were supposed to do something creative with the plants to replace protein in your diet, not turn to *bugs*." He sniffed at my food and recoiled. "I could lose my position on the committee over this. I'm supposed to bring back something succulent like tofu in all its variation, fried, simmered, marinated..." He sighed and shook his head. "You don't even know what tofu is, do you?"

I shrugged. Why should I? It couldn't be better than my grubs. Even the bitter widow who lives nearest the fence agreed I cooked the best bowl anywhere.

He tapped the metal thing in his mouth and started talking to himself, staring at his food. "Yes, I'm here. No, they're eating bugs. Maybe if the presentation's spectacular, everyone will still eat them. Here's a picture." He opened his mouth wide and tapped it again. He must have been talking to another skyman, because he paused like he was listening. "Poisonous?"

He whipped his head up. "These are *poisonous?*"

"Not the way I serve them." I folded my arms. No man had ever insulted my food in my kitchen, and skyman or no, I wasn't keen to start having that now. "They ate the broadleaf."

Grandma had told me the story a hundred times. With the raven-cattle fenced out, people were hungry. There were so many grubs, without the ravencattle munching, that some people ate them. They died. Some people ate the broadleaf, but they died, too. The ravencattle ate both, so we figured it out: broadleaf and grub make each other safe to eat. Getting the grubs to eat the leaves by coating them in honey-water? That killed the grubs, made them safe, and tenderized them.

Mine were the tastiest.

"I agree, this expedition's a complete waste of time," the skyman said, not looking at me. "We can't feed this to the ship. The locals could have just developed an immunity. Since we're still looking for new smoking, grilling, or rotisserie techniques, I'll...no, I'm perfectly capable of being in charge...oh. Oh."

The skyman tapped the silver thing in his mouth, then slumped into my hammock, digging the heels of his hands into his eye sockets.

"You want a cup of freshwater to go with?" I asked.

"No. I have to go."

"You came for one meal?" I frowned. It seemed like a long way to come.

"Our chefs can only invent so much. Some of the most delicious foods were invented from necessity, and we'd hoped for something spec-tacular here. What did you think your colony's for?"

Bile burned up my throat. I must have heard wrong. After all, the skypeople gave us lights and hotplates. "You're saying you took away our ravencattle, then came back a hundred years later hoping for a treat?"

Grandma never lets us forget about the people who died when they fenced out the ravencattle. Her brothers, her niece, her mother.

He glared. "It doesn't take a hundred years for us, not with how fast we move. You were the most promising planet, you know. We restricted fuel on the last two worlds, and they only reinvented stir-fry and kabobs. We'd hoped for something spectacular down here. I can't believe we got bugs. *Poisonous* bugs."

He marched out my door and across the dusty red ground. The women spilled in after he streaked back into the sky, in his teardrop of silver. They asked me what he wanted. I held up the plate of grubs.

Grandma smacked her gums and shook her head at me. "Was your skyman everything you thought he'd be?"

"No." I didn't see any point in lying. I expected Grandma to lecture me, but she just hugged me tight, like she wasn't sure she'd get another chance to.

The other women muttered about how crazy she was, but I didn't pay them any heed. I hugged Grandma back, as if a single hug could apologize for all the times I'd rolled my eyes at her, too.

It was a good omen that the skyman left before my wedding. I watched the grubs munch the leaves the women painted. They only ate the honey-water part, leaving the patterns behind. Then the grubs shivered and curled into balls, ready to cook. I sewed the leaves together for my veil while the women made the feast for the wedding guests, then I personally fried up my groom's dinner. That skyman was crazy for not trying grubs in oniongrass.

I fed it to my groom before both our families, both our villages. The skypeople lights from our houses flooded the red ground and the snaking roots of the broadleaf trees we stood between. He blushed and smiled, looking shyly down, then up at me. His eyes were the rich color of grub guts and he almost smelled as nice.

Our parents draped the veil with all its pretty wishes over both of us. Mother told us we had to make the wishes come true; his father said something about patience.

The lights flickered. I froze; that had never happened. Then they blackened, turning the world to shadows. Murmurs hissed through the crowd. One of the women ran inside her hut, then rushed back out, shouting that the lights wouldn't come back and the hotplate didn't work.

I clutched my groom's hand. He shook, too. The hotplates always worked.

When I heard the stomping hooves, I looked towards the lightfence.
It wasn't there.

The ravencattle charged faster than I could think, eyes wide and wild in the moonlight. They trampled a man to death, right there, right in front of me, squishing his guts out like a grub's.

My groom grabbed my wrist and ran. Villagers panicked around us —some shrieking, some running—but his parents hadn't lied in the wedding bartering when they said he was fast. He yanked me inside my hut and barred the door.

It was dark, dark like the inside of my eyelids, dark like the blood of the broadleaf tree. People shrieked and shouted. Other doors slammed shut. Not even my new, thick thatch could keep out the sobbing of my village and the crunch as the ravencattle chewed at our trees.

I held my groom and he held me through the dark night. When the sun rose, when light came, we cracked the door and peered outside.

The broadleaf trees looked like skeleton hands reaching from the ground, leaves gone. Our cages of grubs at their bases were smashed open, empty. A few ravencattle peered at us as they chewed. Their hooves squashed the faces of our dead. Ten bodies, twelve? I couldn't tell.

We shuffled back inside the hut. I waved my hand over the hotplate. Nothing.

"We'll starve." My groom's handsome eyes trembled.

What had the skyman said? I didn't know what grilling was, but I did know smoke. Grandma talked about how her mother had cooked with fire every time we cremated one of our dead or burned out a rotted broadleaf tree.

I peered out the door. A ravencow snorted at us. I took my veil—maybe the last bit of broadleaf in the village—and tossed it to the side. The ravencow charged after it. I dashed out, snatched sticks from under the broadleaf trees, then ran back inside.

I grabbed a piece of flint and my silvery knife.

His eyes widened. "We don't need a pyre yet."

"Of course not, but I won't have a hungry husband."

I sparked the sticks and blew gently. While they burned, I rubbed down a yellowroot with the last wisp of oniongrass, then laid it on the coals to roast. Hopefully, it would cook.

I counted my baskets and jars. The other huts would have about the same. It couldn't last.

I looked at my knife. I didn't want to face wild ravencattle up close, so I lashed it to my broom, then slipped out the front of my hut, scrambled up the side, and perched in the thatch.

My groom scurried after. "What are you doing?"

"We'll need more food soon." I eyed a ravencow as it wandered towards us. "Everyone will."

Maybe Grandma could teach us how to cook it.

# Freefall

### Eric James Stone

F reefall was the best part of a jump.

As she fell, Gina Wright looked down at Earth, half shadowed beneath her as dawn crept toward her landing target in Kansas, and relished the knowledge that she was about to demolish the world freefall record by more than 20,000 miles. This was going to be so much better than her spacejump from the old International Space Station. She would have forty minutes of freefall before she even entered the atmosphere.

Using the gyros in her pressure suit, she turned away from Earth. The space elevator cable stretched like a strand of spiderweb past her toward the rotating hub-and-spoke wheel she had jumped from: GeoTerminal 1.

A brilliant flash behind the terminal forced Gina to blink even as her visor darkened to compensate. After her visor cleared, she saw a ripple moving down the space elevator cable.

Had the cable broken? No—the LED lights strung along it were still on, so power still flowed from the terminal. With a dad who was chief engineer for the elevator and a brother who drove one of the crawlers, she knew more than she wanted to about the elevator. "How high is it?" and "Can I jump off it?" were the only things that really mattered.

She told her suitphone to call her dad.

"What?" he answered.

"What's going on? I saw a flash and—"

"Working on it. No time for idle curiosity." He hung up.

Typical, she thought. *If I were Kyle, he'd explain things, expect me to help solve them. But no, I'm the idle child who wastes her life jumping.*

She shouldn't let her dad's attitude spoil the thrill of the jump. Activating the gyros, Gina turned her back on the terminal.

MINUTES LATER HER SUITPHONE BEEPED. SHE ANSWERED IT.

"Gina?" Her father's voice was strained.

"Yeah?"

"Sorry about before. We lost the counterweight."

Gina sucked in a sharp breath. The geostationary terminal had to be at the center of mass for the space elevator. Without the asteroid counterweight beyond the terminal, the weight of the cable would pull the terminal—and all the people on it—down to Earth. "How'd it happen?"

"That's for later. What matters is what we do about it."

If the terminal was falling, that meant her dad was falling with it. "Dad, do you have a way to evacuate?"

"No," he said. "But we'll be fine once we detach the cable. Without its weight, the terminal will settle into a stable orbit."

"Oh." Of course they had contingency plans.

"Is there any way you can get over to the cable?" he asked.

"I've got some backup rocket thrusters for maneuvering in case the gyros go out," she said. "Why?"

"You've got a vibroknife that will cut through nanofibers, right? For cutting your chute cords if they get tangled? I remember you telling me that."

"Yeah." Gina was surprised he remembered anything she'd told him about jumping. "Again, why?"

"Kyle's bringing a cargo crawler up. If we detach the cable up here, he'll fall."

Despite the fact she was already in freefall, Gina's stomach seemed to sink inside her.

"I'll let him die if I have to." Her dad's voice cracked. "One life against thousands. But if you can get over there and cut through the cable underneath his crawler, then he can keep coming up and we'll all be safe in orbit until the company sends a rescue ship."

With the gyros, she oriented herself toward the cable. The station's slingshot had flung her in the opposite direction of its orbit to put her into a freefall path to Earth. She hoped she had enough fuel to cross the distance in time.

"Usually it's good old dependable Kyle coming to rescue me after some crazy stunt." She chuckled, trying to laugh away the sudden weight of responsibility. Risking her own life was easy—having someone else's life depend on her was different. "Whose plan is this, anyway?"

"Kyle's. He said if anyone's crazy enough to make it work, it's you."

A FEW FEET AWAY, THE CABLE LIGHTS FLEW PAST GINA IN A CONTINUOUS blur. But her fuel readout flashed 1% in crimson. It had taken almost all her fuel to change her trajectory enough get to the cable. But there wasn't enough left to slow her descent relative to the cable. She needed to wait until Kyle's crawler moved past her in any case—she had arrived at the cable above him. But soon her fuel would be gone entirely, and her freefall path would take her away.

Still thousands of miles out of the atmosphere, her chute was useless. There was no way she could stop herself, and that meant she could not cut through the cable—the vibroknife would be torn from her grip if she tried cutting at this speed. She was going to fail Kyle, fail her dad, unless—her mind raced as she saw the possibility—unless she could get Kyle a spacechute.

"Dad?" she said.

"Still here."

"Can you patch me through to Kyle?"

"Hold on."

After a few seconds, Kyle's voice came on her phone. "Hey, sis. How's the view from up there?"

She ignored his banter and began unbuckling her chute. She was falling fast toward his crawler, so time was limited. "You're the only person on board the crawler, right?"

"Yes." Kyle must have sensed her urgency, because his voice became all business.

"You have a spacesuit?"

"Yes. Why?"

"I'm falling too fast to be able to stop and cut through the cable," she said. "But I'm removing my backup chute and I'll attach it to the cable just before I pass you. It'll slam into the crawler at a pretty good clip, but it's nanofiber so it should be okay. Then you can go out and get it."

"I've never done a spacejump," he said.

"I'll set the chute for auto, so it'll release at the right altitude. You'll be fine. Trust me." She used a tiny bit of fuel to get close enough to the cable that she would be able to attach the chute.

A pause. "I trust you."

Gina smiled. "Good."

She set the chute to automatically deploy as soon as it detected atmosphere, then removed the final straps.

She could see the blinking lights of the crawler approaching rapidly from below. Careful not to touch the cable itself, she pulled the chute straps around the cable and fastened them. Then she used the last of her suit's fuel to start moving away from the cable.

The chute hit the top of the crawler as it whizzed past her.

"Your chute is ready," she said. "And Kyle . . ."

"What?"

I love you, was what she was going to say, but their family had never been one to express maudlin emotion. Besides, he would know she loved him when he found out there was no such thing as a detachable backup chute. "Safe landing."

"Thanks, sis. Same to you."

Gina turned off the phone. Using her gyros, she turned to face Earth one last time. The familiar thrill welled up inside her.

Freefall was the best part of a jump.

# Launch

## Daniel Friend

"Do you swear to tell the truth, the whole truth, and nothing but the truth, so help you God?"

*So help me God*, I thought. *So help me, God. I do.*

"I do."

The cameras hovered all around me, little insects with quietly purring rotor wings. There were no flashes like in the old lawyer shows, though. The courtroom and the witness stand were already lit perfectly.

"Where were you the day before the launch?"

"Cape Canaveral," I said, giving in to my nerves and putting a strand of hair back behind my ear. "I was seeing my sister off before the launch. She was sad because she'd have to leave her teddy bear behind."

"And how old was your sister?"

"She had just turned four."

The prosecutor let the word hang in space for a beat. He turned, rubbed his balding black head, and then turned back around to face me, his fingers now stroking his neat, kempt mustache. He had finished questioning most of the preliminary witnesses already.

The NASA program director had been called in to explain to the court exactly how the colony ship had been constructed with modules of colonists in suspended animation to protect them from the rigors of the trip; the string physicist, who had needed an assistant to translate his techno-jargon into understandable English, had testified about how every unaccounted-for gram of mass would throw off the ship's hyperdrive exponentially, marooning it who-knows-where in deep space.

All of it had been pretty standard, really; the information was the same stuff anyone could look up on WikiNews. The only point in rehashing it was so that it would be in the court's official record. And, of course, to remind the nations of spectators watching the trial.

And now it was my turn. The first question had been standard procedure; the second, and its pause, were calculated to remind the viewers in the twenty-six countries who had contributed colonists how much they had lost, how much they hurt, and how much they wanted someone to blame. I knew exactly how they felt and then some.

"Ms. Penn, why weren't you emigrating to Regulus with the rest of your family?"

"It didn't make sense at the time. I had my job here at the Cape, I had a boyfriend, and by the time that didn't work out, it was too late to change plans. I was thinking about joining the next colony ship in a few years, but...I don't think there'd be much reason to now."

"We all know," the prosecutor said. "After you had seen your family, what did you do next?"

"I went back to work. It's a busy day before a launch; we had to make sure that the payload module's systems checked out, we had to make the final adjustments to the mass calculations so that in-orbit fueling could continue, we had to prep the cryogenics for the people who were about to . . ."

I tried to bite back the tears welling up in my eyes. The rotor wings of the cameras whirred. Real grief is better than any Oscar-winning performance. The prosecutor took a step closer and tried to look kindly. "Charity, we all understand your loss. We know how much it hurts. But right now we need to establish the guilt of the person who caused all this. Okay?"

I nodded. The prosecutor continued, finally getting to the meat of the case, the reason I was up on that stand.

"After you left your family, did you see this man at work?" The prosecutor pointed to the man in the defendant's chair, Lee Talley.

Lee Talley. The man the entire world wanted to crucify. The man every developed nation wanted to turn into a scapegoat for what would probably come to be known as *The Horizon Disaster*, or maybe *The Horizon Disappearance*. It didn't matter. The point was that there were five hundred people that would almost certainly never be heard from again.

Scrawny, young Lee Talley, with his black hair, brown eyes, tan skin, patchy goatee and plastic-framed glasses, barely two years out of college, was going to take the fall for the lives of those five hundred people. Fate had decreed it, and from the way he looked vacantly down at the court-room floor, I guessed that he knew it too. He was the reason I was here. He was the person my testimony could condemn.

And there I was, with my lame brown hair and stupid violet contacts and pressed pinstripe skirt, about to say all the words that would bring "justice" crashing down upon this lanky, quiet boy. Heck, he was only two years younger than me. I could've gone out with him if I hadn't been with Brad, and if Lee had ever said more than two words at a time. He was always so quiet that I never really knew him, even after working together for all those months. Now somehow his life depended on my testimony.

"Yes," I said, "I saw him at work."

"You work preparing the launch payload, correct?"

"Correct."

"What were each of you doing that particular afternoon to prepare the stasis module?"

"I was running the final check on the intravenous interface of each stasis alcove—the system that administers the sedatives before launch, the cryogenic preservatives during stasis, and the stimulant to wake the colonists up. Lee was final-checking the module computer systems that administer drug flow and life support when the colonists wake." I took a deep breath, steeling myself. "He was also in charge of uploading the final mass calculations to the computer that would interface with the hyperdrive."

"So you're saying that it was Mr. Talley's job to upload to the computer the final mass calculations of the module and all its occupants?"

"Yes, the combined masses of the module itself, every person that was about to board, and all the equipment that was to be loaded with them."

"This is the same mass measurement used in the calculations for the crucial hyperspace jump, correct?"

"That's correct."

"So any error, even a slight one, in Mr. Talley's calculations would have interfered with the hyperdrive computer's calculations, correct?"

That strand of hair had come loose again. I put it back behind my ear. "That's what the string physicists say."

"In your estimation, Ms. Penn, how difficult would it be to change those calculations on the spot?"

"Objection, Your Honor, these questions have already been asked to an expert in the field," the defense lawyer said. "There's no need to belabor the point." The cameras whirred to face him, as though transmitting back to us, through their movements, the excitement of the millions of people watching the broadcast. Then they whizzed back to cover the prosecutor as he responded.

"Your Honor, I believe Ms. Penn can provide a unique point of view on the topic that is relevant to these proceedings; that is, what it is like to do these calculations in a work environment rather than a university."

"The witness may answer the question," the judge said. "Objection overruled." The defense lawyer's sandy hair seemed to droop along with his eyes.

"I'm not sure if I'm qualified to answer that," I said. "Lee was hired because his degree prepared him for that kind of string calculation. I really don't have the training for that part of the job. But I saw on other launches that it could take him a long time to readjust the calculations if something wasn't as expected."

"How long a time, Ms. Penn?"

"I don't know; I never timed it. Several minutes, maybe."

"How much time did he take to check the calculations before this launch? More than usual?"

"I can't say exactly. It wasn't a short one, but it wasn't one of his longest, either. It was longer than his average time, though, I'd say."

"Did he mention anything being out of the ordinary about the mass of the capsule?"

"No."

"Did you see anything unusual regarding Mr. Talley that day?"

This was the pivot question. Everything in the case turned on how I answered it. *"Do you swear to tell the truth, the whole truth, and nothing but the truth, so help you God?"* The words echoed in my mind. *The truth, the whole truth, and nothing but the truth.* I reached up to put my hair behind my ear, but it was already there, so I put my hand down again. I answered the prosecutor's question. I told the truth, and nothing but the truth. Just like we had planned.

"Yes. When we entered the capsule, Lee had a small package with him. It was about the size of a burrito, wrapped in a silver foil that looked like a heat sealant. He put it in his pocket as we entered the capsule for the final check. I don't think he realized that I saw him."

"And what was so unusual about that? I'll save my colleague the trouble of a cross-examination question later and ask it now: couldn't the item just have been a regular burrito?"

"I don't think so. They don't let those in past security, technically, but he was more careful with it than anyone I know is with Taco Bueno. And the really strange part about it was that he didn't seem to have it when we left."

"Are you sure about that?" the prosecutor asked, suddenly intense.

"Yes," I said. "It was big enough to see in his pocket. He didn't have it when we came out."

"And why didn't you say anything to anybody about this before?"

"I assumed that it was a part or tool or something that Lee needed on the ship. Lee never says anything about his work—well, about anything at all, really—so I just assumed that it was . . . normal."

Of course, as soon as the investigation about the *Horizon*'s disappearance had been launched, I had told them about it. In exchange for my testimony against Lee Talley, I wouldn't get charged with criminal negligence and involuntary manslaughter. I went along with it all the way. And here I was, finishing it.

"No more questions," the prosecutor said.

The sandy-haired defense attorney asked me some questions, mostly, I think, for the sake of appearances. But my testimony was damning and he knew it. And as I got down from the witness stand, I could see in Lee's eyes that he knew it, too.

Lee didn't even look at me, but even so, I looked away. I couldn't risk meeting his gaze right then. As I walked, stumbling, back to my seat with the in-house spectators, I tried to fight back my tears. The camera bots stopped looking at me once I sat down, and then whirred away to whatever argument was taking place between the two lawyers.

Finally, I let the tears come out. Silently, I cried and trembled in my seat. I couldn't see the courtroom floor through my own saltwater. All I could see through the tears was my baby sister's face as she handed me her teddy bear, and I promised to take good care of her. That tiny teddy bear, with her pink and white plaid dress and her pink bow.

All I could see was Lee discreetly hiding his package in a cryostasis alcove. I knew when he did it that he was reworking the mass calculations to include it. I didn't even know who he'd left it there for. All I could see, through my tears, was my hand placing that tiny pink bow from my sister's tiny teddy bear in the chamber that I knew would be hers, in a place that I knew wouldn't be noticed before launch, but that she would be sure to find it when she woke up. What a look of joy on her face that would have been! Surely that tiny bow wasn't a gram, was it? Surely one minuscule gram couldn't throw off the calculations!

I know Lee didn't see me place it. I know because when it was his turn to testify, he didn't mention it. He was resigned to his lot, nothing more. He was going to die, and that was the truth, the whole truth, and nothing but the truth.

The whole truth.

*Oh, help me, God!*

# Glass Beads

### Emily Martha Sorensen

The first evidence that aliens existed was a junk heap. A trashy old ship that was barely running, strapped with a broken hyperspace drive, barely afloat, dead in space.

And it wandered aimlessly into our solar system.

We didn't realize, at first, that it was a trash heap. We went ballistic trying to contact it. When we discovered it seemed to be just dead in space, we prepared a mission to visit it. For political reasons, I was selected as one of the first explorers, representative of the Native American Consensus that had taken over North America after the collapse of the United States economy.

My other team members were experts in engineering, programming, sociology, and linguistics. So I was set adrift from the rest of them in our three-month journey, nominally the leader, in fact treated with the cold politeness due to one of my rank who did not have the expertise.

As we docked, the other members' excitement was palpable. Anna Lewis, our programmer, actually licked her lips.

"What do you think we're going to find?" Don Sanchez, our sociologist, asked nervously. He twitched and bounced, his ADHD even more apparent now that our goal was so near. "Do you think we're going to find anything worth salvaging? Do you think we're going to find frozen corpses, or real, life frozen crew members? Do you think—"

"I think we're going to find what we're going to find," Chinue Ndiaye, our linguistic, said coolly. She was always calm and rational, and

Don had irritated her more than once on this trip. They had had this conversation multiple times, and she clearly disliked him distracting her now, once again, with it.

"Just hope we'll be able to salvage something," Garth O'Harris, our engineer, said gruffly. He had spent most of his trip avoiding the rest of them, his skill with people mainly at its best when he ignored them and kept working.

Tensions were high, so as the nominal team leader, I stepped in.

"Whatever we find, the United Nations will receive gratefully. No matter the outcome, our names will go down in history . . ."

A chorus of groans came from the rest.

"Jono, no offense, but we've heard that speech before," Don told me.

"Yeah, we don't have to hear it again right now!" Anna cried.

"Better we focus on the matter at hand," Chinue murmured.

I schooled my face to keep from showing my annoyance. This team had not been vetted sufficiently to make sure we got along together before sending us off to space—the United Nations had been too eager to get a team out there to study it to do more than the rudimentary of psych profiles before putting us up there. Theoretically, it was my job to keep everything running smoothly, but when tempers were high, all too frequently I was chosen as the common enemy.

"I just want us to calm down," I said soothingly. "Just breathe . . ."

The pressurized hatch made a sucking sound.

"That's it!" Anna screamed. She dove forward to read the display. "Vacuum-sealed," she said. "And it's oxygen in there. Pure oxygen, nearly. We'll have to be careful not to create too much friction. One spark could be deadly."

"Environmental suits," I ordered. "Just in case."

Despite the tension, nobody disagreed me. Encumbrance as those could be, nobody was stupid enough to risk their lives over it. I said a silent prayer of thanks.

Chinue went first, Garth a short second. Now that we were here, now that we were starting, the tension was dissipating to make a well-oiled team. Anna went third, nervously bouncing in the low gravity, and Don followed last, after me.

A series of vents came on over us, and Anna shrieked. Garth pulled out his pocket reader and checked for the composition.

"Hydrogen. Helium," he noted. "Not air we can breathe."

"Do you think they're trying to poison us?" Don asked nervously.

"Don't be stupid, Don," Chinue said. "It's probably what they breathe."

The derelict looked more and more useless, the further we moved into it. The reason it had been abandoned seemed clear to me. But Garth took a different perspective.

"Much of this is like the technology we use already," he said gruffly, examining a doorway. "It's twenty years ahead of our own, maybe. This is something we can analyze and make use of immediately."

And Chinue was riveted by the scrapes and scratches over doorways. She noticed a regular pattern and started taking notes on her tablet to analyze it.

Despite my advice, once we'd gone over the tiny ship together twice, the experts broke into different teams. Anna gravitated towards ops, or what we assumed was like it, to see if she could get more than the environmental systems working. Garth tried to figure out the drive, or what looked like the engine, to see if it really could have come from that far away. And Don hovered near Chinue, making notes and sharing with her. Irritated as she could be with him when they were not working, as soon as they had a project to share, they were a well-oiled machine.

I headed up to ops to see what Anna had gotten functioning.

THE REST OF OUR JOURNEY WENT MUCH MORE SMOOTHLY. THE SHIP clamped onto our own firmly, we visited it daily on our journey back to Earth. Chinue seemed to be determined to work out the alien language before we got home again, and when Garth had gotten sufficient systems fixed that Anna was able to download some video records, Chinue and Don poured over them almost constantly. I had to remind them over and over again that they required more than two hours of sleep per day.

Through all of it, I started to get an unsettling feeling. Not that it could be put-my-finger on precisely, but it all seemed just a little too easy. Of course, when I tried to explain this, nobody listened to me.

"*Easy?* " Anna asked incredulously. "You think this is *easy?* I suppose you think they write their software in C! I'm flying blind here; I can't even work out what kind of machine code they are using. You think figuring out a system just by picking options at random is *easy?*"

Don just laughed when I said the same thing. "This is an alien culture, Jono. It's nothing like our own. It's amazing."

And Chinue, halfway into her list of tentative nouns, verbs, and particles, simply ignored me.

Garth, surprisingly, was the only one who listened to me.

"The technology bothers me," he said. "I don't think this was accidental."

My heart hammered. "What do you mean?"

"Well, this." He knocked the wall. "For one thing. The whole spaceship seems so similar to what we have right now, it's eerie. It was built much like we build things, and it doesn't have any real comforts and luxuries. It has no drive other than basic impulse either, for another thing. It was built for use inside a solar system."

"Could it be from our future?" I wondered out loud.

Garth laughed. "Einstein disproved that. Communication to the past might eventually be possible, but not sending back a whole spaceship."

"Besides, that doesn't explain the linguistics," I murmured, looking back at the corridor where Chinue was working. "The bug-eyed alien video files could be faked, but I find it hard to believe anyone could build a language built so differently from ours that it would take Chinue weeks to analyze it. No known analogs at all in our languages, she says. All the artificially-created languages on Earth were built on something—be it Spanish, German, Gaelic, or Old English . . ."

Garth nodded. "Yes. There's that, too."

Still, the technology so eerily like our own continued to bother me. Until the day that Anna discovered what she thought was a communications protocol.

"Look at this, look at this, look at this, look at this!" she shrieked, running down the corridor and jabbing her finger back the way she came. "Everybody! I think I've found the way they communicated! And it's *talking!*"

Of course we all dropped everything and booked it. My game of Solitaire forgotten, Garth's nap, even Don's notes back home about the apparent color that meant danger to their people (yellow, where red would have been the human equivalent).

Breathless, Don panted and waited. Chinue's face looked impassive, but her knuckles gripped the seat before her so hard they had turned white. And then Anna turned on the machine.

There was loud static for a moment. Then palpable silence. We waited, our hope matched only by our terror. And then the voice came back again.

"What it is saying?! What is it saying?! What is it saying?!" Don shouted.

"Shut up! Let me analyze it!" Chinue snapped, recording it to run through the program Anna had written for her. The voice kept talking in clicks and snarls, talking and talking, and repeating itself in a pattern. She sighed in frustration after several minutes. "We don't know enough yet. I think it might be saying something that means 'spaceship'—or perhaps 'people aboard the spaceship.' I don't know yet whether we've triggered a distress beacon, it's just a pre-recorded message, or if this is actually somebody speaking."

"That's all we need—an outer space 'out of service area' message," Don quipped.

Anna laughed tightly.

"Hello?" Garth asked, taking what looked like the microphone. "We can't understand your language. Not yet. If any of you have better linguists than we do, we speak a language called English. Um. We could send you samples if you need . . ." He trailed off, looking at us. "Think that's a stupid idea?"

"Better than nothing," Chinue said.

Anna turned on her voice recorder and played back several of her reports. The voice on the other end went silent. It kept on going. We waited for almost an hour, but even after Anna shut it off, the voice was silent.

"I think that's it for the day," Anna said finally. "Tell you what—I'll keep it turned on, and I'll call you if I hear anything."

"Keep the voice recorder going," Chinue said tightly.

"Do I look stupid?" Anna retorted. "Of course I'm going to keep it going."

It was several days before we heard the alien voice again.

THE NEXT FEW WEEKS, CHINUE AND ANNA WERE AT THE COMMUNICATIONS center almost constantly. Don forwarded reports to Earth at least every day, and Garth spent his time trying to triangulate where the signal came from.

"That's where the problem is coming," he explained. "I can't find that signal *anyplace*. We're five weeks out of communications range from Earth, so we can't ask for advice yet—they haven't even heard the news that we have alien contact yet. No doubt they'll be sending other experts out to meet us, but in the meantime . . ."

". . . We're stuck on our own," I finished.

After awhile, it seemed Chinue and the alien speaker had gotten some real understanding going. Within a week, Chinue was speaking in bits and pieces of its language, while it conversed with us in broken English.

"Those aliens must be real language savants," I said, impressed.

"Don't be an idiot," Chinue said without looking up. "I'm speaking to one of their *experts*, not common folk, and we're both using technological aid."

"It's basically Babelfish," Anna put in, bouncing in her chair. "It's simple enough that I barely had to tweak it. Basically, just had to fix the way they refer to things indirectly instead of directly, so most of their stuff comes out in a passive voice equivalent, and their subject-object terminology, which has six extra divisions ours doesn't. There's self-as-social-group-perceives-it, for instance, or outsider-as-self-perceives-it, inanimate-object-that-doesn't-perceive, inanimate-object-that-does-some-how-perceive things—"

"Hush up," Chinue said tightly. "We're talking."

"— Five world," the microphone said, then a series of growls and clicks. Chinue tapped through her dictionary for a moment, then carefully repeated half of what he said, ending with the slightly-louder inflection that indicated a question.

There was another loud alien burst of static, then more monologuing. Chinue scrutinized her tablet for a minute, made several notes, asked another question, and then sat back, stunned.

"He's trying to open trade negotiations," she said.

We rocked back on our heels. Trade negotiations. We weren't qualified for this sort of thing.

"Don't promise anything," Don said immediately. "We'll wait until the experts can do it. Explain to them we need to wait until we understand each others' languages better. We can't negotiate anything without UN authority."

Chinue nodded. There was another back and forth for several breathless minutes. Then her face got even paler.

"He said, in his people, to refuse a trade negotiation is seen as act of aggression. If we don't want to offend the superiors, and perhaps spark a war, we need to start hammering out something now."

I let out my breath in an explosive exhale. Nobody had sent a diplomat here. Then I realized everyone was looking at me.

"What?" I asked nervously.

"You," Don said. "You're the one who's good with people. You're the closest thing we have to a politician here. You negotiate."

I stared at him, arms tightening in horror. "You can't be serious. I'm not remotely qualified for—"

"He says he wants Jupiter," Chinue said, looking up from her screen. "'You've taken our technology. You can have it, if you wish. In return, we want possession of fifth planet.' I believe that's what he's saying."

"That's fair, isn't it?" Anna asked. "We can't use it for anything. Here, let's say yes—"

"*No!*" I shouted.

Heads turned to me.

"One junk heap spaceship for an entire planet?" I asked through grated teeth. "You must be crazy. Tell him we will *lease* some portion of the planet in exchange for *equivalent* technology. We will need blueprints of this communications system he is using, to begin with."

Chinue nodded and went back to talking. There was back and forth for several minutes.

"The concept of 'lease' is unfamiliar," she reported. "Or I do not understand the terminology. I think 'use, not keep' is understandable, however. He agreed to it."

I rubbed my forehead, which was tense with fear. I couldn't believe this had been left to me. "Okay. We need . . . we need . . . what else do we need?"

"We need blueprints of this spaceship," Garth said immediately.

"Information about their society and history," Don added.

"We probably want some kind of dictionary of their languages, both spoken and verbal," I said.

"A manual of their programming languages," Anna put in.

"And information about this alloy." Garth knocked his fist against the wall of the ship. "I haven't seen anything like it."

Chinue nodded and began speaking into the microphone again.

"Do you really think we're going to get it?" Don wondered out loud.

"In exchange for Jupiter?" I retorted. "We'd better."

There was a lot more back and forth.

"Tentative agreement," Chinue said finally. "We will pick up the negotiations again in the morning. It is now their rest period."

We all let out sighs of exhaustion and relief.

As we were heading back towards our own ship, Garth was pondering.

"You know . . . I've been thinking . . ." he said.

"About the negotiations?" I asked.

He nodded. "Yeah. About the convenience of it."

"You think they sent the spaceship here to force us into negotiating?" I asked. "Same thought had occurred to me."

"Don't know why they want Jupiter, of course," he said.

"No." I shook my head. "Which is why I'm so worried. I don't know what we're bargaining away. I'm afraid what we're asking for is glass beads."

"Glass beads." He looked questioning.

"There's a myth about my people that they sold the island of Manhattan for a handful of glass beads," I said tightly. "It's not really verified by history. But it does illustrate what I fear we're doing."

"Trading something without knowing how much value it has," he said.

I nodded. "Or the value of what we seek."

"And yet, the invaders have the upper hand." He rubbed his beard, looking troubled. "We can't refuse to negotiate, or they'll just take what they want by force anyway."

"Exactly."

He frowned and pondered for a moment. "Well, I'm glad you said 'lease,'" he said finally. "If nothing else, we'll get it back eventually."

"And I'll try very hard," I said grimly, "not to trade our land for glass beads."

# Sweetly the Dragon Dreams
## David Farland

*Life finds a way. We dropped planet-killers on Mursadoni, scorching all three continents, and when I returned forty-two years later, the land was covered with green ferns that provided food for clouds of lightning moths.*

*So I searched the heavens further. On Remiseas, nine hundred years after its immolation, I found forests and birds and lizards—all which should have been decimated—and I discovered new life-forms rising from the ashes of the old.*

*On Danai, the infestation was much worse. A few of the higher life forms were gone, but after six thousand years, I found wide variations in the flora and fauna. Included among the survivors is a thriving population of humans led by a hive of skraals. My supply of planet-killers and sunbusters has been exhausted. I will drop flash-heads into the hive with the hope that the resultant nuclear contamination will wipe out the skraals' queen. Further steps will be required to eradicate the biological contaminations.*

—final transmission from the cycor drone ship *Death's Head*

In the dry days on Danai, the moons lure the damselfly nymphs from the slow-flowing waters. Soft of flesh they come, minute hunters from the marsh, climbing ashen stalks of cattails or perchance some slender green reed.

At the rising of the sun, they settle at the base of a frond, letting the light take them and transform them, until their old bones crack and their new form breaks free.

For a moment they will hesitate, poised, their new wings still wet, waxen and thrumming, as they examine their own glory.

Soft new carapaces shine in the sunlight—glimmering like cinnabar or rubies, or the green of dappled leaves.

That is how young Tallori found them that summer morning as she waded along the shores of the marsh. The rising sun hung like a golden shield upon the shoulders of the world, and the young damselflies just seemed to be waiting for her to pluck them from their perches.

She had caught nearly a hundred in a dozen different hues, placing them in a reed basket. She felt happy to be catching them. Tallori would be paid one silver penny for every five damselflies. She could make a small fortune in a few weeks.

Tallori was a bright child, but not bright enough. She had not been found worthy of schooling. She was a mere human, and thus far inferior to skraals that ruled Danai.

The damselflies were to be food for the Holy Maiden Seramasia, and Tallori felt grateful to be of service. Not only would she make more than she had ever dreamed, she would also be assisting a goddess.

Tallori was large for an eight-year-old girl. Her hair was yellow sunlight, and her eyes, set deep beneath her brow, were greener than the sea. She sang a rhyme as she picked the damselflies from the stalks:

> *A blue one to ease my lady's cares,*
> *A red one to make her grow.*
> *A white one to match her skin so fair,*
> *A gold one to make her glow!*

That is when she found the monster.

Tallori tiptoed over a break in the cattails, a space less than ten yards across, when she noticed how rough the ground felt beneath her feet. The dark water was as brown as her father's beer, and she could not see through it, yet at times she could feel clams in the mud with her toes, or find small freshwater crabs to eat. The rough surface made her wonder.

She stopped to pick a scab from her knee and eat it. That's when she looked down. A vast eye stared up at her. She screamed.

"OVER HERE!" TALLORI SHOUTED, DRAGGING HER FATHER, ANGAR, TO the edge of the wide river. At the child's insistence, he'd brought a huge ax. He stopped, unwilling to muddy his sandals.

He suspected this was all some plot on his wife's part to get him to do some work. When Tallori had come with her story about a monster in the bog, Angar's wife had said in a businesslike tone, "Bring back some reeds, and I'll weave some baskets."

So he was skeptical of Tallori's motives in bringing him. He was a fat man with fondness for strong drink. Rather than wade off into the mud, he squatted in some reeds and rubbed his temple, wishing the sunlight did not aggravate his hangover so much.

"Come quick!" Tallori shouted. "The monster is over here. You can see its big teeth!"

Only when Tallori tugged his arm and became frantic did Angar pull off his sandals of woven reeds and bother to step into the mud.

Twenty feet from shore, he saw it there, beneath four inches of tawny water: an eye as large as a platter, reflecting the golden sun. It was set in a serpentine head that looked to be some nine feet long and four feet tall. The whole of it lay in the water, staring out.

Mankind had been living on Danai for over a hundred thousand years. From time to time, something odd turned up in the bog—petrified men or ancient tools.

But this was too good to be true. "I know what this is," Angar said, trying to convince himself of his fortune. "It's a dragon!"

A *dragon* was a flying reptile, one of the first biologically advanced beings that mankind met when they had first ventured to the stars. In some ways, the dragons were even superior to the godlike skraals, and had been friends and counselors to the skraals back in the days of Bliss—before the cycor began their great war and turned the heart of the galaxy into a great void.

The last dragon had been expunged more than six thousand years ago in an attack that had left Danai a wasteland.

Angar inspected the remains. Last winter's flood must have stripped mud from the banks of the river, uncovering the creature.

"My, look at those teeth," Angar said. The beast had great teeth as long as his hand. Each was stained yellow from millennia in the mud, and the cutting edges were serrated.

"I'll bet folks would pay nicely for one of those," he mused. Maybe even the holy maiden. He seemed to remember hearing that even now, the goddesses took a peculiar interest in the remains of dragons.

Yet he had to wonder. Three months earlier, a cycor scout ship had come to Danai and rained flash-heads upon the capitol. The supreme mother had been killed, the holy maiden wounded, and though the scout ship was destroyed, it was only a matter of time before the enemy returned with greater weapons. Now Holy Maiden Seramasia had gone into hiding, preparing to meet the cycor threat.

Yet Angar suspected he could find her: all he had to do was send a message through the boy who was buying the damselflies.

THAT NIGHT, DEEP IN A FOREST CALLED SHADOWFEST, A TWELVE-YEAR-OLD boy named Anduval inched along the limb of a boa tree covered in white spirit fungus. The tree was large so close to the ground, perhaps four feet in diameter. Boa saplings tended to snake along the forest floor, rising and dipping at random, until they sensed a hole in the canopy high above. Then the trunk would twist upward, seeking the heavens. Thus, for long stretches, the trees sometimes formed a path above the forest floor.

Twenty feet below, a sounder of wild pigs lay asleep, half-hidden, having rooted beneath patches of wild fungus and plates of spongy lichens. The colossal boars weighed as much as three tons each and stood eight feet at the shoulder. A full-grown boar had a mouth large enough to swallow a man whole; their enormous tusks were as sharp as sabers. The boars were savage hunters, fiercely protective of both their young and the patches of mushrooms in their territory.

An old sow grunted curiously and opened her eyes. Anduval halted, heart pounding. He dared not move. With each step, spirit fungus dislodged from the log and rained down on the wild boars.

He couldn't see exactly how the tree twisted ahead. He was guided only by the light of a jar filled with tiny glow beetles whose green luminescence carried only a few feet. But Anduval had memorized the trail over the years. The glass mushrooms were about ninety feet ahead, where the boa tree dipped down and touched the forest floor.

Anduval wrapped his hand around his jar, obscuring the light, and waited for the sow to return to sleep.

One slip, and he would fall to the forest floor. The ground was spongy, covered with layers of leaves and old lichens that had rotted here for forty thousand years. He'd probably survive a fall, but not an attack by the boars.

So he held tight. The boles of the boa trees twisted crazily in a tangle, and their foliage in the canopy blocked out the stars, so the forest floor lay in perpetual gloom.

The only sound was the dripping from above—sap falling in an ever-present mist, spiders dropping lifeless from old age. A huge growler swept overhead, uttering a soft rumble as it sought for flying insects. The air smelled of ten thousand varieties of mold.

After long minutes, the even breathing and occasional grunts of pigs assured Anduval that they were dreaming contentedly. Morning was coming, and the pigs would soon waken. Time was short. Anduval would have to sprint back to the palace when he got his prize.

Breathlessly, he inched along in the dark, feeling his way across the log until bones cracked beneath his feet. He pulled out his light. A small, lizard-like creature lay dead on the log, having fallen from the canopy, its wings akimbo. Fungus grew over the body in colored patches, reclaiming the moisture and minerals.

Ahead, water tinkled down the boles of several trees, forming a pool. At the water's edge, ghostly mushrooms rose up like spears, some to a height of three feet. Anduval raised his light, inched forward, and spotted a mushroom dripping with its own sugary dew. It looked to be newly sprouted, for it was still the color of tinted glass. He pushed his way past older mushrooms, those that had been trampled by pigs or had dried out, and examined the new one closely. He reached into a pocket, drew a harvesting scythe, and slashed through the mushroom's stalk. Using a wet cloth to lift the mushroom so that it would never have been touched by human hands, he placed the mushroom into a pouch woven from twisted leaves, and smiled. It was a good harvest. He suspected the mushroom weighed seven pounds.

Anduval glanced up, searching for a second mushroom, when he heard a startled grunt at his back. A boar scrambled up from the detritus and let out an angry squeal.

He had been found.

He whirled and raced back toward the bole of his boa. A huge black boar rushed from the darkness. Anduval leaped aside. The boar barreled past and went splashing into the shallow pool.

He lifted his light. The boar squealed in outrage, whirled, and gave chase.

Anduval sprinted where the bole angled up gently. The boar charged, but it could not see in the dark, and it had to take care not to slip.

He realized it had to be following his light. The bole veered left, then right. Below him, wild pigs squealed in anticipation. Seldom did they get fresh meat beyond the occasional insect or worm.

The huge boar grunted and redoubled its speed. Anduval could feel its breath at his back. He reached out and held his light far to his right.

The boar veered toward it—and slid from the damp bole of the tree, just as Anduval had hoped.

The pigs squealed in delight at the fresh meat that thudded down around them.

IN A SUBTERRANEAN PALACE DEEP BENEATH THE MOUNTAINOUS TREES, Anduval arranged his fungi on a platter.

He had three spears of yellowcap, firm and meaty, set beside a clump of ruffled young brain fungus, all in shades of gray with blue fringes. A dozen "black buttons" took up the center of the platter, while his single clear glass mushroom—as long as a baby's arm—curved around the platter's rim. Sprinkled over the glass mushroom were tiny "blue dot" mushrooms no larger than grains of sand.

When he felt certain the arrangement would be pleasing, he carried it through the arched alcove and into the dining hall of the Holy Maiden Seramasia.

Other attendants had arrived earlier and placed their offerings upon the table. The offerings included a wide variety of fungi, but Anduval felt certain that they would not please his mistress. The pile of dark green swamp lettuce looked too stale to be appetizing. A single, white sweet globe was overly large, and thus its dark center would be flavorless. Others looked slightly more palatable.

He thought to shove the central platter aside, but he knew it contained the offering of the kitchen steward, and he did not want to get a beating.

Anduval's offering was last to the table, as he had hoped. His would be the freshest of the fare. But he had to take care to leave soon, for ancient custom dictated that he could never occupy the same room as the maiden or pass within two hundred feet of her.

He set his platter upon the outer edge of the table, hoping that if the holy maiden chanced to circle once, she would be tempted by his offering. The other attendants had all put their platters near the door to the maiden's meditation chamber, hoping to be first to be seen. But there on the far side of the table, his platter stood alone.

He took one last second to turn his platter, just so, to better display his rare and succulent glass mushroom as he prepared to flee.

Footsteps issued from the maiden's entrance, and he glanced up.

Terror took him. The holy maiden stood beneath a white marble arch, glorious and resplendent, not twenty feet away. Skraal guards flanked her.

The guards were taller than men. At eight feet, their height was imposing enough, but it was the guard's reputation that most frightened him: in their zealousness to protect the maiden, they sometimes got rough. The guards were far more powerful than humans. The least touch of a skraal could leave a bruise. Should one of the creatures grasp him, their slender fingers would rip through his flesh as easily as rice paper and would shatter his bones as if they were made from straw.

Trembling, heart pounding, Anduval dropped to his hands and knees and prostrated himself. "Have pity on me," he cried, "for I am but a foolish child."

He closed his eyes. He had seen the holy maiden up close, which was forbidden, and he relished that instant. She was naked, for skraal nymphs rarely wore clothes.

She had been beautiful. Though she stood upon two legs, her similarity to humans ended there.

She had no breasts or hair.

Her face had been as white as the petal of a swamp lily, as white as the lining of a cloud, and fleshy around her silver eyes. Her legs and arms were slender. Her abdomen, shaped like an inverted pear, was full and fat.

She had a gracefulness to her, like the elegance of a crane or a roe deer. In the way of skraal nymphs, her oral-dactyls, the fingerlike appendages that shoved food into the vertical slit of her mouth, were clearer than crystal.

He could see little evidence of the wounds she'd received in the cycor attack. She had nearly been killed when the drone ship had dropped its flash-heads and then smashed into the capitol so hard that debris flew up from the far side of the world. Seramasia had been a hundred miles from ground zero, yet the radiation burns had left part of her exoskeleton pitted.

Anduval's heart pounded, but not from fear. He had seen the holy maiden up close, and he hoped to savor the image.

Then she spoke, her mouth-fingers playing rapidly, her voice deep and mellow like a woodwind. "Have no fear, frail one," she said. "Your presence here pleases me. And though you may be young, I believe that you are wise beyond your years—perhaps wise beyond all understanding."

Anduval braced himself, not trusting ears. Humans were never allowed near skraal nymphs. In all of his life, he had never heard that the maiden had spoken to any human except Magus Veritarnus, a mysterious man who strode through the palace in black robes with his head hunched in thought.

"Now," she said, "stand before me, and do not avert your eyes. I have questions for you; choose your words well, for I will permit you to continue in my presence only if you speak perfect truth."

Perhaps at no time in his life had Anduval felt more frightened. Tears flooded his eyes, and his stomach clenched alarmingly. Though he had not eaten since yesterday, he felt that he might vomit on the floor. When he managed to stand, his legs quivered, and it was only with great effort that he stilled them.

He looked up and peered steadily upon the holy maiden. She strode toward him, and her guards stiffened in alarm. Their instinct demanded they protect her. And, like dogs, they wished to lead the way, to stand between her and Anduval, but she brushed them aside.

"My lady, please," a guard begged. "The danger—"

"There is no danger from this one," Holy Maiden Seramasia declared. "I sense only . . . devotion."

As a skraal nymph, Seramasia had powers of the mind that no human could match. She was not mature, and had not therefore transcended, but she could still see into a man's mind as easily as a child might gawp at tadpoles at the bottom of a clear pool.

Anduval gazed into her eyes. She had four of them, two large ones that peered forward, and two small ones upon her temples. The large ones did not have whites. Instead, they were silver, like the eyes of a fish, and deep in the center was a dollop of light blue, as if from summer skies. The eyes upon the side of her head were dark, like bits of onyx.

He saw now that her skin was not really white. It was gelatinous, almost, and only looked white from a distance, though he could see that it was beginning to harden. Beneath the clear skin, he could make out tiny blue veins. Her muscles, in fact, were opalescent, and her fine bones were as clear as glass.

She smelled sweet and earthy, like vanilla poured over moss.

Anduval had never seen anyone with such breathtaking beauty.

There was movement in the fine musculature of her face, a skraal smile as her lips tightened. "How old are you," the holy maiden asked, "in human years?"

"I am twelve years and three months," Anduval answered softly, filled with awe.

"You are young, even for a human. Do you know how old I am?"

"Two hundred seven years, nine months, three days, and almost nine hours," Anduval answered.

The holy maiden laughed, a clear melodic sound like an oboe. "So perfectly honest. You please me. Your offering pleases me. Did you know that for nearly three months now, I have not eaten from any other platter but yours?"

Anduval fought back the urge to gasp. He'd never known what had become of his offerings. Each morning and evening he delivered his platter, but at the end of her meal, all of the offerings were thrown away. "I am honored," was all he could manage to say.

"Three months," she said. "Since the attack, your offerings have revived me and healed me."

She gestured at his platter. As a nymph in the early stages of her life, she could not eat anything but fungus. "Your yellowcaps, so bright and crisp. These ones sprouted in the night. You had to have harvested them well before dawn, before any sunlight could beat down through the swamps and touch them. And this glass mushroom—you had to travel miles into the forest to find it, for the steward tells me that the nearest ones grow only at the base of Mount Dimlock."

Now she peered into his eyes. "You know my tastes—my needs—better than I know them myself. How did you guess that I craved glass mushrooms?"

For a moment, Anduval stood frozen as he tried to choose his words.

The libraries of Magus Veritarnus were filled with ancient tomes that detailed the feeding habits of nymphs. It was a vital subject. Some nymphs developed vast powers. Most did not. So scribes had recorded the feeding habits of past nymphs, trying to unravel the secrets as to which would succeed.

Anduval had studied the texts tirelessly, and had gone much further—charting Seramasia's growth against that of other maidens, studying texts that plumbed the secrets of various fungi—the content of their vitamins, minerals, phytogens, and hormones.

A truly great skraal mother had not risen in more than six thousand years. The world needed one; it needed a mother right out of legend.

Anduval suspected—as did the skraals—that there were inadequacies in the nymphs' diets. Many species of fungi had been lost in the ancient cycor attacks.

Of course, Seramasia knew all of this. So Anduval tried to explain his choices.

"The air is dry this morning," he said. "I thought you would relish the glass mushroom's moisture. I know there is some variation, but skraal maidens crave certain foods, according to their age, their closeness to ascension, the heat and humidity. The injury you sustained in the attack, this too amends your needs. As I studied the records, I began to see patterns."

"All of my other attendants are skraals, and they are supposed to be intellectually superior to humans. Why could *they* not see these patterns?"

Anduval did not want to admit it, but sometimes he thought he was smarter than most skraals, even though tradition held that it was impossible.

"As I pondered what you might want, I felt the answer in my bones."

"Then tell me," she asked, "what I will want to eat tomorrow."

"Your ascension is almost upon you," Anduval said. "Your skin is hardening. Tomorrow, or sometime soon, you will begin to crave insects with your fungus. You will need the protein to build your chrysalis. Tomorrow I will bring mallow mold, and I have hired children to collect young damselflies."

The holy maiden considered his words. "You traveled by foot into the dimmest part of the forest this morning, beneath boa trees so vast that the ground never sees light. Were you not afraid of being eaten by a colossal boar?"

Anduval almost decided to lie, to boast at his courage, but the holy maiden had demanded the truth. "I was."

"Then why did you do it?"

"I wanted to please you," Anduval said.

"More than you cared for your own life?" the holy maiden asked.

He was afraid she might laugh at him or mock him.

"Yes."

"Do you *love* me?"

At her back, a guard hissed. Cessari was her personal attendant and the most dangerous skraal on Danai. Indeed, he held the title of Consort, and in the fullness of time he would become the holy maiden's mate.

It was dangerous for Anduval to confess his feelings for the maiden. He was only a boy, and he had been told he was not old enough to love. But he knew what he felt.

"I do love you," Anduval answered, afraid that the consort might crush him for his boldness. "I have loved you from the first time that I saw you at a distance, two years ago."

The holy maiden peered into his eyes and smiled in satisfaction. "I know what you want from me," she said. "You hope that in time I will learn to love you, too."

Among the skraals, she was but a child, like him.

He did not have to confess his feelings. She could divine them.

"You understand," Seramasia said, "that human emotions are but a shadow compared to what I feel. If I were to love you, you would never understand the depth of my passion. If I were to love you, our minds would meld into one, and my love would destroy your ability to reason. There is a purpose behind the law that keeps you at a distance."

"I understand," he said.

She grew thoughtful. "You please me," she said. "It is my hope that in time you will find a human woman to love. I will go into transcendence soon, and when I do, I will be gone for a number of years. Seek for a human woman to love.

"I fear the cycor will return soon. I do not know if we have four years or four hundred, but we must prepare to defend ourselves. Yet I fear that our preparations will be in vain.

"Therefore, we make the best of the time we have left.

"As for now, your devotion must be rewarded. You will continue to bring my morning meals until I go dormant, but in the afternoon you will begin an apprenticeship under the magus. You, too, shall become a magus."

Anduval considered. There were technologies that were undreamt of by men, and it was the duty of a magus to master them. It would greatly add to his duties. But he was only a human and did not have the strength or endurance of a skraal. He did not know how he might manage it.

More importantly, he would arouse the jealousy of the maiden's skraal servants, and that was a dangerous thing to do.

Suddenly Anduval recalled something, a message that he had hoped to deliver to the magus, a message for the holy maiden. Compared to the dangers posed by the cycor, it seemed rather inconsequential.

"Milady," Anduval said with a bow. "I have heard a rumor that might interest you: in the bogs outside the forest, the skull and body of a dragon have been found."

The holy maiden drew a breath in surprise, and her guards leaped forward eagerly.

"Is the skull intact? Has it been opened?"

Anduval shrugged. "As far as I know, it has not been taken from the bog."

"We must go look upon it," she said, glancing toward Cessari. "This is a great treasure."

"Beware, milady," Cessari said. "This may be a trap to lure you from the safety of the forest!"

But the holy maiden whirled and peered to the east, as if her mind sought out beyond the miles. "No, I can feel it now. There, at the limit of my powers. How sweetly the dragon dreams . . ."

They would have to go under the cover of darkness, Anduval realized, when the creatures of the forest ventured out to forage. She would want to go in secret and hide her heat signature from cycor ships.

The holy maiden riveted Anduval with a look and said, "Go and tell the magus what you have heard."

ANGAR WAS DRUNK BY MIDDAY. HE WENT TO THE PUB AND TOLD THE TOWN about his dragon, and as the tale spread, many an oaf just like himself came and offered to pay for rounds.

By early afternoon, the size of the dragon had grown enormous in the telling, and many a man gaped in disbelief at stories of a talon a yard long and a wingspan of a hundred feet.

There were offers to buy teeth. "I'm the best scrimshaw artist in Moonravis," one fisherman boasted. "Lend me the ivory, and I shall double its value!"

But Angar did not like the man's work. It was true that he was the best in town, but with a find like this, the ivory should go to the best carvers on Danai.

"I'll bet I could make fine boots and belts from its skin," the cobbler suggested in a wheedling voice, his hands making little groping gestures.

The innkeeper offered, "Five gold rings for a tooth—and all the beer you can drink for a year!"

"Two years!" Angar demanded.

"Sold!" the innkeeper shouted instantly, and Angar rued the bargain.

"I should have demanded more," he grumbled.

But the innkeeper forced a mug of his finest into Angar's hand, and in moments Angar was so happy that he was dancing on the bar while the other guests serenaded him with drinking songs.

"You know," a blacksmith called out in the midst of the song, "that it is not the teeth or hide that is the greatest treasure of a dragon. It is found in the dragon's skull!"

The blacksmith pointed to his own skull and nodded wisely.

Angar's head was reeling by then, but somehow the blacksmith's image, his message, kept whirling about in Angar's mind. It was like a piece of oat straw caught in a dust devil. It spun around and around.

Suddenly Angar fell from the table, and several peasants leaped to be the first to help him up.

"Leave me, leave me alone," he said. "I've got to go get that dragon out of the bog."

With superhuman effort, he hauled his massive belly off the floor and began to weave in the general direction of his home. But the patrons of the bar all shouted, "We'll come and help!" and Angar was still sober enough to realize that he would be grateful for twenty strong hands.

So the townsmen went to the edge of the bog and, with picks and shovels and pry bars, they dug into the mud and freed the dragon, pulling its half-petrified corpse into the sunlight on the riverbank. Flies buzzed around it curiously for awhile, then rejected its ancient flesh as an unworthy home even for maggots.

The townsfolk gaped in amazement at the dragon's size. Surely it would have had an eighty-foot wingspan. And its talons really were over two feet long.

But the leather did not look to be worth much. Most of it had been devoured by worms and discolored by the tannins in the peat, it seemed.

Meanwhile, the ivory in its teeth was discolored and had gone soft with age. Angar feared the innkeeper would rescind his offer of two years' free beer.

One of the townsfolk even laughed at Angar, saying, "I would not like to have to bury that thing!"

As Angar fell into despair, a skraal warrior came to the bog and ordered the people not to disturb the dragon's remains.

"The holy maiden will pay well for a skull that is still intact," the warrior offered.

So Angar shooed the townsfolk off his property and stood guard over the rotting corpse. He settled in the shade of a hazelnut tree and lay in the tall grass for a long while, trying to figure out how to make the most money from his smelly prize, when he fell asleep.

Two full moons were up when he finally roused himself.

"The greatest treasure *is found in the dragon's skull!*" he recalled, the thought whirling about him like dry autumn leaves.

He wondered at that. Angar was not an educated man. Education was for skraals; farming and petty labors were for humans. But Angar knew a bit of folk wisdom.

Sometimes, when a large bird died, it would leave piles of small stones as its craw decomposed. There was an old wives' tale he had heard about a farmer who discovered diamonds amid such remains, and a further search revealed that a nearby hillside was covered with them.

Perhaps dragons did the same. Maybe dragons swallowed rubies or emeralds, or maybe such gems just formed naturally in a dragon's skull!

Why should the skraals get all of the treasure? They got the best that men had to offer, and what did the hardworking people get in return?

With that in mind, he staggered home to find his ax.

"Magus Veritarnus, my name is Anduval. I am to be your apprentice."

The magus shot Anduval a dark look, hesitated for an instant, and said, "I can't waste time on such nonsense." He turned his back on the boy.

Anduval had found the magus in his operations center. The magus was a tall man with a lean physique and a haggard look. His skin was as midnight-black as Anduval's. He had his long hair braided in cornrows and slung over his neck onto his chest. The magus peered up at a glass wall where squiggly chains made from green, red, yellow, and blue were wrapped into cords. The magus had a crystal wand, and when he pointed at one of the rods, he would speak, and the chains would break. The colored blocks would then rearrange according to his command.

"Let's have a look at chromosome twelve, gene one hundred eleven, marker four, shall we?"

The image on the wall shifted, rushing down the coiled chains, until it stopped. The magus squinted at the image on the wall, ignoring Anduval.

Anduval prompted, "It is the wish of the holy maiden that I be your apprentice."

"Go and tell her to mind her own business," Magus Veritarnus shot back. "We are in a state of emergency."

"The holy maiden seems to think that I can help."

The magus turned, looked down. "Time that I spend with you is time taken from more important duties. Do you understand?"

Anduval understood far more than most adults thought he should. For weeks now he had been gathering bits of information overheard in palace halls and in the markets outside of town.

"You are preparing for the cycor attack," Anduval said. "You only have a few years to do it. You're gathering seeds and spores, and hiding them here beneath the fortress. I know, because I know of the children that you've hired to begin the work.

"You hope to weather the attack, as our ancestors did. But you are afraid that it won't work. Six thousand years ago, the cycor hit us with planet killers. But that didn't work, so you're worried that they'll be more thorough this time.

"You're trying to save what you can, the seeds of humanity. But you are doomed to fail, for there are hundreds of millions of people who will die. There isn't room to protect them all, down here in the depths of the palace."

The magus straightened his back, sighed, and peered down at Anduval as if in defeat.

"You're damned smart for a twelve-year-old." Anduval hadn't told the magus his age, but then, the magus was rumored to have phenomenal powers of observation. "I wasn't that smart at your age.

"This isn't a palace, you know. It is a bunker, designed to withstand cycor attacks. That is what it was built for."

He studied Anduval as if weighing him; Anduval realized that the magus needed time to make up his own mind.

"I was told to inform you that the body of a dragon has been found."

"Frozen?" the magus asked hopefully. "Preserved in ice?"

"No, it was found in a peat bog. I hear that it has not decomposed. The holy maiden has asked that I lead you and her to it."

The magus stopped for a moment, breathless, riveted by the news. He nodded slightly, eagerly, black pupils shining.

Then a look of defeat entered his eyes once again, and he said softly, "Let us hope that it is whole."

Anduval had to sprint that night to keep pace with the quicker skraals.

Their entourage was small—the holy maiden, a pair of guards, Anduval. Magus Veritarnus ran at the tail of the group, his black cape flowing behind.

Anduval led the way. The light of two small full moons, the angry twins, shone red and glaring on the fields of dry grass, bathing the night in blood. He ran, and in doing so he tried to hide his humanity. He dared not slow or stop. He could not beg for rest. Anduval wanted to prove that he could move as swiftly and effortlessly as a skraal.

So he sprinted through the fields, his heart pounding, lungs heaving like bellows, until he was dizzy with fatigue. His feet winnowed the dry grasses, knocking ripe grain from stalks of wheat.

The scent of grass and stinkweeds carried on the warm night air.

The others raced behind him. They did not have far to go outside the great forest, but the stars overhead seemed threatening to Anduval. At any moment, one of them could turn and dive—a cycor warship that would explode like the sun, washing the planet in fire.

*It is only a matter of time,* he told himself. *They will come, and the world will become void in a flash.*

A wind came from the deserts in the east, blowing a thin veil of red dust high into the air. Lightning flickered in the empty heavens, and the skraals, agitated, ran faster.

The skraals moved swiftly and effortlessly, and Anduval knew that they wished his small legs would go faster. But Holy Maiden Seramasia did not condemn him. She jogged at his back, sometimes whispering words of gratitude and encouragement.

Thus they reached the cottage where the farmer Angar lived. The house was made from squares of sod, with poles angled up at the top. Bundles of cattail reeds served as a roof.

The girl Tallori answered Anduval's call at a door made from scraped sheep's hide, her mother being too weary to rise, and the child led the way to the dragon's corpse, racing through the tall cattails.

There, beside the slow-flowing river, they found Angar under the starlight, standing upon the dragon's skull, his ax raised overhead.

Magus Veritarnus saw what he was about to do, and let out a cry of shock.

Putting all of his bulk and might into it, Angar let his ax fall.

The dragon's skull split easily, the rotting bone breaking with a sound like a melon.

What happened next, Anduval could never clearly describe.

Shimmering lights rose from the dragon's skull, as soft as fog, as bright and sparkling as opals. They gave off no sound, no smell. Instead, they only glittered, rising up like thistledown.

"Catch them!" Magus Veritarnus shouted, and the holy maiden leaped magnificently, bounding perhaps twenty feet in the air and seventy feet in distance, so that she seemed to fly over Anduval's head.

He raced forward, seeking to catch a light in his cupped hands, but the lights did not move on currents of wind. They seemed to be alive, darting about of their own volition. Angar the drunkard stood, eyes wide with amazement, and Anduval saw lights pass right through him, then circle back around his head, as if seeking entrance and finding none.

One of the coruscating lights drew near, and Anduval reached out and caught it in both hands. Strange currents passed through him. He felt his hair stand on end, and the light rose up. It was as long as a small serpent, but its body was flat and eyeless, much like ribbon, yet it waggled a tail to propel itself through the air.

Opening his mouth in amazement, Anduval was about to shout a question when the light burst upward and into his brain.

In the way that sometimes happened with Anduval, he dreamt two dreams simultaneously. It was a gift he had, a gift that he had only recently discovered.

ANDUVAL WAS A DRAGON, HUNTING BESIDE THE RIVER. HIS SCALY HIDE was the tan of dying reeds, with stripes of dark green and silver. With such camouflage, he could easily hide among the rushes and ambush the hippo-like creatures that waded near.

He looked up and spotted wings in the sky. Another dragon with a soft-blue underbelly soared above the clouds.

A thought struck him, an argument so lengthy and complex that a human could take months to unravel and comprehend it; yet Anduval recognized that it was an argument over territorial boundaries and disputes.

The dragon vocalized, sending loud clicks in the air so swiftly that no human could have decoded their meaning.

A SECOND DREAM STRUCK SIMULTANEOUSLY, IN WHICH THE DRAGON piloted a starship. The creature was hanging upside down in a cockpit, sending his mind out among the stars, feeling ahead for meteors and bits of space debris, then weaving a safe path through the void.

The cycor were following his ship doggedly, and he glanced back in anger. He so desired to turn the ship and face the enemy . . .

ANDUVAL FOUND HIMSELF LYING FLAT ON HIS BACK, BLINKING UP AT THE stars, while the girl Tallori knelt at his side. Magus Veritarnus hunched over him, two fingers pressed against Anduval's neck, checking for a pulse.

"You will be well, child," the magus said. Those were the first words the man had spoken to him all night.

Tallori was weeping. Anduval could not be sure if she wept from fear for him or in awe of the holy maiden or simply because the combination of events left her overwrought. Humans that lived outside the palace were simple creatures.

The magus turned aside, as if listening for some inner voice, and then whispered. "It is not for humans like us to touch a dragon's dream. Doing so was unwise. The dragon's memories, its hopes and lore, all are stored in a brain that is nothing like ours.

"The dragons came from a far world, you know. Humans cannot even pronounce the name of their species—much less speak their tongue. So our ancestors called them *dragons*, after creatures from legend.

"We cannot even begin to comprehend the math they understood, their mastery of flight. Perhaps if we had a floccular lobe to our brain, as birds do, we might understand some of the things that are innately known to dragons.

"The skraals can sometimes unravel it." The magus jutted his chin, and Anduval peered a few yards away. The holy maiden stood atop the dragon's body, and the lights were circling her, as if greeting an ancient friend, their opalescent hues sometimes bursting into colored sparks.

"The creatures that you see are called *piezoelectric life-forms*. They're symbiotes. They grow and reproduce in the minds of dragons. Our thoughts and memories are stored in twisted strands of DNA—which is so much less efficient than the crystalline structure of a dragon's brain or a skraal's brain."

Holy Maiden Seramasia stood for long minutes, and one by one the dragon dreams entered her. As they did, her eyes filled with tears, and her thorax trembled as if she might shatter.

Anduval worried. "Should we stop her? It looks as if it hurts."

But the magus shook his head. "She does not hurt. Those are tears of joy, tears of revelation. The dragon dreams must find a home quickly, or they will die. So they are lodging within her skull. Like hermit crabs, they need a place where they can survive. A skraal's brain is not exactly like a dragon's either—the dreams will not survive there for long, a few years at the most—but our holy maiden is learning things that none of her kind have been able to comprehend on this planet for more than six thousand years."

The magus turned to Anduval, looked into his eyes. "You're right about my fears. The cycor will make sure that nothing on this planet survives the next attack. They'll hit us with a sunbuster, send a missile to the planet's core, and let it explode so that we are shattered into fragments."

Anduval was horrified. He knew of border disputes that sometimes happened among human tribes, but that was all that he knew of war. "Why would they do that? I mean, if they wanted to take over, that I could understand. But killing everything—that seems like such a waste!"

A few feet away, a snoring sound arose. Angar had sat down in some thick weeds and fallen asleep, too drunk to keep his eyes open any longer.

"The cycor don't need plants and animals to feed upon," the magus said. "Biological life forms evolve, and highly evolved creatures are a danger to them—so all life represents a threat.

"For millennia, we have hoped that a dragon would come to our world. We're trapped here. Oh, we could build little ships that float through space like rafts upon a lake and try to escape, but the cycor would only find us that much sooner. The dragons alone have the knowledge necessary to build the fast starships that we so desperately need if we are ever to escape.

"But I fear that the last of the dragons have been hunted to extinction. Indeed, this world may even be home to the last vestiges of humanity. The center of the galaxy is nothing but a void. The stars have all gone dark, and the planets that whirl around them are destroyed. The home world of the dragons is gone, along with the ancient home of mankind. Perhaps some of our brethren have fled the galaxy, but if so, we may never reunite with them again."

Magus Veritarnus glanced down, the whites of his eyes reflecting the lights of the piezoelectric creatures.

For long hours, they waited in silence as the moons slid inexorably down to the horizon and beyond the shadowed hills. The stars had begun to fade, though the sun was not yet up, when the last of the opalescent creatures entered Seramasia.

Anduval could see them there still, deep within her crystal skull, their lights sparking from time to time.

He could not understand completely what was happening. Perhaps such things were beyond the comprehension of mere humans. But Anduval peered up at Magus Veritarnus and saw a change in the man. He had always walked about with hunched shoulders and a careworn look.

Now he had hope in his eyes.

When the last of the creatures had burrowed into her skull, the holy maiden looked around at her small crowd of followers.

"It is done," she said. "I know how to escape, but time is short if we are to build a worldship."

THE WEIGHT OF THE WHOLE PLANET FELL UPON ANDUVAL'S SHOULDERS that night, as he bade goodbye to Tallori's and her find, there by the river, and trudged back through fields misted with morning dew, he understood why the magus always walked with his head bowed. It was full daylight when they reached the palace. It became a madhouse as the holy maiden began to issue orders to her skraal attendants, demanding that they begin to gather vast amounts of rare metals from across the world.

Over the coming days, the skraal nymph closeted with Magus Veritarnus for unending hours, discussing her plan to create a worldship. Sketches were drawn and sent to far cities, where modules for the great ship were to be produced.

Amid this bustle, Magus Veritarnus seemed to forget that he had been assigned to be a mentor, and Anduval felt as if he had been cast aside.

It was not a feeling that he could live with. Anduval had no mother or father that he knew of. He had been raised in a crèche in the palace beneath Shadowfest, one of nine human children.

All of his life, he'd craved to belong, to find some sort of companionship. He'd hoped that by working hard, he could prove himself and win acceptance from others.

Somehow, as a child, he'd proven himself well enough to become the holy maiden's attendant. But the skraals were not humans. They showed nothing in the way of affection, and the other workers never offered any praise.

Yet Anduval hoped.

So he continued his duties as an attendant, bringing fungus and damselflies for the holy maiden each morning, hoping to prepare her for transcendence.

But with each passing day, he grew more concerned. In his brief vision, he had seen into the mind of a dragon, and the threat of the cycor was a shadow that flooded his mind. The cycor were not human. Properly speaking, they were not even alive. They had no compassion, no emotion, no hope or love in them.

There could be no swaying such creatures from their wanton destruction.

And the end would come swiftly, he knew.

Cycor ships were fast. When a spaceship accelerated, the force of acceleration exerted pressure upon its occupants. Thus, a ship that was constantly accelerating created its own artificial gravity. But it also had certain limits. Accelerate too quickly, and the gravity field would crush its occupants. The safe speed for acceleration over an extended period of time was only a little more than one gravity.

But a cycor ship carried no living creatures within; it could safely accelerate at a speed of one hundred gravities.

Human ships were infinitely slower.

*Our only real hope is to hide from the cycor,* Anduval reasoned.

But hiding was no longer possible. They had been found.

The holy maiden wished to build a worldship, but it could be destroyed as easily as a planet.

*What shall the holy maiden do?* Anduval wondered. *What can she do?*

After two weeks, Anduval was finally able to corner his master. He found the magus bleary-eyed and swaying from fatigue as he left the holy maiden's meditation chambers. Anduval had just returned from his nightly run to gather fungus.

"I want to help build the worldship," Anduval begged. "We are in a race against the cycor, and every moment is precious."

"I agree," the magus said, "and someday you shall help to build our ship. But the holy maiden's personal needs are more immediate."

"She has twenty other attendants," Anduval said. "Surely they can bring her food. I can even tell them what to collect."

The magus studied the boy for a long moment, weighing his argument. "You, too, have been touched by the dragon's dream," he said, "if only for a moment. How much do you understand?"

Anduval bit his lip, struggling to explain. The dragon's dream hadn't come to him in his native tongue. It was like pure intelligence that had flowed through him, only for an instant, and much of what he knew was just stray impressions.

"The scout ship that found us could not have been a long-range vessel," Anduval said. "It had to have come from a mother ship. That means there is a warship nearby, or possibly a fleet of them."

"Agreed," the magus said. "If a vessel had been stationed in this solar system, the cycor would have destroyed us by now. Our nearest stellar neighbor is nearly two light-years away. Let us hope that there is not a warship so close."

Anduval bent his head in thought. It would take two years for a message transmission to reach the nearest star, and if a warship was there, it would take a few months more than two years for the enemy to reach Danai. "The cycor will be near a planet, won't they?"

"Mining," the magus agreed. "They do not need food, but they may be mining asteroids for minerals or mining the gravity fields of a nearby sun for fuel."

Even the dragons had not understood how the cycor could mine and store gravity.

"Can we build a ship in four years?" Anduval asked.

The magus shrugged. He was not reassuring. "We must try."

*Even if we can build a ship,* Anduval wondered, *will it be fast enough to outrun the cycor? How far beyond the edge of the galaxy must we go to escape them?*

The magus rested a hand on Anduval's shoulder. "Let us hope that the cycor are farther away than that. I will consider your request, but until further notice, you are the head steward. There is nothing more important than the feeding of Seramasia. Even in ancient times, only one in a thousand holy maidens truly transcended. I can find no genetic reason for this, and so it must have to do with nurture.

"The holy maiden has begun to talk to me about the requirements of our ship. We will build it in modules—engines, the hull, life-support. It must be a large ship, large enough to carry every man, woman, and child in the world.

"It will be a complex task . . ." A look of defeat passed across the magus's face. "I confess, I do not understand how it all works. We can only hope that the holy maiden will guide us."

FOUR DAYS LATER, ANDUVAL WAS SUMMONED INTO THE HOLY MAIDEN'S meditation chamber. The deep gray room itself was vast, with a sixty-foot ceiling, and perfectly round. Within this space, white silk sheets tangled on the floor, creating something that was not quite a bed, not quite a chair.

Holy Maiden Seramasia lay cradled in silk. Candles in glass cups provided footlights around the room, but brighter than the candles was the holy maiden's womb.

Her abdomen, that perfect inverted pear, glowed brightly from inside. Anduval could see her ripening eggs through her skin, like clear marbles.

Along the backs of her arms and legs, and all down her spine, mucilage had begun to ooze out—a clear gel that would harden within a few hours into a chrysalis.

Her courtesans crowded near, like bucks in musth, and from time to time, they would stoop and nuzzle her abdomen, pushing against it, trying to arouse her.

The sexual tension in the room was electric.

Anduval felt grateful to see the holy maiden, but not like this. There was a soft glow all about her, and she was more beautiful and sensual than ever. He had no desire to watch the skraal males fight over her.

Even being here was dangerous, lest one of the males inadvertently strike out.

"Come near, little one," the holy maiden urged.

Anduval trembled and drew close, until the big male, Cessari, snorted and charged.

Anduval leaped backward, and Cessari lashed out with one long arm. Anduval ducked beneath the blow. The holy maiden reached out and grabbed Cessari, restraining him.

"Stay back, little one," Cessari growled. "This one is not for you!"

The holy maiden calmed her consort, patting his head. Cessari crouched beside her and placed a hand over her womb, as if claiming it for his own. He glared at Anduval, but dared not resist the will of the maiden.

"You have served me well," the holy maiden told Anduval. "As you can see, I will be going into my long sleep soon. I will eat no more until I wake."

"But it's not time yet!" Anduval objected.

"Many factors help determine the time when a skraal nymph goes into transcendence. I have been under a great deal of stress these past few weeks, and that has tipped the scales.

"I hereby release you from my service," she said. "I will no longer need you to attend me."

She would be gone for years—somewhere between three and twenty —sleeping in her chrysalis, lost to the world.

This was bad. An ancient adage came to mind. *Early to the cocoon; late to bloom.* Chances were good that she would sleep for many, many years. The ancient tomes suggested that the long sleep was a coping mechanism, a way for the nymphs to deal with hard times.

Anduval had read tome after tome about the holy maidens. He knew that a maiden who went into chrysalis phase early would come out stunted—both physically and mentally. Seramasia would not come out with the great powers that Anduval had hoped for.

Panic took him. "But, milady, you're the only one who understands how to build the worldship!"

Seramasia nodded sadly. "I have left what instructions I can with the magus. Much of the work can proceed without me. While I am gone, you will grow, and you will help build our ship. I wish you well. I hope that when I waken, it will be to a better world for us all.

"Young man, find love with one of your own kind, if you can. The girl with the damselflies, do you still see her?"

Anduval nodded.

"Bring her to the palace. She wishes to fight the cycor. She will need someone to teach her, to watch over her. I want you to care for her as you have for me.

"Reward her parents. I will prepare a payment for them, to ease their loss."

Anduval recognized what she was doing. She hoped to deflect his affection. She hoped he would fall in love with some human girl.

But Tallori was only a child, and he had no interest in her.

"Go now," the holy maiden said, "and get her. By bringing her to the palace, you may save her life."

Anduval stood for an instant, wondering. The holy maiden could sense things about people. She could read their thoughts and emotions. Was it possible she knew something he didn't, that Tallori might someday grow to be someone that he could love?

*Perhaps,* he thought. But the holy maiden was not an adult yet. She had not transcended and gained all of her powers, and nothing guaranteed that she would. Not all maidens broke free of their chrysalis. Many died in the attempt. Even those who broke free did not always develop great powers. Years of meditation and good food might help ensure that a maiden became a powerful adult. Yet most of the time, maidens awoke with little more psychic power than they'd held before.

So if the holy maiden suspected that Anduval might find love with this girl, it might still be nothing more than a hunch.

Ever so gently, Cessari reached down and positioned the maiden's womb so he could gain entrance, rolling her onto her stomach, and then leaning above her.

The holy maiden let out a little piping call of desire, and Anduval felt the touch of her mind.

It was like being dragged into a whirlwind of desire. The longing for her came upon him so strongly that it drove all other thoughts from his mind. He was only twelve, but at that moment he felt a man's desires and found himself staggering forward.

*She wants me,* Anduval thought. *She wants me as much as I want her.*

But then the maiden caught herself, and her desires withdrew, leaving him empty and embarrassed.

"Go," she pleaded. "Get out of here before it is too late."

She was almost mindless with the need to mate. Anduval turned and ran.

THAT NIGHT, THE STARS WERE BLAZING OVERHEAD WHEN ANDUVAL walked to Tallori's sod house.

He breathed in the rich scents of the night air as he walked. It was late autumn, and the farmhouses along the path boasted trees ripe with fruit—tart peaches, sweet pears, and fat plums.

In the night, the deer had come from the shadows of the forest. They huddled under the apple trees, sometimes rising up on their back legs as they picked fruit with their mouths.

Anduval saw a herd of four deer under Angar's apple tree. The small buck that led them showed no fear of Anduval, but simply held his ground, as if claiming the tree for his own.

At the sod house, the rich smell of peat and earth mingled. The hide flap that served as a door allowed easy entry, but Anduval stood outside and clapped until, at last, Angar came to the door.

The huge man was drunk and wavering on his feet.

"What do you want?" Angar demanded.

"I've come to pay you for your service to the holy maiden," Anduval said. He produced a pouch and handed it to the drunkard. "The price of a dragon's head."

Angar shook the pouch and frowned when he did not hear the clinking of coins. "Wha's this?"

"Rubies, emeralds, and diamonds," Anduval said. "Enough so that you can swim in a lake of beer, if you like."

A maniacal grin spread across the man's face. Excited shouts issued from inside the house. His wife had heard the news.

The young girl, Tallori, appeared at her father's back, peeking out from the shadows.

*She isn't really pretty,* Anduval thought. Her face was plain and freckled, her hair too bleached by the sun. She was not a promising child.

*Does the holy maiden really know something about her?* Anduval wondered.

"The Great Lady wishes to bless you, too, Tallori. Your damselflies served her well. What boon would you ask of her?"

The girl looked down at the ground as if studying the dirt on her bare feet, then glanced back toward her mother. She was obviously poor. Her dress was little more than a sack made of the crudest brown cloth. It looked as if the only comb that had ever gone through her pale hair was her fingers. Anduval waited for her to ask for money. Peasants were such simple creatures that wealth was the only reward they could imagine.

"I want to fight the cycor with you," she declared. "I want to come live in the palace and help build the worldship. If the holy maiden has any power at all, then she knows this."

*If all children spoke with such ferocity,* Anduval thought, *even lions would fear us.*

Immediately, Tallori glanced back into the room where her mother hid. Regret was stamped upon the child's face, as if she had betrayed the family.

"The lady bids you welcome to the palace," Anduval said.

Tallori stared at her mother in the darkened room and asked, "Can I go?"

There were sobs from the mother then, and the peasant woman came and gave her daughter a hug. Angar made a huge show of hugging his daughter, and Anduval had to wait at the door while her mother got Tallori's things and kissed her good-bye time and time again.

Anduval had never had anyone treat him so, and he stood for a long moment out in the shadows, watching the stars twinkle overhead. As he watched, one of them flared for an instant and then winked out.

Somewhere, he knew, a distant star had exploded. The cycor had struck again.

He heard a gasp and saw Tallori standing outside the doorway with a small bundle of belongings tied together with a rag. Her face was tilted upward. She had seen it too.

So they took off, running through the warm night, Tallori struggling to negotiate the path in the darkness with her bare feet.

Once again, Anduval felt the weight of the world falling upon his shoulders. He was no skraal nymph, but he could sense the cycor out there in the heavens, hunting him.

Tallori surely felt it too. She looked small and frightened as she hurried under the starlight.

Somewhere along the path, she reached out and grasped his hand for comfort.

ANDUVAL BECAME THE BIG BROTHER THAT TALLORI HAD NEVER HAD. He began that night as her mentor and tutor, but she had been raised in a world where the most complex tasks included weaving wool on her mother's loom and churning butter.

In theory, Anduval was an apprentice to the magus. But after only two weeks of instruction, the boy's understanding of physics soon dwarfed that of the magus. It was widely rumored he had been blessed of the dragon, had accepted its dreams, and Anduval went to work as head of construction for the most complex system of the worldship—its navigation system.

Anduval tried to make Tallori his assistant, but she often became frustrated and wept when Anduval tried to teach her. She grasped basic math well enough—simple things like trigonometry and calculus—but Anduval's mind was far more powerful than her own.

His memory was flawless. He recalled everything that he both saw and heard, but his mental prowess went far beyond that. He could multiply or divide any pair of numbers in his head, or calculate pi to a thousand decimal places.

More importantly, when confronted with a mystery, he could often consider it for a moment and intuitively recognize the answer.

She tried to keep up with him, but one day as she tried to multiply two six-digit numbers in her head, she began to sob uncontrollably.

Anduval put his arm around her, patted her on the back, and said, "Don't cry, little sister. Don't cry."

They were in Anduval's room where he was studying a sketch of the celestial navigation system for the worldship. He had been making notes about gravitonic sensors, red-shift resolution equations, and skraal brain-wave-computer interfaces.

Even with all of his understanding, he struggled to make sense of the holy maiden's often-crude schematics.

"I can't keep up with you!" Tallori blurted, wiping her nose.

"It's not your fault," he said. "The skraals can't keep up with me, either. Even Magus Veritarnus has been humbled. But all of us must learn as fast as we are able.

"It's not your fault that you were raised in a stone-age existence," he explained. "The skraals willed it to be so for many reasons. Technology carries inherent dangers. If we had used ancient telecommunications equipment, it would have unleashed radio waves that would have alerted the cycor to our presence. Power plants would have left energy signatures that cycor scouts could easily pick up. And even the simplest of electric machines can emit energy fields that adversely affect a skraal.

"Danai is a world in hiding. Now, we must come out of hiding and escape before the cycor attack.

"We must master a hundred thousand years of technological advancement in the next four years. Everyone must do all that they can, or we shall all die in the attempt.

"We can't lean upon the skraals for help. We can't hope that some great leader will save us. The time has come for each of us to be great."

Anduval stood for a moment, looking sober and hopeful.

"I don't know if I can be great," Tallori said. "But I know I can do more than other people believe a child can do."

Thus, as Tallori began to understand the dangers, she often longed to return to blissful ignorance. Just as she wept for her ignorance, she soon learned to weep for her enlightenment. She began to understand why Anduval was such a brooding and driven young man.

He worked for twenty hours a day, napping for a few minutes in the afternoon, sleeping two hours a night, taking only moments to cram a bit of food into his mouth. Then he would get back to work.

He became a shell of a young man, and Tallori became more than just his pupil. She began to feed him, care for him.

She soon found that the entire world was in turmoil. Their world was called upon to evolve, but the going was extremely slow.

Before a ship could be built, Magus Veritarnus had to design and manufacture its various components.

Before the components could be constructed, factories had to be erected, tools had to be created, and workers had to be trained how to do their jobs.

The factories in most cases required nuclear power systems to run the various smelting and metal-working tools.

Of course, before the power systems could run, the fissionable metals had to be mined.

So the skraal consorts ventured across the land, urging potato farmers to dig for uranium here, begging that sailors manufacture selenium crystals there.

At every step, the lack of technology and training became a stumbling block. It seemed that for every day of progress that was made, Magus Veritarnus discovered three more days of work to be done.

For instance, to build the basic hull of the ship—the easiest component to fabricate—the people needed to create selenium crystal beams and plates capable of resisting impact with space debris while traveling near light speed.

The selenium first had to be mined from rock, ground up, and dissolved in an acid bath.

The selenium solution was then placed in tanks and an electric current passed through it. The charged selenium particles would bind to a titanium plate and begin to form crystals. In this way, beams and plates could be "grown."

But once they were grown, the selenium crystals were so tough that even diamond could not cut through them. So in order for them to be shaped and fastened together, laser cutting torches were needed.

Thus a single rod for the hull could not be finished until the titanium was also mined, the acids and their containers created, the electrical systems installed in the baths, the laser cutting torches made, and so on.

Confusion reigned, and the people of Danai hit setbacks at every turn. Much of the planning for the construction took nine months to complete. Too many questions had to be answered. What facilities needed to be built, when and how? Who would do the work, and who would manage the workers? How could you train a stone-age woodcutter to build a gamma converter or a crystal AI?

Some work was done in fits and starts while other projects were planned, but farmers who had to dig for ore with picks and shovels proved too slow, missing deadlines. The factories were not completed on time.

After a year, the work had hardly begun, and some of the skraals began to worry about human saboteurs. Cessari called the magus and Anduval to task, insisting they launch a search for the imaginary saboteurs.

But good work did get completed. Anduval helped devise an early warning system in case of a cycor attack. Graviton-detecting telescopes were built and aimed toward the heavens. The gravity drive on a cycor ship would register as a massive planetoid or black hole racing toward Danai. Simple farmers were trained to man the scopes.

Listening stations were constructed to eavesdrop on cycor ships.

Meanwhile, the magus provided holographic interfaces for himself, Anduval, and dozens of project leaders around the world. The devices were simple silver bands that went over the forehead and wired straight into the optic and aural nerves. Thus, they could relay sights and sounds from one leader to another, so that the magus and Anduval could personally monitor situations and take care of training from afar.

But in the third year, a hurricane hit the hull's manufacturing facilities, and the factory was swept into the sea. A week later, at a separate construction site, a small nuclear power plant went into meltdown, and four hundred square miles of land had to be evacuated—along with a newly completed re-breather for the life-support systems.

Upon learning the news, Cessari himself burst into Anduval's laboratory.

"Now will you search for the saboteurs?" he demanded.

Anduval had only learned the news of the meltdown the day before; he'd spent a sleepless night trying to figure out how to get the work back on schedule.

"No, I will not," Anduval said. "There are no saboteurs. None of our people caused the hurricane, and the meltdown was an accident. The fuel rods are cooled by water from a nearby river, but the floodgates that control the water flow broke. They froze shut, and could not be reopened."

"Where is the man responsible for opening them?" Cessari asked. "I want to question him myself."

"He died this morning from radiation poisoning," Anduval said. "He stayed far too long at the site, struggling to cool the reactor's core even after it had gone into meltdown."

Cessari raged in the way of his kind, striding back and forth, striking the air with his empty fists. Finally, he turned back to Anduval.

"The deadline for completion of the project is coming quickly. You must meet the deadline."

"We all are doing the best that we can," Anduval said.

Tallori knew that even their best was not good enough. "But we will not meet the deadline. Our only hope is that all cycor ships are far, far away."

At this, Cessari rushed up to Anduval. He did not dare strike the young man, but he warned, "You cannot fail our queen. If the cycor attack before we are ready, I shall make sure that you are the first to die."

Anduval bowed his head in acquiescence. "I assure you, under such circumstances, I would have no wish to live. Yet I must also warn you, even skraal law prohibits murder. I will be within my rights to protect myself."

Cessari blurted an obscenity and stalked away.

"What are you going to do?" Tallori asked Anduval when the skraal was gone. "You have to protect yourself. The skraals are faster and stronger than us."

Anduval merely shrugged. "But I am smarter than they are."

TALLORI GREW FROM A CHILD TO A YOUNG WOMAN. SHE FOUND THAT SHE could not comprehend the math that Anduval was mastering, but she found her niche. She planned Anduval's meals, freeing time for him and making sure he did not fall ill due to fatigue.

When a plant manager looked as if he would miss a deadline, Tallori ran interference for Anduval, bolstering men's spirits with praise and honors, offering bribes when it was prudent, and, when necessary, reminding them that failure meant death.

Time and time again, she marveled at what her people had accomplished. There were farmers, working their crops by day and mining by night, breaking their hearts in order to meet a deadline that they did not understand so that their ore could be turned into something that they could not comprehend.

Old women and children worked in factories from dawn to dusk.

The world was full of heroes, she discovered.

In another age, no one would have given her the time of day. But as Anduval's assistant, it was rumored that she had the ear of the magus, and all men gave her high regard.

Thus, she became the mother that Anduval had never had.

But as she neared her teens and her body began to morph from that of a child into a woman, she wanted more.

Anduval loved a skraal nymph, and Tallori began to realize that she was in love with him.

She wondered if Anduval would ever even notice.

So the day came when, at the age of twelve, she sought out Magus Veritarnus at his laboratory. He'd spent long years collecting seeds, spores, and animal embryos, and then freezing them for storage. As she had anticipated, he was busy when she found him. He was always busy.

The world on Danai had been divided into ecological zones, and the plants and animals from each zone represented species selected from various worlds. The deep forest at Shadowfest was comprised of plants and animals from the skraals' home world. It was an impenetrable jungle where boa trees rose up in vast tangles for thousands of feet. The ground beneath them was a silent tomb, filled with fungi that digested the fallen leaves and dead animals.

Most of the alien proteins in the creatures and plants within Shadowfest were inedible to humans, though some terrestrial animals—like the wild pigs—had begun to evolve the ability to eat them.

Around the skraal forests, humans lived in the plains and wooded hills.

So the magus had to store specimens from both zones. Even a few plants and animals from the dragon's home world still thrived here. Women still planted dragon's breath vines beside their homes. The vines were prized for the mildly narcotic smell that its flowers emitted in high summer. Old folks, bowed by arthritis, loved to take their ease beneath an arbor of dragon's breath.

Tallori had little interest in the magus's efforts to save the specimens from this world. Whether the people of Danai fled on a worldship or simply tried to weather another cycor attack, the magus's work was vital. But everyone's work was vital, from the farmwife who simply tried to feed her husband, to the husband who mined a little each day, to the factory worker, to folks like Anduval—each was essential to the effort.

But Tallori was too focused upon Anduval's efforts to build a prototype of the celestial navigation system. So she dared to interrupt the magus, hoping for a moment of his time.

"How comes the prototype?" Magus Veritarnus asked as she neared. He stood squinting up at his monitor, repairing the damaged DNA of some embryo before he sent it to the freezers.

"Well," Tallori said, managing only a mildly sarcastic tone. "We are only fourteen months behind schedule. Anduval hopes to have it finished in three months."

"A full-sized starship can be piloted even with a simple prototype. If he gets it working, we will be able to make do."

The magus did not bother to mention that everything else was behind schedule, too. The prototype ship would be small, only able to carry a few hundred people.

But it was vital to the efforts. So many of the holy maiden's sketches were . . . mysterious. Knowing what a starship's drive system was supposed to do was one thing, building it so that the nuclear-powered lifters, ion propulsion units, gamma-wave converters, and so on all worked in unison was another.

"You know we will not make our deadline of four years," Tallori said.

The magus nodded. "Some of the skraals hope that it will be done in five years. Anduval imagines that if all goes right, it will take eight. Personally, I do not believe that we can get it done in twenty."

He said it casually, in the way of one who has accepted that he will die in a vain struggle.

"Anduval is not like other people," she said. "He's smarter. He sleeps very little, in the way that the greatest of geniuses do."

"Anduval is not like other people," the magus agreed.

"The thing is," Tallori said. "I love him. But I feel that I'm too stupid for him. I can't talk to him about math or physics."

The magus had been staring up at his monitor, switching out little blocks of ATGC. Now he peered at her.

"A man can love a woman for something other than her native intelligence. He can love her for her goodness, her kindness. I know that Anduval is fond of you."

"But I can never be his equal," Tallori said.

"Intellectually, no," the magus admitted. "Anduval is a special boy. Evolution does not always take place in tiny steps. Sometimes it comes in giant leaps. Anduval is the next leap."

The magus fell silent for a moment, and Tallori stood her ground, waiting for him to explain. Reluctantly, he said, "Two million years ago, a manlike creature roamed the earth, a creature called Homo habilis. It had a small brain that could comprehend little. It could make a leaf-shaped house and use a few simple tools—a stone knife, an awl to poke holes in furs, a needle.

"But one day, one of the creatures evolved. The gene that told the brain how large it should be simply formed a double string, and suddenly a new specimen was born, one with twice the brainpower. It was called Homo erectus.

"It created a few more tools, better weapons, and over time its genetic superiority was confirmed. The old species died out, and those with the new, larger brains took their place.

"Eventually, a second mutation occurred, and mankind was born—a creature with dual brains that were connected by a bundle of nerves, so that the two halves of the brain could talk to one another. Each half of a brain was dubbed a 'lobe,' and that is where you come in. You can feel the evidence of those two brains. Often you will feel them arguing, struggling for control. When faced with a moral dilemma, one of your lobes may argue one course of action, while the other lobe demands another.

"But always, it was suspected that evolution would take its next bound forward. As had happened time and again before, a new form of human would be born, one with doubled cranial capacity."

Tallori could not understand everything the magus said, but she understood there were genetic reasons why Anduval was smarter than she was. "So, Anduval has a larger brain?"

The magus shook his head. "He has four brains—two frontal lobes and two posterior lobes. Each pair of lobes is connected by its own corpus callosum, its own bundle of nerves.

"When you hear two voices arguing in your mind, Anduval hears four in his."

The magus now turned and looked her full in the eye. "There are those who would argue, rightly, I think, that true intelligence is not merely the ability to recall correctly, but to make intuitive leaps, to use the stored information to unforeseen advantage. That is Anduval's gift."

Tallori was thinking furiously. She was wondering what that might mean for her future.

"Anduval cannot have children with you," the magus said gently. "You are from common human stock, and he has been greatly modified. Even if you were to try to have children, they would not be viable."

The words hit her like a punch to the gut, taking the air from her lungs.

But the magus said softly, "Yet he needs someone to love, and his line must be preserved. If you marry him, I can take your eggs and a few cells from his heart, and create a child, one that will express the best traits in both of you."

Tallori looked up at the magus, and for the first time she understood the significance of his oversized head, the bumps on his temple. "Anduval is your son, isn't he?"

The magus appeared to be at a loss for words. "Close. His full name is Anduval Nine. My birth name was Anduval Eight."

THE MEMORY OF SERAMASIA HAUNTED ANDUVAL THROUGHOUT THE years. At night he dreamt of her, sprawled out on her silk sheets, her womb glowing with urgency.

At such times, he was filled with longing, and he rededicated himself to his work.

But a thousand days after Holy Maiden Seramasia entered her long sleep, Anduval had a special dream.

In it, he was preparing his celestial navigation system for testing on the prototype, and he worried over the artifact, a glowing ball of crystal with engravings upon it, shot through with colored wires and bound in platinum.

The navigation system was meant to be used by a skraal navigator. But would a skraal be talented enough to pilot the ship?

Originally, all navigators were dragons whose minds were uniquely adapted to flight.

Anduval had boosted the ship's long-range detection capacities in an effort to make it easier on the skraals. Beyond that, he had eliminated the need for physical manipulation of the controls. The skraal's crystal brain structure created a powerful electric field, a psycho-electric cloud that could easily interface with the control mechanisms without need for physical contact.

All he needed to do was tune the interface to the proper frequency so that it did not damage the delicate neurons and axons in the skraal's brain.

A holographic display would appear in the pilot's mind, showing the space ahead, and revealing obstacles that could include anything from clouds of dust or plasma to small planetoids.

As the ship neared such obstacles, lasers would pulverize smaller debris, and the ion shields would route the particles into the fusion drives for use as fuel.

But the pilot would have to weave a path through the larger obstacles. At slow speeds, that would not be hard.

Yet he worried still. A skraal would be able to pilot the ship, but would the pilot be talented enough to outrun a cycor vessel?

Anduval had no way to know. His limited information on cycor vessels was six thousand years out of date.

So in his dream that night, he was pondering how to speed up the system when Holy Maiden Seramasia suddenly appeared at his side.

She was a holy maiden no more. In the dream, she was filled with glorious light. Gone was the fat and fragile flesh. Now she was all hard lines. Her skin had turned to blue crystal, and the brilliance radiated from her abdomen, her thorax, even her head.

Tiny baby skraals were crawling on her back, like large scorpions made of glass. Even as he watched, the newly hatched were exiting her womb.

Anduval hardly dared look at her, for it hurt his eyes so. A feeling of rapture overwhelmed him as the holy mother addressed him, her thoughts a storm that beat upon him, her love a gale that blew through him.

"It is beautiful," Seramasia said of his navigation system. "Have no fear, my friend. It will work, and it will save us all."

"Do you know this," Anduval begged, "or is it merely a hope?" He was no longer sure if he dreamed or if Seramasia had indeed transcended and now communed with him through a mind-touch.

"I see the future, frail one. I see all things. I see your love for me, and it is not nearly as great as my love for you." Her voice trailed off. She glanced to the side and down, and Holy Mother Seramasia suddenly disappeared.

Anduval woke in his room. It had not been an hour since he had gone to sleep. His eyes still felt gritty, and were probably bloodshot.

Every bone in his body ached from fatigue.

For years he had been afraid of failure, but the dream had comforted him. Yet he worried that it was false comfort.

*Was it a dream,* he wondered, *or did Seramasia really appear to me?*

It was possible for a powerful holy mother to send dreams to her subjects, to communicate from a thousand miles away.

He raced down from his bedchambers, past the crèches in the human quarters, and took the grand corridor to the royal chambers. He entered through the old dining hall and reached the closed door to the meditation chambers.

There, a trio of skraal courtiers guarded the chrysalis. Twisted ropes of bone, yellowing with age, still bound the holy maiden. The chrysalis only vaguely hinted at the shape of the woman sleeping within.

The skraals leaped to readiness.

"Halt!" one warned. All three held disruptor rods—pale white rods that emitted a killing jolt.

Anduval stood for a moment panting, staring at the egg-shaped chrysalis in disbelief. He'd expected to see it cracked open, the new Holy Mother standing resplendent and glorious.

But it had only been a dream, and now he felt the fool.

"Any movement?" Anduval begged. It was not uncommon for the queen to grow restless inside her chrysalis, to stir for months before it opened, even to cry out to her courtesans or speak briefly.

"She sleeps deeply," a courtesan answered, "and moves not at all."

*Of course it was just a dream,* Anduval thought.

It was too early for her to emerge from her chrysalis. She would still be deep asleep, comatose.

*Even when she does awaken,* he thought, *Seramasia will not be a vessel of light. She will not be glorious and powerful. She will come out of her chrysalis with a hardened skin, nothing more.*

Two days later, an emergency meeting was called in Magus Veritarnus's laboratory. The skraal lords in charge of palace security were there, along with dozens of guards. Tallori stood at Anduval's side.

"The cycor are coming," the magus said. He flipped on the screen of his workstation, which took up one vast wall. It showed an area of space

—a bright star like a glowing world, with tens of thousands of lesser stars beyond.

Static played, and suddenly there was a loud squeal that seemed to emit from the star.

"That squeal is a signal burst," the magus said. "A cycor warship sent a message to its command center. They are coming to Danai."

One of the city guards asked, "How long will it take to get here? It looks as if they are far away."

"The drone scout that discovered our world relayed our whereabouts," Anduval explained. "It sent a message burst, similar to the one that you heard. That message traveled at light speed to the star that you see. The warship received the message, and then sent out a report of its own before moving out. That ship will be racing toward us now, at near the speed of light. It will take only a day or two to reach maximum speed."

"So you're saying that we have four years?" the guard asked hopefully.

"I'm saying," Anduval corrected, "that the cycor learned of our position two years ago, and set out immediately. Depending upon their speed of acceleration, they will attack shortly—within days."

Suddenly, up on the screen, there was a distortion in the star field. A dark blur erupted, as if a planet had formed, and immediately began to enlarge.

A cycor ship was approaching quickly.

"Well," the magus said in resignation, "here they come."

The world was about to end, and he had given up. After all of their preparations. Yet Tallori could not give up hope so easily.

She thought frantically. It would take years still to build a worldship. Most of the components for the prototype had been completed, but the hull was a thousand miles away, being towed across the ocean by sailing ships, while the drive system was scattered over the southern half of the continent. It would take weeks to gather the parts, assemble the prototype. And even when it was completed, it would only be able to carry the elite of the planet, three or four hundred people.

*But we'll never finish it,* she realized.

Heart pounding, she looked to Anduval, and realized that everyone was staring at him, waiting for an answer. But Anduval had none.

"We must hide," Magus Veritarnus said. "Tell the people everywhere to seek out their assigned shelter—deep in caves or bunkers, wherever they can! They will need food to last a year, at least."

Anduval studied the approaching doom and then turned and strode away. Tallori followed him back to his personal quarters, her mind racing.

The palace was about to become a madhouse. The simple farmers at the edge of Shadowfest would rush here for safety, hoping to gain entrance. The smarter ones would bring animals and food to eat, whatever they could carry.

But the palace wouldn't be able to hold them all. It might be able to protect a few thousand, but it couldn't hold the *hundreds* of thousands who would come.

The skraals would be forced to drop the shield walls and block all entrances.

Tallori's heart pounded, and she imagined that it sounded like the drumming of closed fists upon the shield wall doors. She imagined her mother and father, trying to break into the palace, crying out for help.

She found Anduval kneeling on the floor in his spartan quarters, staring at the wall. There were storage containers built into the wall for his personal effects, a toilet, a sink, and a bed low to the floor. Nothing else. The baths and commissary were down the hall.

She knelt beside him. "What can we do?"

He shook his head slowly, staring at the wall as if at some private horror. "Nothing," he said. "We can hide, but the gravity field emitted by that ship is too large. If they even draw close, they could siphon off our atmosphere or rip the crust of the planet apart. They won't even need to use weapons."

"Can we fight them?" Tallori asked.

Anduval shook his head.

He turned, and there was infinite pain in his eyes. "I've failed you, Tallori."

A shock of fear pierced her, more powerful than anything she'd ever felt. The skin on her forehead tightened, and the hair rose on the back of her neck.

"I love you, Anduval," Tallori said.

He nodded slightly, as if to say that he knew.

"Will you kiss me?" she asked in a small voice.

Tallori was only twelve and a half, far too young to marry. But she had been in love with him for nearly four years, and she did not want to die without having felt the touch of lips against hers.

*If I'm going to die,* she thought, *I want to die in his embrace.*

Hesitantly, Anduval reached out and stroked her face.

He was not the kind to lie to her. If he kissed her, she knew, it would be an admission of what he felt.

He leaned close. Their lips met, and she wrapped her fingers in his long hair. She leaned into him, so that she felt his heart thrilling, and just enjoyed the taste of him.

Anduval pulled back and said, "You deserve better than I can give you. You deserve a full lifetime of love."

Tallori shook her head. "This will have to be enough," she whispered, when the door to his room burst open.

Cessari stood in the doorway, a disruptor in hand. "You have failed," he said coldly. "You shall be the first to die."

With superhuman speed he attacked, aiming the disruptor rod. Anduval shoved Tallori aside, out of harm's way.

A burst of electricity arced across the room, a bolt of violet lightning. It struck Anduval's silver headband. Sparks flew; Tallori smelled a rush of ozone.

Cessari let out a trumpeting call, a skraal cry of pain, and collapsed to the floor.

The skraal lay convulsing.

Tallori gaped at Anduval in wonder.

He stepped closer to Cessari, and the skraal's muscles all clenched simultaneously. His mouth flew open, his oral-dactyls spasming, and his eyes jiggled. His head turned up and to the side, while his legs and arms curled in. He gasped, struggling with every fiber of his body to breathe.

"I told you I would protect myself," Anduval said. He removed the silver headband, pulled free the platinum leads that hooked into his nerves, and threw the device down upon the skraal.

Cessari went completely rigid and quit moving, a gray-green effluvia exuded from his pores.

He stopped breathing, stopped moving.

Tallori was confused. She stood, staring down at the skraal. "What . . . what did you do?"

"I built a skraal brain-wave interface into my headband," Anduval admitted. "It had no power source, but it was designed to accept the electrical impulse given off by a disruptor. When Cessari shot me, the electric charge overpowered the interface, which shattered his brain."

The skraal consort was dead, his life fleeing as smoothly as a candle going out.

"He could have hit you," Tallori said. "How did you know he would use a disruptor? All he had to do was crush you like a bug."

"He brought a disruptor when he threatened me earlier," Anduval said reasonably.

He stood for a long moment, peering down at Cessari.

The skraals would be angry. Tallori had never heard of a human killing a skraal. They were faster, stronger, smarter than humans. They were biologically superior.

Anduval had only acted in self-defense.

She wondered what his punishment might be.

Suddenly the floor began to rumble, and in the halls, a warning horn sounded. Tallori looked around, wondering if there was an earthquake or if this signaled the beginning of an attack.

"They're closing the blast doors," Anduval said, "sealing the palace."

It had not been fifteen minutes since the warning had gone out. The people who lived in the nearby forests hadn't had time to reach the palace. Tallori's mother and father probably hadn't even learned of the danger yet.

Suddenly Anduval's eyes lit up, and he shouted, "There is one thing that we can do!"

He turned and raced down a hallway toward his laboratory, and Tallori struggled to catch up. She found him at his console, where he grabbed the navigation system—a ball of crystal shot through with wires of gold and silver and veins of turquoise and crimson.

ANDUVAL SPRINTED TO THE HOLY MAIDEN'S MEDITATION CHAMBER AND found that the doors had been thrown wide open.

The skraal courtesans knelt before her chrysalis, that great mass of yellowing bone.

One of the skraals was pounding upon the chrysalis as if to break it with his fists, while the courtesans all chanted in reedy voices like wood-winds, supplicating in their musical tongue, "Waken, O Holy Mother! Waken, O Bearer of Light!"

But all of their pounding, all of their prayers, would not waken Sera-masia, he knew. It was too early for her to waken, perhaps months or years too early.

He strode to the base of the chrysalis and held up the orb, as if to show it to Seramasia. But in fact, he only needed to get it near her skull.

"Back away," he shouted to the skraal supplicants. "Get back, all of you!"

Confused, the skraals began to retreat. Anduval pressed the power switch on his navigation unit and pleaded, "Wake up, great lady. Behold the danger. Our enemy approaches."

He held the device near. He knew what it should do. Active sensors down in his laboratory were constantly mapping space for a light year in every direction.

Sun, planets, moons, and meteors—all would be thrown up against the backdrop of space.

And the image would pierce the holy maiden's mind, show her the advancing threat. Even in her deepest sleep, even in her comatose state, Anduval hoped to reach her.   .

Whether Seramasia could do anything to stop the cycor, he did not know. Most probably, if she became aware of the danger at all, she would only be able to shrink away in horror and despair.

Magus Veritarnus stood at his console. He peered up at the star field and struggled to come to grips with his imminent death.

The cycor ship had grown large. It was less than a tenth of a light year distant, according to the sensors. He could see it clearly, a large dark orb rushing toward them.

Inside that orb was a black hole, sucking all light and matter into it— all but the cycor warship, a silver needle that floated ahead of the great pearl.

The cycor ship defied the laws of physics as the magus understood them. It should have been sucked into the black hole.

*Ah,* he thought, *but there you have it. Death is a mystery. Should it not come in a mysterious fashion?*

He watched the field growing steadily. The warship was slowing, decelerating at fifty G's. Yet still it seemed to be rushing upon them.

In a heartbeat, the whole ball shifted, as if making a course correction, and a puff of blue smoke issued from the silver needle as if something had exploded.

Instantly, the ship disappeared.

For a long moment, the magus merely stood, heart pounding, unable to accept his good fortune.

*A malfunction,* he thought. *That is the only explanation—a mechanical failure aboard the cycor ship.*

The black hole had turned and was veering away. It would bypass Danai entirely and exit the solar system in a matter of hours.

In the hallways, warning horns were still blaring.

But suddenly a new sound arose, a clarion call like a thousand flutes and oboes, a song sung by skraals only upon transcendence of a holy maiden.

*She has left behind her pharate form and ascended to imago,* the magus realized.

Magus Veritarnus whirled and rushed to worship at the feet of the new holy mother.

SERAMASIA BROKE FROM HER CHRYSALIS. SHE DID NOT DO SO WITH A pounding of fists, with kicks or shouts. Rather, a fierce light sprang up, playing through the corded ropes of bone, sparking in hues of gold and green.

After a tenth of a second, the chrysalis burst outward. Seramasia crouched within the effluvium, blazing with a light so fierce that Anduval was forced to cover his eyes with his arm. Tallori shouted in awe.

Every bit of Seramasia was as clear as crystal. Every bit of her was filled with light whiter than the sun. Not in ten thousand years had such an imago taken form.

"Holy Mother!" Tallori cried out, breaking into tears.

The skraals raised their voices in triumph, singing to the goddess in a symphony of praise.

"Fear not," Holy Mother Seramasia called out. "The cycor threat has been overcome!"

From all through the palace, people came running—skraal teachers and physicians, the old human women who mopped the floors, the chefs and servants.

The people broke into song, their hearts breaking with relief and joy.

Last of all came the magus, striding through the halls, his black robes flowing out behind him. Amid the shouts of praise and wonder, he clapped Anduval upon the back, and whispered in his ear, "Should we thank the god who saved us, or should we thank *you*—the man who made the god?"

Anduval glanced at his mentor and smiled in satisfaction. "Our world is full of enough heroes," he said. "Let Seramasia take the praise."

THAT DAY, THE PARTS TO THE PROTOTYPE OF THE WORLDSHIP CAME together.

The hull that was floating out at sea, towed by a great-masted sailing vessel, broke free of the cords and rose slowly into the air. Two thousand miles away, the propulsion systems cracked through the roofs of their warehouse. From all across the world, pieces rose into the sky and raced through the heavens until, at last, they rested in the blue skies above Shadowfest.

When the pieces had all fitted themselves together, the ship hovered in the sky. At sunset, Anduval found himself rising up through the dense foliage as easily as dandelion down borne on a summer wind.

A blast of wind greeted his upturned face.

Seramasia floated above him, a great light in the sky, while Tallori and the magus and dozens of technicians and scientists from the palace rose up to meet her.

Stores of food floated up as well: great casks of water, sacks of grain, all of the fruits and vegetables of the field, and all things that might appeal to a skraal.

At the edge of the world, a sliver of red sun straddled the horizon, an ember among darkening ash.

Down below, the sounds of the jungle rose up from Shadowfest—the squeals of colossal boars, the rumbling call of a growler, the shrieks of flying reptiles.

Anduval reached the hovering ship and entered the threshold, wondering what to do.

He felt a touch in his mind and heard Seramasia's voice. "Be at peace, my truest friend, and rest, for we have far to go."

Anduval took Tallori's hand when she arrived, and he felt content. Together they walked through the ship's corridors and up to the navigator's console.

Holy Mother Seramasia was at her seat, resting easily. As the ship smoothly accelerated out of orbit, she peered up into the field of stars displayed on the console above.

The ship veered and set a course—not for the far dark reaches beyond the borders of the galaxy, but toward the void at the galactic center.

"Of course we cannot run," Anduval whispered aloud, for he too had been touched by a dragon's dream, and the dragon dreamt of vengeance.

ON THE DRY DAYS ON DANAI, THE DAMSELFLIES TAKE THEIR MAIDEN flights, rising into the summer morn in all their glory.

Lightning bolts of blue, bright sparks of molten fire, the small creatures from the marsh take leave of the earth and climb the sky on trembling wings, tiny hunters on the wind at last.

# Working on Cloud Nine

## John M. Olsen

There aren't a lot of luxuries on a space station. That's why it annoyed Loralee when the radio links all died.

With only four of them on the prototype waste recycling station, they each wore a lot of hats. She was the station chemist, biologist, and botanist. She floated in the command center of the Cloud Nine station with Penelope Devonshire, the station electronics and radio guru. "Pen, you told Phil to be careful on his EVA. I heard it."

Pen nodded her head. "Yes, I told him."

Loralee thought Pen's British accent gave a classy touch to everything she said. She liked Pen even though she alternated between a prim professional and an alter ego that swore like a sailor.

She drifted near the station's status displays for the rotating one-gee ring. The whole station was a prototype designed to make space stations self-sustaining.

Pen continued, "He even managed to take out the local radio and intercom. Remind me again why we let managers touch expensive things?" Pen wasn't angry yet.

Loralee rubbed a hand across her stubbly head, having shaved it the week prior for a hair sample. The others said she was impulsive, but she preferred to think of herself as efficient. She had grown her hair out for months for that experiment.

She spread her arms out wide and rolled her eyes. "It gets worse. If Cloud One is on their toes, they'll have a shuttle on our doorstep within twenty hours. Once they launch, they'll come all the way over even if we fix the com system." Travel between the nine geosynchronous satellites of the Cloud network didn't take much work since they all shared the same altitude in the Clarke belt. All it took was one well-aimed rocket boost to get going, and another to slow and stop at the destination. The trip only used a lot of fuel if you were in a hurry to cover the thirty-seven thousand clicks between stations. Solar sail tugs worked well but had much lower acceleration. A complete loss of communication would put them on a fast track visit from Cloud One even if their telescopes saw no signs of damage. She didn't want that kind of attention because of her unauthorized research.

Pen gave a resigned sigh. "I'd better send the spider over to the dish cluster to see if I can put a camera on what he ruined." She looked at a screen showing a view outside the station on the opposite side from the antennas. "Wireless still works, but it will take two hours for the spider to crawl around." She typed some commands, and the robot stretched out its limbs and crept through the vacuum along the guiderails on the outside of the station.

Loralee brightened. "Hey, maybe you can use the spider to fix whatever he knocked loose. It's a regular Swiss army knife with legs."

Pen said, "It depends on what he broke. I'd better see if Roger has eyes on Phil. If not, he'll be half way suited up with a rescue kit in hand. And here I thought you and Phil would enjoy a quiet shift."

"Yeah, thanks. I'll be in the ring for a bit, but I'll meet you back here when he comes in." Loralee gave a cheery wave as Pen left to check on Roger. Roger Adams handled the mechanical systems, and propulsion, and watched Phil's lifeline and vitals at the airlock data station.

Loralee had her work cut out for her to prepare for an unexpected visit from Cloud One. She pulled herself through the halls at full speed to the ring. Everyone acknowledged her as the champion hall flyer. Even scientists needed to invent games from time to time, and nobody could traverse the station as fast as she could. Roger had sprained a wrist once trying to match her, and had earned a reprimand from Phil.

The one-gee ring took up the center of the station, and consisted of a tube with a ten-meter radius, extending thirty meters along the hub. It spun fast enough to generate one gravity on the inside surface. She climbed into the ring's shuttle, a cab about a meter square, and gave it the command to spin up and synchronize with the ring. The crew could only enter and leave the ring via the cabs.

Exercise equipment helped to stave off bone loss, but she had repurposed most of the space on their ring, crowding the fitness equipment into one small area. She walked out between rows of dark mulch to the narrow running track exposed along the middle of the ring. To either side grew her prized fruit trees, apples to her left and oranges to the right, with room for two more rows near the outside of the ring to increase the variety. High yield grains and small vegetables surrounded the trees at ground level.

The humid air inside the ring carried a faint smell of both loam and blossoms. She loved working in the ring, and she spent as much time as possible with her plants and trees.

She checked on the status of the newest apple seedlings. She had almost enough now to duplicate her ring of apple trees in each of the Cloud stations. Rather than sit directly in the rich loam, the seedlings sat in rows of makeshift pots.

The older trees on both sides of the aisle reached to within a meter of the center of the ring due to the enhanced growth she had stimulated in them. The plants had responded well to the gravity differential as they reached from standard Earth gravity on the ground to zero at the center of the ring. She had spliced the tree tops together as they grew, sharing nutrients in the critical upper reaches. Based on her research, the low gravity environment would improve fruit production by almost an order of magnitude above that of a ground-based tree. Her initial experiments had verified she was on track.

Loralee checked on the approved projects first. Oxygen production and carbon sequestration through the growth of "green slime" as they called it, did as well as expected, but some of her vegetable crops matched the oxygen production of the slime and had the benefit of both looking and tasting better.

She finished an inventory of her rogue project and figured it would have to do. She could use a few more months to assemble a presentation, but didn't have that luxury. With the emergency response ship on the way, she couldn't hide her off-hours research. If they ran an audit, they would find everything. She had to beat them to the punch. She might get in less trouble for having hid her private research if she shared it all now.

Loralee headed back toward the ring shuttle but stumbled over Phil's exercise bag near her storage lockers. It wasn't like him to leave it here. Station training demanded you never leave anything loose because zero gravity could turn any loose object into a lethal projectile. The discipline carried over into the ring, even with the force holding everything down to the floor.

She decided to take it to him and remind him not to leave it in the ring, so she picked it up. The weight of the bag surprised her. Setting it back down, she unzipped the bag and saw labeled seed samples from her private research stacked inside with gym clothes and a book.

Something was up. Loralee didn't know what, but she knew it was big. First, Phil had somehow cut off their communications, and now he planned to do something with her seeds. She scowled. If communications were up, it would be awkward for her to report the theft of unauthorized research materials. This loss would have crippled her plans.

Time was short. Phil must know she would discover the missing seeds soon. Whatever he had planned, it would be in the next few hours.

She stored the seeds with meticulous care, locked the rack, and loaded the duffel with matching empty containers. She also grabbed a quarter liter jug of ninety-five percent ethanol from a fuel refining experiment. Phil would sometimes ask her for samples of her cleaning fluid, as he called it. After the first few times, she realized he must drink the stuff.

Loralee didn't know Phil's plans, but she knew she would do whatever it took to stop him. It was time to find out what he was doing. She dug through the first-aid kit until she found the sedatives she was after and dropped a heavy dose into the alcohol and swirled it until the tablets dissolved.

She took the duffel and the jug with her to the command center to wait.

Within a half hour, everyone had gathered back in the command center. Loralee had stored the alcohol in a cabinet and clipped Phil's exercise bag to a wall ring. She seethed inside as she waited for her chance to act.

Phil frowned as he looked around at the team hanging from various handholds around the room. "The plug-in module seated when I replaced it, so I'm not sure what went wrong. I'll check the wiring on the inside first to see if we blew any breakers. Roger and Pen, you two are late for your sleep shift. I need you to be alert and ready eight hours from now if Loralee and I don't fix everything while you sleep."

Roger unclipped a little mirror-tipped pen from his shirt pocket to twirl around as he drawled, "Well, if'n you think you won't have it fixed on your shift, I'll be ready to suit up and see if I can fix whatever got tore up." When they had first met, Loralee had mistaken his slow southern speech for a sign of ignorance or laziness. She'd soon discovered neither was true. Roger had proven himself as one of the best and brightest rocket scientists and mechanics she'd ever met.

Phil scowled at Roger. "Are you implying something? I don't want to hear it. Get out of the way, get some rest, and I'll tell you what to do in eight hours."

Roger held his hands up palm out and floated toward the door. "No problem here. Just said I'd be ready to go when you need me."

Phil seemed as surly and demanding as ever but seemed even more on edge. Loralee wanted to say something to confront him but waited. She looked over as Pen pulled herself out into the hallway after Roger. Once out of sight of Phil around the corner, Pen pantomimed and mouthed something to Loralee about two hours, and made a walking spider motion with one hand on the other. Pen would check on the spider when it got around to the dish side of the station, but didn't want to incur the wrath of Phil since she wouldn't sleep through her full rest cycle.

Loralee gave Pen a satisfied nod. She waited to let Roger and Pen get to their respective rooms, then took a breath and hoped to sound casual.

"I saw your exercise bag in the ring, so I brought it back here for you." She pointed at the bag hooked to the wall. "Oh, do you need some cleaning solution while you do your inspection?"

Phil looked up, scowl gone. "Oh, thank you for bringing the bag. And yes, I've run out of cleaning fluid again."

Loralee pulled the drugged alcohol out of the cabinet and tossed it to him. Phil licked his lips as he stowed the small jug into a large plastic toolbox.

Loralee asked, "So, do you have any idea what to look at first?"

"I said I'll check the breakers in the far hall first. I need to get some tools and supplies together." Phil glided to the tool storage locker and loaded things into the portable tool box, then unhooked it from the wall.

Loralee said, "Let me know if you need help with anything."

Phil pushed his oversize load out into the hallway along with coils of conduit and pressure tubing. In zero gravity, a bigger load only meant you had to slow down to steer a larger mass. There's no actual lifting involved; it's all pushing and pulling.

Now she needed to wait and see if his self-control was as weak as she hoped it was. Loralee hated waiting but gave him an hour to settle in and get drunk. She had nearly decided to go hunt him down when a low-pressure alarm sounded. The methane storage tank monitor blinked, having lost a significant amount of gas. The methane was compressed and stored for use as shuttle fuel. She checked the station air mix on the displays, and it was within normal tolerances. It wasn't a leak.

Her worry became panic as she remembered the pipe and conduit Phil took with the toolbox. What had he done this time?

She hauled herself hand over hand through the main hall and looked down each side passage as she flew past.

She found him tucked partway into an access passage leading to a large unused storage compartment. "What did you do, Phil? I have a huge pressure drop!" She gave him a tentative poke.

He didn't respond. Loralee tugged him from the access hall by his feet and spun him to face her. She caught a strong whiff of alcohol on his breath. He was out cold. Her quarter liter jug floated from his grasp, empty. Well, thank goodness for small favors. Her plan had worked, aside from not preventing whatever disaster he'd pulled off in the past hour.

"This has got to take the cake as the stupidest, most dangerous thing you've ever done." She listened for any leaks to see if he'd opened a flow valve nearby and heard nothing. Good. She switched her attention to Phil. Based on his size, he would be out for several hours. Even if this methane leak was the only thing reported, he was done on the station. They'd send him down, and he'd never go back into orbit again. That suited Loralee just fine. She considered sending him in an emergency pod to but figured the real evidence against him was enough.

She hauled him by the collar to his room a short distance down another side hall, and then hooked his jumper's belt to the wall to keep him from drifting. For good measure, she sealed and locked his door from the outside with her personal lock code. She continued to think about what had happened and realized the consequences might not end with him. She might get grounded herself if someone went on a witch hunt because of her special projects. All her work and all her success to prove stations could become self-sustaining could come down to mean nothing. She was the first to grow full size producing fruit trees in orbit. Up in smoke. And all the optimizations to their experiments? They might keep everything she'd done, but they'd sweep her under the rug. She had wanted to show off, and make the big flashy announcements rather than produce the slow, plodding by-the-rules experiments.

She had only one real choice now if she wanted to come out of this with her career intact. She had to get Pen and Roger and tell them what she knew about Phil and work to keep the team from getting taken down in the fallout when the repair crew arrived and took stock of the degrading situation.

Loralee knocked on Pen's door first, suspecting she was awake to track the spider on her personal console. Pen opened her door almost immediately. "What's up? Did you find something?" Pen saw Loralee's expression. "What's wrong?"

Loralee held up a hand to hold off the questions until she had knocked on Roger's door and woken him up. He came out into the hall rubbing his eyes. "Ain't this a bit too early?"

Loralee took a deep breath and said, "I, um, drugged Phil. He's passed out, and I locked him in his room."

Pen and Roger stared, trying to parse what Loralee had said. Finally, Pen said, "Drugged? What were you thinking? He'll have you grounded so fast your head will spin for a week."

Loralee interrupted, "He's done something dangerous, and the sedative got him out of the way. I'm pretty sure the dish failure wasn't an accident. He tried to steal all my latest generation of seeds, and he caused a methane pressure drop I can't locate."

Roger sighed and said, "Whoa, backup. That's a big load to dump on Phil's back. I'm not ready to accuse him of anything, but we can work on this while he sleeps it off. We got to get the station working before visitors get here, anyways. Sleep time's over, I recon." He took a deep breath and rubbed his face. "We'll get through this. Where was he working?"

Loralee told him where she had found him. "He was scheduled only to check wiring, so I wasn't worried. I didn't hear any leaks near him and the air mix is good."

Roger floated down the hall and said without turning back, "I'm on it. I'll see what he was up to."

Pen said, "I was about to check the spider anyway. I'll head to the command center with you and connect from there."

The spider had made it far enough to aim its camera at the dish assembly, so Pen stopped its march and made it focus in at maximum zoom on the dishes and their access panels. Plain as day, Phil had cut the cables not once, but twice with a piece removed. They would have to splice in a new length of multi-strand cable to get communication back up, which would take several hours in a space suit. It would be hard, tedious work.

Pen smacked her fist into a bulkhead and said through clenched teeth, "I hate to say you were right. He had to have done it on purpose. Is he trying to get us all grounded, or is it worse than that?" She continued with a string of scatological curses aimed at Phil which would have shocked a marine. She had, in fact, surprised Roger with her ability to maintain a stream of unrepeated curses, and he had served as a Marine before he joined the Cloud Consortium.

Loralee looked at the blinking methane gauge which had leveled back out at a constant but lower pressure and said, "Good. The pressure is stable. What's the chance your spider can fix the cable cuts to the dishes?"

Pen said, "It has tools, but not the supplies it would need. I'm sending it to the airlock for storage. It won't do us any more good out there."

Loralee pushed off toward the door. "I'll go see if Roger has found the pressure drop."

Pen said, "Right. I'll keep an eye on everything here."

A half minute later Loralee was looking over Roger's shoulder.

Roger complained, "I don't know what he thought he was doing here. I looked through his tool box and found a few non-standard doodads. He's got some wireless switches in his bag." He tossed a switch from hand to hand and then spun it in the air in front of him before he picked it back out of the air and tossed it into the toolbox for safe keeping.

Loralee said, "Well, he sure wasn't fixing the wiring. The spider got a good picture finally, and Phil chopped the cables to the dishes in two places."

"Well, being right don't mean the job changes any. But yeah. I'll grant you got it right." He continued to inspect Phil's work.

Loralee asked, "Anything on the gas leak yet? He had some tubing that could hold high pressure."

Roger sniffed. "Huh. I was wondering what was. It smells like he's got a tiny methane leak. I'm surprised you didn't catch it. Our methane's got some leftover smell from the compost." He traced the new lines, aligned to blend in with the existing piping. "See back here? He tapped into these two lines. This top one comes right out of the methane refueling line. Then they go down that way and through the wall. It looks like he tied it into some one-way valves in a junction box in the empty storage room. It'll be a pain, but we can pump the gas back out of that room once we get some equipment hooked up."

Loralee went ashen-faced. "Two lines? What's the other line?"

Roger traced the other line back to a valve on a different pipe.

Roger's eyes opened wide as he almost yelled, "Oxygen? You mean to tell me he turned the storage room into a bomb?"

Loralee said, "I didn't think to check the oxygen tank since there was no alarm."

"Yeah, it has different alarm thresholds since we use it for lots of things." He sat in thought for a moment and then continued, "That does it for me. I say we pile into the emergency pods and let Cloud One handle the damage control. Fixing this ain't what we signed up for. Let's go tell Pen."

The station's two pods could each hold two people, so the station had a maximum crew of four. The highly durable pods had life support and an emergency beacon, as well as an automated flight control system which would activate upon launch. It was possible to override the launch flight path, but the default action de-orbited the escape pod, landing in a New Mexico desert.

They entered the command center with the large plastic toolbox to see Pen looking through Phil's duffel bag.

Pen held out a book. "Did any of you know he followed the Anti-Orbiters? They protest the exploration and use of space and believe money spent in orbit is wasted, or even dangerous. They're anti-research, and anti-expansion. They've become more radical lately."

Loralee gaped. "I had no idea. Sure, he's a putz, but I never pegged him as loony. Maybe that's why he tried to steal all my seeds." She hadn't ever tried to keep her research secret from the other crew members since they used the ring daily.

"You've been breeding plants for orbit-friendly traits. They have better survivability, higher radiation resistance, and whatever else you've been breeding into them. Remember, Anti Orbiters? They hate everything you stand for in your research."

Roger held his hands up like a sports timeout signal. "Hold on, everybody. From what we know, he's trying to blow up the station, and you're worried about seeds? He's a total nut bar! If he's with the Anti Orbiters, then we have even more reason to bail and let the pros deal with the problem." He opened the case and pulled out one of the remote switches, handling it with a great deal more care now he suspected what it could trigger. "I think he put some of these switches out, but I don't know what they do. My guess is it's something designed to make our room full of volatile gas explode. We need to leave the station, and we need to do it now!"

Pen said, "I think he planned to leave, too, except he drank himself into a coma. Thank heaven for idiot alcoholics. I like Roger's idea. We get in the pods, eject, and wait for pickup. We can put the pods into a holding pattern rather than drop us out of orbit."

Loralee said, "Then we take him with us."

Pen tilted her head to the side in confusion. "Take him with? Why?"

Loralee replied, "Because we're better than that. Besides, I don't want him to blow himself up with the station. More than our lives are at stake. You two can take one of the pods if you like, but we have room for four between the two pods. Four of us leave. He's a total jerk and wants to kill us all, but he's a human being."

Roger gave a matter-of-fact shrug and said, "Fine by me. I'll go open them up. Be ready to go in five minutes." He pushed off and coasted through the door to the main hall.

Pen pulled herself up to the console with the Spider's camera view. An error blinked on the screen.

"What is it?" Loralee coasted near to look over Pens shoulder.

Pen said, "It saw an obstruction and stopped. It never made it past the docking ring." She panned the camera around until she saw something clamped onto the ring. "See that? It looks like one of those accursed switches."

Loralee's eyes went wide with horror as she realized what else Phil had done on his spacewalk, and that more switches could be in place anywhere on the station. "He put out traps." She turned to the door and yelled, "Roger! Don't open the hatches!" She shot out into the hall at racing speed and repeated her warning as she arrowed toward the escape pod hatches.

She arrived as Roger exited the first escape pod. He said, "What's all the yelling for?"

"Booby traps! He set switches up as traps! I've spotted one on the docking ring. He had time to put more of them out. He could have put them anywhere."

Pen yelled from down the hall. "Spotted another. It's on the outside of the airlock door."

Roger looked around and then reached out to grab one of the handholds to keep from drifting. "Okay. Slow and careful-like. I'll inspect the other escape pod door while you watch. You keep hold of my feet, so I don't drift into anything."

Loralee wedged her toes into two of the handholds across the hall to stabilize her position then grabbed Roger's ankles while he went hand over hand to get into position for a close look at the second hatch.

Roger talked himself through each step. "It's not sealed tight. See the gap?" He held on with one hand while he got his mirror-tipped pen from his pocket. "I'll check around the edges. He probably left it ajar on purpose."

A tense half-minute went by as Roger eased his tiny mirror into various nooks and crannies around the door while Loralee held his legs steady as a rock. At each position, he muttered, "Nope." She wanted to warn him of cramps forming in her hands, but he grunted and pulled back away from the door before she could speak.

Loralee let out a sigh of relief. "So it's okay?"

"Nope. I finally got a good view of the far side of the hinge. It's trapped. I might could get it out without pushing the button, but I ain't sure. Now see, this is why I left the Marines and got a safe civilian job."

Loralee wasn't sure she wanted to know what he'd done in the military if living on an experimental space station was considered a safe job. She said, "So if you had opened this escape pod hatch first …"

Roger flicked his fingers out as he said, "Boom."

Pen, who had stopped a safe distance down the hall to keep from distracting them, said, "So we can only evacuate two, we can't use the airlock, and if we wait for the shuttle from Cloud One to arrive, it will hit the switch on the docking ring. And if we bump anything too hard, like with the one working escape pod, we might blow up the station anyway!" She grew louder and angrier as she spoke. She finished, almost at a yell, "That tears it. He's covered all the bases!"

Pen's outburst devolved into a convoluted stream of curses aimed at Phil which ranged from his uneducated choice in music to his toiletry habits.

Roger looked impressed. "Ain't never heard half of those before." He winked at Loralee to lighten the mood. "Guess she's finally mad now."

Loralee thought for a moment. "Roger, we know where he put all the oxygen and propane. How much adjacent wall space do we have? It wouldn't make sense to have an active detonator earlier because he could press a button by accident, like with the escape pod door or the airlock trigger."

She knew Roger had most of the mechanics and layout of the station memorized, so she waited as he looked up in thought and ticked off something on his fingers.

Finally, he said, "We got about thirty linear meters of hallway and forty meters of maintenance crawlway. It's divided between where he put in the new piping and a second hall across the top of the storage area." He seemed to catch on to her idea as he continued, "Do either of you know the mechanical systems well enough to spot something out of place in the pipe runs?"

Both women shook their heads.

Loralee said, "Not if he tried to hide it and make it match the other equipment. I'll come along with you as a gofer. Pen, can you cover the electronics side and watch for anything unusual?"

Pen said, "That sounds good, but I think we're pretty well past unusual by now. I can put the spider out where the shuttle can see it's in the way. They won't dock until we can get those switches cleared." She paused in thought, then continued, "Could I drill from outside to empty the explosive gas? It might take a while, but I think the spider's battery could last long enough."

Roger shook his head. "There's too much chance of sparks or heat. It might set it off instead. Better to park it in the way of docking like you said. Best chance is to find and disarm the detonator since it might could destroy the station even without the explosive gas. We can't tell how much damage it can do, so we have to assume the worst."

Loralee tagged along behind Roger as they traversed the main hallway. Roger pulled himself into and out of the crawlways as they searched. He had crawled into a tube up to his ankles when she heard a yell, followed by Roger breathing hard and fast.

She asked, "Need me to pull you out?"

His breathing slowed to about twice its normal pace, and he replied, "No. Not yet. Got a box strapped in place, and it's plugged into the network. The network cable has its lock tab removed, so it came out when I bumped it."

Loralee asked, "So didn't he hook it up then? Can you move it?"

Roger said, "A timer counted down from three minutes when the network connector fell out. It stopped counting when I plugged it back in. It says two minutes and fifty-six seconds now. I think it's a failsafe. If we unplug this thing for more than three minutes, it goes off no matter what."

Loralee talked her way through the options. "Airlock? No. It's rigged. Keep it plugged in? We could get a cable without the broken tab, but it could have another internal timer. We have to get it off the station, and I see only one good way to do it."

Roger chimed in, his breathing close to normal now. He drawled, "Once you eliminate the impossible, whatever remains, no matter how improbable, must be the truth."

Loralee gave a nervous laugh. Her adrenaline levels were pretty high, but she couldn't imagine what Roger felt as he sat face to face with a detonator. "So, you read Sherlock Holmes, huh?"

He replied, "Yup. I read them all as a teenager. Now, what's your improbable option? I'm a little distracted here, what with the detonator and all."

"We can eject it using the working escape pod. The default program to de-orbit should get it away from us fast enough. It goes off once it's well away from us. That will cut down the local debris if it blows apart."

Roger said, "Okay then. I've got nothing better. I need to cut some tie straps loose. Hand me the wire cutters from the toolbox, then get out the red can of leak-stop adhesive foam. We also need Pen."

She handed the cutters past his leg and asked, "What do you need the foam for?"

"That's not for me. That's for Pen to spray into the opening of the other escape pod hatch. It'll set up and hold it in place so the launch can't bump the door's trigger. Give her the can and the instructions, and then get set to fly this box down the hall."

Loralee handed off the can to Pen who sprayed it around the opening to the booby-trapped escape pod. The foam, a special adhesive designed to set in ten seconds, held the door in place so it could no longer shift if it got bumped. Pen said, "I'm starting to feel a bit punchy here from lack of sleep, so I'm not taking chances. I gave it a good slathering. I pity the person who has to clean up this foam."

Loralee said, "With any luck, that'll be us. I need a practice run so we can time it. Be ready at the hatch with the spray can. I'll stop long enough for you to spray it, and then I'll stick it inside the escape pod. The can should have plenty of glue for a test run with a fake detonator. I don't want a bomb rattling around loose when a three-gee booster goes off."

Pen said, "Got it. You fly to me and stop, I spray the box, and then you stick it inside. You come out, we shut and latch the door, and then we hit the launch button."

Loralee fingered the activation tag used to enable the launch sequence. "Pull the safety tag after my test run. We don't want to launch it empty by accident."

Back where Roger's feet poked out into the hall, she asked, "What are the rough dimensions? I need a practice box."

At first, he lay still, but after a few seconds he shifted in position. "Yeah, I can measure this for you."

"Did you fall asleep?"

"Nah. Just sending off a prayer."

"I never took you for the religious type, Roger."

He answered, "I don't parade it around, but I spend time on my relationship with God pretty regular-like. You never know when you might end up face to face with Him. But you asked for measurements. Let's see. I'd estimate about ten by twenty by fifty centimeters."

"Great. I'll use one of the smaller toolboxes for a test run. Are you holding up okay? I'm not as ready as you are to meet God right now."

Roger said, "My fingers are a bit stiff, but I think your plan will work out okay. I suspect you'll die of old age surrounded by a horde of beautiful, intelligent great-grandchildren."

She couldn't tell if he said it to ease her stress levels, but it worked regardless. She transferred tools from a small toolbox into the larger box and prepared for her test run.

She called down the hall, "Pen, ready to start a timer on my mark? Three, two, one, mark!"

She sat in place to allow for the time it would take to pull Roger out, then grabbed hold of the toolbox and shot down the hall at full speed.

Her time on the college swim team meant she knew how to do a flip turn at the bend in the passage. She pulled and kicked her way down the straightaway to where Pen waited, then flipped and stopped herself against the handholds with her feet.

Pen gave the toolbox a quick spray of foam, and Loralee sprang into the escape pod and mounted the toolbox to one of the seats, holding it in place until the foam hardened and locked it in place.

She pulled herself back out, then called, "Time!"

Pen looked at her chronometer. "Just under fifty seconds. We will have over two minutes for the escape pod to boost away. That will be plenty of time. Worst case, even if it doesn't contain the explosion and the whole pod turns into shrapnel, the parts will all travel away from us by then and should burn up in the atmosphere. I hope." She pulled out a data tablet. "Let me aim the spider's camera along the pod trajectory to record it." She tapped for a few moments then continued, "We're as ready as we'll ever be. If we're alive ten minutes from now, I'll buy you a drink."

Loralee checked the toolbox. The foam had sealed it down tight, so she drifted back to Roger and tapped him on the foot. "Are we ready to do this? Do you need to work on your relationship some more?"

Roger answered from inside the access way, "Nah, we're good. Give me a countdown, and then pull me out. I've got the detonator with both hands."

"On my mark again. Three, two, one, mark." She pulled on his feet with her own feet braced against the wall next to the narrow access tube.

Roger's head glanced off the corner on his way out, causing him to grunt in pain.

He steadied himself and handed off the package. "You have control. Fly, girl."

The practice should have made the real trip feel more ordinary and less terrifying. Neither was true. Loralee's adrenaline rushed through her bloodstream as she shot down the hall with the box. Its timer counted down in a cool, monotonous parody of her emotions as she flip-turned at the corner.

Pen pulled the pod's safety lock free as Loralee approached.

Loralee got a better grip on the container as she flew to meet Pen, and noticed the back of it had a recessed area. As she stopped, she gasped out, "Use more foam. It's not flat."

Pen, ready with the can, slathered on a double portion and called out, "Go!"

Loralee pushed through the escape pod door and flattened the container against the second seat, then held it in place with her forearms. With the odd shape and their good safety margin, she decided to press it into place a little longer to guarantee it sealed down tight to the seat.

She felt the warmth as the foam cured, then heaved a sigh of relief. As she let go, she realized why she had felt the heat from the foam. It had sealed her right forearm to the side of the box where excess foam had squeezed out.

"Got a problem, Pen. I'm stuck. The foam sealed me to the box!"

Pen yelled, "Stuck? Pull it loose!"

"Working on it. I can't reach any farther than the inside control pad. Hurry to the hallway first-aid kit down by Roger and get the yellow spray can from it. Now!"

Loralee tried various forms of leverage to peel her arm loose, and then gave up on halfway measures. She planted her feet on both sides of the box and pushed with all she had.

She screamed as a narrow strip of skin pulled away, now a permanent part of the escape pod.

Loralee pulled herself out with her good arm, leaving a crimson smear wherever her bad arm touched.

She pulled the hatch closed and jabbed the launch button and held it in as its calm prerecorded message called out, "Ejecting in four, three, two, one, Eject. Eject. Eject."

The walls rumbled as the pod detached and its boosters fired, shooting it away from the station at three gravities.

Loralee heard the vilest curses she'd ever heard from around the corner, interspersed with her name. She looked up in time to see Pen execute a spin-turn to rival her own and rocket up the hall toward her. Pen froze mid-flight, mouth agape and holding a yellow can from the first aid kit.

Loralee tried to catch Pen with her good arm as Roger also came around the corner.

Pen yelled, "You got me out of the way! I thought you had ejected yourself with the pod! You don't even need this, do you?" She waved the can at Loralee.

Loralee held out her bleeding arm. "Yes, I do. It's an anesthetic. Spray, please. Now. This hurts. Bandages would be nice, too. Butterfly bandages to hold it together." She bit her lip and hissed her breath in and out as she felt the full force of the damage to her torn, bleeding skin. She was starting to go into shock and fought it off as she talked.

Roger spun and retraced his path to fetch the rest of the first-aid kit as Pen applied equal parts profanity and anesthetic.

Once Roger bandaged Loralee's arm, they headed back to the command center.

Roger said, "I didn't hear any impacts of debris on the hull. That's a good sign." He got some painkillers out of the kit and handed them to Loralee.

Pen pulled up to the spider's console and rolled back the recording to replay it from the time of the launch. At about the time they expected the detonation, they saw a bright light flare through a pod window for several seconds. The pod remained intact. The escape pod thruster continued to fire as it faded into the distance. "So, it was a dud? No bomb? Did we do all that work and eject an escape pod for nothing?"

Loralee added a question of her own. "Could we have missed the real detonator?"

"Nah, we got 'er." Roger scratched his chin. "You don't need to go boom to put a hole through a hull. We should still check the station to make sure there weren't no secondaries."

They scrambled to do an exhaustive search but found no more detonators or gas pockets.

The next order of business was to get rid of all the switch triggers. The tension peaked when the switch on the remaining escape pod clicked as they removed it, but nothing happened. Their fear reduced to mere urgency as they spent the next few hours removing triggers and cleaning adhesive foam from the hatch of the remaining escape pod in preparation for the arrival of an emergency response shuttle.

Roger fetched a new section of cable for the dish repairs and suited up to pull the triggers from the docking ring and the airlock hatch, but a full mission to patch the wiring was out of the question. Roger and Pen had been awake straight through most their sleep shift, so they were all ready to drop. Loralee volunteered to take a watch and sent them off to catch a little rest. She should have gotten some rest herself, but the combination of anesthetic and other painkillers had acted as a stimulant.

Part way through her solitary shift she heard a docking sequence. Someone had arrived ahead of schedule.

Pen and Roger both floated to a stop at the airlock rubbing their bleary eyes. Loralee pulled up with her left arm out in front of her to protect her right which was strapped down in a snug sling.

A solar sail tug sat linked to the docking ring. Tugs gathered dangerous bits of debris and dead satellites, shuttled equipment between stations, and refueled live satellites to extend their life expectancy. The pilot stepped out of the airlock in a full pressure suit. Since the crew didn't have suits on, he pulled his helmet off. Loralee recognized Zachary Brown, a pilot they knew from previous refueling and salvage runs. "Cloud One diverted me when you went dark. Would anyone care to tell me what's going on here? Where's the station manager?"

From down the hall toward the crew quarters came the irregular sound of metal banging on metal, accompanied by muffled screams of rage.

Zachary stayed on with them after the emergency response shuttle arrived. It took three people to pin and sedate Phil so they could transport him back to Cloud One, then to Earth at the next drop. Loralee gave the shuttle crew a supply of fresh vegetables and fruits as they left. The secret of her personal experiments was out now, so she might as well make the most of it with goodwill offerings accompanied by her full disclosure reports. It was up to the Consortium managers to decide how to proceed, but Loralee felt she'd made a good case with her research and results.

After the shuttle left, the crew gathered with Zachary in the tiny mess hall. Loralee asked, "So now what? We've been so busy with reports and repairs that we haven't had time to see if we're all fired."

Zachary said, "I got some news on that. Ground crews recovered the escape pod. They say it had a rather large thermite charge inside, which is why it didn't explode. The multiple layers of reentry heat shielding kept the thermite from melting through the hull, but they couldn't identify any parts from the seat you used as a mounting point. The base of the seat was all that was left, with aluminum slag splattered everywhere. Good thing the pods are tough."

Zachary sucked on a water bottle as if he had nothing more to report.

Pen prodded him with a toe. "And? Continued employment? Charges of destruction and endangerment? Hero parades? Somewhere in between? Where do we stand?"

Zachary answered, "This had the potential to be the worst disaster in orbital history. You prevented that. I sent a preliminary report describing how you stopped it, and an audit of your assigned experiment results. I also added a summary of the results you've seen on your undocumented experiments. Between my advance warning and Loralee's more formal report, it seems the Cloud Consortium has changed its policy on project approval since you're several years ahead of some board member's high-level unpublished goals. Your continued employment is guaranteed if you continue to make complete reports on everything and can produce a viable plan for self-sustaining ecosystems like you have promised. It's not all roses by any means. They might not be so impressed with the moonshine and a few misappropriations, but I'll see what I can do to gloss over those. I think we can make this work."

Roger chimed in. "Well, that'll do. I guess this means you took the job as the new boss-man here on Cloud Nine then, did you?"

Zachary nodded. "I've got your back, but don't mess this up. Everyone will watch you now. You'll live in a fishbowl." He grinned as he reached into a bag Loralee held open for him. "Besides, those nutrition patties only go so far. Where else can I get fresh produce in orbit without waiting years?" He tossed a radish into his mouth and crunched down on it for emphasis.

Loralee smiled. Plans didn't always work out the way you expected, but she still had her lab. Her botany experiments could move forward as she had hoped, reducing their reliance on deliveries from the ground. She wondered what the Cloud Consortium board would think of building solar smelters next. Maybe Roger could use a new metallurgy project.

# Fido

## James Wymore

I still have some control of my mind. If anybody else knew me, they might think I didn't. But I do. It's just been broken down into pieces, analyzed, and put back together so many times now. The connections might be a little bit off. I know a few ticks. It's part of the game. I have to hide things from myself if I want to hide it from them. Why would I want to hide it from them? Because it's my mind, and it's the only thing I have left of my own. Let me try to put enough parts together to explain.

STANDING IN THE DESERT WHEN THEY CAME DOWN, I COULD FEEL THE HOT wind on my face. I couldn't see anything. Nothing registered on radar or seismograph, but for a few seconds, even in the middle of a desert, my cell phone had four bars.

Once they were below the mountains, their ship became visible. Unlike the expected saucer shape, it had building sized cubes sticking up at odd angles. Despite being larger than several city blocks, it was undetectable except for the hot wind. It landed without making a sound.

A door opened on the side of the closest angular protrusion. It looked for all the world like a car salesman coming out of an office to see if I liked anything on the lot. There was no bright light or strange music. If I hadn't watched it appear before my eyes, I would have thought some guy was coming out to ask me if I'd seen his lost cat.

He sported a big smile and a tie the same color as his shirt. It was after dark. But I left my flash light off because it seemed like the polite thing to do. He waved and said, "Do you want to come with us and see the stars?"

"Why me?" I asked.

"Because you know about us." That wasn't true. I had seen a blip, which I suspected was something important. I secretly hoped, against all the odds grilled into me by seven years of college, we'd someday make contact with extra terrestrials. I guess it was enough for them. "And because we think you want it. It's your choice. We will take somebody. It can be somebody else if you don't want to go."

"Will you ever bring me back?"

"We won't return in your lifetime." His mouth moved, but only as an afterthought. It seemed a little bit out of sync with his words.

I took a quick mental inventory of what I'd be leaving behind. A few college buddies, some Facebook friends, a boring job in Astronomy, and a girlfriend that wasn't sure if she loved me. None if it compared to what I expected I would learn and see on that ship. Still I was hesitant to just up and jump aboard.

"How do I know I can trust you? Where will I stay? What will I do?"

"We have an exact duplicate of your apartment and all the food or supplies you will need. You will not be required to do anything you don't want to."

"Can I go back and tell my friends? Can I get some things to take with me?"

"I'm sorry. We can't stay long." When he said long, his mouth didn't close for three seconds after the sound was already over.

"I want to go with you," I said. I knew if I didn't go, I would regret it for the rest of my life.

He smiled and began walking back to the door that looked like it opened into the most normal strip mall in the world. I followed him.

WHAT AN IDIOT! IT WAS ALL A LIE. THEY DIDN'T LOOK LIKE SALESMEN, this ship didn't look like a bunch of buildings, and it wasn't a store front I walked through. You see what they want you to see and hear what they want you to hear.

One thing I learned for sure. Friends from college, some Internet pen pals, a boring job, and a timid girlfriend were definitely worth staying for.

Still it wasn't all bad. They more or less gave me the run of the place. Three squares and a half-decent house with no job; it was all most people ever asked for. I didn't ask for it. At least, I don't think I did. My memory is a little sketchy in places. At least I remember how I got here.

My apartment, an exact copy of the one I lived in on Earth, isn't bad. The big TV, a computer, clothes, and food are just like what I left. Framed art decorates the living room and movie posters line the bedroom. The only real difference is here the fridge never gets empty. I'm not sure when they fill it. Probably when I'm asleep. Sometimes my worn clothes show up new, too.

I think they downloaded the whole internet the day I got on this ship. I have thousands of movies and books, all from that year or before. It's enough to keep me busy for a lifetime. But there is something stale about knowing there will never be any new books or movies. I can look up endless websites, but nobody updates them. Naturally, I refuse to start reading any series not published through completion already.

The TV works. I have two hundred channels and no season premieres.

The weirdest thing is that if I send an e-mail, somebody answers it. I know it isn't the right person. Somebody on this ship takes a wild guess at what I want to hear and writes back. Creepy, right?

I'm not completely alone. I have a girlfriend here. Well, sort of. She lives in the apartment across the hall.

She goes somewhere she calls work every day. I meet her at the mailbox in the hall. I get junk mail and bills, but I never pay them. Nobody has yet come to evict me or turn off the utilities. She talks about her job, and how hard it is to deal with an unreasonable boss. She usually invites me over to her place for dinner. I don't have any other plans, so I usually go. Sometimes I invite her over. It's nice, really.

The thing is, her words don't match the movement of her mouth. That's the tell. The aliens obviously communicate telepathically. So the business of aligning mouths with words is a bit off for them. If not for that, I would have thought I hit the jackpot being the only human male on a ship with a gorgeous woman. Like I said, I can't trust my eyes or my ears.

For a while, I tried not even using my brain. I figured out they can read my thoughts to some extent. I'm not sure how much. So I tried not to have any thoughts for a while. I looked up Buddhist meditation and attempted to keep my mind clear. Eventually, I completely gave up. What was the point? I'm like a goldfish in a glass bowl. So I let them have free run of my brain for a while. I regret it now. I should have kept something back, even then. Live and learn.

I assumed they brought me here to observe human behavior. That's probably why they set up the hot blond next door. As far as I can tell, the other doors in the apartment's hall are empty. Maybe if I played nice with whatever it was they were projecting in my mind to be the hot neighbor, they would have installed some friends and an eccentric landlady. But I don't want that. It's hard enough holding onto the few threads of sanity I have left, without going all the way into their imaginary world.

Still, she's a better cook than I am. And we have some deep conversations.

ASTRONOMY USED TO BE MY LIFE. LITTLE DOTS IN THE SKY. I WOULD squeeze them for every tiny bit of information possible until I'd wrung all I could from the light they sent across the great abyss of space.

I found a planet orbiting a nearby star. I documented it, named it, and walked away with a Ph.D. I was a hot scientist for twenty-seven. The world was my oyster. Then the government hired me to join a team working with the Hubble Space Telescope. It was a dream until a few years later when I started to realize how boring it was to catalogue space dust in various configurations. Sure, I was mapping the universe for blue and red shifts, looking for the location of the big bang. Still, it just became tedious.

I was about ready to look for a new job when I found the blip. Less than that, it was just a blurring on the edge of a star. I showed it to dozens of people. Most of them discounted it as an aberration. But I couldn't let it go. So I made a dozen wild hypotheses and began looking for the same thing. Weeks later, I saw it in front of another star. It looked like heat was warping the light at the star's edge.

I wrote it up in a paper. Nobody believed it. I didn't bother to tell them when I saw it streak across the full moon. I did the math, projected the trajectory, and went to the desert by myself. By then I was sick of trying to make them believe me.

I don't know what I expected to find there. A weird meteorite, maybe?

THINKING THEY WERE STUDYING ME WAS NAÏVE. THEY WEREN'T. THEY are so far above us that there's nothing for them to learn from studying us. A dog has more intelligence compared to us than we have to them. And that is all I was to them. I was an exotic pet they mused over in moments of boredom. That's why, when I met my neighbor for the first time and she asked my name, I didn't tell her my real name. I told her to call me Fido. And she did.

IN SOME CIRCLES, I WAS KIND OF A BIG DEAL. INCIDENTALLY, THE PLANET I found early in my career orbits the star known as "the dog's ear" in Canis Major. So I named it Fido. Pretty funny, right?

Anyway, the joke was on me. I didn't appreciate what I had when I had it. And I could never go back. There were windows on this ship. So I knew the starscape was slowly changing. Only a little, of course. Most of it still looks the same.

Not here in my apartment, though. My windows are 3-D movie projectors. You can make shadow puppets on the street with your hand. Even so, it really looks the same as the city outside my apartment used to. The video loop restarts every week or so. When it was real, I never bothered looking out my window at those people. After a year on this ship, I memorized every single face and action.

I DECIDED TO GO FOR A WALK ONE DAY. I'D SEEN EVERYTHING IN THE HALL outside my apartment. But I needed to get out and move around before I screamed. Most of the time I'm okay, but sometimes it gets to me. You know?

I left the door open. It wasn't like anybody was going to walk in and steal something. Predictably, the blond was just leaving for 'work.' I have clocks. So I know she doesn't keep anything like regular hours. She usually leaves for or returns from work whenever I happen to be in the hall. What are the odds?

"Hello, Fido. How was your morning?" Her voice expressed genuine interest. She made eye contact with dazzling blues that seemed lit from behind.

"Same as every day, Monster." She had a made up name back when. But I just called her Monster to keep it real. She played along and now it's stuck. "I'm alone on an alien spaceship and I have never even seen one of the aliens."

"I'm here. You can see me now."

"Yep." Usually I'm cool with it. I made the choice to come here. And as far as I know, I'm the only human ever to live on an alien space ship. That's pretty awesome, right? But once in a while I get down on it. I really shouldn't have taken it out on her, though.

"Why are you so sad?" she asked. Her lips twisted into a short sneer during the 'you.' It was like a nervous twitch except it didn't alter the sound that came out at all.

"Because you're not human."

"I'm almost human."

"And that's not what you really look like."

"Why does it matter what I look like?" This time when she said 'matter' it actually looked like 'vacuum.'

"Because it's a lie. If you won't show me what you really look like, I can't trust you."

"I can look like whatever you want." This wasn't a new conversation. And it didn't sound sexy like a movie with a shape shifter dazzling all the male imaginations.

I said, "I want you to look like what you are when I'm not looking at you."

"That's impossible."

"Why?"

"Because perception is in the mind. It's a negotiation. You don't have sensors capable of perceiving my natural form." Her mouth completely stopped moving after 'mind'. She always said something like that.

"Then tell me about your people."

"You cannot understand them."

"Then use small words and similes."

"I am that already." She put her hands out, dramatically.

"So frustrating!" I punched the mailbox mounted in the wall. The door to my box popped open and a dozen letters spilled out onto the dingy carpet. I ignored them. Somebody would probably clean them up. "I came here to learn about you."

"Would you like to talk about it over dinner?"

"Sure." I'd had dinner with her hundreds of times. It was always great, but I never learned much about her or her kind. I was just feeling a moment of self-pity. Otherwise, I never would have said, "Sometimes I wish I could go home."

"I'm sorry." She wasn't.

She waited until I started back toward my open apartment before she went out the front door. Suddenly a new idea hit me. I turned and followed her.

Outside the apartment was strange. Everything was flat black with recessed lighting. Sharp corners jutted out from the walls making the path crooked. I can only assume alien artistic architecture was the reason. I used to think the angular protrusions and twisting halls were the actual shapes of the ship's interior, but now I don't believe that. I can't trust my eyes.

I stayed far back and followed as Monster zigzagged through the main corridor. Her high heels didn't click against the hard floor. My shoes were making no end of noise. I slipped them off and followed in much quieter stockings. The floor was icy cold.

I'd memorized all these halls some time before. There were a few branches leading off the main hall. Most terminated at dead ends. A few ended in closets with cleaning supplies or utility access panels. I had no idea what the panels controlled. The indicator lights didn't blink. I fiddled with some of the controls once. Nothing happened.

Knowing all the juts and switchbacks of this hall made it easy to follow from a distance. So far, Monster hadn't turned back to look at me once. Most likely, she and every other alien on this ship knew exactly what I was doing. But I held out hope that even telepathic beings would have to intentionally concentrate to access my mind. There was no way I could shield my intentions now. My hope was that they didn't bother to 'look in' on me very often. It wasn't something I planned. It just came out of following a sudden impulse.

Toward the far end of the long corridor, Monster turned down one of the small branches, which I knew previously to be a dead end. I dashed for the edge and looked down in time to see her move through a wall without making a sound. It disturbed me, just like when her mouth went out of sync when she talked. I rushed to the same wall and plunged my hand straight through.

The rock was not an illusion. I could feel a barrier there. I had thoroughly explored this hall, like all the others. I had pushed and kicked this exact wall, looking for seams or moving parts. Yet now my arms pushed through it like soft sand. See what I meant about not trusting my eyes? I only hesitated a moment before rushing bodily in.

The walls shifted. Instead of black and angular, they were white and round. The light came through semi-transparent panels blended seamlessly into the walls. Equipment jutted out from the ceiling, mounted on white metal bars. There were no tables or computers, but as a scientist, I recognized this equipment as something used in experiments. It resembled the equivalent machinery on Earth. I thought I could identify an oven, spinners, shakers, containers, and maybe refrigerators storing samples I couldn't see.

Distracted by the plethora of new information, so rare since my arrival, I forgot to hide from Monster. Looking around now, I didn't see her. Where had she gone?

There were a few places unbroken by equipment or lights. They matched the one behind me. So I figured they had to be more of those doors.

I walked over to one and pushed through. It felt just like plunging my hands into a warm beach or gritty clay.

For a moment, I am positive I remember seeing two floating sparks of light rapidly twisting around in a tall column as if a small streak of lightning trapped in a high, invisible cylinder. We were in some kind of castle dungeon with medieval torture instruments everywhere. I remember a rack, stocks, an iron maiden, and several others I couldn't identify. I know it's crazy, but that's what I saw. One second later, the lights flared and Monster was standing there next to a UPS deliveryman. The room was still gray, but the heavy rock walls shifted to look like metal and all the devices suddenly became computers.

"Fido?" Monster couldn't suppress her shock at seeing me there. I was thrilled to have surprised them. I'm positive the other guy entered my mind and did something. Maybe he changed what I really saw into those torture devices and then computers.

I long suspected them of messing with my mind. Why hadn't they erased my memories completely? No idea. Either they had limits on how much they could mess with my thoughts or they possessed some ethic, which prevented them from changing too much. Or maybe they just didn't care. It's not like I had anybody to tell, anyway.

I refused to let go of the instantaneous image I had seen before it shifted. I closed my eyes and memorized it. Even then, I knew it was morphing somehow. I don't know if they did it or my own brain somehow re-created what I saw with images it could understand. It's the only explanation for why there would be gothic torture devices on a spaceship.

"What are you doing here?" Monster pressed. The other guy's projected image had dark skin and brown clothes. Monster was wearing a white lab coat I am sure she hadn't had on when we talked minutes before. "You're not supposed to be here."

"Why not?"

She reached to the side of one computer and suddenly a lever appeared there. She pulled it. I knew computers didn't have levers—I swore it wasn't there before or after she pulled it. She pushed some random buttons on the keyboard. "My boss will be angry if he finds you here. Go home. We can talk about this over dinner."

"Why am I here? Why did you bring me on this ship? Who is that guy?" I crossed my arms and leaned to one side. I wasn't moving from that spot without some answers. To them it must have been like a cat hissing to defend its interest in some morsel of meat fallen from its owner's plate.

Monster glanced at the being behind her. "He's somebody I work with. Please come out of this room. We can talk in the foyer." Her mouth was moving twice as fast at the end as she went through the portal.

I followed her. I could learn nothing more from that room now.

We went through the same door, but didn't come out in the same place. The white room was square now with light fixtures on the wall and shelves of books hung in strange places where equipment used to be.

"I already saw all of this," I said. "There's no point in hiding it from me now."

Monster bit her lower lip. I guessed she was trying to express concern, but it just looked manic. "You shouldn't be able to go through those doors," she said in an urgent voice. "If my boss knows you've done it, you will be in danger."

"Why? I can't tell anybody what I see here. How could it possibly be a problem for me to see what you do?"

"I don't have time to make you understand right now. Please go home. I promise I'll tell you all I can later."

"Okay," I said. I knew I wasn't going home. I finally had access to more than the corridor outside my apartment. I wanted to see everything before they changed the barriers. I had given up my whole life to see aliens and technology. I wasn't about to surrender now because of some vague threat.

"Don't," she said. How stupid! I had forgotten she could read my thoughts. Now she knew what I was planning. "I chose to take care of you because others of us will not be kind to you. They will not let you live if you don't follow their rules."

I let that sink in. I absorbed it and understood the threat. "Okay," I said flatly. I didn't want to die. I turned and walked out before I could think anything else.

I moved slowly toward my apartment, trying to make sense of everything. They had designed these doors to keep me confined to the black hall. Why not just keep me locked in my apartment? And what had changed to let me through the doors now? Was it some kind of security setting? When they fixed it, the locks would confine me to the hall and my apartment again.

I knew Monster would have her mental eyes trained on me now. I also knew they would be fixing those barriers soon. It was unlikely they would ever make that mistake again. Normally I'm sane, but just then I didn't care if they killed me or not.

I turned down a random branch and moved to the end. I found a wide, un-broken expanse of wall and pushed through. On the other side, the room was blue. It resembled a sphere with some kind of spiral path working around like a screw to the top and bottom. My socks soaked in water from the twisting platform. It was so humid. Water actively condensed on and ran down the sidewalls. It collected at a drain in the floor. What purpose could this room serve? It made no sense.

Seeing no other obvious doors, I pushed back out into the black hall. I moved further down the path to another open expanse of wall, leaving wet footprints, and pushed through again. This time the room was green. It was unbelievably huge, maybe half a mile square and fifty feet tall. Despite the green walls, the ceiling was white with warm light. Wide, serrated leaves attached to thick vines covered the whole floor. I was standing on black soil. The smell was bitter and overwhelming. There were dozens of doors all around the outside of the room, but I doubted I could work my way through the gnarled jungle that knotted together and poked up all across this vast space. A huge hole in the center of the ceiling pumped air in that moved out through hundreds of ducts on the sides. So they needed oxygen, and they used plants to produce it. The satisfaction at having finally learned something about them set my head spinning. My eyes began to tear up and my breathing went heavy. This room was beautiful. It filled me with emotions. In here, I felt no homesickness.

I didn't stay nearly as long as I wanted. I was manic. Every moment I knew my precious time was running out. I pushed back out into the hall and ran to the next branch. Now I was leaving bits of wet dirt to trace my path.

Each room was another revelation. I saw something that looked like a processing plant. I saw huge towers in a hot warehouse that I could only guess were fuel. My mind saw nuclear cooling towers, but I couldn't even pretend to know if that was what they were.

Most of the rooms had doors leading in other directions, but I only ever went back into the black corridor. In one room, I saw some rapidly orbiting lightning at the far end and turned right back around. I was sure those images were what the aliens looked like to me. However, if they needed oxygen, they had to be more, right? Maybe they used the oxygen for the fuel? No time to process. I rushed to another branch. If this was the main corridor, why hadn't I ever seen any of those aliens in it except Monster?

The next room I explored was adjacent to the corridor closest to my apartment. Fleshy pink color and very dim lights greeted me. Huge cylindrical containers revealed a storage house of some kind. They were clear with bluish fluid pumped in at the top and out the bottom. A grayish cloud floated in the center of each one. When I moved closer and looked inside one, my euphoria ended.

The grayish clouds were people wrapped in what looked like gray yarn. Some curled up in fetal positions. Others stood like proud soldiers. Even though I had little background in biology, I knew they were preserving these people. The humans inside were definitely alive. A quick survey showed me they represented a full spectrum of genetic phenotypes. Each was a different race with the full range of hair colors. If their eyes were open, I was sure at least one would have every color. Tall and short, wide and thin, it was a collector's set of representative samples of human DNA.

I studied them all. One woman in the middle of the group caught my eye especially. She was near my age with medium skin, dark hair, and a cute expression. They didn't seem to be in pain. The whole thing made me sick to my stomach. How could I have been stupid enough to think they just wanted to take me along as a novelty?

I didn't know what to do. I wandered, in shock, back through the black hall to my apartment. I closed the door and curled up on my recliner. We were all just lab rats they wanted for some unfathomable science project. Unlike the others, I was the behavioral science specimen.

I wanted to lash out. I wanted to scream. Instead, I started to cry. What was I supposed to do now?

I wanted to go back and free everybody they had in stasis. What good would that do? It's not like we could go home. The aliens would probably just gather them all back up and put them back. Except one. One they would keep out to replace me. I would get to see just how medieval those machines in Monster's lab could get.

Even if we somehow managed to escape and hide, what could we do? We'd still be on this ship, far away from Earth, with no possible chance to get home. There simply was no solution. Those people were better off in stasis. Too bad they didn't have one extra capsule. I'd have volunteered to join them.

I wanted to personify my captors as horrible, wicked creatures. Nevertheless, deep down I knew they did not act out of malevolence. They were just like me. Driven by an insatiable curiosity, they forged across the dark abyss. If we possessed the technology of this ship, humans would do the exact same thing. They found cute little animals of comparably small intelligence, and deigned to study them. As much as I wanted to hate them, it would be hypocrisy.

That's probably why they chose me. They knew, despite the emotional trauma, I would understand the driving principle behind their behavior. They had tried to make me happy the best they knew how. Monster even looked a lot like the girlfriend I left behind.

As we sat over Italian food that was actually worth the exorbitant price I paid for it, Giselle had a big smile on her face. I asked, "What are we celebrating?"

"I just got a big promotion at work. They made me manager over the entire service center!" Her voice was low, perhaps too well enunciated. I never figured out if she had been good at working in a credit card call center because of her diction or if it had become a part of her as an adaptation to that job.

"That's great," I said, lifting my glass. "Now you won't have to spend all day on the phones, right?"

"Not as much," she said. "I'll spend more time training people to take calls instead. I'll still have to deal with the worst customers, of course." She meant the ones that wouldn't work with the regular callers to fix their overdue accounts.

"I'm really happy for you. Does it come with a big raise?"

"Of course." Her eyes were half closed and she was looking down at me over her nose. She only did that when she was sizing me up for her plans. "How was work for you today?"

"The same as always," I said. "No new world changing information yet."

"So you haven't decided if you want to stay with it or not?"

"I don't know. It's okay, but it's not great. It's just not what I expected."

"What would your ideal be? What is everything you could hope for in a job?"

"I don't know. Something strange and impossible to believe."

"Stranger than astrophysics?"

I laughed. "Good point." She looked off into the distance while I continued to struggle with my inability to appreciate what I had worked so hard to become. I knew she didn't love her job. She still made more than I did. To her, work was just something you did to pay the bills. In that moment, her face changed. She was dissatisfied, too. Just not with her job.

I LET THE TEARS FALL FREELY NOW. HOW COULD I HAVE MISSED IT ALL this time? Giselle had loved me. I was the one that hadn't appreciated her. I couldn't even be happy at her celebration dinner. I defined myself by my job, and it left her playing second fiddle. She would have been okay with it if I had really loved the job. But being lower in priority than a job I didn't appreciate was too much. That was on me.

It had taken me years in solitary confinement aboard a spaceship and a shocking foray into how small our minds really are for me to understand. One thing for sure, the aliens had chosen very poorly. I was a terrible specimen of human behavior. I lacked the best human quality: love. For all my star charting, I had failed to see the only good thing in the universe was right next to me.

No wonder they weren't surprised at my not warming up to Monster. If they could see into my mind, they knew I was a cold, selfish jerk. Obviously, that was why they chose me. They thought I would be happy alone with just a puppet of a person to fill whatever small need I had for other people. Until now, they were right.

I was deluded enough to give everything up for a chance to see what real aliens were like. Now, years later, it was ruined. I'd had a glimpse of what they really are, but all the excitement was gone. All the drive to learn died. Or maybe the discoveries had just been anticlimactic. In retrospect, none of it was surprising.

I expected them to have some advanced technology for cloaking the ship. Now, I think they just picked a remote location and depended on their telepathic ability. I thought they must have had some advanced power source that let them fly through space at relative speeds. However, it really just looked like some kind of nuclear power. The plants for oxygen and food were exactly what a ship would need for sustained flight through space. The only thing remarkable was their form—some kind of pulsing lightning that twisted around a central column.

I'd finally seen what I came for, but the vision of so many humans just sitting there in stasis ruined it. I think because that's what I was, too. Sure I was moving, eating, and watching old television. Yet I was little better than a body in stasis. It's debatable which of us got the better deal. I was so tired of pretending to live. I was so sick of just spending time to spend it. I needed somebody. I needed another human being.

Sometimes when I have a really great idea, it's like an electric buzz from my mind sets every cell in my brain dancing. This wasn't one of those moments. It was more like, one plus one... duh! I wasn't the only human on this ship.

What should I do? Was it even possible for me to bring them out of stasis safely? Where would they go? The aliens would be furious. What did I care about that? So what if I mess up their demonstrative collection? I was positive they'd have samples of DNA, too.

Then I remembered the medieval torture machines. There was no reason to have those on a space ship. The deliveryman next to Monster had made me see them somehow. I know he changed that memory. Obviously, it was some kind of threat.

They would know my plans. They probably already knew what I'd done and were deciding what to do with me. Still, I had managed to surprise Monster. So their telepathy was limited. Maybe they were too preoccupied to notice. Or maybe they just assumed my small brain was so primitive and uninteresting that it wasn't worth bothering to look inside. Either way, it made the gamble worthwhile.

Would there be some way for me to do this without them knowing? What if I could pull some people out of stasis and the aliens never found out? The thought was like an infection. It filled my mind and ran over into obsession in mere moments.

The configuration of the capsules and the people in them burned in my memory. There were fifteen of them secured in a triangle like bowling pins. One of the three center pins contained a woman. Her face was round and fleshy. In many ways, she was the physical opposite of

Monster and Giselle. She wasn't a candidate for being a super model, but she had a hint of a smile. Obviously, they were all dreaming. Whatever she dreamed, it made her look fun and whimsical over a kind of deep strength.

I can't really explain how I came to decide so much about a complete stranger based on an expression her face made in stasis, but she caught my eye. With her capsule being in the middle, I suspected that I might be able to arrange things so the aliens didn't even know she was gone. As long as she stayed in my apartment, they might never know she was here.

It was a ridiculous long shot. One scan of my brain would tell them everything.

It didn't matter. I was committed. I didn't care if they tortured me. I just needed another human to talk with.

Once I decided to act, I went fast. By rushing, I hoped to avoid detection. I pulled out some old jeans, a shirt, and some towels. I used one brown towel to make a head shape and used the rest to stuff the clothes like a scarecrow. It was a pathetic decoy. If, as I suspected, their perceptions were other than sight, this would be a complete waste of time. Still I brought it on the chance it might keep them from looking closer at the tanks. I also grabbed my toolbox.

Grateful the room was close, I hurried down the hall carrying my life-sized fabric doll and toolbox. I pushed through the sandy barrier and into the pink room. Heart racing, I didn't waste a moment. I climbed up onto the platform that was halfway up the round walls and walked around to the back of the stack of cylinders. My damp stockings failed to protect my feet from the bite of metal corrugated for traction. I could feel tiny snags making Swiss cheese out of my socks. The platform wound past a few more pieces of alien equipment. I was sure one was a centrifuge. Another was a small freezer. I ignored them and moved on.

There was a little space between each cylinder. I slid between the six that were closest to the back wall to the person I had chosen. Her shoulder length hair was floating free in the tank. She was biting one lip now as if deep in thought. They all had on gauzy gray clothes, which seemed to be nothing more than protein strands in the plasma, which adhered to their bodies. It fit tightly with loose threads floating at strange angles in the light blue goo.

I found an access panel in the back. Two round screws made of the same clear acrylic as the case fastened it on. They didn't match any of the screwdrivers I owned. I grabbed some pliers and began mashing and twisting the hard plastic. The top pulled off the first one. I jammed a flat screwdriver under the second screw before twisting with pliers until it came free. The panel popped open under the pressure of the goo behind it and smacked me in the face.

The stuff inside smelled like a disgusting mixture of broccoli and ether. Most of the fluid oozed out of the hole and ran down to the floor where it pooled around the bases of all the stasis chambers. As soon as the air hit her, the woman inside began to cough and convulse. She doubled over and hit her head on the side of the tube.

I reached in and put my hand between her and the clear wall, guiding her out through the opening as she heaved blue goo out of her lungs. The tube responsible for filling the chamber kicked into overdrive and started showering us with more of the clear sludge. Luckily, it provided enough buoyancy that I could easily slide the woman out of the tube despite the opening being waist high.

I made sure she settled onto the floor safely before I jammed my scarecrow into the tube feet first and slammed the door shut. It took some jiggling to get the one working screw back in place. Then I knelt down in the smelly stuff, next to the woman. She wasn't choking now, but her lungs sounded raspy. I assumed she had been breathing the blue stuff. Some of it was still in her lungs and sounded like pneumonia. She had one hand touching her mouth and the other shielding her eyes.

I shouldn't have put her through this trauma. What gave me the right to decide whether she stayed in stasis or not? Too late now, I hoped she would prefer this shock to never ending dreams. Once her eyes could open a little, she grabbed my hand. She wasn't expressing thanks. She needed support. She was terrified and she didn't want me to leave.

I curved my hand so she wouldn't crush it. I wanted to move her out of this place as soon as possible. However, I could tell she was weak and in shock so I waited. The puddle of blue stuff we sat in was sinking slowly. At first, I thought it was spreading out. Then I realized there must be a drain somewhere.

Not wanting to cause any more hurt to possibly sensitive ears, I whispered, "Are you okay?"

She didn't acknowledge me. I spoke louder. "Can you stand up?"

She turned toward me then, her eyes focused off in the distance. Then she turned the other way and closed her eyes again. Slowly she pulled her knees up to her chest. A raspy whisper escaped her throat. She wasn't trying to answer. The sound was just an instinctive act. She flailed the arm that was holding my hand and then let go so she could curl all the way up into a fetal position. Whining softly, almost a purr, she fell into a shivering sleep.

At that moment, I would not let myself believe what I suspected. Instead, I roused her and tried to help her up. She couldn't stand. Her legs were too weak. Whenever she opened her eyes, she winced. All she wanted to do was sleep right there between the stasis chambers. I knew that couldn't happen. I had to get her back to my apartment.

With a great effort, I slid my hands under her arms and dragged her between the cylinders and out the door. At first, the blue liquid acted as a lubricant and left a trail. Once we hit the black corridor, there wasn't enough and her ankles squeaked across the cold floor. I stopped to open the outside door of the hall in front of my apartment. Suddenly my heart stopped. Monster might have been in there checking the mail and waiting to ask me for dinner. I looked in. It was clear.

I dragged the squirming woman across the cheap industrial carpet. Her gray body suit kept snagging on the carpet and tearing like wet tissue. So I had to lift her higher, straining my back, to get her into my living room. I didn't want her on the couch. That seemed wrong. So I took her straight to the bed. It took a lot of work to get her arms and legs under the covers. She couldn't help at all. Each time her foot or other limb would be stuck in the covers, she would try to cry out in pain and instead release a tiny whimper. It was a cute sound. Then she would shut her eyes tight and curl up into a ball.

I changed my clothes and took a shower. When I came back, she was still fast asleep. I stood in the door of the dark room, watching her halted breath. I thought about what condition I had seen before that this woman reminded me of.

She couldn't focus her eyes the few times they opened. She couldn't control her limbs. She couldn't speak. The gravity of the situation slowly settled on me. Whatever I had imagined was shattered with the sure realization of one important fact I had never imagined possible.

This full-grown adult woman was mentally a baby.

I told you I was a moron, right? I realized too late that these people might not have been abductees. The aliens probably had not kidnapped anybody. The people in the chambers were probably cloned, or grown in test tubes. As the result of gene splicing, the aliens most likely selected them for demonstrative variety. The equipment in the room was for combining DNA into zygotes. Those giant tubes served as artificial wombs. The people in them had never lived. They were just fetuses that had been growing up into adulthood. And I, in my usual self-centered manner, had just barged in and birthed an infant in her late twenties.

What would the aliens do when they found out now? Would they just kill her and start growing a new one like some aborted experiment? Would I be destroyed, too? It was pointless to try guessing their ethics and motives. I had made a choice and now I had to live with it.

It was now my responsibility to care for and teach this innocent person. In a way I could never have fathomed, my life had changed forever. At the very least, for as long as it lasted, I wouldn't be alone.

"THAT COULD HAVE GONE MUCH WORSE." MONSTER ZIGGED HER LIGHT manifestation into a smile. "I told you he just needed another human. They are pack animals. They can't exist in isolation."

"And you think he will be happy now?" Her boss arched his spark to emphasize the question.

"I do. His mind needed to feel responsible for the choice. They have some vague need to believe in freedom." Monster morphed to display the equivalent of arched eyebrows.

"That's absurd. What you are saying is paradoxical. You say he feels free, but he is making choices that bind him through the distant future?" The same arch of question flashed.

"I know. Nevertheless, their thoughts often oscillate between two irreconcilable opposites. I have observed it many times in our dinner conversations. We had to wait until he was ready to make a big change. Then it had to be his idea. Now he will be happy with the choice he made. That's how they all live on their home planet. They make choices, which bind them, and then they are happy about being free."

"It's funny to think about, but I'm glad we aren't stuck with such incongruent thoughts and behaviors." Her boss zagged to show the conversation was almost over. "You really have an interesting hobby. Too time consuming for my liking, though."

"It's something to do on the long trip. Anyway, I suspect he won't need me around as much now." Monster smiled again and zipped off to tend to her work.

# Knowing Me

Eric G. Swedin

A screen above me constantly replays a permanent reminder of what is now gone. My wife places the drill on the dirty snow, checks the orientation readout, then flash-freezes the clamps to secure it against the comet's surface. A blizzard of ice sublimates off the comet around her, visible only as a hint of haze tickling the edge of my vision. I can hear her humming to herself. Her suit is painted in bold rainbow colors, the full glory of which is only visible when the cone of light from her head lamp illuminates an arm or leg.

She does not know how many times that she has drilled holes for guidance rockets, but I kept track. It is in my nature to be thorough. In the last seven years, she drilled nine hundred and thirty-seven holes. The laser turns the ice and dust into vapor that sprays around her legs. She is my angel, a goddess of love and perfection.

Strange to think of gods at a time like this, since the universe is truly a godless void that creates aberrations like me and angels like her. That same universe conspires to bring two events together on the screen. The laser stutters, a wobbling of light, and she pulls herself closer to check her tool. The laser pierces a gas pocket.

Released after untold millennia, the explosive expansion of gas shreds her suit with shards of ice. She jerks backwards, arms flapping as if she wants to take flight, her legs twitching. There is no sound. Her body drifts slowly away, the tail of her severed tether undulating gently. I have reviewed the telemetry many times and am grateful that she lived only seconds.

My analysis shows that her new vector will lead to an unstable orbit around the sun, gradually decaying into incineration in about twenty thousand years. The same end would happen to this comet, much sooner, if we did not have other plans.

And so ended the only person, other than my mother, into whose eyes I was willing to look.

I MET MY WIFE ON MY TWENTY-FIRST BIRTHDAY. MY MOTHER ALWAYS insisted on a party, an excruciating parade of blank faces and noisy words. Already my talent at world modeling was unequaled. The government provided all the equipment and CPU cycles that I desired. In return, I occasionally worked on their projects instead of my own. Even then I was deep into my life's work, modeling the two greatest of all the wars in human history.

My mother thrust a woman up to me at the party. She had broad shoulders and wide hips, with stout legs and hair cut short. Her smile was different. I have learned when people smile at me, they are trying to establish something called social rapport. It doesn't work with me.

Then she touched me. I don't like to be touched, but her touch was comfortable and soothing, like my mother's.

She stayed at our house that night and strangely enough, I was not upset. I am a man of routine, a slave to order. Having a book or a chair out of place irritates me. Not to have my meals on time makes me angry.

She stayed and after a while I learned to live for her touch. My mother said that the new woman was now my wife. My mother even tried to move away to an apartment of her own, but I didn't like that. I stayed in bed and cried until my mother came home and the three of us became a family.

THE PROPULSION ENGINEER AND THE LIFE SYSTEMS ENGINEER ARE HUSBAND and wife, the other couple that formed our crew. They live in another pod, built to be redundant, separated from my pod by the wispy mist of the comet's surface. Only communications lines and a life support feed connect us. My pod is a nest of steel, a warren of six rooms and stale air. I don't much use the other rooms anymore, other than the toilet, and occasionally the shower. Every week or so I get a sack of emergency food packets from the storeroom and secure it to the bulkhead within easy reach. My wife used to cook, using the staples in the galley, but I just hydrate the emergency packets and microwave them.

The propulsion engineer sends me a message: It's about time to get over your grief and move on. It's been four weeks. I know it's hard to get on, but we are coming up on our next burn phase and we need those settings. Remember the mission. Everything is about the mission.

I send back a short reply—Message received—because if I don't, they will keep resending the message.

Another screen displays my lists. My mother taught me that if I made lists, I would remember what I needed to do and thus bring order to my life. Order is the sweet taste of sanity. The burn settings are completed and on a ready list, but I want to keep them to myself for the moment. Last night the two engineers tried to force their way into my computer systems. Their feeble efforts amused me.

I began my Second World War model when I was fifteen years old. Surrounded by the comfort of my bedroom, geometric shapes on the wallpaper, all the furniture painted blue, I worked on my computer sixteen hours a day. Some call it obsession, but I call it focus. The only reason I picked that conflict was that my birthday occurred exactly one hundred years to the day after Hitler sent his army into Poland. At first, each system of equations represented a country; then I modeled the leaders and major generals. Each iteration added a new layer, a new level to the fractals of history.

After I posted my model on the Net, people all over the world started running the model. By good fortune I had picked an even-sided war. Germany won sometimes; other times the Soviet Union stood on the eastern shores of the Atlantic, master of Europe; even Japan occasionally found glory in a stable empire covering half the Pacific Ocean and half of Asia. For most users, my model provided amusement, though serious historians began to appreciate what I had wrought.

When I was seventeen, a man in a general's uniform knocked on the door of our small apartment in New Memphis. A pudgy man with eyes that darted around the room, taking in everything but only glancing across us, he informed my mother that he represented the military government and wanted to give me more computing power. That was an exciting day; now I could seriously drill down on my model. The number of agents in the model grew at a geometric rate. My fame grew and soon I was recognized as one of the best systems modeler in the world.

When I was twenty I received an e-mail from a respected historian. Text only. Everyone knew that I preferred to keep it simple, no video, no audio, and no olfacts. Anything beyond plain text defocused me. He asked why I was expending my talents on a long-ago war? Why not concentrate on the most recent wars? His query revealed his self-interest, since his speciality was the Ice Wars.

I thought about the question while cutting my hair. I always cut my own hair, a snip for each individual hair. It took about six hours and gave me time for my thoughts to wander down new paths of creativity.

The Second World War model had grown to bore me, and the Ice Wars provided a new challenge. So I shifted course. Some of my users objected, but their concerns no longer held my attention. Occasionally I did a little something on the older model, tweaking an algorithm or adding an agent, but my mind wanted to only concentrate on the Ice Wars.

The new model began with the winter of 2035, when the winter snowfall did not melt until July. The next year the snow only turned to slush during the summer. And the following year, the snowfall did not melt at all. The snow turned into hills of ice and then into mountains. I was born on the plains of Texas, where my parents helped build New Memphis. What had once been dry prairie had turned into lush farmland.

The wars began as the peoples of the planet struggled to migrate and feed themselves amidst crop failures and famine. The oceans retreated, exposing land that had not seen sunlight since the last ice age. In the universities, the purely academic debate over how quickly ice ages came and went became moot. Now the answer was in. Having vast mantles of ice at both poles was the natural state of the Earth. Global warming had not stopped the return of the ice. The warm interlude that provided a nest for human civilization to flourish was an aberration.

It all went into my model.

THE PSYCHIATRISTS HAVE NAMES FOR ME, NEAT CATEGORIES TO CONFINE my mind. All my life the psychiatrists knocked at my door with their tests and questions and I have never opened the door. Only my mother and my wife got inside.

My wife changed my life. I still worked sixteen hours a day on my modeling, but she filled the rest of my time. Mother was still there, her presence surrounding us, a womb of comfort.

My wife lived in my bedroom with me, keeping quiet so as not to disturb me. Sometimes she and my mother went shopping or out to have fun. I didn't go with them.

She liked to do things in our bed and I wanted to make her happy. It was exciting. She relaxed me on days when I was so jacked up that I could not form even a simple equation.

One day about a year after my wife arrived, the general came to our apartment again, dressed in his uniform and looking official. My wife saluted him. He explained a plan to us, conceived as a way to reverse our present ice age. He said that the physics engine in my Ice Wars model showed that the plan would really work. All we had to do was crash a comet into the Earth. Not just any comet. The comet needed to have the right mass and velocity to survive entry and hit at just the right spot during the right season.

The general summoned a map on his tablet. The target point lay off the old Yucatan peninsula, where the receding waters had exposed a large deposit of iron ore; ironically enough, the ore came from the asteroid that had ended the time of the dinosaurs. Back then, the asteroid had put enough water vapor and dust into the atmosphere to cool the earth and change the environment, killing all the large animals. This time, the iron particles from the collision, cast into the upper atmosphere, would provoke a greenhouse effect, melting the ice mountains, refilling the oceans, and ending the ice age. Humanity could reoccupy the rest of the globe. Truly, multiply and replenish.

Think of it. To reclaim what was lost and defeat a foe that had handed us so many chilly defeats. The idea appealed to my fighting instincts.

Why a comet? Why not use nuclear weapons? The weapons would have to be so strong and numerous, churning up deposits of iron ore into radioactive fallout, that the planet would be poisoned. An asteroid could have been used, but a comet of the right size had already been located, coming toward the sun in a languid orbit.

To guide a comet into Earth required a crew on its surface. The comet was not a single mass of dust and ice, but a chaotic tumbling mass of separate planetesimals constantly shifting as the sun heated them on their long fall in from the Oort Cloud. Guiding the comet was a difficult process, requiring constant corrections as the planetesimals shifted, and the cometary halo interfered with data transmission, so they needed a modeler with the crew to provide navigation.

I did not want to leave our apartment, but my wife asked me to do it. She did not ask for much and so I agreed. Mother came with us. The government built a new apartment for us near Houston, an exact duplicate of our apartment, and moved all the furniture into our new home.

We began to train for spaceflight at the Johnson Space Center. Apparently my wife had trained as an astronaut before she came to me. We didn't ever talk about her past and it really didn't interest me. The training was stressful, so many people, too much emotion. My wife thrived on it, enthusing about her life's destiny. Anything that made her happy at least made me less cranky.

Just one time did I ever venture out on a trip. Other people had field trips, so why not me? My wife and I drove for a day to the south. She didn't care for self-driving cars and she knew how to drive, a skill completely unnecessary for me. The four Secret Service men assigned to protect us, bulky with body armor and bristling with weapons, dutifully tagged along in their own car. We reached a ridge overlooking the Rio Grande near Brownsville. In the past two decades, the river had revived from a muddy trickle depleted by irrigation to a raging torrent fed by the glaciers in Colorado.

No one wanted to live near here, though it was good cropland. Fibulas and tibias, ribs and skulls, and grey fragments of smashed bones littered the ridge. Amidst the bones were pieces of clothing and the debris of makeshift weapons: knives, hoes, clubs, a few hunting rifles, an occasional pistol.

Here was one of many places where the Ice Wars turned nasty. Starving Americans flowed across the river, a desperate horde seeking the fertile crops of Mexico. The Mexican army massacred them. They called it inoculation, as if people were a disease. There was not enough food for everyone. Eventually there were not enough people left to fight and the Ice Wars ended.

Many more graveyards of the Ice Wars littered the world, monuments to the struggle to survive, yet avoided in shame.

I FORGET MY MEDS AND THE GRIEF OVERWHELMS ME. ROARING A TONELESS howl, pounding the keyboards with my fists, punching a screen repeatedly until a lattice of cracks satisfies me, and bouncing around the room, eventually exhausts me. The equipment is built to be strong and my flailing limbs are weak.

Something within myself, perhaps a shade of her memory, helps me find the determination to put my arm in the autodoc and key up an injection. The meds bring an edgy sulkiness that is nothing like the calm that my wife once brought. Those same meds got me through the worst time of my life, when we lifted off and I left my mother behind on Earth. I was in a stupor for weeks. I only left because the fate of Earth depended on me leaving and the general guaranteed that she would be safe.

Another message comes from the engineers: Where are the coordinates of the next burn?

I send back my standard response—Message received—and am surprised when they instantly answer.

A threat: We are going to cut off your oxygen and water supplies if you don't talk to us. What are you doing over there?

Are they lying? Intellectually, I know that a person can lie, but when I watch them, I can never tell. I check the emergency supplies for my pod. Three months of oxygen and water and an intact filtration system that will last for more years than I planned to live; that is, if I didn't mind the faint whiff of urea in my drinking water.

NOW THAT MY WIFE IS DEAD, MY ICE WARS MODEL CONSUMES ALMOST ALL of my time and most of my computing power. The processors and memory units in my living pod are as powerful as anything I ever used back on Earth.

Over and over again I run my Ice Wars model, sometimes with the comet crashing into the iron ore deposit, sometimes without the comet crashing. There is no doubt that the comet will reverse the mountains of ice. The oceans grow again, drowning the new cities, forcing the population to flee. A new Ice Wars erupts as people fight for food amid a rapidly changing climate. A field that grows a good crop one year might not grow any crop the next year. Where only desert plants now live becomes flush and fertile the next year. Starvation haunts the land once again, and exotic diseases prune weakened populations. Hard times for all.

Without a comet, the ice age keeps its lock on the planet. In fact, only an external event like a comet or asteroid can pull the planet out of the ice age. Of course, if I expand the timeline of the model to forty million years and include continental drift as an agent, the ice ages eventually end when Antarctica drifts north and allows the world's oceans to permanently warm. A tropical paradise last seen by the dinosaurs arrives.

My model clearly shows me that the comet I ride will provoke a rerun of the Ice Wars. A sobering conclusion.

I have never considered the nature of my mission. That my wife wanted to do it was enough for me. To not fulfill the mission would make the death of my wife meaningless, but her death is only one of many possible deaths.

MY MODELS NO LONGER INTEREST ME. WE ARE ONLY FOURTEEN DAYS from Earth. The time passes with memories playing on all my screens. Many are of my mother, who I have not seen for some eleven years. Others are of my wife back on Earth. Still more show us as a family of three and I still wear a sweater that my mother knitted for me, though the threads are now bare. On one screen, my wife dies over and over again.

A vibration shakes the memories. We are starting our last course correction. One screen switches from my mother smiling at my ninth birthday to a view of the comet's surface. The rockets burn brightly like candles on a misshapen cake. The planetesimals of the comet shift, sending seismic waves shivering through the pod. A few waves are strong enough to even rattle the equipment.

For the first time in my life I have deceived someone. The calculations that I have fed into the rockets will take the comet past Earth. No one will notice for several hours.

The burn completes. The engineers, in their elation and ignorance, congratulate me through a video feed. They are sucking on champagne squeegees, hoarded for this occasion.

I finally send the engineers a message. We have completed the last course correction for the comet and we now coming up to an optimal launch point for Earth. If you launch the escape vehicle within two hours and fourteen minutes, you can make it home. I have already downloaded the proper burn sequences into the escape vehicle.

A quick response from the life systems engineer: What about you? Don't you want to go home?

An easy question to answer.

I have no home anymore.

I will not be the one to renew the Ice Wars; and soon, as the comet is sucked ever deeper toward the sun, I will join my wife.

# Making Legends

## Jaleta Clegg

Neptune hung in space like a giant, blue jewel. Jack Williams, captain of the *USS Kepler*, rested his chin on his steepled fingers as he mentally composed an ode to the planet. His crew, all well-trained and probably much more qualified than he would ever be, functioned perfectly without him. First Officer Emily Kaile kept them in line with utmost military precision and decorum. She was a decorated career officer, born to the service and probably bred to the service. Her parents were both admirals, and her grandparents and so on back for generations, or so it was rumored. Jack was a frustrated poet. His appointment as captain had happened only because of his mother. The meddling witch.

Not that he wanted to complain. He'd seen sights, unbelievably breathtaking vistas, on this voyage. Saturn, resplendent amid rings and moons. Jupiter's atmosphere swirling in grandiose curlicues. Even Mars had its moments. And now Neptune. Another six months and the *Kepler* would swing back towards Earth with her crew of intrepid explorers. Three long years before they reached Earth again. Humankind's first long-term venture through the solar system. At least in person.

"Status on the *Ares?*" He spoke as Kaile passed his command chair in her endless pacing of the bridge.

"Resupply ship is on schedule to rendezvous at Nereid in three days' time, sir."

Jack nodded acknowledgement.

She paced away, her back straight and unbending as the proverbial iron rod.

If only he had some way of getting her to speak more often. Her voice was low, musical, sweet, and easy on the ears. But bridge discipline must be maintained and the conn was not the place for idle chitchat. Perhaps tonight over dinner.

He turned his thoughts back to his half-composed poetry featuring the blue ice planet and its glimmering necklet of moons.

EMILY KAILE SAT IN HER PALE BLUE NIGHTGOWN, HER BACK RAMROD straight, as she prepared for bed. She pulled pins from her hair, one by one, letting it escape into soft ringlets. Captain Williams had been different at dinner. He'd tried talking to her about non-Navy topics. He'd even quoted poetry over the sorbet served for dessert. Bad poetry, but nonetheless, poetry. She pulled the last pin anchoring her bun. Soft curls framed her face, changing the sharp lines she showed when in uniform, which was pretty much any time she wasn't actually asleep.

She pulled her brush from the drawer under her mirror, running it slowly through her hair. The gold locket around her neck glinted in her reflection. Someday, she'd escape the military life. She'd break free of her family and do something wild, like wearing a dress and going dancing. She'd marry an insurance adjuster or an accountant and settle for a life in a little seaside cottage where she could be nothing more than a neighborhood mum. She'd have at least four children, all sweet little cherubs who messed about and got dirty and did not in any way wear uniforms. She'd put their pictures in her locket. She fingered the bauble as she dreamed.

Emily had spent her life in uniform, ever since she was first enrolled in a military school at age three when her mother had gone back to active command duty. Emily bounced back and forth between boarding schools, military internships, and time with her parents, which was just another form of military training. Career Navy, both in space and on water, ran through her veins instead of blood.

She pulled her hairbrush through her ringlets and imagined the roses that would bloom outside her kitchen window. Fat pink blossoms that smelled of traditional grandmothers. Her grandmothers smelled of moth balls, official insignia, and Naval offices. She would smell of lavender and roses and vanilla cookies when she became a grandmother. But that would require that she have children, which required she marry, which required Emily to find a man to date and fall in love with. First officer on a Navy ship was not the place for such a search, no matter how politically and militarily advantageous for her career. The Space Navy frowned on romantic entanglements, especially involving higher ranking officers.

She whispered curses down upon her mother for arranging her appointment to the *Kepler*. Although if Emily played her cards right after she returned, she could land herself a—

Her thoughts cut off abruptly as alarms shrilled. The lights flickered and faded to solid red glow.

She stood, reaching for her uniform. It wouldn't do for the First Officer to appear in a lacy nightgown for a uniform drill.

"Kaile?" The ship's purser hammered on her door. "Captain wants you on bridge, now!"

She shouted acknowledgement as she jammed her legs into the uniform. Was that real panic in the man's voice? Was this not a drill? What emergency would summon her to the bridge in the middle of the night? The crew knew their jobs and fulfilled them perfectly. They'd had the last three and a half years to work out any kinks. Emily was proud of them, and they knew it. They gave their best. They wouldn't be summoning her for a routine event.

She yanked the zipper up on her jumpsuit as she opened her door. The corridor was a madhouse of crewmen rushing to and fro in the red lights, shouting over the howling alarms. Emily grabbed the first officer she spotted, the ship's engineer.

"What is all the fuss about?"

The man jerked his sleeve from her grasp. "Meteor swarm. Dark albedo, impact in five minutes." He hurried away.

Emily stared after him for a long breath. The space rocks had to be very large and dark to be missed by their scanners and radar. Especially if they were so close. She whirled on her heel and ran for the bridge. Her hands fumbled her hair into a messy bun as her feet carried her to the center of the crisis.

The first meteor hit the ship as she was scrambling up the last ladder to the bridge. She clutched the rungs as the ship shuddered. These were not tiny ice chunks that their electrified grid could deflect or melt. These rocks had to be at least the size of her fist. The sound of them smashing into the hull echoed over the shrieking alarms. Emily bit her lip and climbed faster.

"GET YOUR LAZY BUTT DOWN THAT TUBE! SEAL OFF THE SEWAGE LEAKS. Can't have those pipes bursting." Davey, the head engineer, threw a roll of duct tape at Nigel Jones. The burly man turned away, shouting orders at the rest of his engineering crew. Alarms shrilled as the ship jerked. "Get those engines shut down!"

Nigel glared daggers at the man. The last place he wanted to be in an emergency was down in the septic chamber, patching holes in the sewage lines. He pulled a hazard suit from the locker and yanked it on. He should be the one balancing the containment fields for the ion flux drive. Nigel knew more than the grease monkeys clambering their ham-fisted way into the engine of the *Kepler*. But did any of the engineers appreciate his self-taught particle physics expertise? No, they sent him into the cramped septic containment chamber to wade through filth as he taped the flexible conduits leading to the biomass digester.

Air hissed in his mask as he sealed the suit. The environmental filter unit started automatically. It kept out potential toxins and gases, but not the smell. Nothing could keep out the smell. Davey said it was all mental, in his head, but Nigel knew what he smelled, and it wasn't pleasant. He squeezed his narrow body into the tight space. The ship lurched as another swarm struck the hull. Even here, in the heart of the ship, Nigel heard the clang.

He slapped tape over leaks as he bitterly recited his list of grievances. He'd jumped at the chance to join the crew of the *Kepler*. Finally, his theories of quantum particle energistics would have a testing ground. He'd be able to rub shoulders with others who loved the practical applications of entanglement string theory. Or so he'd thought. Out of the six engineers and fourteen engineering assistants, Nigel was the only one not Navy or former Navy. And none of the others knew anything about subatomic particle energy transference, in the lab or otherwise. Nor did they care. They smashed wrenches into things. They banged about like giant, lumbering bilge rats spreading carnage and destruction in the heart of the ship. They didn't care about the delicate tuning of the engines or the beauties of quantum field theory. If it worked good enough, they were content.

Nigel had plans. He had designs to increase the energy output of the drive exponentially. If implemented, they could have cut this miserable seven-year voyage down to a much more enjoyable four months. He had a few kinks to work out, but he was hoping to test his prototype during the voyage. But had they given him the chance to even discuss his work with Davey? Oh, no. Davey wasn't interested, so no one else was, either.

They'd laughed him out of the lower decks mess hall. They'd kept laughing all the way to the engineering bunkroom. Then Davey had posted his assignment to the sewage lines and made it permanent. Nigel would gladly watch the lot of them freeze in vacuum. He hated them all.

He was glad of his suit as he crawled through the crowded access ports. The emergency lights bathed everything in red light, which only made the sewage harder to distinguish from the rest of the garbage that collected in the septic chamber. He muttered curses as he worked his way through the nests of tubing, patching the holes as he found them.

When he finished, he climbed free of the septic chamber. The alarms had shut off but the lights stayed red. He clambered out of the access hatch and reached for the fasteners on his helmet.

Then paused. Where was everyone? Why was the engine room so quiet and deserted? What had happened?

He stumped across the floor, leaving stinking footprints. The air valves showed atmosphere within normal operating parameters. All of life support seemed fine, at least according to the gauges. He flipped open the helmet and stripped off the suit, leaving it lying in the puddle of sewage that had dripped off it.

The other gauges showed the ship was still functional, at least the ones Nigel knew how to read. So where was everyone?

"We don't have a choice," Captain Williams spoke. "Navigational controls are completely destroyed. The ship is on a collision course with Neptune. We have to abandon ship. The *Ares* will not be able to reach us in time."

"The port lifeboats were hit," Emily reported from the damage station. "Only three of them are still functional. We won't have room for everyone, even if we crowd the lifeboats."

"Someone will have to stay behind." Jack Williams stood beside his command chair. "Abandon ship, Commander Kaile. Give the order."

"Sir?" She met his gaze with a questioning one of her own. "We can institute repairs—"

The damage officer shook his head. "Life support is still online, but the engine control systems are completely destroyed. One week and the ship will be caught in Neptune's gravitational pull. We don't have the parts or the expertise to repair guidance systems before then. If the *Ares* speeds up to catch us, she'll go down with us."

"And leave those in the lifeboats to perish." Jack struck a heroic pose. "We will fit as many as we can into the lifeboats and launch them towards the *Ares'* flight path. Send a message to her to slow and prepare for rescue operations. All hands, abandon ship. Proceed to the designated lifeboats in an orderly manner."

The hooting call echoed through corridors painted red with emergency lights. The scientists among the crew scrambled to download data. Crew members grabbed what small objects they could stuff into their pockets before reporting to the lifeboats. Emily stood guard, maintaining order and keeping the boats from too much crowding. She pulled the release lever as each one was filled and sealed.

The stragglers hurried to the last functional lifeboat. Emily counted them off as they boarded. She stopped the last two from boarding. "The lifeboat is at maximum capacity. I'm sorry."

The purser traded glances with the galley assistant. "We aren't staying here to die."

Captain Williams spoke from behind. "First Officer Kaile, what is the problem?"

"Lack of room, sir. We have one remaining seat on the lifeboat. And four of us left on the ship."

"Correction," Davey said, poking his head out of the hatch. "We lost a couple of men down in the engine rooms. We have two seats on this boat."

"And still four of us," Emily said.

Jack drew in a deep breath, puffing out his chest. He squared his shoulders before speaking. "I shall remain to die with my ship. It is the captain's duty."

Emily shot a sidelong glance at Davey and the lifeboat crowded with crewmen. "Then it will be my duty and pleasure to also remain behind. It has been an honor serving with you, Captain Williams." She snapped her heels and gave him her best salute.

He returned the salute, keeping his hand pressed to his forehead until the purser and galley assistant had scrambled past Davey into the overcrowded lifeboat. The hatch clanged shut before he snapped his hand away. The lifeboat launched with a hiss of escaping air.

Emily's lip trembled, but her back remained straight. "I guess it's just the two of us, sir. How long until we are crushed by Neptune's atmosphere?"

"A week, maybe ten days. And since we're the only two left on board, there is no need for formality." Jack let his shoulders sag. "Might as well get comfortable." He slouched off to his quarters.

Emily flexed her hands. For the first time in her life, she had no schedule to keep, no duty to fulfill. She had no idea what to do with her freedom. She glanced down at the bulge of her nightgown beneath her uniform.

She grinned as a wild notion entered her head. No one would ever know. Who would report her to the captain? The lock light on his door flashed red. Emily allowed a small giggle to escape as she stripped off the uniform and let her hair down. She left the uniform on the floor as she danced away with her sky blue satin nightgown swirling around her bare feet.

Nigel's mouth hung open in shock. They'd abandoned ship and left him behind? He stared at the deserted stations, the tools left behind where they were abandoned. The screen flashed its ominous message: Abandon ship, all hands, abandon ship.

"No one thought to tell me? To use the radio or even the intercom?" He slammed a fist into a bulkhead. Then shook his hand and winced. Well, at least he no longer had to worry about Davey bossing him about. He ran his hand over the control panel, dismissing the alert and opening the status.

"Steering is full red, attitude jets are gone. That might be an issue." He muttered to himself as he worked his way through the system status reports. "Engines are still operational, mostly. Yellow lights on half the systems. Life support shows green. Hull integrity might be a little problem. Not bad shape, considering. As long as we're not headed straight for —" He pulled up the feed from the external cameras. "Of course we're headed straight for the planet. I might have enough time, though, if I can get the engines to slow us a bit."

He tapped his way through the controls. Davey hadn't let him touch them, but that hadn't stopped Nigel from stealing the simulator programs and running them on his personal tablet in his bunk. He could fly this ship, given the opportunity. And it seemed to be right in front of him. The ship was abandoned after all. It was just Nigel and his dreams. He could do as he pleased.

He set the engines to reverse burn. It would slow the *Kepler* only slightly, but it would buy another day or two. That might give him enough time to set up his experiments. And if he could pull it off? He'd go down in history as the man who brought the stars within reach.

He, Nigel Jones, would be known as the man who invented the first faster than light stardrive.

But only if he could get it online before the ship smashed into Neptune. He couldn't stop whistling and grinning as he fetched his plans and started gathering tools.

"O BEAUTEOUS BALL OF CERULEAN HUE—"

Jack stopped and tapped his lip with his pen. He could only write poetry by hand, on real paper with an old ink pen. Or so he told himself, his excuse to never actually commit his words to paper.

He crossed out *ball*.

"O beauteous orb— Closer, but not quite right."

He tapped his lip as he stared at Neptune. He'd routed the feed from the main camera to his room, then messed with the computer until he'd projected it onto the bulkhead wall. The blue planet, in all its swirling majesty, watched him back like an omnipotent sea god waiting to crush an insignificant bug beneath his feet. Impressive, despite the ripples from the compartment's doors.

"Truly, you were well-named. And truly, I would give my command for a decent thesaurus."

Jack threw the pen in the general direction of his desk.

"Face it, thirty years of the Navy has not freed your inner poet. You are still shackled, haunted by your mother's ambitions for you. Damn you, mother!"

He shook his fist at the ceiling.

"Do you wish me to retrieve the latest message from your mother?" the computer asked politely.

"No." Jack hesitated, then let his lips curl in an evil smile. "Actually, yes. Play it and overlay the entire video with flames. Burn her. Burn her to ashes!"

"Please rephrase your request. Query not understood."

"Just delete it. I never want to see her or hear her voice again."

The computer complied.

Jack fidgeted, unhappy with the quiet resolution. Burning all ties with his mother and her ambitions for him should have been accompanied by trumpets and fanfares and wild symphonies.

"Computer, can you play music?"

"I have seven thousand three hundred and twenty two songs in my library."

"Can you play the music on the bridge?" It would be more dramatic with Neptune swelling on the screen. Death was certain, but he would face it his way.

"Certainly. What do you wish to hear?"

"Do you have something about the *Flying Dutchman* perhaps? Doomed ship of the damned seems very appropriate."

"I have *der Fliegende Holländer Ouvertüre* by Wagner. Is that suitable?"

"Perfect. Please play it once I'm on the bridge."

Jack opened his closet. He should wear something befitting the occasion. He was going to the bridge to stare at Neptune, listen to Wagner, and court his poetic muse. He had a week to compose his magnum opus. The captain's command chair was the most comfortable place he'd found to sit on the whole ship. And with no one to impress, he could wear what he liked. He settled for his white dress uniform jacket with the thick gold stripes on the sleeves and his green silk pajamas underneath. He would have worn a tuxedo if he had one. Green silk was close enough. He thought the pants looked rather dashing under the white jacket.

He gathered his notebook and pen and strode from his cabin to the bridge.

EMILY SCOOPED ANOTHER SPOONFUL OF ICE CREAM INTO HER MOUTH. SHE danced her way down the corridor as she let the creamy cold slide across her tongue. The half empty carton dangled from her hand. She closed her eyes and twirled through the hatch into engineering. She shivered at the delicious taste of freedom. No more rules or regulations. No more rationing. She could eat what she wanted, wear what she wanted, keep whatever hours she pleased. At least for the next week. She'd pull out her dress whites and wear them for their funeral plunge into the ice giant Neptune, but until then, she'd rebel in whatever way she pleased.

A wrench clanked on the floor.

Her eyes snapped open. A man was bent over the fluctuator assemblage for the engine manifold uptake. "Who are you? Why didn't you abandon ship when the order was given?"

The man stopped fiddling and spun around. "Why are you still on the ship?"

She pulled herself to attention. "I asked you a question," her eyes flicked over his collar. "Yeoman," she finished when she found no insignia there.

"Rank doesn't really matter anymore, does it?" The man retrieved the wrench from the floor. "I'm Nigel Jones, and I'm the one who's going to save our lives."

"You can fix the engine? The head engineer said the steering was completely destroyed, and we didn't have the parts or the time to repair it." Emily set the melting carton of ice cream on a nearby control desk.

Nigel shifted the ice cream to the floor, his lips pursed in disapproval. "Did you have your heart set on suicide by gravitational crushing? Because I don't."

"Why did you stay if you weren't willing to die?" The man intrigued her. He didn't act like a yeoman, or even an ensign. He acted like a man with a plan. She had nothing better to do.

"I was in the septic tank and didn't hear the alarm. Faulty radio system in my suit. By the time I climbed back out, everyone was gone. Or so I thought." He shot a glance at her. "Is it just you and me, then?"

"The captain's somewhere around." Emily shrugged. Jack had made it clear he wanted to be alone. She'd track him down later, once she worked up the courage to tell him how she felt about him. Ever since that first day she'd come aboard and seen those dreamy brown eyes, poet's eyes, and that sad little smile of his, she'd been smitten. But a good officer didn't let it show. Not that it mattered now. They were doomed, and no one but Jack would ever know how she truly felt.

"Anyone else?" Nigel glared at her, as if her staying behind was a personal affront to his plans, whatever those were. "I have to recalculate everything."

She licked a stray drop of ice cream from her finger as she shook her head. "Just the two of us. And you. You should have heard the alarms. You should have abandoned the ship. We're going to crash into Neptune and die in about a week."

"Not if I can help it. Didn't you hear me? I can save us." He thumped the wrench onto the desk as he trapped her with his intense and slightly cross-eyed stare. "I can build us an FTL jump drive. We'll pass *through* Neptune, and pop out the other side. Once through, we call for help, then wait for the *Ares* to catch up to us."

She stopped licking her finger. "FTL is impossible. That's why the *Kepler* is on the grand tour, to see if mankind can handle long-range spaceflight. It will take years to reach the nearest star. If we can make it that far."

"You're wrong. I can build an FTL drive using our drive as a basis. I've been working on these calculations for years. See here, if we cross connect the flavinator with the hexachromic converter—"

Her eyes glazed over as he poked and prodded and talked his way through the engine. She had no idea what he was saying. Her expertise had been command tactics, not engineering physics and definitely not subatomic particle theory.

"—and that creates the thrust that will shove us to the proper acceleration. But I need at least an ounce of gold to get the reaction to stabilize." His gaze dropped to the locket dangling between her breasts. "Is that twenty-four carat or eighteen? I can refine it if needed, but I have to know how pure it is."

Emily clutched her hand around the locket. "You can't have this." It held her dreams, her escape from the military life.

"It won't matter in a week, will it? We'll all be dead. Or you can give it to me and I can save us all." Nigel held out his hand.

"I don't think I like you. I think you're a nasty man, mean and small and twisted and—" She let her voice trail off. She couldn't think of any more insults for the rat-faced man. She turned on her heel, her night-gown billowing around her.

"I need gold. Either your locket or someone else's, but if you want to live, find me gold. And quickly." His nasal voice followed her as she marched out of engineering.

She faltered outside the door. She'd left the ice cream behind and it was the last carton of her favorite flavor. She didn't want to die. She wanted to retire from the Navy and buy that seaside cottage. She imagined her future four children watching her, sad frowns on their faces. She turned back to Nigel.

"Can you really save us?"

"There's no guarantee, but I'm ninety-five percent confident it will work."

She fingered her locket. "Ninety-five percent?"

"Okay, eighty-three percent certain. We have a good shot at making this drive work, but I need your locket. And a few other things."

Emily slowly unlatched the chain and slid her locket free. What good was it if she were dead? She could buy another one. She pictured her children, all with Jack's soft brown eyes and dreamy smile. Yes, it was a worthy sacrifice. She held the chain out to Nigel. The locket spun at the end.

"What else do you need?" Her voice quavered only a little as the nasty little man snatched it from her.

"I'll get you a list."

She grabbed the carton of ice cream from the floor and fled as tears threatened to fall. She really hadn't wanted to die. She just wished Jack was the one with the plan to save them, not this horrid Nigel man.

Her bare feet whispered down the empty corridors. Somewhere, wild dramatic music crashed in a tangle of violins and horns. She followed it, searching for Jack. It was time to tell him of her dreams and their chance at surviving long enough for them to come true.

JACK WAVED HIS HANDS, CONDUCTING THE DOOMED *FLYING DUTCHMAN* through a wild symphonic storm. The music raged through his thoughts. He was Captain van der Decken, cursed to sail forever through the black void of space. Words swirled in his mind, phrases of poetry half-formed then rejected. He'd write his magnum opus later, after the symphony had inspired his muse. Or when his arms grew tired of conducting the doomed ship on its cursed journey.

Or perhaps he'd go to the galley and eat whatever delicacies he found. No reason to horde them now, not with only a week of travel left before their journey ended.

Would it be with a blaze of glory? Would they explode as they plowed into Neptune's atmosphere, or would it be more of a slow quiet death by compression as the pressure rose the deeper they plunged into the planet? He paused, frowning at the view as cymbals crashed.

"Jack?"

He turned to find Emily framed in the doorway, carton of dripping ice cream clutched in her hands. Her hair was loose around her shoulders, framing her face in a way that made her seem soft and delicate, not controlled and in command as he was accustomed to seeing her. She wore a flowing blue gown. He briefly wondered why she'd brought it with her on a space voyage with no possibility of a formal dinner that would require such a dress instead of her uniform.

"Yes?" He finally spoke as the overture died in a crash of timpani drums.

Emily fumbled her way onto the bridge, her face flushed in a most becoming manner. She set the carton of ice cream on a chair, then brushed at her dress with one hand. Her other hand tangled in her hair, attempting to twist it into its usual tight bun. But her eyes caught his, pleading for something. Her hands moved as if on their own.

"I—" She opened and closed her mouth soundlessly for a long moment. Her hands played with her hair, tugged the neckline of her dress, plucked the skirt.

Jack caught them and held them still. "We're alone on the ship, Emily, and about to perish. I think we can dispense with formalities. That dress is lovely. It suits you well."

Her blush deepened. "That isn't entirely true, sir. I mean, Jack."

"What? Someone is listening in? I shut down the comm system. No need for them to hear us in our death throes."

"You may want to turn it back on, sir."

"Whatever for? Emily, there is something I wish to say, that perhaps I should have said years ago."

A smile creased the corner of her mouth. "I know, Jack. I feel the same way. I've known since I first met you."

"You've known that my deepest desire was to be a poet not a starship captain?"

"What? No, not that. I mean I knew you enjoyed composing poetry. You shared it at officer's mess. I rather enjoyed the one about the peony and the apricot blossom. Very touching."

He beamed. "Yes, that one did turn out rather splendid."

She pulled her hands free and stepped away. "I can't do this." She twisted her hair into a tight knot, then realized she had no way to hold it in place. She let it fall again. "Sir, Nigel Jones is in Engineering. He claims he has a way to save us. And prove FTL travel is possible at the same time. He says he can build his jump drive on our existing engines and push us through Neptune and out the other side. We don't have to die."

He blinked as the soprano in the opera launched into a soaring descant. "We don't have to die? We aren't doomed?"

"That's what he says. He needs a few supplies, though."

Jack turned, leaned on his command chair. That cursed seat his mother had forced him into. His journal of poetry slid from its cushion to thump to the floor. So much for escaping her through death. He'd have to find another way. "Fine. Give him whatever he needs."

She reached towards him, as if to comfort him, but her hand stopped short of his sleeve. She hesitated, then pulled it back, clenched it into a fist. Her shoulders slumped. "Yes, sir." She turned on her heel and marched from the bridge, her back straight as a rod, her bearing all military.

He spoke only after she was safely out of earshot. "Ah, sweet Emily. Perhaps I'm not the only one with a family heritage I'd rather not claim. Your sapphire dress and wanton curls were truly charming." She did not need to know how desperately he wanted to dance with her, whisper loving words into those waving locks, hold her close to him and feel her soft warmth.

Now that they had a chance, he would have to be the captain again. All military precision and uniforms and protocol.

The opera wove a soft melody, counterpoint to the thunder of the drums.

Being Captain could wait, at least until the Flying Dutchman was safely rescued by his one true love. He conducted the chorus with vigor.

"Is this enough?" Emily dumped her armful of wires harvested from the damaged section of the ship.

Nigel didn't bother to look as he answered. "Should be. Just leave them over there." His voice echoed from inside the housing of his contraption.

"Are you sure that thing is large enough to push the whole ship into jump space?"

"Plenty large enough. Hand me the converter assemblage." Nigel stuck a hand out behind him.

Emily looked over the tangles of junk scattered across the once-pristine engine room. "Which one is the converter?"

"The one with the red and white bushings on the outside."

"The one that looks like a chicken?"

He pulled his head out of the engine long enough to glare at her. "It does *not* look like a chicken."

She twisted it in her hands, examining different angles. "It does resemble one. See, here's the head and over here are the wings, and this is the beak."

He snatched it out of her hands. "It's a converter assemblage for the ion diffuser. It is not a chicken!"

Emily leaned over the housing and peered inside as Nigel crawled into the tubing once more.

"Is that the ion diffuser? It looks kind of like the turkey I made out of macaroni and dry beans in grade school."

Nigel shoved the chicken converter into the back end of the turkey ion diffuser.

Emily giggled. "My grandmother tried to make turducken once. That's where you shove a duck inside a chicken inside a turkey."

Nigel whacked his head on the housing as he whipped around to face her. "Get out of here, you bird-brained woman! This is a delicate experimental engineering marvel, not a strange bird dish you serve at Thanksgiving! Go find me something I can use for carpathian strickenings."

"Sure, I'll just go do that."

Nigel's reply was muffled by the engine parts. Probably a good thing, Emily thought as she danced from the engine room. She had no idea what he wanted, but she'd find an armful of strange bits and bobs and he'd be happy for a while. The closer they got to Neptune, the less optimistic Emily was about their chances. Nigel was certifiably insane. And so was his project.

She drifted down the corridor to the personnel quarters. Jack had disabled all the locks. She wandered in and out of rooms, stirring through drawers and lockers as she pleased. The crew had left most of their possessions behind. Not much of it was very interesting, it was mostly pictures of people she didn't know. And would never meet now.

She twirled in her blue nightgown in front of mirrors, dancing to the music in her head. She'd tried ballet, years ago. But her family was military, or so her grandparents had insisted. She learned to dance the waltz and the foxtrot and a handful of others appropriate to officer's balls. She attempted a cha-cha, then giggled as she tripped over her feet. Cha-cha's were never played at the formal affairs she'd been allowed to attend. She'd always wanted to go slumming with the enlisted folks. Their dances sounded much more fun, with wild music and shouting and drinking songs. She wanted at least a taste of wildness before being locked into dress whites and protocol that would make anyone's spine calcify in an upright position. She'd never gotten what she wanted.

Until now.

She laughed and twirled, spinning until her skirts flared wide.

Jack caught her as she tumbled sideways, dizzy from the spinning. She blinked and scrambled backwards, out of his hold. Her cheeks burned with embarrassment. No, she'd never gotten what she truly wanted. Not even now.

"Sorry, sir," she panted. "I was just—"

"Dancing?" Jack smiled. "Computer, play a waltz, please, and pipe it throughout the ship."

"Do you have a preference?" the computer asked in its clipped slightly feminine voice.

"Yes," Emily spoke quickly, interrupting the captain. "Brahms, opus 39 in A-flat major."

Jack smiled like the sun breaking through clouds. "One of my favorites. Would you do me the honor?" He offered his hand.

The sweet piano music filled the corridor as Emily stepped into the circle of his arms. Her skirt flared as he swept her into a graceful waltz through the empty ship.

Nigel grimaced at the saccharine strains of an orchestra in full voice. Whatever the captain and that floozy of a first officer were doing, it wasn't looking for the parts he needed. He'd have to go scrounge them himself.

Again.

He stomped from the engine room. He needed personal entertainment devices so he could strip out the control chips. He started in the officer's quarters. They were more likely to own the expensive versions he needed. He yanked open drawers, then pawed through the contents, leaving a trail of destruction behind. The mess didn't matter. Nothing would matter if he didn't get his drive working. Four days until they were too close to Neptune. Four days until the planet sucked them down.

Four days until they plunged to a slow death as the atmosphere slowly crushed them into nothing.

If he were a romantic, he'd console himself with the thought he'd end up as a rain of diamonds deep inside the blue swirls of Neptune.

He snorted. He was about as romantic as that stupid turducken Emily had been babbling about.

"My drive does not look like a roasted chicken. Or any kind of edible fowl." He threw a handful of uniforms onto the floor and rooted in the back of a drawer. "Ah, yes. Perfect." He stuffed the small video player in a pocket then moved on to the next cubby.

JACK WATCHED, ENTRANCED, AS EMILY SPOONED ANOTHER GLOB OF sundae into her perfect mouth. She insisted it was too wide, but he liked the way every emotion sent it shifting. Like now, a little pouty and puckered as she let the ice cream melt on her tongue. She wiped a drop of hot fudge from her chin, then licked her finger.

"You haven't touched yours," she said after she swallowed. She met his gaze, stared deep into his hazel eyes. "You're staring at me."

"And you're staring right back. You have beautiful eyes." He stirred his spoon through his sundae, scooping up a lump of cherry.

Emily set her spoon in her dish, her fingers holding it precisely, placing it carefully at exactly thirty degrees off-center. Her smile of a moment before had disappeared. She looked haunted, resigned, disconsolate. Jack rolled the words through his head, searching for a poetry form to fit the emotions rolling through his heart.

She pushed to her feet. "We should help Nigel."

He caught her hand. "You know his drive is not going to work. It's hopeless. We may as well enjoy what little time we have left, Emily."

She reluctantly pulled her hand free. "We are both officers. We should act in accordance with our rank."

His heart broke when she added, "Sir."

"Why?" He blocked her exit from the wardroom. "No one will ever know, will they? Our communication system is off."

"And it shouldn't be, sir. We should call the *Ares*, get a report on the rest of the crew. At least let them download the science scans we have of Neptune." She plucked at the blue satin of her nightgown. "I apologize for my lapse in discipline, sir."

"Emily, please. We can turn on the equipment, make a status report, if that will make you happy. I'll even let the computer send all the data scans we've got. We can even set it to keep running scans automatically, all the way through the atmosphere. Until. . ." His voice broke. He cleared his throat. "Until we're gone."

"I should go change into something more befitting."

"That dress is beautiful. You are beautiful. I've wanted to say this for years, ever since you first walked onto my bridge." He reached for her hand again.

"Sir, we can't do this."

"Why not? We're doomed. We're going to die, and I am going to do it on *my* terms. Not the Navy's and certainly not my mother's. Computer, play that song I told you to save."

"Acknowledged."

The sweet strains of a violin playing Salut d'Amour dripped from the speakers. Jack wrapped his arms around Emily, drew her into his embrace, reached for her lips with his.

"Oh, please!" Nigel's sarcastic remark destroyed their moment. "Computer, shut that crap off."

The song broke off mid-note.

Jack rounded on the weaselly little man. "You, sir, are out of line and out of uniform!"

"You're one to talk." Nigel shot a pointed look at the captain's green silk pajama pants. "While the two of you are eating ice cream and swooning, I've been working to save us. Two days to doomsday, people. But I think I've got the last problem solved."

He shoved between them to slap a sheet of paper on the table amid the puddles of caramel and whipped cream. He tapped a tangle of scribbles to one side. "See the transducer array here? It needs the power inducements tripled and the confabulator transmogrified with a three-pronged hamiltonian stack."

"What?" Jack wrinkled his nose in confusion.

"Quantum engineering," Emily answered, with a solemn nod.

"Exactly." Nigel plowed on, ignorant of the look they traded over his scruffy head. "What I need you to find are more of these." He set a control circuit board on the table. "I scrounged that one out of the telescopic binary controller. I also need a gimbal mount and half a dozen steel bearings. The hydroponic plant unit should have the mount. The steel bearings are going to have to come out of the docking port bumper pods."

"I'll get the bearings," Emily said.

"Are you certain?" Jack asked her.

"If there's a chance, we have to take it, sir." She turned smartly on her heel, then marched from the wardroom.

"I should lock you in the brig, you nasty little man," Jack said to Nigel after Emily was gone.

"You can play footsie with her later, after I save our hides." Nigel matched the captain's angry glare with one of his own. "If you want to die, I can shove you out the airlock right now."

Jack flexed his fists open and closed, then open. His shoulders sagged. "What do you need me to find?"

"Video player circuits. Your friend, the computer, should have a bunch in the comm room. Or maybe the ship's library. Go find them, rip them open, and yank these puppies free. I need at least a dozen more."

Jack slouched from the room. His grandmother would be smirking, right next to his mother, if they could see him now. They'd never believed in him, not as a poet, only as a puppet for their ambitions. He'd rather die than return to their influence.

NIGEL CROUCHED IN FRONT OF THE MONSTROSITY HE'D BUILT INTO AND around the engine. His hand rested on a lever painted with bright red nail polish.

"It looks like a giant duck," Jack said. He squinted at the thing. Large wings swung out on either side. A heavy bit that resembled a bill on a head hung over Nigel, as if the giant metal bird were about to eat him.

"It is *not* a duck! It's a highly sophisticated, and very elegant, proto-type of the Jonesian quantum FTL jump drive." Nigel shifted around to glare at Jack. He kept his hand tight on the handle, though.

"I see you named it after yourself. Isn't that a bit presumptuous of you?"

"Hush," Emily ordered, her voice crisp and professional. She stood over a radar screen hastily assembled and mounted over the dead steering controls. "We're down to one hundred thousand kilometers from the highest level of clouds." The ship groaned under the gravitational pull of the giant ice planet. It was only going to get worse.

"Give me a countdown," Nigel shouted, turning back to his invention.

"Still looks like a duck," Jack muttered.

"It does not!"

"Five."

"Are those my command clusters? You shouldn't be wearing those." Jack glared at Nigel, who was in an officer's dress whites stolen from one of the purser's racks.

"I can wear what I want. I think I deserve a promotion after all my hard work."

"Four."

"I'm the captain and the only one authorized to grant field promotions on this ship. If your duck works, then we'll talk about promotions."

"Three."

"It is not a duck!"

"Two."

"Is too."

"Is not."

"One."

Nigel glared at Jack.

Jack pursed his lips, waiting until the last second. "Quantum duck drive," he whispered just as Emily said, "Now!"

Nigel yanked on the lever while turning to shout, "It is NOT a duck!" He slipped, his hand shoving the lever assemblage. Metal screeched on metal as it shifted back an inch.

The giant quantum duck wobbled. A high whistling filled the air. The metallic wings started to twitch. Golden light pulsed out from the breast of the bird, a bubble that grew larger with each laborious beat of the wings.

Nigel cackled. "It's working! It's really working!"

Emily bent her head over her radar screen. Her face was blank, bland professionalism at its finest. "No readings at all on the scope."

"There aren't supposed to be any, not in jump space." Nigel leapt up from the floor, rushing to her side.

Jack stared in despair at the giant glowing golden duck. It had saved their lives at the cost of his soul. His poetry screamed as it died, twisted under the weight of his mother's ambitions. He'd have to face her again. He'd have to return.

"We should be far enough now. I think we passed right through Neptune." Nigel rubbed his hands together, like the evil rat he was. He pranced back to his freakish contraption.

"I'm getting something," Emily said, squinting at her screen. "Wait, if that's Neptune, it's dropping behind us. Very fast. We're gaining speed."

The golden bubble of energy around the bird pulsed as it expanded.

Jack squinted into the light. Maybe they weren't so doomed after all. "Is it supposed to do that?"

Nigel danced in front of the duck, his arms waving. He looked like a demented monkey.

"If this is correct, we're closing in on seven times the speed of light." Emily straightened, her dress whites glowing yellow. "We're way beyond the solar system. Nigel, shut it off." Her voice wavered only a little.

"I'm trying," Nigel shouted. "The control lever is inside the bubble. I can't reach it, not without vaporizing my entire arm and quite possibly the entire ship."

"What kind of fool builds the off switch inside the containment field?" Jack couldn't help insulting the man. Maybe he was saved after all. Death or his mother? Death was preferable.

"It wasn't inside the containment field until you pushed me!" Nigel shot a glare over his shoulder.

"Shut it down," Emily cried. "Pull the power, yank the field generator coils, pull the control switches, shut down the whole ship, whatever it takes!"

Jack backed from the engine room, a strange glint in his eye. Words poured through his mind, snippets of poetry, some of it even rhymed. He had to capture it, preserve it. For one brief moment, he would BE a poet. He would spite his mother with his dying breath. His feet thundered down the shuddering, pulsing hallway. Golden light flickered and danced across the ship's electrical grid, sparking from the walls and conduits. Jack released a maniacal cackle.

"Mad, I'm going mad." He skidded to a stop. He stared at the crackle of energy playing over his ship. A smile burst over his face, one of pure joy. "A sure sign of poetic genius. All good poets are mad!"

He laughed again, dancing and skipping and singing his way through the ship to the control room and its enormous windows.

"How far now?" Nigel's voice cracked.

Emily shook her head. Her bun bobbed. Stray hairs wafted loose around her face. "The equipment can't calculate that quickly. We could be as far as the Andromeda Galaxy, maybe farther." Her voice was flat with despair. Jack had been smiling as he slipped away, but it hadn't been a sane smile. She wasn't sure a raving lunatic was a proper father for her future children. If she ever had any. Her little white cottage by the sea seemed farther than ever at this moment.

"I should have used more gold. That necklace you gave me was not as pure as you thought. It shouldn't be reacting like this. The field is expanding too fast. It's too much like a foam, not a solid." Nigel's words were lost in muttering as he squirmed around the far side of the gracefully flapping duck.

A spark of gold flickered across the control boards. Emily pulled her hands back. Nigel's invention may have saved them from Neptune, but had he doomed them to an even worse fate? Only his feet were visible under the engine housing. His duck continued her maiden flight, wings creaking as they flexed up and down.

Emily stretched her hands wide. She was useless here. She brushed her hands down her dress uniform. This was her family's heritage, their calling. "Not mine," she whispered. She wanted a garden and children. She wanted to wear pretty dresses and go dancing.

And have her husband smile at her.

In her imagination, he wore Jack's face. Not the crazy one she'd glimpsed, but the thoughtful and kind one he wore when he was at dinner with her in the wardroom. She would find him and change his face back to the one she loved if it was her last dying act.

She couldn't save them; that task was in Nigel's incapable hands.

She whirled and ran from the engine room, through the creaking hallways of the ship, towards the bridge. Jack would be there, in his captain's chair, watching.

The ship groaned, lurching to one side. The walls flexed with a horrible cracking noise. Their doom might come much sooner than she'd thought. She ran faster.

She burst into the control room amid a chorus of ship creaks.

"Yes?" Jack spoke without looking up from his notebook.

She hurried to his side. He wrote, *My tortured yearning*, crossed it out and wrote instead, *My doomed yearning*. The windows showed a crackling, twisting tunnel of golden sparks.

"Jack," she started, but emotion closed up her throat, stole her words.

"Emily." He wrote another phrase, frowned, then nodded. "Better. Almost a rhyme that time."

His hair was thinning on top. His forehead wrinkled. He was short, slightly pudgy, with a haunted look in his eyes most of the time. And she loved him, not because he commanded the ship, but because he guided it with a gentle, if somewhat vague, touch. He was not military to the bone. He was like her. He put on the uniform as a costume to cover the softness inside. She rested her hand on his sleeve.

"You want something?" He blinked his watery eyes up at her, then back to his notebook. "I need a word that rhymes with wretched."

"I love you." The words slipped out before she could stop them.

He shook his head. "Not even close. You are not much of a poet."

She worked her mouth soundlessly. Hadn't he understood? "Jack, I love you. I've loved you since I first met you. But protocol—"

"Protocol be damned. We're on a doomed ship, flying forever between the stars. Say what you please." He stopped writing his loopy words and looked up, focusing on her. "You love me?"

The ship gave a horrendous cacophony of noises. The window cleared to show a vast starfield twined through with ribbons of gas.

Emily gasped. "I know where we are. That nebula, it must be!"

"Thousands of light years or millions, it makes no difference." Jack turned back to his writing. "We're not going home again. Welcome to the *Flying Dutchman*, the lost ship of legend. I shall be playing the part of the cursed captain, and you, the part of the doomed crew."

Emily straightened, her body snapping to attention as it had for most of her life. "I have an idea. We can go home again."

Jack rose to his feet. He set his notebook and pen carefully in his chair, then turned to her. He took both of her hands in his. "Say it again."

"We can go home." She smiled.

"Not that, the other. You said before."

She let her fingers curl into his, her gaze meet his. "Jack, I—"

"I did it!" Nigel burst into the room, rushing up to the conn where they stood. He held a contraption trailing wires and connectors in one fist. "I had to recalculate for the reduced mass of gold, but after pulling the concatenator and readjusting the plasma flow, I shut down the drive. I can control it now."

Emily felt her cheeks flushing. She pulled her hands from Jack's. Her military indoctrination was still too deep. "If we turn the ship one hundred and eighty degrees—"

"And reactivate the drive," Nigel interrupted, "we can shoot for home again. We'll have to guess on the duration, but we should be able to get close. I've reworked the numbers adjusting for the new configuration."

"We're going home?" Jack's face fell.

Emily's first flush of excitement died in a rush of sorrow. Her dream was fading, turning into a nightmare of a lonely career in the Navy, dying alone far from her perfect seaside cottage. She drew in a long breath, straightening to something beyond military posture, drawing herself up into a woman fighting for her dream.

"Nigel, go back to the engine room. Prepare to activate the drive on my signal." Her voice snapped, crisp and commanding. Her dream did not include the weaselly engineering assistant.

It did include Jack. She turned to the navigation console.

"Mark!"

Nigel gingerly pulled the switch, now located halfway to the door and well outside the radius of the containment field.

The quantum duck flexed its wings once again. Golden light pulsed and grew. This time the field stabilized quickly. The ship shivered less than before. The wings lifted high, swept low, repeated in a smooth motion.

"Yes!" He pumped his fist, though no one was near to share his triumph. He knew, and that was enough for now. Soon, the whole world would know. He, Nigel Jones, had invented a faster-than-light space drive. The Jonesian Quantum Tunnel Drive. He liked the ring of that.

He punched the big red button he'd installed. "Flight duration countdown initiated."

"Acknowledged." Emily's voice answered from the speakers.

He relaxed, lounging in the chief engineer's seat as he watched his bird fly. Not a duck, never a duck. Ungraceful, waddling, nasty bottom-feeders. He'd grown up with ducks and hated them. They stank. They stared with their beady dark eyes and narrow heads. They attacked any chance they got. No, his drive was not a duck but a swan. He nodded. Yes, the Swan Drive. Wait, the Jonesian Swan. Much better.

"Nigel, turn it off! We're going too fast."

He started, fell out of the chair at Emily's urgent command. He scrambled back to his feet. "We shouldn't be. I adjusted for the levels of transducer flux."

"We've overshot the sun, if I'm reading the scans right. Shut it down!"

He mashed the red button without thinking, his body responding to her authoritative command. He hated her in that moment as his swan died, turned inert once again.

"We pushed too far," Emily's voice crackled from the speakers again. "We're almost to Vega. Let me turn the ship around and we'll try again. Reset the drive."

"Yes, ma'am." He hated the snap in his voice. He should be the one giving the orders. He should be the one in command. It was his drive that saved them. He muttered and cursed as he reset his beautiful bird.

"Ready?"

"Yes, ma'am."

"Then activate it, but only for a count of five."

He mashed the button, watched his swan flap her wings, once, twice, raise them for a third. He jammed his thumb into the red button. The bird froze.

"Perfect. We're home."

He waited until he'd shut off the comm system before he pumped his fist. "Yes!" Now they'd see his genius, they'd know how brilliant he was. He'd show them all.

EMILY REACHED FOR JACK'S HAND. IT RESTED LIMP ON HIS NOTEBOOK. HE stared at the familiar glow of Sol with a sad, sick resignation.

"We're home," Emily whispered.

"Yes, we are." His voice was flat, devoid of everything except an overwhelming despair.

Emily twined her fingers through his cold, flaccid ones. "Jack, I'm resigning my commission. I'm quitting the military."

"They won't let you." He yanked his hand free then jumped to his feet. His notebook tumbled to the floor. He rounded on her with an angry glare. "We're heroes now. They'll parade us around in front of everyone. Us and that rat with his ungainly duck he built out of my ship!"

She took a step back. Her chin trembled. This wasn't the Jack she loved. "We can still be together."

"They won't let you resign. Ever!" He slashed his hand through the air. "There is no 'we.' There never will be. We're officers together and we can never be together any other way."

She dropped her gaze. The words he'd written in his notebook caught her eye. *Jack + Emily? Roses are red—* She raised her eyes, new hope blossoming in her heart. "Jack, do you love me?"

"It doesn't matter. It never will. Haven't you been listening to me?"

She stood in full command. "Jack, do you love me? Do you want a future together?" An idea grew with her hope, an awful, glorious, impossible idea.

"It doesn't matter what I want. My mother has won. I'll die doing what she wants. Never what I want." He snatched up his notebook, held it as if he would tear it in two.

She grasped his hands, gentled their wildness. "Jack." Just his name, filled with all the love she'd been hiding in her heart. "I know how we can be together. How we can escape."

He stilled. His gaze met hers, locked with hers. And slowly his smile grew to match hers.

"WHY ARE WE MEETING IN THE DOCKING BAY?" NIGEL'S NASAL VOICE didn't disturb Jack in the least, not today. "They'll be here in ten days. We can just ride it out. We'll be heroes."

"You'll be a hero." Jack's voice was mild.

"Put on the suit, Nigel." Emily's was cold and commanding.

"Why?"

"Because the hull of the lifeboat leaks. I've left you several patch kits and spare air canisters. The engine is completely gone, but you should be fine. The emergency beacon is rigged up for you. They'll find you without any trouble." Emily's smile was cruel and terrible. Jack loved her all the more for it. She was strong where he was weak.

"This is what you've been doing for the past hour while I've been fixing the drive?" Nigel's voice cracked with anger.

"We thank you for that," Jack said.

"And for the lesson in how to fix it if it should break again," Emily added. "Now get in the lifeboat. Unless you want to wander the stars with us."

"You're bonkers, complete raving lunatics!"

He struggled as Emily pushed the spacesuit into his arms. She was stronger, and more determined.

"You can't steal my Quantum Swan!"

"Quantum Duck," she corrected. "All of your schematics and notes are uploaded on the lifeboat's recording system. You can build it again."

He flailed his arms and shouted protests as Emily shoved him into the airlock.

"We'll wait five minutes for you to suit up," Emily said as the door slid shut.

Jack watched Nigel's lips move in vehement curses as he struggled into the suit. "Are you certain this is what you want?"

Emily threaded her fingers through his. "Absolutely. You and I are going to find a perfect world, with an ocean and flowers, and we are going to build ourselves a little white cottage on the seashore where we will raise our children."

She turned to face him as the airlock hissed.

"And maybe someday," she continued as Nigel rushed into the lifeboat before it launched, "they'll find our paradise."

"Until then?" He smiled as the lifeboat drifted away.

She gently laid her hand on his cheek, turned him to face her. Her smile was answer enough.

"Computer," he spoke with more authority than he had during his entire command previously. This time it was for him, not his mother. "Computer, activate Quantum Duck Drive. And play the overture from *The Flying Dutchman*."

The opening chords crashed through the ship as their lips met.

# Neo Nihon

## Paul Genesse

Six years behind schedule, a fleet of heavily armed colony ships with a large escort of military vessels appeared within striking distance of Neo Nihon. First Minister Sachiko Okura suppressed the mind-numbing fear of a global apocalypse and calmly assembled her entire cabinet with a class red nine alert message.

None of her ministers arrived bleary-eyed or disheveled as they entered the brightly lit command center with banks of screens deep below the parliament building at the heart of Neo Kyoto. The nine women and eight men all came within twenty minutes or less and showed few signs of alarm, which was a testament to their exceptional profession-alism as the urgent summons had never been used before and was reserved for the threat of an in-progress extra-planetary attack.

Sachiko wasted no time and made a gesture to begin recording the proceedings. She noted it was 3:34 A.M. As she stood, everyone present followed her lead. The Prime Minister held a polite bow for two breaths with her eyes on the floor. The ancient ritual of presenting one's neck, and head as a sign of trust, had never made her feel so vulnerable as it did now. The enemy fleet surrounding Neo Nihon made her feel like the sharpest sword ever made was about to cut off her head.

The ministers bowed in return, then sat on the silver and black chairs with sophisticated glowing user interfaces on the armrests and headrests.

Sachiko made fleeting eye contact with each person. "Honored Ministers," she said in formal Japanese, "I regret to inform you of the arrival of hundreds of armed spacecraft. Scans indicate that most of them are the long-overdue colony ships manufactured by our Neo Nihon Corporation. This fact was verified before we lost contact with our spaceport and satellite network.

"The force appears hostile. They are our ships, designed and manufactured because of Japanese ingenuity, but our countrymen are not in command. If our people still live, they are most likely trapped on Earth.

"This is what we know for certain: the fleet came through a Wheeler-Bridge forty-nine minutes ago, suppressed communications, and are now in a high orbit around Neo Nihon. The ships have not answered any of our hails, and have arrayed themselves to allow orbital bombardment of every region of the planet or rapid combat drone deployment."

Frowns and worried expressions flashed across the ministers' faces as they realized the entire fledgling colony might be destroyed at any moment.

Sachiko's confidence wavered and she leaned on the table. She permitted her dark eyes to meet those of Infrastructure Minister Takeshi Okura, her husband of thirty-one years, and the only non-military person present who knew as much as she did about the crisis. Takeshi nodded at her, and she stiffened her posture, regaining her famously serene composure. Takeshi had always been able to give her courage with only a glance. It had been this way ever since they met and married before leaving Japan and Earth forever.

"Our planetary defenses have been activated," Sachiko said, "but we do not have the ability to counter the number of ships facing us. We must seek other solutions." She bowed to Defense Minister Kiyoshi Hinato, whose eyes narrowed. Only Hinato knew the full scope of what she hinted at. His two predecessors had some knowledge, but they had been out of the defense ministry for a decade or more and the secret defensive plans of Neo Nihon had evolved into several unexpected directions, partially because of Sachiko's leadership.

"We will trust in our preparations," Sachiko said, "and after incorporating the new information about the enemy fleet into our models, Defense Minister Hinato and I believe it is as we feared all this time. The Chinese Military Corporation has seized control of the colony program on Earth and now threatens us here. They have used the transport ships meant for our own people to send soldiers and possibly their own colonists. The large number of CMC Jiangdao Class drone carriers confirms our conclusion." Sachiko bowed to Hinato.

"With your permission, Prime Minister Sachiko Okura-sama," the Defense Minister said, "I will present the probability of an attack and our chances of survival."

Sachiko sat down as Hinato spoke. He displayed real-time images on the table and wall screens, sampling from shots of the five-hundred ninety-seven ships arrayed against them. "I estimate the number of soldiers and navy personnel at no more than 600,000. Between 1.5 and 1.8 million combat drones of various models are also with their fleet."

Sachiko hid her dismay behind an expression of cool detachment. The estimates had increased since the first report. This even more over-whelming force would crush Neo Nihon in a matter of hours. The entire population was only three million scattered across the large planet, and only a tiny fraction of them were part of the military or safety officer core.

"To mount any significant resistance," Hinato said, "our builder drones will have to be re-tasked and armed with whatever is available. However, there is no time for such a course of action. The chances of defeating the invaders is close to zero, though we could mount small-scale warfare indefinitely if they spare a significant percentage of our popula-tion." He bowed and sat down.

Sachiko stood solemnly and stared into one of the many cameras recording the meeting. Her performance would have to be perfect if she was to be believed, and the enemy duped into trusting that Neo Nihon was no threat. She willed tears to her eyes by thinking of when her only child was born. Nenji was such a beautiful little boy and had become a perfect adult son, intelligent, respectful, and hard-working. She also remembered the birth of her first grandchild. Nenji and his lovely wife, Esumi, had presented the beautiful baby girl to Sachiko and said, "Dear Mother, to honor you, we have decided to give this child your namesake."

Tears flowed freely from Sachiko's eyes, but she kept a stern visage as if they meant nothing. Many would see this meeting. Friend and foe alike would judge her accordingly. "Honored Ministers, I am very sorry, but it would be fatal to our people to mount armed resistance. I shall offer our total surrender. I respectfully ask if any of you disagree. Let each minister speak freely for the record and if a majority believe differently, we shall make other plans."

One by one the ministers agreed with the futility of fighting such a tremendous force. Sachiko's husband spoke last, his spirit undaunted. "Neo Nihon is the only hope for our people on Earth," Takeshi said. "We shall be resilient as our ancestors have always been. We will endure any hardship. It is what we must do."

Sachiko blinked and wiped her eyes. She opened a channel to send a message to the enemy. The communications officer in the adjoining room confirmed a connection and Sachiko spoke in International English. "To the force in orbit around Neo Nihon, I am Prime Minister Sachiko Okura and speak for the entire colony. If your intention is to forcibly take control of this colony, we offer complete and unconditional surrender. We will not resist. I humbly request that you please refrain from attacking. We desire a peaceful resolution."

The communications officer signaled that the message had been received and that he was awaiting a reply. Nothing came for several moments and Sachiko considered sending her message again.

An alarm klaxon sounded. A glowing red warning kanji flashed urgently on the monitors. Had the enemy responded violently? She glanced at her husband and Defense minister Hinato as the alarm got louder. "Status report, please," Sachiko said into the security line.

"Prime Minister," the communications officer spoke rapidly in a high-pitched voice, "multiple enemy ships have discharged some kind of pulse wave. It's hitting us...now."

Sachiko expected the walls to shake, the ceiling to rumble, but she felt nothing. What manner of weapon was being unleashed? Was her surrender too late to stop the attack or had she provoked it? A few seconds seemed like an eternity as the ministers glanced nervously at each other, expecting the worst.

"*Sachi-ko.*" Takeshi slurred her name, his face drooping so much it appeared he was a ghastly caricature of the man she loved. He slumped to the floor, ineffectually trying to grab onto the table. She watched in horror as he collapsed in a heap as if all his bones had been removed.

Warning kanji filled every screen and lit the room in a crimson light. Sachiko leapt to her husband's side and cradled his head. Several others fell to the floor. Cries for help filled the chamber. Security officers and terrified assistants rushed inside.

"What's wrong?" Sachiko asked as Takeshi's eyes began to glaze over. She felt for a pulse in his neck and found none. "Takeshi!"

Unable to answer, Takeshi let out a wheezing breath.

"Help me, Doctor Ishibashi!" She turned toward the Health Minister, but the older man was also on the floor, apparently not breathing. Defense Minister Hinato lay motionless beside him, spittle leaking from the corner of his mouth.

"Takeshi!" She shouted desperately at her husband.

No response. His mouth hung open. She lifted Takeshi's head just as the light went out of his eyes.

Sachiko put him down as gently as she could and sprang toward the emergency closet. The automatic door slid open as she approached and the med bot emerged.

"Help him!" she ordered.

The six-armed bot instantly sped to Takeshi and began a rapid scan by running a glowing white sensor over his torso, followed by intensive resuscitation efforts to restart his heart. The med bot stopped a moment later and began simultaneously scanning the other injured people in the room.

"Don't stop!" Sachiko shouted.

"The patient, Mr. Takeshi Okura,"—the bot spoke with a woman's voice in an overly calm tone—"has suffered total nervous system destruction. He will not respond to any further emergency efforts and biomechanical support will not change the outcome. Regretfully, there is no chance of revival." The med bot went to each of the others affected by the pulse wave. All eight men were given the same pronouncement.

Sachiko realized with a jolt that none of the female ministers were hurt. She asked for a report from the communications officer. The line was silent. Sachiko opened the side door and entered the communications pod. All three of the male staff lay on the floor while the traumatized female officers stood over them helplessly. Med bots soon pronounced all the men dead and waited for instructions.

"Excuse me, please!" Sachiko shouted to the panicked staff. "I require your help."

"Yes," the four survivors, all women, responded as one and stood at attention. They looked at her with large eyes full of fear.

"Please fill the most critical empty work stations. I need to know what is happening in the entire colony. Report to me and the…surviving ministers as soon as possible. Please, work quickly and have the med bots remove the bodies."

Sachiko bowed and went to kneel beside her dead husband. His face had turned gray, his lips were blue, and his mouth hung garishly open. She considered turning him over as she could not bear seeing him like this, but instead covered his face with her lavender faux-silk scarf, the one he had given her on her sixty-fourth birthday a few months before.

News came in quickly, overwhelming the reduced staff in the communications center. The reports were clear. No females had been hurt by the unknown pulse wave weapon. However, all genetic males on Neo Nihon appeared to have been killed, though it would take days to verify. Men, boys, infants, even unborn male children. All of them. Preliminary tests revealed their entire autonomic nervous system had been ablated—which caused immediate death. An estimated 1.49 million male colonists, half the population, was presumed dead.

Sachiko felt numb. She refused to speak or acknowledge the information as it streamed in. Finally, she called her son. Nenji always answered, but when his wife, Esumi, answered the call, Sachiko's hopes disintegrated.

Esumi, please let me speak to Nenji."

"He won't wake up!" The terror in Esumi's voice made Sachiko feel feint.

"Esumi, please check for a pulse."

"Mother! Send help! Nenji! Wake up!" Esumi dropped the receiver. Sachiko listened to the young woman shout and cry. The wails of a frightened child entering the room and yelling for her father was all Sachiko could take. She terminated the call.

Nenji was dead. All the men were dead. No weapon like this had ever been used in the history of the human race. It had been unbelievable to Sachiko a moment before, but hearing Esumi's voice, and listening to her sweet granddaughter, little Sachiko, wailing for her father had finally made it real.

Updated alarm messages with sharp warning bleeps scrolled down the large monitors in the command room as they had for what seemed like hours. The volume and the flashing lights overwhelmed Sachiko and she could not take it anymore.

"Turn off these alarms right now! Stop all of them! Immediately!" Sachiko shouted as loud as she could and glowered at the duty officer.

Everyone stared at her in total astonishment. Sachiko heard her own words echoing inside her mind. Had she really just snapped like that? In front of everyone?

The alarms were silenced and only a faint beeping continued. The staff kept their distance and Sachiko felt her own rage radiating from her body, an aura of pure hatred that no one dared enter.

Sachiko paced for a moment, then found the scarf on the floor she had used to cover her husband's face before his body was dragged away. Why had she let the med bots take him? She had not said goodbye.

"At least Nenji died in his sleep," Sachiko mumbled to herself as she dropped to the cold floor and lost all track of time.

"Prime Minister, there is a message for you, please."

A communications officer led Sachiko to a terminal and let her watch the short recording. The ethnic looking Chinese man wearing a CMC military uniform spoke International English with a faint Mandarin accent.

"Prime Minister Sachiko Okura, representatives of the Chinese Military Corporation will formally accept the surrender of Neo Nihon. A shuttle will arrive outside your parliament complex shortly and you will get on it alone. Failure to comply will result in further attacks."

"Acknowledge the message." Sachiko returned to inform the surviving ministers. She left them to plan the public announcement and went to the office of Saito Nagata, the Deputy of Public Safety. His body was in the middle of a ring of his surviving staff who were all kneeling as they held a vigil. The other men who had been on duty or responded to the summons were also dead beside their stations. Most of the survivors wept openly. Some were in a daze.

Sachiko knelt beside the Deputy's body and bowed to him. All of the staff stared at her, clearly surprised to see their Prime Minister on the floor with them in this darkest of moments.

"We will not forget what has happened," Sachiko said, her voice trembling. "However, our friend, Deputy Nagata-san would want all of us to carry on and do what was needed for our people. I must request that all of you please help me prepare for my meeting with the leadership of the Chinese Military Corporation. I will soon formally submit our surrender."

"Prime Minister, how may we serve?" A steely-eyed woman, Okina Makoto, Deputy Nagata's Chief Director and one of Sachiko's oldest friends from their days in the diplomatic core on Earth, asked her. Sachiko hoped Okina would be here. Her friend was the guiding force behind Neo Nihon's investigative service and secret research division. Okina had worked closely with Defense Minister Hinato and his predecessors.

"We must learn everything we can about the CMC force," Sachiko said, "about what has happened on Earth, and especially their new weapon. I will require the most advanced surveillance, infiltrator information gathering, and crypto-deciphering bio-nanobots. I will soon be on their ship and they must suspect nothing."

"Yes, Prime Minister," Chief Okina said and began giving commands to her staff who ran off in several directions.

Sachiko worried that the bio-nanobots she would soon use would be detected. They were designed to appear as a person's own cells, and millions of them circulated inside everyone on Neo Nihon, preventing illnesses, helping keep the water supply safe from bacteria and viruses not present on Earth, and allowing the colonists to thrive in the alien environment.

The Neo Nihon colony had spent vast amounts of resources on developing this new technology, but did the CMC have scanners that would detect the spying devices? If Sachiko made it aboard their ship and they found out would they blow her out an airlock? Someone else would have to carry on, but this great task was hers, and she could not fail her people. The lives of the survivors on Neo Nihon and those Japanese waiting on Earth—if they were still alive—were her responsibility.

"Okina," Sachiko said, "The CMC must never know what your office has done tonight. Your staff must be given new identities, memory replacements, and sent away to await your orders. Purge your systems of any records of my being here."

"Yes, Prime Minister. Please, excuse me…" Okina hesitated.

"Yes."

"Our defenses are in place," Okina said, "but what will we do to them in the end?"

Sachiko heard the anger in Okina's voice. She wanted to know about retribution. How would the enemy be made to suffer? How would they be made to regret this barbaric atrocity committed against a peaceful people?

"Okina-san, we will not deal with them as they have dealt with us," Sachiko said. "They have made a fatal mistake which we shall not repeat."

Okina blinked. She did not understand.

"They are greedy, Okina-san, and know nothing of war. They should have killed us all."

GLOWING ARROWS DIRECTED SACHIKO TO FOLLOW THE SAME SHORT PATH out of the unmanned CMC shuttle that she followed in. She paused at the doorway, her legs shaky from the harrowing ride. At the bottom of the ramp stood a squad of human-sized battle drones in sleek armor that reflected the dull gray metal walls. Scanners on the drones' torsos passed over her body from head to toe and she felt a flush of heat. They scanned her a second time, and Sachiko thought they had detected the bio-nanobots.

The drones paused for a long moment before one of them motioned for her to come aboard the ship. Sachiko walked meekly down the ramp and pretended to stumble at the bottom. She caught herself by grabbing one of them, her hands on the machine's chest.

She wiped one hand over a seam near the shoulder joint of the drone, implanting thousands of bio-nanobots that would eventually infiltrate the memory core and communications center.

The squad of battle drones surrounded her and guided Sachiko to a room where a simple unpadded metal chair sat at the foot of a crescent shaped stage. Looming above her were five empty chairs with elaborate armrests and red cushions. She sat and focused on her breathing, ignoring the metallic taste in her mouth from ingesting a solution of bio-nanobots.

Nearly twenty minutes later, a door behind the stage opened and five men in their fifth or sixth decade of life entered. Their CMC military uniforms were filled with red stars over eagles. All were ethnic Chinese in appearance, though one, the youngest at perhaps fifty-five, had a fair amount of European genes in him, judging by his Caucasian facial structure. He was probably descended from one of the powerful North American bloodlines that had mingled with the ruling Chinese caste.

"Prime Minister Okura," a distinguished man with a wide jaw, and silver hair addressed her. "I am First Admiral Zhou Guang and the ranking CEO of this battle group."

Sachiko got on her knees and bowed in the ancient way, keeping her eyes on the floor.

"There is no need for another strike on your colony," Admiral Zhou said. "I wish to end these hostilities. Will you sign an unconditional surrender?"

"Honored Admiral Zhou Guang," Sachiko spoke his name before ending her bow and looking up, though she did not make eye contact, "I will sign as you request."

A large screen lifted from the floor beside her. Sachiko grasped the screen and pulled it toward her, transferring a large amount of bio-nanobots to the device. She read the short document written in the customary legal language, International English. It was brutally simple and precise. The people of Neo Nihon would accept any request from the CMC military authority without protest.

This was not the time for resistance. Without delay, Sachiko signed with her finger, then imprinted both her hands to provide a DNA sample, transferring even more of the espionage devices.

"Our forces will begin ground deployment," Admiral Zhou said. "Do you anticipate any of your people will resist?"

"Honored Admiral Zhou Guang," Sachiko said, "if you allow me to speak to them, the citizens of Neo Nihon will comply with any order you give."

"That is my expectation," Admiral Zhou said, and nodded at his companions. "You will make the speech from here. The key points have already been drafted for you. Please review them now and we shall record the broadcast."

The screen changed and Sachiko read quickly, hiding her horror. The surviving women of Neo Nihon would be forced to serve the invading soldiers in all ways, and would in effect become their property. Women with the ability to bear children would do so as quickly as possible. Birth control was forbidden. The genders of the offspring would be equally divided between male and female, and standard genetic enhancements would be made. The mistake of having too many sons, as had happened on Earth in the United Chinese Republic, would not be repeated.

When Sachiko finished reading, her mouth was dry as desert sand, and the urge to urinate was so sharp it made her whole body shiver.

"Are you well?" Admiral Zhou asked. "I expected a woman with your pedigree and well-known accomplishments to be more resilient."

"Admiral Zhou, please excuse me. The flight was quite unsettling."

"Of course," he said. "Are you prepared to read the speech, or do you need a moment to settle yourself?"

"Thank you, Admiral, if I may have a short time, and also use the toilet."

He grinned. "No, you may not. You will read the speech right now. We do not tolerate delays, and you will comply with our schedule."

Sachiko kowtowed, and thought his juvenile tactics to fluster her were poorly done. She decided to play along, and realized that it would be more advantageous if he did not respect her. "Yes, Admiral," she said timidly, "I am ready."

"You may proceed."

Sachiko remained on her knees and stared into the camera, and at the prepared speech on the screen behind it. "Citizens of Neo Nihon, I have signed the formal surrender of our colony and the Chinese Military Corporation is now in total control. CMC ground forces will commence

landing immediately. No form of protest, even non-violent, will be toler-
ated. The penalty for resistance will be swift and severe. We must fully
comply with all directives.

"Directive one: Dispose of the dead bodies immediately. All bodies
must be buried or cremated within twenty-four hours, starting now.

"Directive two: all citizens selected will be required to house at least
one soldier, and serve them dutifully in all ways requested.

"Directive three: Comply with all orders of the Chinese Military
Corporation.

"We are fortunate to have such a strongly led institution guiding us in
the times ahead, which will be filled with prosperity for our colony. The
two greatest corporations are now combined as one. We are all citizens
under the protection of the CMC. In Unity We Trust."

Sachiko read the last line and bowed low. She desperately wanted to
say more and thought of an ancient speech delivered at the end of a
terrible war the Japanese people had lost. She risked the ire of Admiral
Zhou and said, "Honored citizens, we must carry on as our people have
always done after a great loss. I beg you, on behalf of all the generations
to come, endure the unendurable, and suffer what is insufferable.

"Let us continue as one family from generation to generation,
welcoming the new members of our colony who have traveled from the
dying world of all our ancestors. We must be mindful of the heavy
burden of responsibility to continue no matter what, and of the long
road before us." Sachiko bowed again, eyes on the floor until she heard
one man applauding.

Admiral Zhou stopped clapping. He grinned at the officers beside
him. "You see, this woman will be our mouthpiece."

The men laughed. The one with the Caucasian features made a
crude joke in Mandarin. She thought he said that Sachiko was too old to
warm his bed, but he could find an appropriate use for her mouth if she
stayed on her knees.

She pretended not to understand. "I am your servant, Admiral
Zhou," Sachiko said humbly, while thinking it was obvious why these
men had been chosen to remain behind on Earth when their betters had
been allowed to travel to the Chinese colony.

"You will be our puppet for as long as you are useful," Zhou said.

"Yes, Admiral Zhou. I will not disappoint you, and neither will the
people of Neo Nihon."

Four battle drones escorted Sachiko down a hallway to a tiny lavatory.
She voided her bladder and hoped the millions of nanobots in her urine

would be able to do their job and find their way into the data core of the ship. She also blew her nose and rinsed out her mouth sending even more spy devices into the closed system of the CMC vessel. She had to learn about the weapon that had exterminated the males of Neo Nihon. She also needed to understand what had happened on Earth in the past decade when no communication pods had come with news, and the arrival date of the Japanese colony ships had come to pass six years before. What had the CMC done to the people of Japan and her family specifically? Knowing the fate of her mother and father, since she had lost half her loved ones in the colony, was of utmost importance.

The battle drones marched Sachiko to the same shuttle and she rocketed away from Admiral Zhou's flagship. She expected at any moment for Admiral Zhou's smug face to appear in a monitor. He would taunt her and gloat about his discovery of the espionage devices planted aboard his ship.

The shuttle shook and pitched. The thunderous sound of reentry assaulted Sachiko. Would the CMC just detonate the craft and be done with her, blame her death on an unforeseen problem? Or would they do nothing, as their anti-nanobot systems would prevent any breaches of their networks?

A loud boom made Sachiko flinch. She tried to calm herself and considered an even worse scenario. What if the CMC compromised the bio-nanobot devices and fed false information, setting up Sachiko and her conspirators for a catastrophic failure?

The CMC must not be underestimated. They had somehow captured the Neo Nihon Corporation colony ships and developed a doomsday weapon of unparalleled power. Perhaps she was foolish to oppose them now and the defensive strategy of the colony would come to nothing.

Sachiko met with her spy chief, Okina Makoto behind the thick metal door of a walk-in freezer in the kitchen inside the parliament building. The staff had all gone home to attend to their newly assigned "partners." Okina checked the area thoroughly and deployed counter-surveillance devices. The faint smell of frozen fish filled the room.

Sachiko was desperate to learn if the infiltrator bio-nanobots had been able to broadcast anything. For three weeks she had no indication of success. Her life consisted of dealing with the daily troop landings and the assignment of CMC soldiers to the homes of grieving widows. So far she had been spared the dishonor of her own live in "partner," but Admiral Zhou had visited her once himself, making clear in humiliating fashion that he was in absolute control.

She considered a memory removal of the painful event, but she wanted to remember, and it motivated her to press on.

Okina's request for a meeting had given Sachiko renewed hope. "You have news?"

"Congratulations, Prime Minister," Okina said. "The devices you planted are working. "The transmission started yesterday."

Sachiko felt joy for the first time since the attack. "Is it authentic? Not misinformation from the CMC?"

"I believe it's real. The data was hidden inside normal traffic from Zhou's flagship."

"Will they detect it?"

"The chance of them finding it is not statistically relevant," Okina said.

"Good. What did you learn?"

"Prime Minister, what you planted on the battle drone was unsuccessful in breaking the firewall, but we have a lot of other information. There's a lot to analyze. I'll need help."

"You'll have help," Sachiko said, "but not yet. What strategic information did you find?"

"Most everything we've learned from the CMC soldiers is true. The pulse wave weapon has no defense and can be used against either gender, or both simultaneously. It was used by both sides during the war, but the CMC started it, not the African Federation. Men only were targeted first in the initial attacks, then both genders were hit at the end in desperation."

"Do you have casualty numbers?"

"Remnants of the CMC ground armies, and fragments of the civilian populations are living along the equator in Indonesia, the Philippines, and Central America. Male survivor estimates range from four to five million planet-wide, but no one knows for certain. Virtually all the women are dead. Only those few females in orbital stations or on spacecraft survived the final strikes."

"Wait, how many are dead?" Sachiko asked.

Okina's eyes misted over. "Five billion."

Sachiko covered her face with her hands. The calamity on Neo Nihon was minuscule compared to what happened on their homeworld. The people left behind had destroyed themselves instead of waiting in line for their turn to travel to the colonies and escape the ice age and the wars plaguing Earth.

"Prime Minister?" Okina asked.

"Yes."

"The devices you planted on the computer screen have gotten into the network of Admiral Zhou's staff, but not the most secure files."

Sachiko allowed herself to smile, but when she saw Okina's grim expression her excitement faded.

"We know their plan," Okina said.

"Go on."

"The CMC is the only military left with the pulse wave technology. They will use Neo Nihon as their base and strike from here once they are ready. They're planning to conquer all the colony worlds one by one and bring their remaining soldiers on Earth to live with any sizable population. They will annihilate the males on all the colonies and replace them with their own. We are their first test. They will replicate this strategy everywhere they go in the future. The CMC fleet will return to Earth as soon as they can, and gather more troops before they launch an attack against another planet."

"What news of Japan?" Sachiko asked, a coldness enveloping her whole body.

"The CMC estimates there are many pockets of male survivors in the underground shelters throughout the country, but they're not worth the resources to eradicate."

"How long do we have before the colony ships are ready to return to Earth for reinforcements?"

"The CMC leadership wants them to depart in twenty-two months. It will take that long for their energy requirements to be replenished and for the ships to be made ready for another Wheeler-Bridge crossing."

"How many soldiers will they bring back?"

"The maximum, approximately 600,000. The troops on Earth have been told that two or three men will share one woman here until they are redeployed to other colonies."

"Have we not been humiliated enough?" Adrenaline surged through Sachiko. She took a ragged breath to calm herself. Rage must not cloud her judgment. The CMC was not invincible. They had seized Neo Nihon Corporation colony ships, which were the most advanced vessels ever built. Technical help and orbital maintenance facilities were imperative to them, and they needed help with everything. The CMC had anticipated a passive population, and a secure base on a rich world.

"We must analyze and exploit everything now," Sachiko said. "Contact all your staff and activate our hidden assets according to the defense plans. Use every resource we have available to crack their networks. Have our people work on this project as hard as I know they are able."

"Prime Minister," Okina said, "it will be a great risk."

"Okina-san, we have less than twenty-two months to find a way to defeat our enemy. If we do not succeed by then, our people may never recover. The CMC reinforcements must not arrive."

"Yes, Prime Minister."

"I will also require more of the espionage devices. I will get us access to all of the CMC's data centers and codes."

"How?" Okina asked.

"It may take months, but I will find a way. Admiral Zhou is the key."

"PRIME MINISTER SACHIKO OKURA," ADMIRAL ZHOU SAID, "YOU WILL be pleased to know that the colony ship program is two weeks ahead of schedule. The technicians you have provided are working well, despite the conditions aboard the ships."

"That is welcome news, Admiral," Sachiko said. She sat on the other side of a red glass desk inside his spacious office aboard his personal shuttle, which had landed outside the parliament building.

They were alone and he stared at her, saying nothing for an uncomfortably long moment. Perhaps he was giving her time to ponder why he had made his unannounced visit. During the grueling eighteen months since the CMC had invaded, Admiral Zhou had made only one other visit to the capital, and never before had he stationed so many guards around the parliament building.

"Sachiko, I'm not here to congratulate you."

"Admiral Zhou, I do not require praise. How may I be of service?"

"No, it is I who will help you for once."

"I am honored," she said.

Zhou leaned back in his large chair with data transfer ports and controls on the armrests. "Have you read the reports from your citizens about their level of satisfaction with the current situation?"

Sachiko demurred. "I have avoided them on the recommendation of my advisors."

His expression showed pity. "Sachiko, you are the most hated woman on this planet. Your citizens despise you more than they hate us, and we murdered their sons and husbands."

The people had been told Sachiko and Admiral Zhou were consensual lovers, laughing together and planning the dishonor of the people of Neo Nihon. He had only visited her one time, long ago during the first weeks of the occupation, but she chose not to publicly dispute the rumors.

"Forgive me, Admiral," Sachiko said, "have I displeased you? I have done my best to carry out all CMC directives and pushed my people beyond their breaking point to help the CMC accomplish all its goals."

"I am not displeased, but you have made yourself irreplaceable."

"Admiral, I do not understand."

"Sachiko, there are plots to assassinate you. Your beloved polite and honorable people want you dead."

Sachiko averted her eyes, then showed him an expression of surprise.

"I can't risk leaving you here in Neo Kyoto. I'm taking you up to my flagship. Your new office will be there, where I can keep you safe and we can work more closely together."

She stood up and took a step to the side of his desk. "Thank you very much, Admiral, but is there no way I can remain on Neo Nihon with my family?"

"I will have your staff, your granddaughter, and daughter-in-law transferred with you. They may also be in danger. Your daughter-in-law's dear husband, Major Chun Liu will be my new liaison officer."

Sachiko shuddered when she thought of Chun Liu. His treatment of poor Esumi, and his threats to little Sachiko, who still asked about her father made her blood boil. Sachiko hid her true feelings and stepped toward the Admiral with gratitude on her face and adoration in her eyes. "Thank you very much," she said, and reached for him, intent on touching his face and kissing him on the lips.

Zhou caught her wrists shook and his head, keeping her away from him. "That is not necessary." He gently pushed her away.

"I'm sorry," Sachiko said, averting her eyes and wondering if he knew what she was trying to do.

"I have something to show you," Zhou said.

He sat Sachiko at his desk and showed her a monitor screen with Okina Makoto's face on it.

Sachiko gasped.

"You know this woman," Zhou said.

"She works in the parliament. She's an old friend."

He shook his head. "No, this is leader of the plotters who wants to kill you." He played a recording of Okina in a dark room speaking into a camera.

"Everything I have done was for the people of Neo Nihon. We will no longer allow the cruel and honorless, Sachiko Okura to speak for us. She is a tool of the CMC and cares nothing for our lives. She will cause all of us to pay for her vanity and her schemes must be stopped. She will die for her crimes, and though I will not live to see her assassination, my sisters will carry our the task and fight to the end. Death to the tyrant, and death to the CMC."

Okina put a pistol to her head and pulled the trigger. Her head exploded in a shower of blood and brain matter.

Sachiko pushed the screen away and held the armrests of Admiral Zhou's chair with a death grip.

"My men found her moments after she killed herself," Zhou said. "The message was sent, but not many will see it. Still it's a pity we didn't take her alive."

"What about the others?" Sachiko asked.

"Do not worry," Admiral Zhou said. "I have taken care of everything. My men will track all the plotters down and pull up their organization by the roots. We have captured several of them already and are punishing them now."

He played a live feed from six different rooms. CMC soldiers tortured screaming women. He stood beside her, grinning at the depravity committed by his men. He turned up the volume so she could hear the cries and pleas for mercy.

"This is not necessary," Sachiko said.

"This is their penalty. We have all the information needed to continue our hunt, but they must be taught a lesson. You see here only the beginning of what will happen to those who oppose us. Their children will pay a harsher price."

Sachiko seized her moment and slapped Admiral Zhou across his face, her palm connecting solidly with his cheek.

Surprised, he backed away and drew his sidearm.

Sachiko fell to her knees, touching her forehead to the floor. "Admiral, please forgive me. You are within your rights to do anything you wish. I am a foolish mother and grandmother with a soft heart. I am very sorry for touching you and beg for your forgiveness."

"I have broken your famous composure at last," he said. "Get up. You're an old woman and I have no need of you on your knees. Leave me, now."

She stood, avoiding his gaze and tried to shuffle past him. Zhou put his gun to her head and grabbed her by the throat. "Never speak of this to anyone."

She nodded, fear in her eyes.

He dug his fingers painfully into her, almost choking off her air. "Never touch me again." Zhou pushed her away and she fell to the floor.

Sachiko fled the room as fast as she could, somewhat surprised she was still alive, and hopeful she had accomplished her task. It would take time for the bio-nanobots she planted on Zhou's face when she slapped him to do their jobs. Would they see enough for Sachiko to find a way to take control of his system? Perhaps the bots she planted on his armchair controls or the desk screen would be able to penetrate his data core? Time would tell and she would likely never have another chance.

By the next morning, Prime Minister Sachiko, all her staff, and her surviving family, along with two hundred female technicians and their CMC partners were aboard Zhou's flagship. She stared at the large viewscreen in her new office. The blue planet with vast oceans and beautiful white cloud formations so similar to Earth took her breath away.

She silently thanked Okina-san for her tremendous sacrifice. The spy chief knew too much and had requested to die. It was the best strategic move.

They had come too close now, and Sachiko's plan was also ahead of schedule. The angry women Okina Makoto had recruited did not know they were part of an elaborate hoax, but they would divert the attention of Admiral Zhou's secret police for many precious months. Innocent citizens would be tortured and killed, but they would die for a higher cause. Victory in war without casualties was not only impossible, but foolish to contemplate. The real question was how those lives would be spent.

SACHIKO STOOD BEHIND ADMIRAL ZHOU IN THE BRIGHTLY LIT COMMAND center of his flagship. Crew in crisp brown uniforms and small caps worked diligently as she watched the entire CMC fleet begin their last exercise before returning to Earth, which was scheduled in two days. All of the colony ships, and their escorts positioned themselves for the opening of a Wheeler-Bridge. The long column pointed away from Neo Nihon and toward the yellow sun, almost identical to Earth's.

"Admiral Zhou, the fleet reports their crews are at battle stations," the Executive Officer said. "All ships are at status one A."

"Follow the acceleration protocol," Admiral Zhou ordered.

The fleet began slowly advancing, their systems linked together with the memory cores on the colony ships. Without absolute precision of movement, some ships would be damaged while inside the Wheeler-Bridge, and could be destroyed.

Sachiko observed the drill, as she had several others, ready to assist in any way required. The exercise progressed with nothing more than minor telemetry errors, and at the end Admiral Zhou sent a recording to all the ships praising a job well done.

As the bulk of CMC naval crews were in their debriefing meetings, Sachiko sent a congratulatory video message to all the technicians, engineers, system designers, and all the other Neo Nihon women onboard the ships. She had hand picked and worked with them over the past four months to help make the ready the colony ships, and service the military escorts who would soon leave for Earth. She ended the message by bowing and touching her heart with two fingers.

Some of the women in the video feeds mimicked her gesture. Moments later, Sachiko watched the alarms light up the screens in the command center.

"What's happening?" Admiral Zhou asked, as he stared at live images of the fleet, which was still in a slow moving cylindrical column formation.

"Admiral, we're getting reports that several pulse wave weapon systems have activated, locked on to all ships and are preparing to discharge."

"What?" Zhou and his assistants looked stunned and darted toward the monitors.

"They're going to fire, sir!" A terrified officer shouted.

"Shut them all down!" Zhou screamed. "Send the abort codes!"

"The codes aren't working! The Colony ships are blocking the signal. The weapons are going to fire in twelve seconds. Eleven! Ten!"

"Admiral Zhou," Sachiko said, "allow me to help you understand."

He spun around fast, bewilderment, fear, and anger playing across his face.

"I wanted to watch you suffer," Sachiko said.

"Six seconds!"

Admiral Zhou's face paled and his eyes widened.

"Five!"

"This death will have to suffice," Sachiko said, "but know that your greed and stupidity have lost this war, and when I'm done the CMC will be obliterated."

Alarms flashed and screeched.

Zhou collapsed along with all the men in the room.

Sachiko reached down and took a handful of his silver hair. She jerked his head so he was looking at her then spit in his face as he died. She dropped him as he gasped like a suffocating fish out of water. She let his head bounce hard on the metal floor and admired the quality of the sound.

Female technicians entered the command center and took up positions at key terminals. Sachiko bowed to them before standing in front of a bank of signaling monitors. She tied the lavender scarf Takeshi had given her around her neck, then connected her personal data-pack to the system core, prepared several prewritten commands, and turned on the broadcast channel. She connected to the fleet, and all the receiving stations on Neo Nihon. "This is Prime Minister Sachiko Okura. I am now in command of the entire fleet, including all battle drones. The CMC personnel in the fleet are dead."

The camera tilted to reveal Admiral Zhou's body and the other dead officers. Sachiko watched the startled reaction of soldiers in various video feeds. She also saw groups of women smiling and bowing.

"To the CMC soldiers on the surface of Neo Nihon. Many of you have behaved inhumanely in the past twenty-two months since you've occupied this colony. You have abused the women here and it will not continue. Satisfaction reports have been submitted by all of the colony women, and health reports have also been generated from their medical nanobots. It has been found that forty-six point eight percent of you CMC soldiers have committed heinous crimes and offenses against at least one female colonist. I deem you unfit to live among us. There will be no trials. Please consider these executions as a warning to those of you who remain among us."

Sachiko watched the panicked faces of solders in her video feeds. She pressed the command function on her data pack and verified the order, then initiated the protocol by a DNA scan of her finger. Bio-nanobots had entered all of the CMC soldiers through the water supply and had been tasked hours before to gather near the brainstems of the offending men. Anti-nanobot technology had been bypassed entirely.

Patiently, Sachiko waited for the signal to reach the condemned. A few seconds later micro explosions severed their brainstems and 248,179 CMC criminals died.

"To those of you CMC soldiers left alive, I have this message: you may be asked to leave your assigned residence. Some of you may be allowed to remain. I urge each of you to behave in a respectful manner toward your hostess. If you do so, you will be welcome in our society."

The video feeds showed mayhem and chaos as the survivors reacted to seeing so many men die in front of them. Sachiko waited for a long moment before continuing.

"Residents of Neo Nihon, if I may please have your attention. I wish to inform you that later today I will lead the majority of the fleet back to Earth. Any surviving Japanese citizens will be rescued and brought up to the colony ships. Estimates are that a few hundred thousand have survived. I will bring them here.

"CMC soldiers, and any others left on Earth will be killed with the pulse wave weapon after rescue operations are concluded. The CMC or their allies cannot be permitted to survive and plot a counter attack upon us or any other colony. All manufacturing and tech sites on Earth will also be destroyed. The pulse wave weapon must never be constructed again, and those weapons we possess will be dismantled.

"I thank you very much for your attention, and I ask for your patience in the days ahead. An interim Prime Minister will be selected when Parliament reconvenes in three days. The original constitution and laws of Neo Nihon will be restored and the war powers mandate suspended.

"When I return from Earth I will submit my official resignation as your Prime Minister. The wartime clauses will then no longer apply and I will stand trial for any crime it is deemed I have committed.

"Please understand that everything I did was for the survival of the people of Neo Nihon. I have followed the defensive plans drafted over the past years with a goal to preserve the lives of our people at any cost. I humbly thank the citizens of Neo Nihon for the opportunity to serve you. This has been the greatest honor of my life."

Sachiko's eyes filled with honest tears. She bowed low and thought about her granddaughter, Little Sachiko, and about the family she had lost in the CMC invasion. She wondered what her husband, Takeshi would think of what she had done, then switched off the broadcast channel. Historians might judge her harshly, but her people and the many colonies would survive because the choices she made.

Once the fleet had returned from Earth, Sachiko would consider sparing her people the ordeal of a trial. Others would lead now. Perhaps she would follow brave Okina-san's example, and take her own life. Had Sachiko not suffered enough? She had learned far too much about war, but had done her duty. Thankfully, Neo Nihon was victorious and would prosper. There would be peace, and Sachiko's great task would soon be over.

# The Last Ray of Light

## Wulf Moon

*Editor's Note: The following story was originally published in the May 18, 1978 issue of* Science World, *magazine. Moon was fifteen at the time his story was accepted, and it was his first professional sale. Since then, Moon has gone on to have a story published in a Star Trek anthology, to write a conclusion to one of Nora Roberts' mystery novels, and more. The story is reprinted here with only minor grammar and punctuation edits. Hopefully, it will inspire young writers to submit their stories to a wide variety of venues, and to keep improving their craft.*

*Author's Note: Science World didn't generally publish science fiction, though this story did happen to be about a hyperloop/vactrain, decades before Elon Musk theorized building one through Tesla. While men as far back as Jules Verne's son Michel had written about pneumatic tube travel, I didn't know that. I had nothing to read on such things in our small town in Wisconsin—internet didn't exist, there were no search engines, and the best I had for research was a tiny school library. But here's the point: I wasn't handicapped at all. Like every kid, I had within easy reach the best tool possible: Imagination.*

*This was the Seventies. An energy crisis crushed the country. The news made me dream about a fuel starved future world. How would people travel? What if that system failed? What price would my protagonist pay to save those trapped inside? Forty years later, you get to see into a boy's imagination.*

*What's more, I'm thrilled this tale has been resurrected in an anthology where proceeds help students reach for the stars! Just forgive my naiveté about how computers might communicate in the future—our school's computer lab had the only computer I had seen, and those of you in the know (i.e., Ancient Ones) will understand why the computer in my story says "STOP" at the end of every sentence.*

"This is car PM7-T. Request aid from Dock 5. Repeat, request aid for car PM7-T."

Xenon spun around just as he was about to leave the computer component production plant. Had he heard a voice over the com-system?

"Car PM7-T. Emergency. Request aid."

Again a faint sound passed down the corridor.

Was it possible that someone was still in the building? The computer read-out on the screen had shown that all cars were at their platforms. There shouldn't be anyone left in this sector. Unless…there had been a malfunction.

He raced back down the hall to the terminal of the dock. In five minutes the cooling system would automatically turn off to conserve the planet's dwindling fuel supplies. With the triple suns reaching their maximum intensity in another fifteen minutes, the atmosphere inside would quickly rise to 110°C. If there was someone locked in one of the cars—and he hoped to God there wasn't—their blood would slowly boil.

Standing in the terminal of the dock, Xenon pressed his electromagnetically charged identification ring into the "INPUT" slot. A humming sound came from the computer as it analyzed the ring's clearance data. The screen and buttons lit up, revealing the words, **"COMPUTER SHUTDOWN: 5:07 MINUTES STOP."**

He slapped the side of the panel. Only five minutes of computer aid…and someone may be trapped. The com-system was silent.

"Where are they!" he muttered under his breath.

As if in response, a voice sounded.

"Dock 5, this is car PM7-T. Repeat, car PM7-T. Emergency, car locked in tube."

Xenon took no time to respond as he flipped off the cover to the control panel and fingered down glistening square buttons.

"Perpetual Motion tube 7," he muttered at last. Punching in that information, his fingers moved on to oval buttons. As he pushed in T, the circuits of the computer locked into the transportation system. A second later the screen lit up.

"PM7-T PRESENT AT DOCK 5 STOP SHUTDOWN: 4:17 MINUTES STOP."

It couldn't be. He pressed "VIDEO SCANNER" and again modules and components clicked into place. The three dimensional screen revealed tube 7, but no car was there.

"Great, just great," he moaned as he switched the video scanner to "INTERIOR." The screen revealed the faces of two men and one woman—one of whom he recognized from the research quadrant.

"Argon! What's wrong with the car? You realize, don't you, that in less than twenty minutes we'll be nothing but steam."

Desperation marked the faces of the trapped car crew members. Argon moved closer to the viewer. He ran fingers through his tousled hair.

"The frictional force regulator went haywire. It flew up to a ten and we stopped dead. Drained out the com-system of our car for a full ten minutes. Why didn't this show up on the computer's emergency tables?"

Xenon shook his head in perplexity. "Haven't got the slightest idea. Your dead stop might have overpowered the circuits. Can you get the friction regulator back down to a zero?"

"Already fixed it," replied Argon. "But that stop gave it an awful beating. Only goes down to 1.5."

"Good enough," he responded. "Rock the car forward with your bodies to give it enough force to start moving. After that, perpetual motion will take over and you can start praying you'll make it in time."

"Nothing doing. I've already tried it. The computers shut down the anti-gravity pulsators and we've got one long slope to climb to the dock. We're just sittin' here like a rock. Any more suggestions?"

Xenon pounded his fist down on the computer. "That's just swell. The automatic time regulators switched them off four minutes ago. They aren't scheduled to activate until eight tomorrow morning."

Argon and his companions nervously sat back in their chairs. Though the cooling system was still working, thick beads of perspiration dribbled down their foreheads.

Xenon tapped his fingers on the computer console. He was desperately trying to think of how to get them out.

"Hold on, I might have it yet," he yelled in sudden inspiration.

Xenon put his hand in a pocket and pulled out a lightweight blasting repair tool.

"I'm going to disconnect the time regulator from the anti-grav and it should—I hope—switch on."

"SHUTDOWN: 2:23 MINUTES STOP."

BLASTED BY AN INTENSE BEAM OF LIGHT FROM THE REPAIR TOOL, THE plate covering the time regulator vaporized. Xenon thrust his hands into the space, fingering over a mass compiling of modules, circuits, and components. The anti-gravity modules were in red. Only a computer maintenance specialist would know which controlled which tube, so he blew them all out.

"SHUTDOWN: 1:18 MINUTES STOP."

"Try it now!" Xenon yelled.

Shaking forward, the people in the car got it to move—slower than the force they had exerted because of the frictional pull.

Victory shouts sounded over the com-system as Xenon returned to the control panel. Punching out computer supplied distance figures and rates of speed, he calculated their arrival. He stared, dumbfounded, at the blinking letters.

"PM7-T ARRIVAL TO DOCK 5:26:39 MINUTES STOP."

They would arrive…ten minutes too late.

"SHUTDOWN: 0:37 MINUTES STOP."

Thinking quickly, Xenon pressed "LOCK OPEN" for tubes 7 and 6.

"Be ready for anything," he called into the com-system.

Xenon raced out of the terminal while there were still lights to guide him. Just ahead, he saw the two open locks. He could see the number 6 through the transparent tube on the car inside. Basically, the car was a cylinder of unbreakable glass, powered by a single explosive burst from the rear. He flung himself inside the car just as the lights went out.

Fingers skipping down the control panel, Xenon punched on the auxiliary lighting and reduced the friction to zero. The car lunged forward. Xenon's body smashed against the control panel as the car moved down the tube.

Hands poised over the control panel, Xenon punched in a crossover to tube 7. Then he raced to the rear of the car and pried open the panel over the power mechanism. That mechanism was designed to give the car its one burst of energy. Xenon smiled as he noted that the fuel tank held over a gallon of the precious ruby-red fluid that could be exploded by any spark. That gallon of fuel packed enough power to make the car move all the way into the tube 7 intersection and around the entire building in less than ten minutes. Normally that much fuel would last two weeks, but this was no time to worry about the planet's dwindling fuel supplies.

Xenon flattened himself against the floor and sighted the repair tool at the point of ignition. Eyes closed, he pressed the trigger. A beam of intense light slashed out.

Xenon didn't hear the explosion because there was no air outside to transmit sound. But he felt it. His body bounced off the floor…into the wall. The instrument panel and chairs squeaked with the force—but everything remained intact.

Dizzily, Xenon stood up. He couldn't feel any motion but he realized that the car must be traveling at a tremendous rate of speed. Climbing into the control section, he snapped the impact shield over him in expectation of what was to come. The crossover into tube 7 was a blur, but he recognized it. It wouldn't be long now.

The temperature slowly rose as minutes ticked by. By now the others should realize that they wouldn't make it in time. Xenon had no way of communicating his plans to them. Xenon ripped his shirt off. The heat was becoming unbearable. Sweat seeped down his body and stung his eyes. Breathing became more and more difficult. He tried to remain motionless.

A point of light glowed ahead. Xenon only hoped the occupants of car PM7-T would be ready for the impact. He could not tune up the friction control to slow his car down without losing precious seconds.

If only they could see him, they would have a moment to prepare… BOOM!!! The entire control flew apart, and Xenon was knocked to the floor.

Pulling himself from the debris, he gazed into the other car. The seats had broken off with the occupants still in them. But the control section remained intact. Xenon looked to where the frictional force regulator was located. Only jagged edges remained.

"Get to that regulator!" he gasped as Argon stood up.

Argon pulled himself to the control panel and tuned it up. Xenon could barely see Dock 5 approaching in the dim darkness. The friction increased and held as the cars slowed to a stop. Xenon fell into the corridor as the others fell out—wheezing and gasping. They flung themselves into the exit chute and slid down, down, down into the cool underground city.

"Is that the whole story?" the voice repeated. Xenon shook himself back to reality.

"Yes," he replied bitterly. The computers around him blinked and flashed as they analyzed the information.

"Your actions have been found in violation of laws G-117 and E-523. Destruction of government property and waste of diminishing fuel. Do you accept these charges?"

The voice from the speakers was cold and vicious—as all council rooms were programmed to be.

Xenon gazed around the room, not knowing where to direct his voice.

"Accept these charges? What are you doing, offering them to me on a platter? NO, I won't accept them! I saved three lives—"

"And put us that much closer to the last of our resources," the computer butted in. "Waste cannot exist! Waste must not be allowed. Do you accept these charges?"

"Can't your primitive components analyze what I just said? I will not accept the charges!"

Xenon began to break into a cold sweat as a large glowing object swiveled into place over his head.

"Accept the fact that you caused waste. Accept! Accept! Accept!"

Xenon quaked in fear as the object above his head began to hum.

"Oh, what's the use. Yes, I broke the laws. If a life is worth less than a gallon of fuel, then yes, you bet I broke them. But your programming can't understand that, can it?"

The computers totally ignored his words.

"He accepts," stated one machine, recording it to its memory cells. "Violation will be punished by termination."

Xenon clutched the arms of the chair, knuckles white. The hum intensified above his head.

A blinding flash of intense red light reflected off the shiny metallic sides of the computers.

# Cycle 335

## Beth Buck

An alarm sounded aboard the Imperial Space Vessel *Aryalle*. It startled Julie back to the waking world, away from what she called the "in-between place" she seemed to inhabit so frequently these days. Before she shrugged on her uniform jacket and propelled herself onto the command module, she heard a quiet voice in her head say, *initiate cycle number three-hundred and thirty-four.*

Julie winced. She took a minute to recollect what she had been thinking about: continuously rotating harmonic wave theory. It was very important she not forget. She knew she'd remember when she needed to, but that didn't stop her from wishing she could write it down.

"What have we got?" she asked Lieutenant Draper, the only one currently on duty. She already knew the answer, of course, but she still needed to ask. Although *why* she still needed to ask she couldn't say.

"Another vessel," Draper said.

"We've been in orbit around this world for hours and haven't picked up anything," she said. "Why didn't we see them before?"

"They were in a lower orbit on the far side of the planet. They didn't enter the range of our instruments until just a few minutes ago."

"So the planet *is* inhabited, then," Julie said to herself. She turned back to Draper. "You alert Colonel Miller. I'll be down in the lab taking some more readings. Inform me when we enter communications range. This is the first sign of sentient alien life we've seen and I want our first contact to go well."

"Yes, Ma'am."

Of the four old colony sites they investigated so far, this was the first that – apparently – still had people living in it. Butterflies and nervous jitters wrestled in her stomach. Julie propelled herself below deck to the lab as quickly as she could in the microgravity of high orbit and willed herself to calm down. It had to go well this time, it had to. Or she'd wind up doing all of this over again.

The colonel's voice sounded over the intercom. "You seeing this, Julie?" he asked.

"Yes, Sir," she replied. "Looks like the hull is a composite of –"

"I don't need your report. I just wanted to know if you saw the ship," he grunted. "We're still not picking up much radio traffic from the planet, so it could be a ghost ship; some relic from the early days of the colony. Keep running your scans until further notice. I want a full set of readings."

"Yes, Sir," said Julie. She switched on the voice recorder as she continued. "Hull composition: metal alloy. Spectrometer indicates inclusion of aluminum, platinum, and beryllium. Low but constant energy signature, directed towards us, probably scanning. Wait, what's that?"

She double-checked her readouts. Infrared scans showed two heat signatures consistent with humanoid life. No, not human*oid* – *human*. She felt the thrill of discovery. This was it: the reason for which the Empress had personally invited her to be a part of this mission, and the reason why she accepted. A chance, after centuries of isolation, of reunification.

The intercom crackled, and Colonel Miller's voice ordered, "All crew report to the command center and prepare for battle!"

Julie panicked. She didn't want to blow this again. Julie pushed the communicator button. "Colonel," Julie shouted into the mic, "Weapon ports are closed, I am not reading any energy surges that would indicate an increase in shields. Scans indicate the other ship is holding their non-aggressive position. Recommend you cancel preparations for military engagement."

"Quit the save-the-world trash, Pandergast," growled the colonel. "I said battle stations!"

Julie ignored him. "Recommend attempt at communication, Colonel. The psionic translators won't work over such a distance, but they may still have in their database methods used before the Diaspora. Ancient Morse Code –"

"*Battle stations*," the Colonel insisted, enunciation every consonant in those words as if Julie was a deaf toddler.

Julie ground her teeth. She unhooked herself from her workbench and propelled herself back through the hatch and through the corridor into the command center.

Lieutenant Draper already wore the rail gun targeting goggles. She grabbed a stabilization bar to keep from drifting around the room but did not take her station.

Colonel Miller sat strapped in the forward command chair, muttering. "Useless pacifistic female bureaucrats, always getting in the way of the real work..."

Miller gave Julie half a glance and turned back to Draper. "Power up the forward rail guns."

"Colonel, what are you doing?" Julie asked.

"Fulfilling the parameters of our mission," he replied.

"You can't just attack them! We were sent to *make contact*."

The Colonel snapped at her, his blue eyes alight with cold fire. "I know what we were sent for, Pandergast. *Much* better than you do." He asked Draper, "Are they in range? Hopefully we'll be able to dispatch them quickly. Then we will evaluate how to deal with the rest of the colony."

"We'll be within firing range in twenty seconds, Sir," said Draper.

"No!" Julie yelled at the top of her lungs. Draper, *do not* fire. The Empress charged us with initiating peaceful first contact with our sister colonies we can't just attack without provocation."

"I told you to sit down, Captain. We do not have time for this."

"Ten seconds," said Draper. Julie didn't move.

"I GAVE YOU AN ORDER!" Miller bellowed.

"The Empress —" she protested.

"The Empress isn't here! She has no idea what we are up against and neither do you, so SHUT UP!"

"I will not! Stop this *now*!"

"Firing," Draper said dispassionately.

Julie's blood froze as a spate of fire tore across the space between the two ships. She braced herself for the scene of fiery carnage she expected would follow.

Nothing happened. It took a full second for her to realize it. *Nothing* happened. The projectiles didn't bounce off, they didn't penetrate the hull, they...stopped existing.

The Colonel's face turned purple as he rounded on Draper. "What kind of stupid idiot could miss the only target within a million miles of here?"

"I didn't miss. I couldn't have. You saw it yourself, Sir." Draper looked pale and shaky.

"Then what just happened?" he shouted.

"I don't know, Sir," confessed the Lieutenant.

"I thought you said they weren't as technologically advanced as we are?"

Draper shifted uneasily in his seat. "I said they didn't *look* like they were."

Julie broke in, "If you had asked *me*, I could have told you that the scans were inconclusive. If we're lucky they'll refrain from blowing us out of the sky. As we are in orbit around their planet, it's not unlikely that they'll launch more ships to finish us off."

Anger flashed across the Colonel's face. "This is your fault, Pandergast," he said.

Julie scoffed. "*My fault* that you failed in killing the two people on that ship?"

"If you hadn't been screaming in his ear...! But *no!* You just had to assert your petty little female ego!"

Before she could deliver a well-placed retort, but Draper said, "Sir, I am reading some activity coming from the alien ship."

"What kind of activity?" Colonel Miller asked urgently.

Julie glided to her chair and strapped herself in, the better to see the events unfolding on the view screen.

When Draper didn't answer right away, the colonel barked, "Well? Are you stupid as well as blind?"

Draper squinted at his computer screen. "They...they appear to be launching some kind of analog weapon."

Julie looked through the viewport. "Confirmed. It looks like a mace. If a mace can also be like a sword."

All three of them peered at it quizzically as inertia carried it inexorably closer to the *Aryalle*.

Miller's face tightened suddenly. "Evasive action!"

Too late!

*Boom!*

"REPORT!"

Draper cursed. "That thing went right through our shields like they weren't even there. So far we don't have much damage, but I hope they don't have many more of those."

"Return fire," ordered the Colonel.

"I can't. I can push the button, but the rail guns aren't responding."

Another projectile hit seconds after the first.

"Repolarize the shields," suggested Julie. "Maybe that will keep the next volley out."

It didn't.

Draper said, "I don't think we can take another volley, Sir. Recommend we run."

"Negative," Julie said. "The deployment mechanism for our solar sails got shot to bits. Unknown whether the sails themselves are still intact. Either way, we're stranded until they can be repaired."

Julie took a quick look at her stuttering instrument readouts as the *Aryalle* shuddered. "Colonel, that last one punctured our hull! Automatic airlocks are in place to seal the breach, but we've lost 75% of our power. If we want to survive, we'll have to make an emergency landing."

"Oh, God," Julie didn't know if Draper was praying or swearing. "Their hatch is opening again."

Draper locked eyes with Julie for a second. She did not like the look on his face at all, but it reminded her about what she'd been thinking about just before the alarm had awoken her. She knew what she needed to do.

"Colonel," said Julie as she calculated the parameters at lightning speed. "I'm inputting a continuously rotating phase harmonic algorithm into the shield matrix. If we can constantly repolarize our shields' electromagnetics quickly enough, it should work."

"Proceed!" he ordered.

Julie held her breath as the last projectile made its way toward them. She felt relieved when it bounced harmlessly off their shields, but horrified when the rebound made it strike the alien ship.

"No," Julie cried, knowing that this would undoubtedly mean failure.

Colonel Miller did not share her horror. "Good work, Captain," He said. "Lieutenant Draper, what's their status?"

"They're losing power, Sir. Atmosphere is leaking."

The *Aryalle* jolted to one side.

"What was that?" asked Miller.

"The power core, Colonel," said Julie. "It must have destabilized. We will have to jettison the aft section."

"But if we do that," said Draper, "We won't make it through the atmosphere. We'll burn up!"

"Not necessarily," said Julie, as she madly entered more calculations into her console. "When we unload the aft section we can use the forward momentum to bring us closer to the alien craft. We can extend our shields around them and with the extra mass we might just make it."

"It's too risky," said Draper. "The shields will fail, and we don't have the hull integrity —"

"No, but *they* do. They're dead in the water. Use the grappling claws to attach to them, and use the thrusters to reorient our descent so that we're riding in their wake. Their hull can take it." Julie insisted.

"It's suicide!"

"Shut your whiny mouth, Draper," said Colonel Miller. "Do what Pandergast says."

Julie considered the large number of things that could go wrong. The other ship could fire at them again; or explode, taking the *Aryalle* with it; or perhaps she had miscalculated their hull density when during her initial scans, and they'd both incinerate.

Draper executed Julie's instructions exactly, which was to his credit. Julie was pleasantly surprised, as she always thought of Draper as a sycophantic toady who only existed to do whatever Colonel Miller told him to do. Those maneuvers were tricky; there was more to him that met her eye after all.

After docking successfully, both ships careened as one toward the planet. The *Aryalle* rocked and swayed as extraneous bits not shielded by the alien craft melted in the heat of atmospheric friction and broke off. For a second Julie wasn't sure her harebrained scheme would work.

Draper's shoulders relaxed. "We're through the atmosphere," he announced.

"Very good," said the Colonel. "Take us in for the landing, Draper."

"Undocking."

As they neared the planet's surface, Julie saw many cities, roads, and other settlements arranged over the craggy landscape. *The colony didn't just survive,* she thought to herself, *They thrived. They'll have so much to teach us, so much to trade.* Excitement over the possibilities fluttered through her. But then she thought, *They won't be happy to see us when we land.*

The colonel noticed something different. "Lieutenant, why aren't we slowing down? Reverse thrusters full!"

"I can't, Colonel! My controls must have been damaged upon reentry, unless the thrusters themselves are shot."

"Pandergast, do something!"

"I'm good, Colonel, but I'm not a miracle worker!"

"Brace for impact!"

Julie was back there again, floating in that in-between place once more. She didn't know what else to call it. There was no light, no color, neither cold nor heat. She wasn't aware of having a body, so she assumed she existed only as a consciousness.

*End cycle three hundred and thirty-four*, announced that soft voice, so quiet that Julie might have thought she had imagined it if she didn't know better. *Outcome: failure. Only one possible option remains.*

"No, don't send me back again," pleaded Julie. "I can't, I can't."

*"There is only one acceptable outcome. Only one possible option remains."*

A sob escaped Julie's throat.

"How many times are you going to make me relive this?"

*Until there is a satisfactory outcome.*

"I've tried everything. Everything! I've even piloted the *Aryalle* myself. We always crash, every time. And it's all Colonel Miller's fault. He is the one who always orders to fire on them first."

*There is one thing you have not yet tried. One possible option remains.*

"What is that? What do you want me to do?"

*You will figure it out. Initiating cycle number three hundred and thirty-five.*

"No!"

Sirens blared. Julie opened her eyes and found herself back in her cabin aboard the *Aryalle*, just as she had three hundred and thirty-four previous times.

"Only one possible option remains," she repeated to herself in a half-whisper. After hesitating for only a moment, she reached under her bunk and pulled out the locked box the Empress had given her. She opened it and saw the silver pistol inside. It gleamed red in the glow of the flashing alarm lights.

She took the pistol and headed straight for the colonel's cabin across the hall.

He opened the door just as she was about to knock, as if she was waiting for her. "Captain," the Colonel said. "What is this meaning of this?"

"I cannot let you ruin our only chance of peaceful first contact," Julie explained.

"Pandergast," Miller said, "I don't think you understand what is happening here. This situation isn't what you think it is."

"I won't let you lead us to our deaths again," Julie said.

"Captain," Miller warned. "It's the alien ship. Don't look surprised, of course I already know about it. They have this weapon, it messes with your head. If you knew, you wouldn't –"

Julie fired. Her heart tore all around the edges and through the middle to take the life of another person. But she had no choice. All other options had already been explored in great, excruciating detail and Miller's death was the only way out.

There was no blood, the energy beam cauterized the wound. In the weightlessness of space, she merely had to shove his body back into his cabin and let inertia take care of the rest. She threw her pistol in after him and closed the door. She'd have to pay for what she had done later. She went straight to the command module.

"How soon will we be in communications range?" asked Julie.

"Only a few minutes," Draper answered. "Should I summon the colonel?"

Julie paused. "No," she said deliberately. "I informed the Colonel. He's probably still sleeping; he was up all night last night typing out paperwork, from what I understand."

"I'm sure he wouldn't want to miss first contact," Draper offered.

Julie changed the subject. "Are you proficient in Ancient Morse Code, Draper?" asked Julie.

Draper laughed. "You're kidding, right? My mom thought I was nuts for studying it when I should have been working on my biology homework."

"Your mom will be proud to know you didn't waste your life. I have a message for you to send to the other ship, using Ancient Morse."

A quarter of an hour later, an itinerant beeping sounded through the ship's speakers. Draper translated the message. "Overjoyed to meet representatives from sister colony. Hope for much trade, exchange of knowledge. Request to dock and come aboard."

Tears of joy pricked at Julie's eyes. "Give them permission." *Success at last*, she thought.

Draper unstrapped himself from his workstation. "I'll get the colonel."

"That's not necessary, Lieutenant."

"Why?" asked Draper suspiciously. "You seem anxious to keep the colonel away."

"No, that's not it," Julie lied.

"I can always tell when people lie to me," Draper said. "What did you do to Colonel Miller?"

Julie could not meet his eyes. "You don't understand. It had to be done. We're about to meet our colonist friends in about thirty seconds, so we'll have to have this conversation later."

"Captain," Draper said, "What did you do?"

"No time," Julie said. The two ships had docked. Julie wasted no time in opening the airlock.

Two men came aboard. They were similar in height and build, both with brown eyes and nondescript, sandy-blonde hair.

"Thank you for allowing us aboard your ship," one of them said. Julie was even more delighted. The psionic translators worked perfectly.

"This will allow us to capture it intact for study," said the other. They brought out weapons and leveled them at Julie and Draper. "Thank you, Julie, for complying."

Draper looked betrayed. "Complying? Captain, what are they talking about?"

All the blood drained from Julie's face. "I don't know. There must be some mistake, some misunderstanding, some glitch in the translators."

"There is no glitch," said the first man. "We tried your Colonel Miller first, but he saw through our plan almost immediately. He must have had some previous experience with our temporal replay technology that allowed him to see it for what it was. We had to go through nearly five hundred cycles with him before he gave up. We should have known from the beginning you'd be the weak link, Captain Pandergast. Thank you again for your ship. I hope you don't mind too much that we will have to kill you, now. It's not personal, of course."

Both men fired at the same time. Draper took his shot in the chest, killing him instantly. Julie's wound was just a little off-center, so she was still conscious when she hit the ground. Just before she died, she heard that quiet voice in her head one last time.

*End cycle three hundred and thirty-five. Outcome: successful capture of the Aryalle. Thank you, Captain Pandergast, for your cooperation.*

# Sea of Chaos

## Julia H. West

M aster Navigator Winin settled into the contoured couch of the starship *Sally Ride*'s navigation tank. He closed his eyes and said, "VR, Puluwat." The splash of waves, mew of seabirds, and creak of his canoe's rigging replied. He raised his face, breathing deeply. Stale ship's air. "Damn cheap VR."

He opened his eyes and saw Puluwat, his home island, its white sand beaches lapped by the waves of Earth's Pacific Ocean. But though the sun shone in the tropical sky, no welcome rays warmed his face. He shifted his weight on the navigator's bench, evaluating how ripples rocked the canoe's hull beneath him. He looked behind, to the canoe house sheltered by palm trees, and ahead, to where the other islands of the atoll rose from the ocean. Palms on Allei's beaches swayed in a slight breeze, and he could hear children calling to each other from the breadfruit trees on tiny Elangelap, to his right. The virtual reality had what he needed to navigate a starship—but just barely.

"VR Off." The nav tank was small, only the main and an auxiliary couch, with a tiny lavatory built into the wall left of the main couch. But the equipment was clean and well-cared-for; someone knew the importance of a starship's nav tank. Winin pressed the door release and slid out of the couch, his bare feet slapping the deck. He tugged his red and yellow loincloth straight as he stepped through the irising door. "Awfully primitive equipment, Captain," he said to the short, round-faced woman fidgeting in the corridor outside the door.

"But will it do?" asked Akiko Teramoto, captain and owner of the *Sally Ride*.

"I haven't used equipment like this for twenty years, but I explored the Maelstrom in a ship very like this one, when I was young. It will do."

"Good. I'll have your things stowed in your room. The other navigators are waiting aft, in the galley."

Winin followed the captain through the door into the ship's common area. Around a corner, in the tiny galley, three people sat at the tables. A young couple, their hair and skin dark as Winin's, looked up expectantly when Winin and Captain Teramoto entered. The third man, slender and with silver-lined dark hair, didn't raise his eyes from the computer solitaire layout in the table before him.

"Pete, Amy, and Tevita, this is Master Navigator Winin Davis. Galaxy Starliners brought him out of retirement for this mission."

The couple stood hastily. "I'm Navigator Amy Lolohea and this is my husband, Junior Navigator Tevita Lolohea," the young woman said. "I'm —we're really glad to have the opportunity to work with you, Master Navigator Davis. We studied under Hipour."

Winin shook their hands. "Please, call me Winin." He was pleased; Hipour had been one of his better students twenty-five years ago.

The other navigator finally looked up from his solitaire game. He pushed himself from his chair and said, "Senior Navigator Pedro Sanchez." He neglected to put his hand out for Winin to shake.

Captain Teramoto waved them all into seats. "We need to get moving, so I'll brief you and let you work out the navigation details among yourselves.

"You should have heard by now that Galaxy Starliners discovered a safe route through the Maelstrom Overspace Hazard. All their small ships got through safely, so they arranged a special cruise, with one of their biggest liners, to advertise the new route.

"*Old Earth's Pride* left Tufar on a heading for Earth a week ago. Somehow, overspace interference, a 'storm,' nobody knows, the liner got lost in the Maelstrom."

Winin shrugged and nodded; he had guessed as much from things his various escorts said on the way from Puluwat. But Sanchez's face changed; an intense, excited look. His hands curled into fists, then relaxed as he looked down at them.

Teramoto continued, "A distress call came in from the *Old Earth's Pride* by overspace relay two days ago. They hit something, damaged the overspace drive, and haven't the power to exit overspace. There are eight hundred people on that liner, and they're trapped in the middle of the Maelstrom.

"Galaxy hired us to go into the Maelstrom, repair the *Pride*, and get the tourists out before overspace psychosis takes its toll. Winin, you're here to supervise the Maelstrom overspace navigation; you've traveled into, and out of-, the Maelstrom more often than any other navigator."

The captain left them, and Winin turned to face the other navigators. "I've got Galaxy Starliners' calculations for *Old Earth's Pride*'s position in the Maelstrom," he said. "We need to figure our quickest route to the ship, but keep our safety in mind as well." He turned to face Sanchez. "Sanchez, you were chosen for your Maelstrom experience, yes?"

"Yes."

"How about you two?" Winin turned to the Loloheas.

"No, sir," said Amy, shaking her short, dark curls. "We've always skirted the Maelstrom."

"You're in on this because you come with the ship?" Winin grinned to make his question less insulting.

"Yes, sir," said Tevita.

"Please, call me Winin." He shifted in the hard chair, settling his big body more comfortably. "Now, look here." He brought out a hand computer and enlarged the display projection above it for the other navigators. "I've got headings for the trips I took into the Maelstrom, and collected every other relevant scrap of data I could. I've talked to most of the other navigators who've explored the Maelstrom, and extracted data from the logs of the probe ships that found Galaxy's 'safe' route. We'll need all this to find *our* safe heading through overspace to rescue the *Pride*."

Half an hour later all three table-top displays were full, and the four navigators still had not chosen a route.

"The route to Delta Trianguli is shortest, and the *Pride* was heading toward Tri on the first leg of her journey to Earth. It's more likely she's in that narrow arm of the Maelstrom than off in the direction of Kappa Reticuli." Sanchez leaned his chin in the palm of his hand and spoke patiently, like an adult explaining to children.

"The message from the *Pride* gave their calculated position as galactic west of Tufar, almost too close to that big whirlpool I charted twenty years ago," Winin countered.

"Whirlpool?" asked Sanchez.

Winin said, "Shorter than calling it 'Maelstrom Overspace Sub-hazard 14AA.'"

The two younger navigators sat quietly, listening to the arguments and contributing little.

"I don't think they estimated their position correctly," Sanchez said. "How could they have strayed that many parsecs out of their path? No, don't show me that chart again. I've seen the 'safe' path through the Maelstrom. In fact I've been along part of it, from the Tufar side."

"We must take their data as a starting point," said Winin. "It's all we have. We'll take the Epsilon Eridani to Kappa Reticuli route. Tufar is east of Reticuli; the *Pride*'s navigators could easily have missed their mark after entering the Maelstrom." Winin folded muscular arms across his chest and stared straight into Sanchez's eyes.

"I still say—"

"No more arguing," Winin countered. "We need to set a heading, agree on our landmarks, and set up watches."

"But time is important!" said Sanchez. "That liner is stranded in over-space; how long will it be before those soft tourists start going crazy? If we waste time coming in from Reticuli—"

"We head for Epsilon Eridani and on to Kappa Reticuli, then into the Maelstrom on this heading." Winin pointed one thick finger into the display projection above his pocket computer. "We will argue no longer."

Sanchez drew himself up, shaking with anger. But before he could speak Amy Lolohea pointed out quietly, "Winin *is* chief navigator on this trip.

"All you wayfinders stick up for one another," Sanchez said, his voice dripping scorn.

"You're not a wayfinder?" asked Tevita.

"I learned *modern* navigation."

"Enough," said Winin. "I need your help to chart the heading."

"Why not use the nav tank?" asked Sanchez. "Why ignore resources?"

"A good point. We should all fit—two in the couches, two standing behind." He stood immediately and strode toward the nav tank.

Once there, Winin climbed into the main couch and slipped his cartridge into the slot. "VR, open sea," he said, and the virtual reality came up around him. Pacific waves rocked and pitched his canoe beneath him, and the sun shone on the white sail above. He smiled and drew a deep breath . . . ship's air. He sighed. It would be a long trip.

"Twilight." The sky darkened as the sun disappeared below the horizon, and stars began to appear overhead, spreading down the sky to the horizon. Winin felt the other navigators behind him and pointed straight ahead, toward the east. "The Big Bird—Altair." He swung his arm around to the left. "The rising of the Big Dipper. This is the heading for Epsilon Eridani. Do you all know the route?"

"Yes," said the Loloheas, standing in the center of the canoe, grasping the handrails.

"Put up the star chart," Sanchez said. "*This* doesn't show me the heading."

Winin turned on the navigator's bench. Sanchez perched on the lee platform, staring at the star-filled night skies of Earth with his mouth pinched into a dissatisfied line. "How do you take your headings?" asked Winin.

"With the star chart, of course. Don't you feed all this data into the AI?"

"I do that as well. Computer—star map up. Limit—Sol to Epsilon Eridani."

A three-dimensional star map filled the nav tank; the canoe sailed through a mist of stars. Winin pointed to a star swimming below the constellation of the Big Dipper. "Epsilon Eridani."

"You can tell that without the labels?" Tevita asked.

"I've learned."

Sanchez said, "Computer, label the stars." Even with the illusion of the Pacific Ocean all around, four occupants crowded the nav tank. The stars and their labels, like a swarm of insects, added to the stifling atmosphere. But Winin had a heading to teach. "Add known hazards." Multicolored wisps and spirals appeared among the stars.

"Oh, for God's sake, turn off your canoe. It's too crowded in here."

"I need to construct a heading; we can do it with a drawing out in the galley, or the constellations in here, but I require my canoe. I believe Amy and Tevita will learn the heading this way."

Amy nodded. Tevita moved his gaze from star to star, reciting something under his breath, apparently unaware of the conversation.

"Go on, then, we're wasting time." Sanchez pushed his cartridge into the slot by the auxiliary couch. It seemed to disappear into one of the timbers of the lee platform.

Star by star, Winin recited the entire overspace heading from Sol to the entrance of the Maelstrom. "Under the rising of the Big Dipper to Beck's Star, follow the Eridani reef, keeping to the west side, under the rising of Cassiopeia to Epsilon Eridani. Then, still under the rising of Cassiopeia, keep to the east of Elliot's Pool. . . ."

The Loloheas paid strict attention, reciting the heading along with Winin. But once Sanchez had it recorded in his nav cartridge he leaned back against the lashings of the lee platform and closed his eyes, rubbing his temples.

"Have you got it?" Winin asked finally.

"Yes, sir," the other three said. Sanchez stepped off the platform into the bottom of the canoe, crowding Amy and Tevita.

"Before you go, Sanchez, we'll set watches. Since there are four of us, and we need to conserve strength for the Maelstrom passage, we'll rotate through six hour watches. Six in twenty-four's not bad—I'm sure Amy and Tevita usually run eight-on, eight-off."

When the other three navigators had left the nav tank Winin killed the star chart and leaned into the handrail behind the navigator's bench. Since Sanchez had earned the rank of Senior Navigator, he must be skilled at his craft, although a navigator of his age had usually made Master. And since Galaxy had asked him to come on this mission, he must have Maelstrom experience. But Winin needed cooperation on a tricky Maelstrom passage. And this man balked at every command. Winin could not work with him. "VR off." He popped his nav cartridge out, slipped it into the waistband of his loincloth, and set out to see if a Galaxy rep was available.

"I'M SORRY. THERE'S NO TIME. I DIDN'T REALIZE THERE'D BE A PROBLEM." The Galaxy rep's flat black-and-white image on the tiny screen didn't seem very sorry.

"But I tell you, I can't work with this man. He's insolent and sullen, and our styles of navigation clash. This Maelstrom crossing is dangerous. Defiance on his part could cause problems."

"There's no one else on-station. Other Maelstrom-qualified navigators are out on ships or planetside. Your ship needs to leave immediately. We can't wait. You're good with people, Mr. Davis. I'm sure you can handle the situation." The blurry picture blanked.

Winin expelled an angry breath through his teeth. He'd come out of retirement for *this*?

THE THREE MEN ON WININ'S VIRTUAL CREW RAISED THE MAST AND RIGGED the sail of his outrigger canoe. A breeze filled the sail, and the canoe slid out between the small islands and over the barrier reefs to open water.

"Mr. Davis, we're ready to enter overspace," came the *Sally Ride*'s real-space pilot's voice.

"I have the con," he answered.

Winin turned on his seat near the center of the canoe to get a back-sight. The Puluwat atoll lay behind him; he could no longer see his canoe house, where his family and friends stood watching him leave.

"Master Navigator Winin ready for overspace insertion," he said for the log book. "Let's go." Over the sounds of ocean and seabirds he heard the roar of the starship's engines, readying for the great leap into overspace. A ripple shot through canoe, island, and ocean; nausea twisted the navigator's stomach. But his surroundings settled, and the nausea gave way to the internal itch of overspace, felt even through the ship's environmental protection.

"Successful overspace insertion," the pilot's voice said. "Out."

Winin's steersman looked over at him. The navigator turned again for the final backsight, lining up the trees on the eastern tip of Allei with the southeastern edge of Elangelap—the heading for Beck's Star, the first leg in the trip to the Maelstrom nearly fifty parsecs out from Earth. "Teruo," he called to the steersman, "come around this way." He gestured to the right with one muscular arm. "More, more, that's it. Hold that heading."

The sail caught the wind and filled above him, its fabric dazzling white in the westering sunlight. Here the waves no longer rolled gently, as they did in Puluwat's lagoon, but pitched and tossed the eight-meter-long outrigger canoe beneath Winin. He held the line that controlled the sail, adjusting the canoe's course as the wind and waves changed. This felt right.

A woman's voice—not anyone on the canoe's crew—asked, "Sir, do you require a star map overlay?" Winin chewed his lip. Ancient Micronesian custom dictated that women did not sail canoes; *his* crews were always male. "Computer?"

"Yes, sir," the woman's voice replied.

"Computer, what are you called?"

"Sally Ride, sir."

"Sally Ride, will you respond to the name "Kurua?"

"If you're sure that's what you prefer, sir."

"Computer, give Kurua a male voice. I'm not used to female crew in my canoe; I'm afraid it would distract me."

"If you're sure that's what you prefer, sir."

Cocky AI. Computers weren't that cheeky five years ago when last he'd navigated a starship. "That *is* my wish. Kurua, you are now part of my canoe's crew. Call me Winin, without the 'sir.'"

"Yes, Winin."

The voice was deep, Network English with just a hint of Micronesian accent. Trukese? Someone had done some homework.

"Do you wish a star map?" Kurua asked.

"No thanks, Kurua. I don't need one." He had recited the heading until it rang through his head. He knew it without a star map. "Under the rising of the Big Dipper to Beck's Star, follow the Eridani reef, keeping to the west side, under the rising of Cassiopeia to Epsilon Eridani. . . ."

A swift trip from Earth—in this fast little ship it would take maybe three weeks. Already they were far enough from Earth that he felt the strong overspace flow, the one his VR software translated into the current of the North Wave flowing beneath his canoe. "Come around this way, Teruo," he called to his steersman. "A little more. There." Now the waves passing beneath the canoe felt right, the heading was correct.

The early dark of the tropics fell, and the stars of the big dipper twinkled before him. Forgetting where he was again, Winin drew a deep breath. Recycled ship's air, not salty sea tang, filled his nostrils. He exhaled in a snort and stretched. His muscles didn't cramp in the contour couch like they did on the navigator's bench in his real canoe.

"Senior Navigator Sanchez is waiting outside the nav tank to relieve you, Winin," said Kurua in his deep new voice.

The timelessness of the voyage had lulled Winin. Six ship's hours passed already? "Kurua, save my VR settings. VR off." Canoe, crew, and sea disappeared, to be replaced by the soft pastel walls of the nav tank interior and a minimal navigational display. Winin hit the release, and the door irised open.

Sanchez slouched against the corridor wall, tossing his cartridge negligently from hand to hand. "Ready to relieve you, Mr. Davis."

Winin had given up asking Sanchez to call him 'Winin.' "We're still in the hazard-free zone near Earth, but with this ship's speed we'll pass the Eridani reef during one of the next few watches. I'm sure you know to keep west of it; please remind Tevita when he comes on. I've set the heading for Beck's Star, and we won't need to change that course for several watches."

"Right." Sanchez stepped through the door and it irised shut. Winin stared at the door for a second, sighed, and headed toward the galley for food.

During the next week and a half Winin met often with Amy and Tevita. They pored over star maps and fine-tuned the heading through the Maelstrom, and they talked endlessly of their islands in the Pacific. The Loloheas were from Hawai'i but had taken their wayfinding training in Micronesia, so the three had much to share.

Sanchez avoided all but necessary contact with Winin. His course reports were terse, extra conversation nil. Although the two shared a cabin, Winin's only reminders of Sanchez were rumpled shipsuits left on the floor and blankets hanging down from the unmade top bunk.

But now the Maelstrom disturbed the waters beneath Winin's canoe, and occasional tremors shook the *Sally Ride*. Sanchez did not know the refinements on the heading that Winin and the Loloheas had made.

When Winin's watch ended, he irised the door open and, backing into the head to give the other man room to enter, beckoned Sanchez into the cramped nav tank. "This is it, we're coming to the bad parts. We've tried to make a detailed heading of the next few parsecs, but these are the parts where most star maps say 'here be dragons'."

Sanchez stared at him as if he had no clue what Winin was talking about. Winin wondered what school had taught him; he would never have lasted under Winin's tutelage.

Winin slipped into the auxiliary couch and said, "Kurua, give us the star map." The interior of the nav tank disappeared, to be replaced with the deep black of conventional space, stars blazing huge around the two men. "Kurua, tone it down some." The stars dimmed to 20-watt bulbs.

Winin pointed upward. "You've been in the Maelstrom before; you know there are no star congruencies in this part of overspace so we have to follow landmarks. I came in here once; we never made it all the way through the Maelstrom, but we did get past the whirlpool, so I have my notes and those of several others who tried this route."

Winin pointed at a yellow line amid the various Maelstrom land-marks. "Kurua, bring up the reef." The line grew until a golden curtain shimmered in the center of the tank. "This is the western end of the great reef. We follow it for parsecs straight toward the whirlpool. It's fairly safe, but there's a lot of turbulence. That tosses the ship around, but if you move too far south you'll lose the pointer of the reef. There's a bad storm—permanent as far as I know—due south and considerably deeper than the reef. Avoid it, it's dangerous."

"Space isn't flat like the ocean; why not move 'up' to avoid the storm?"

"Too easy to lose sight of the reef, and that entire area is completely uncharted. It could be easier sailing; it's more likely worse. We're not here to take chances." Winin looked over to where the other man lounged in his couch; Sanchez wouldn't meet Winin's eyes. "We need to sail a fine line between the reef and the storm to reach the whirlpool; you'll have to pay attention to all the signs. Oh—the floaties love this reef, so watch out for them."

"I let the AI keep track of most of it for me. She can tell me this."

Winin took a deep breath and let it out without voicing the biting words he was thinking. Areas of overspace like this made human navigators necessary; artificial intelligence had not been developed to the point where it could deal with the continual fine judgement calls needed to navigate through the hazardous areas. Finally he said, as mildly as he could manage, "Let the computer be your backup; *you* pay attention to the signs and keep the ship on course and out of trouble."

It sounded like a lecture to one of his students, and Sanchez bristled. "Yes, sir," he spat. "Is that all?"

Winin would have liked to say much more, but held it in. "It is." He slid from the couch and stepped to the door. As it irised closed he heard Sanchez say, "Stuck-up old-fashioned wayfinder."

WININ SPENT MOST OF HIS NEXT WATCH KEEPING CLOSE TO THE REEF while fighting the waves that pitched and rolled his canoe. His attention was so completely on the ocean that he jumped when Sanchez suddenly appeared balanced on the lee platform.

"Here to relieve you, Mr. Davis." Of course the man stood in the spot where Winin had to slide out of the couch, as if daring the other navigator to push him aside. "Pardon me," said Winin, refusing to be baited. Sanchez reluctantly stood aside, and Winin slid out, moving quickly to the auxiliary couch. Since Sanchez hadn't given him time to shut down his VR, he brought up the star overlay over Pacific waves.

"There have been a lot of floaties this watch," Winin said without preamble. "We've missed 'em all, but you'll need to pay close attention. Keep skirting the reef; we're getting close to the whirlpool—right about *here*." He pointed with his finger and Kurua lit it without his having to ask. He might get to like this AI after all. "Since we've slowed down, we shouldn't reach the whirlpool on your watch."

"You loaded all this into the computer, didn't you?" asked Sanchez as he popped his VR cartridge into the slot.

"Of course I did."

"Then I'll get it from the computer. Sally, Davis VR off, Sanchez VR up." The waves gave way to the blackness of deep space.

The insolence of the man struck Winin speechless. But he couldn't think of anything to do, short of dragging Sanchez out of the couch and punching him in the face, so he stepped through the anomalous hole in space out into the corridor.

Winin knew he ought to talk to Captain Teramoto about Sanchez. But it was ship's night, and he didn't want to wake her. So he grabbed a box lunch from the galley and retired to his room to think things over before he slept.

Dirty clothing in the corner did nothing to soothe his mind. Even in his own room he was reminded of the man. He folded down the table, dropped his dinner on it, and collapsed onto his bunk. What was with Sanchez? When one of Winin's students acted like this, he usually had something to hide. Was that Sanchez's problem?

Winin opened his locker and pulled a soft bag from beneath his extra loincloths. This was his joy, the model of his sailing canoe. He carefully unwrapped it, caressed the smooth wood, checked every tiny lashing that held hull and outrigger and sail in place. This was real. Made with his own hands, from wood and fibers he'd collected on Puluwat, this was something warm and human, not cold and electronic. *This* was a ship.

The starship shuddered, as it often did while passing through the choppy overspace 'waters' around the reef. A loud crash reverberated through the metal members of the ship. Winin grabbed a handhold, staring uselessly in the direction of the nav tank. Had they hit a floaty?

Then his stomach tried to crawl out of his mouth. Damned souls screamed, and blood writhed up the walls. The starship disintegrated into a billion tiny sparkling fragments that formed unintelligible words in the luminous gray matter of a giant's brain.

Overspace. At initiation every wayfinder navigator experienced it— raw, without the protective buffers the starship raised. So they would know it, and just maybe have enough presence of mind to hit the resets . . . but he wasn't in the nav tank. Sanchez had the reset controls.

Winin couldn't find his hands; no, they loomed before him, big enough to pluck a canoe from the ocean. No! The model, hands are not melting, set it on the bed, feel the spikes, sharp coral, cut me, no! Feel my way through the giant's gut, warm, pulsating, black blood coursing around my knees, screaming at my steps. <u>Door—open?</u> This VR's good, has smell, but gone wrong, thousands of crabs rotting on luminous green sand, white-hot sun blisters the skin from my bones, no!

Look, look, my bones are out and my skin is in! A crab, to skitter sideways down the slippery pink seaweed, dead men's fingers, opening and closing, deep-throated terror roar ebbing with the tide to leave me naked, stranded—*door button?* Whirlpool to suck me down and in, coral shatters my feet, perfume of anemones moves slowly through the viscous water. No, don't fight the whirlpool, *door irises open!* Too deep, too deep, golden syrup sighs around my thighs. No movement, space solid and brittle, cracks and lets the red, oozing hearts of suns leak over all the silver starships, deep bell tones crush the futile jellyfish.

Any god—that floating one will do—help me! His arms don't work, my tentacles reach out, feel rough cratered skin, *right there!* The blades flash past, slice my scalp, forehead, eyes, ears. Oh, ears, I must climb out, escape my head. Lava flows back up into the volcanic crater, so sparkling green it cuts my eyes. But there, there I must push the skeletal tree away and feel the deep oozing fur-covered slime of the leaves.

*Push the reset.* Did the god say that? I will, I will, but I cannot hear it, in all the sighing thunder. *Hand is on the reset, fool, just push.*

Winin collapsed against the god's soft side. Ragged panting, whimpering, filled his ears, the cool smoothness of metal supported his legs, his buttocks. He raised his head. Dim emergency lights illuminated the interior of the nav tank.

Drawing a deep breath, Winin pushed himself to his feet. When his stomach protested, he barely made it to the head in its alcove behind the couch. Relieved of its contents, his stomach settled. He drank two large glasses of water and, less shaky, took stock of the situation.

The whimpering came from Sanchez, who lay unconscious in the nav couch. Winin would have to reset the VR, which hadn't come up with the environmentals. The aux couch would do—all the controls were duplicated there.

"Kurua?" His voice sounded loud over Sanchez's raspy breathing. No answer. "Computer? *Sally Ride?*" Nothing. The computer must be down; thank God the enviro was on another circuit. He had never considered how a self-aware computer would react to the chaos of overspace without the interfaces that shielded it and the ship's crew. Could a computer go mad?

He'd best see how the rest of the crew were. He knew nothing about avionic or computer repair. And he needed the VR up soon; there was the reef, the storm—and the whirlpool.

How long had the enviro been down? He looked at his chronometer. An hour had passed since the end of his shift. Winin felt the customary throb of the drive; the ship was still in motion. It would continue indefinitely on the last heading Sanchez had given it, and Winin had no idea what that setting might have been, and how long ago. VR—navigation—became priority.

He met a pale, shaking Captain Teramoto in the companionway, her round face haggard in the dim emergency light. "Thank God you're all right!" she cried when she saw Winin. "I just checked on the bridge. Rafe's unconscious. What happened?"

"We must have hit something. Environmentals failed. The backup didn't come on until I hit the reset. Neither the computer nor the VR came back up."

"Oh no. I've heard overspace is hard on AI. Poor *Sally*."

"Ma'am, we've got to get the VR up. I don't know what heading Sanchez had us on when this happened, and we're in a hazardous area."

"You weren't in the tank when the enviro went out? How did you reset the systems?" She swayed a little, but caught herself with a hand against the wall.

"Ma'am, I taught space navigation for fifteen years. The final test—the initiation, as it were—for every navigator who gets a certificate from me is a full eight-hour stint in the tank, in real overspace. I monitor from the aux couch. At the end I turn off the tank enviro."

She stared up at him. In the dim light he didn't know if he imagined a smile quirking the corners of her lips. "You and my old master were stamped from the same mold, I see. He did that to me, to see how I'd react. I didn't do too well. I screamed, and shook, and threw up all over his nice clean bridge." She shook her head at him.

"But did you find the reset?"

"I did! Even with my guts crawling away and my head on fire, the reset on the armrest wasn't that hard to find." Her hands shook uncontrollably. She closed her eyes.

Winin nodded. "Then you passed with honors, Captain. Here, let me help you. Where do we need to go?"

"Hang on a sec while I pop up to the bridge and slow *Sally* down, then come to Engineering."

WININ, MASTER NAVIGATOR, FOUND HIMSELF LITTLE MORE THAN AN awkward extra pair of hands for the next twenty minutes.

"Can you run the diagnostics again?" Captain Teramoto's voice came, muffled, from within a hole in the wall.

Winin punched five keys on the portable troubleshooting console plugged into the wall and watched words scroll over the screen. "Card 46D8EW-33 bad," he read aloud.

"It's here, I know it's here. Man, somethin' fried this thing. Even back-up's nuked." She pulled her head from behind the panel, wavered for a moment, and collapsed into a sitting position against a wall.

"Ma'am, are you all right?" Winin was on his feet and at her side in seconds.

"Too much blood to my head, hangin' upside down in there. I'm okay." But her face was pale and her hands shook.

"Have you taken the overspace medication?"

"Not yet. It makes me dizzy. I need all my concentration for this." Winin couldn't argue with that. He hadn't taken anything either, for the same reason.

"Rest a moment. I'll find the card." They were all labeled in raised letters, which was a good thing. To Winin 46D8EW-33 looked just like all the others.

"Have you pulled the old one?"

"Yeah," she held it up to show him.

"Is it obvious where it goes?"

"Yeah, well, no. There are some empty slots in there too. Here, I'm okay now." Winin helped her to her feet.

She leaned back into the hole with the card. "Tight connection," she said. "Try the diagnostics again."

"Right." Punch five letters with a finger, watch symbols float by on the screen. "Diagnostics complete. Virtual Reality and Navigation checks good."

"Yo!" She pulled her head out of the hole and clapped Winin on the back. "Go, man, and keep us out of a mess. I'll button this up and see who else is semi-functional."

SANCHEZ STILL LAY UNCONSCIOUS IN THE NAV COUCH, HIS COLOR BAD AND his breathing harsh, but Winin didn't have time to do anything for him. He plugged his cartridge into the slot—and met resistance. Sanchez's cartridge popped out when Winin hit the button; Winin stowed it in the waistband of his loincloth.

The time his data took to reload stretched on and on. Could the navigation equipment still be broken? Though he used virtual reality and had adapted it to his needs, he still had little idea how the avionics behind it all functioned.

The load light winked off and the ready light glowed. Relieved, Winin popped his cartridge out and stowed it safely beside Sanchez's, then settled himself into the aux nav couch. Better fasten the restraints; the trip could get rough.

"VR, Puluwat, current voyage, night." Starlit ocean appeared all around him and he knew the canoe was in trouble. The feel of the waves was all wrong, the stars were in the wrong places, and the smell . . . no, the smell didn't come with the VR. It was Sanchez, who lolled limp in the bottom of the canoe and had reacted to its pitching like most seasick mainlanders did. Winin didn't have time to clean him up; he'd have to live with the smell.

How close to the whirlpool were they? And where was the reef? "Kurua, bring up the star map." Nothing happened. Captain Teramoto had brought nav up, but the computer was still down. He'd have to do this blind, like his ancestors had, navigating with only his knowledge, memory and senses. He had just spent the last five years teaching young navigators wayfinding in his canoe in the Pacific; was this so different?

The feel of the rough water told him the ship was close to the whirlpool. The reef ran almost directly west to east, the whirlpool at its center. It was too late to skirt the whirlpool by moving southward; they were already being pulled, however gently at this point, toward its center. The *Sally Ride* was too small to be able to call up the massive amounts of power needed to break them free and send them straight out. Such a ploy, if it failed, could spin the ship straight into the whirlpool's depths. He would have to use the whirlpool's motion to give them momentum, then break the ship free as it headed northeast, over the reef to the west of the whirlpool, into uncharted waters.

Crossing over the reef would be dangerous, but less so than to risk discovering what lay at the center of a whirlpool. No one had ever learned if matter was the same in overspace as in realspace, but when a ship hit a reef—or a floaty, or any of a score of other hazards—the results were usually disastrous.

In the nav tank, the stars of Earth's skies shone reassuring above him —Polaris, the Dippers, Cassiopeia. But now, though the stars could keep him on course, he must find his way by the feel of the waves generated by whirlpool and reef. "Teruo, come around, more to the north. This way." He pointed to his left. "More, come on, there."

Winin leaned left over the canoe's side, watching the waves hit its hull. He looked right, noting the difference between when a wave hit the outrigger float and when it touched the hull. The canoe headed at an angle across the reef, the whirlpool to the northeast.

"Navigator Winin, can you hear me?" A woman's voice—Captain Teramoto's.

"Yes ma'am."

"Will you be able to come give me a hand any time soon?" Maybe it was poor reception on the intercom, or maybe she was really as sick as she sounded.

"Ma'am, I'm trying to head us away from a whirlpool. Could take hours. I'll come out as soon as sailing's clear."

Silence. Then, "Are you having problems?"

"No, but be prepared for some rough handling. I'll have to take us straight over a nasty reef."

"Can you cope?" It wasn't just the intercom. She sounded more than weary.

"Yes, ma'am."

"How's Sanchez?"

He glanced at the limp form. "Still unconscious. I haven't been able to take time to do anything for him. As soon as this heading's stable I'll give him the meds."

Teramoto mumbled something, then said, "I don't want to alarm you, Winin, but the main environmentals blew and we're running on auxiliaries. They weren't meant to hold this kind of load for long." He heard her sigh. "Garrity's up, too, but we're both too shaky to fix much. We need you whenever you can come. Amy's awake, but she's in pretty bad shape. D'you think she could handle this?"

Winin closed his eyes and drew a deep breath—then regretted it, for the stench of Sanchez's vomit was still very much present. "Ma'am, if we were anywhere but between a whirlpool and a reef I'd let Amy navigate and I'd come down immediately. But it's too tricky for a novice."

"Understood. I wanted you to know the situation. Garry and I will do what we can until you're free. See you then."

Twenty minutes passed. Winin fought the crosswaves, kept the course steady, and waited. He didn't know exactly how wide the reef was, nor how close they were to the whirlpool. He wished he had Sanchez's data, but when he slipped the other cartridge into the VR slot, nothing happened. Its matrix must have been scrambled when the VR went down.

He needed light to watch the waves and look for the reef, so he called the sun into the eastern sky. But his eyes did not find the reef first, his body did. The wave patterns changed, the interference becoming more and more obvious.

A floaty sailed past. His VR was programmed to picture them as big birds, of no Earth form. Were they overspace life forms? Starships? No one knew. It circled his canoe once, then flapped off away to the north.

Now that Winin had found the reef, he slid from the navigator's bench into the bottom of the canoe to look at Sanchez. The man's skin was pale and waxy, his breathing harsh. Shock? Winin peeled back Sanchez's sleeve and slapped the patches for shock and overspace exposure on the inside of the other navigator's elbow. At the back of the canoe he relieved himself and brought back a wet towel to clean some of the foulness from Sanchez's face and chest.

Winin dropped the disgusting towel overboard and climbed with difficulty, because the canoe pitched and rolled so, onto the navigator's bench. All around the canoe he saw dark patches under the water, sharp rocks to catch his canoe and tear it open. This was the VR's analog of matter not only below, but above and all around them in space.

"Winin?" Teramoto's voice sounded even more tired. "Garrity has started to repair the main environmentals. But he's in bad shape, can't control the shaking. I'm afraid there's nerve damage." Winin remembered how the captain's hands had trembled as she replaced the nav cards. "The computer won't come up. Poor old Sally." There was something tender in her voice—for a computer? For her ship?

"I'll be there soon. Perhaps you should both rest until I can make it." *What good will I do? I can't fix machines, electronics, unfeeling, unalive metal and plastic. Why can't you just leave me to navigate?*

Winin pushed hysteria down, hoping it was just an aftereffect of the exposure to overspace. He watched the waves break over sharp reef rocks. He couldn't afford to lose concentration.

The chaos of waves beneath the canoe strengthened, and Winin could see Teruo gripping the steering paddle hard, putting all his strength into holding the heading. "A little this way. Hold it." They needed to pull away from the whirlpool *now*, Winin knew with a sureness born of a life-time of practice. A little to the west of the course they had been on. The canoe struggled, pitching and rolling. "More sail," Winin ordered.

"Winin, are we all right?" Teramoto's voice broke his concentration.

"Yes ma'am." Winin's voice betrayed the strain he was under. "Right between the reef and the whirlpool. With luck, we'll survive them both." So it wasn't just his VR, wasn't just the canoe. The starship was taking a battering.

Winin clutched the navigator's bench and the line to the sail, while Teruo clung to the steering paddle. The canoe moved at full speed through the rocks, and there were so many of them. Floaties soared and dipped, circling, circling. Winin's voice cracked as he called directions to Teruo and the rest of his crew, and his arms ached from his efforts in adjusting the sail. The canoe's timbers creaked, but held. A scrape, just missed a rock.

And then there were fewer rocks, and the insidious pull of the whirlpool's motion rippled the waves, but no longer tugged the canoe toward its center. The flock of floaties circling the canoe flapped into the sunset. They had crossed the reef and pulled free of the whirlpool.

"Winin to captain. We're clear, ma'am." It did seem clear, this side of the reef. So far.

"Thank God. Should I send Amy up?"

"Yes. I'll give us a new setting, slow way down, and be down in a few minutes."

"Thank you."

Now Winin needed the stars again. "VR, nighttime." The last of the sunset faded from the sky, and Polaris appeared, winking through light clouds at the horizon on their left. "Teruo, set our heading for the Big Dipper." His arm swung right, pointing. "Easy, easy, hold it there. Now reef the sail and hold this heading." Winin slid his VR data cartridge into the slot, recorded the new information, and retrieved the cartridge.

"Winin?" Amy Lolohea said, behind him. The younger navigator's face was greenish, her eyes dark-smudged, but she stood straight, shoul-ders back. "I'm ready to take over."

"Just hold this course, and call me if anything comes up. Watch for rocks; we've just passed over the reef. And please, rest yourself."

"Yes, sir."

Captain Teramoto hunched over some kind of electronic card, turning it over and over in shaking hands. The stench of burnt plastic, metal, and paint nearly gagged Winin.

The captain looked up when Winin's bare feet hit the floor at the bottom of the ladder. Her face was as waxy and drawn as Sanchez's had been, and soot streaked her forehead. "Thank heaven you're here, Winin. Whatever hit the ship fried the main enviro cards. There's too much damage there. Until we get an overhaul we'll have to run on the auxiliaries. One of the aux cards sizzled, it probably kicked in when the mains fried; good thing they're redundant. You kicked the other aux in when you reset."

She pushed straggling hair out of her face and further smeared the soot on her forehead. Her eyes were dull with exhaustion. "Problem is, when we put in a new aux card, it blew. And we'd already replaced one during the trip out. We've got no spares."

"What can we do?" Away from the stress of navigating the ship past the whirlpool, Winin realized how weary he had become. Something within him cried *just let me sleep now, we can worry about it all later.*

"How steady are your hands? These things are LRUs, never designed to be repaired—and we'll have to repair one."

Winin looked at the cards in dismay. Electronics! Metal and plastic, unnatural. "I don't know how to do it," he said slowly, controlling his reaction. "I've never learned electronics."

"I'll tell you how," Chief Engineer Garrity had wriggled out of the repair passageway and now stood behind them, pushing thinning blond hair away from his forehead with sooty fingers. "I'd do it myself, but . . ." He held up the other hand, shaking uncontrollably, to display. "It's taken me nearly six hours to fix the connection that blew the other card. Too bad those Galaxy drive techs haven't come around yet. So you're it, Winin."

I've got to do it, Winin told himself. Will I die here, and kill twelve other people, because I don't understand electronics? He took a deep breath and turned to Garrity. "Okay. Tell me what to do. Be real specific, because I don't know what *anything* is." He squatted on the steel deck and peered at the bright-colored bits.

"There are actually two main and two auxiliary enviro setups," explained Garrity. "The main is mostly slag. One aux is fine, the other . . . well, you see it before you. But they're designed to switch back and forth, so one doesn't have to take all the load. We want it to work that way; we've got days more before we reach the liner, and can't chance running on just one. I don't *ever* want to feel raw overspace again." A whole body shudder joined the trembling.

"Luckily each card has redundancy, too, so the components on this whole side aren't needed. It won't be pretty, but we can rebuild the network outside the card, with wires and components rather than solid state."

Winin blinked at him. It made sense when he heard it, but his retention wasn't good. He could not have repeated it back. Redundancy? Rebuild the network?

"Use the microwelder to join the components. Press the button, once, when the components are placed correctly." Garrity told him how to hold the tiny parts, under a portable magnifier, with tweezers and minuscule clamps, and patiently repeated himself when things fell out, or got in backward, or didn't touch properly.

Winin looked down at his broad brown fingers. They were too big, too clumsy, meant for pulling ropes or clutching a steering paddle. These little colored insects of parts were too small. But he kept at it, though it took almost an hour.

"There. All together? Plug it into diagnostics." Garrity rubbed his eyes with dirty hands.

The diagnostic board flashed with red and yellow warnings.

Garrity smothered an obscenity and bent over the screen. "That first warning's okay. We know card integrity has been breached. What's this? Short. Open here and here. Unknown factor? Never seen that before. Oh, man." Disgust colored his voice.

So many errors! But these baffling items, these little pieces of plastic. How could *he* put them together to make one of these machines?

Winin's chrono beeped. "Sir? Ma'am? I'd like to check on Amy. She looked pretty bad, and we're sailing in unknown waters. We should be all right, but. . . ."

"Go for it. We'll rest," said Teramoto. "We're all on the ragged edge." She and Garrity followed Winin up the ladder to the quarters deck.

In the nav tank, Amy's canoe sailed through seas too peaceful to be true. "Amy, update me. What happened while I was gone?"

"Nothing, Winin. The sea is calm, we continue slowly on a northeasterly heading." Amy huddled on the navigator's bench, the sail's line slack in her hand.

Winin closed his eyes, felt how the canoe rode gently over the waves. He could feel how the reef and the whirlpool, behind and to their right, affected the wave patterns. And, maybe, something up ahead. But too faint yet to tell what it could be, just a minor ripple in the waves. "Have you seen any floaties?"

"None."

"Continue as you are, then. Call me on Engineering Deck A if anything—I mean *anything*, happens." Winin checked Sanchez, who still slept under medication. He breathed more easily and his color was better, so the meds must have helped. Winin left the nav tank again.

He joined the captain and engineer in the galley, where they sipped drinks—alcoholic, by the smell—in tense silence. "We're okay so far," Winin told them. "This side of the reef is much calmer; if nothing else comes up I'll suggest it as a possible route. I'd have to go back and find out what's on the western end, though. . . ."

Teramoto offered him a drink. "Kick back, Winin, relax. You've been through two whole shifts, or more, and overspace besides. Where do you get your energy?"

Winin politely declined the drink, pulling chilled fruit juice from the fridge. "At home, on the ocean in a canoe like those my ancestors sailed, the trips between islands may take weeks. The navigator owns and guides the canoe. I have learned to get by without much sleep for long periods of time. At home, they say you can tell a master navigator by his blood-shot eyes."

"You people—navigators—amaze me," said Garrity, his words a little slurred. "Doing something for a starship that even a computer can't do, a job that requires human reasoning, logic, and decision-making. I could never learn it."

"And I don't know electronics. We all have our talents. My ancestors on my mother's side have been navigators for millennia." Winin finished his juice and leaned against the cartoon-covered wall of the galley, closing his eyes and pressing the heels of his hands against the lids.

"How're Amy and Sanchez?" asked Teramoto.

"Amy's doing fine, and Sanchez looks better," Winin answered without opening his eyes. "The meds seem to be doing their job. How about the rest of your crew?"

"I had the few who were up drug the rest of 'em to the eyebrows. Maybe by the time we're burnt to a frazzle they'll be feeling well enough to take over from us. But it'll be a long time until they come around. We've got to get the enviro up to speed before that; I doubt we could take another bout with overspace, as fried as we are now." She swirled the liquid in her glass, then swallowed the last of it.

"Let's get back to it, then," said Garrity, gnawing a ragged fingernail. "There are at least five faults we need to correct before we plug the card in and see if the fixes hold under use."

THE REPAIRS WERE NOT GOING WELL. WININ HELD THE MICROWELDER TO a bad connection, then peered at it through a magnifier. "How do you know what to do?" he asked. "You flash this and scrape that, and it works." He wielded the tiny knife blade clumsily.

"Hey, don't cut that trace on the side. How do I know? Practice. Study. Years of work. You said you handmade your canoe? How do you know how to do that? I wouldn't have any idea where to begin. There. Done? Plug 'er in and see how we did."

The diagnostic board lit again. "That's the breach of card integrity red, but here's another open—a different one. How could that be?"

Winin looked at the screen himself. Seven flashing lights—all red. He just wasn't doing it, had no talent or aptitude for this finicky work. But he had to. If the one remaining enviro card blew, the only buffer between them and raw overspace would be gone. Winin wanted to die at home, on Puluwat, not screaming in a sea of chaos.

He had to do *something*—but what? "I'd like to check on Amy before we go on. I need a break. My hands. . . ." His big, brown hands, usually so steady, were starting to shake with fatigue and frustration.

"Go for it. Wake me up when you come back down. But don't take too long." Garrity leaned against a wall and closed his eyes. Teramoto slept curled in the corner.

Winin climbed the ladder slowly, feeling every rung carefully with his feet. What could he do? Every minute he delayed might mean death for himself and twelve others. But he knew what those new mistakes on the diagnostics were. He'd cut too far, or unflashed the wrong connection, or . . . stupid things. Beginner things. Things he'd done in that basic electronics class he had to take so long ago. It was required for anyone wanting a license, but he must have received the lowest grade ever. It had been humiliating. They probably passed him because they looked at his record and said, "Oh, navigator, he'll never need *this*."

But I'm a *good* navigator, he thought, one of the best, I've been told. I love the sea, and even the far different sea of overspace. I just . . . can't . . . do . . . electronics.

He had to pass his stateroom to get to the nav tank. As he went by, he noticed he'd left the door open when he stumbled out, so many hours ago, to find the reset. He could see his bunk from the door, and on it his model canoe. Could he spare a few minutes?

He settled on the soft blanket, resisting the almost overwhelming urge to curl up on it and sleep, and picked up the canoe. He had made it his last winter at home, when the seas were too rough to sail and he'd finished the overhaul on his big canoe. It was the sort of toy his parents, the "authentic folkways" advocates, loved. He'd twisted the coir twine from coconut husk fibers, carved the hull from a scrap of breadfruit wood, even woven the sail of pandanus. The breadfruit sap glue was still slightly sticky.

The canoe trembled in his hands, and he stared down at the model, complete in every detail. He'd carved the tiny steering paddle, punched minute holes to lash the hull together, worked with twine as fine as the electrical wire for that cursed enviro card.

He'd seen tiny replicas of starships—from the big liners he'd navigated for so long to the tiny nine-person courier "squids" like this one—built with loving care by spacers. Some spacers went so far with their passion for similitude that they'd carefully added dents and scratches where the real ships had them. Was it just a hobby, something to while away boring shipboard hours? Or was it a labor of love? When he held this model, checked its lashing, worried about a splitting seam, it was as if he worked on his own canoe back home, a tie to his home, his life.

Winin was a navigator. No Puluwat navigator had lost a canoe in one hundred and fifty years. He might build a new one, trade his old one away, but he always had his canoe.

He remembered Captain Teramoto's face and voice when she said, "Poor Sally." Was she just thinking of the artificial intelligence in the computer, or was she thinking of her ship? Could it be that spacers felt the same about these plastic and metal conveyances as he did about his canoe?

He was a wayfinder and a starship navigator, but a navigator was nothing without a ship. And at this moment his ship was the *Sally Ride*, not a breadfruit-log canoe in Earth's Pacific ocean. The enviro card he'd sweated over and hated was as much a part of the *Sally Ride* as the rigging and caulking and sail and mast of his canoe.

He ran his fingers over the lashings of his model's hull. Those holes were smaller than the components he tried to assemble on the board, and the lashing twine as fine as the gaily striped wire. Those big fingers had constructed this toy without feeling awkward and incompetent. What was the difference?

The difference was in Winin. I'm a silly old man, he thought. I'm named for the navigator who discarded the old taboos and rituals, then sailed away—and came back again safe and sound. And yet I won't accept the electronics that give my occupation new meaning in these days, when sailing a canoe on the oceans of Earth by dead reckoning is an outmoded art. Without starships, without VR and enviro, the art of navigating by the stars, by the feel of the waves and the current on the hull, would have been lost.

This ship, this *Sally Ride*, is as much mine as my canoe at home. I must embrace her. Would I neglect the rigging on my canoe because I didn't want to fix it? Never. But I don't *want* to fix the enviro. Or didn't. . .

.

Winin dropped the canoe on the blankets and hurried out the door, along the companionway, down the ladder. Garrity snored, collapsed against a wall, in the engineering bay. Winin wished he could fix the card without waking the man. Garrity's skin was pale, his eyelids bruised-looking, his hair sweat-sticky and awry.

"Engineer?" He shook Garrity's shoulder gently, then with some urgency. "Garrity? I'm back. We've got to fix this card."

Garrity groaned, pushed himself up. "Is there any water around? My mouth tastes like . . . well, I'd rather not say."

Winin took a squeeze bottle from the tiny fridge built into the wall.

"Oh, yes." Garrity held the cold plastic to his forehead, his eyes. "Feels wonderful." He squirted some into his mouth, then into his cupped palms and rubbed it over his grimy face.

Without a word Winin handed him a towel.

"Well, I may be back from the dead. Now, where were we?"

"The faults on the board."

"Yes." Garrity scowled. "What a disaster."

"I'm sorry."

Garrity shrugged and studied the screen, chewing a ragged fingernail. "Okay, let's try this again."

"I have an idea," said Winin. "Let's start over, on the other damaged card, and have you explain this to me as if you never had before. I'm tired and cranky and so are you, and we may have been working at cross purposes before, despite ourselves."

"Ok-a-ay," Garrity drew the word out in a long drawl.

They plugged the other damaged card into the diagnostic console. Winin listened intently as Garrity explained what each fault code meant, how each component worked. Just as he had found analogies for the bizarre happenings of overspace, given each of them an analog his VR software could translate into something familiar, now he tried to do the same with the components on this board. And he repeated back to Garrity each concept as he understood it.

"Now you've got it, man," said the engineer. "Let's go to, because that enviro card's been workin' overtime for hours now. Let's start with that open."

As Winin worked, Captain Teramoto awoke. Garrity found her another water bottle and towel, and when Winin looked up for his next instructions she had scrubbed most of the soot from her face and hands.

"Still at it? You've got a lot of stamina."

"Yes, ma'am."

"Does talking bother you while you're working?"

"No, at home we all sit in the canoe house, twining cord or working on the canoes, gossiping all the while. I like to talk while I work." Winin hit the *remove* button on the microwelder and a bit of offending plastic disappeared.

"Tell me about your island. I've never been out to the Pacific."

"Since we're one of the 'Living Past' islands, there are very few modern structures. The apartment buildings and grocery stores erected there in the early 2000s were razed, and we built it all back up with traditional houses. The people who just can't stand not having Coke and Vids, usually the teenagers, leave. I did. But we come back."

Teramoto said, "My ancestors were Japanese, but I've never been there. I grew up in America, in Arizona."

Winin asked, "Have you always wanted to go to space?" He squinted at the card, then remembered the magnifier and used it.

"Since my earliest years. The stories we'd hear—they sounded so romantic. I toyed with the idea of becoming a navigator, but I wanted my own ship. *Sally* is my dream come true." Winin looked up at her, saw her caress the cold metal wall and shake her head, smiling gently.

"That's how my canoe is. It's part of me. I built it—with my apprentices, of course—but all the design, the new ideas for a swifter hull, all are mine. So I know its strengths, its weaknesses."

"Yes. It . . . it *hurts* to have *Sally* damaged like this. Especially the computer. She's built up quite a personality."

The cheeky computer, thought Winin. Another facet of the captain's mind.

"OKAY, GARRITY, IT'S DONE. PLEASE LOOK AT IT UNDER THE MAGNIFIER and see if it's good." This time he'd tried hard, seen it as part of an almost living organism, the *Sally* whom Captain Teramoto loved. With the disappearance of his reluctance, the job had flowed smoothly.

Garrity leaned over the magnifier, nose almost touching its glass. "Good," he grunted to himself, "clean one here, good connection, cut that bridge, yes." He pulled back and studied the entire thing. "Looks like a nightmare, but this time should do it."

The diagnostics ran, and only one line of red type flickered across the screen. Card integrity breached.

"Yo! Now we can plug her in and see if she really works." Garrity's face looked more alive than it had since the overspace accident.

"Here, let me," said Teramoto. She took the card and crawled into the hole in the floor.

"What if it doesn't work? Will we lose our protection from overspace?" Winin was reluctant to experience that again; it would probably incapacitate the other two.

"No," answered Garrity, "The other circuit will kick back in immediately." He crouched over the diagnostic screen, keying in responses to the overall diagnostics test. "I miss the computer. It's easier to ask her to run the test. Good thing I remember how to do this myself."

Winin and Teramoto stood behind him, watching the screen. "Okay, here we are." He pointed to one of the tiny images on the screen. "Here's the dead main enviro—and some auxiliary damage we'll have to sort out later. Here's the aux—damn! Still running on one circuit."

"Is it the damaged or undamaged circuit?" asked Teramoto.

"The undamaged. It tries to transfer—see, the other one flickers, but doesn't come up, and it goes back to the undamaged one. This is even harder on it than running straight. What can be wrong that the diagnostics didn't catch?"

Winin had an idea. "There's a lot of soot around, from the damaged systems. You two have it all over your faces and hands. If some of that got on the card, or in the slot, would it affect its performance?"

"Yeah, probably. Okay, Garrity, pull that thing again. Winin, get an air can and some swabs from that workbox. Good. Here's the contact cleaner. Blow the slot clean, then swab that sucker down."

Winin wedged his bulk into the passageway and carefully cleaned the slot from which Garrity had pulled the repaired card. The first swab came out black. He tossed it behind him, out of the hole.

Garrity's voice came, muffled, to his ears. "Look at that carbon —filthy."

Winin patiently ran damp swabs through the slot time after time until one came out clean. He felt a tap on his back, and backed out of the passageway. Teramoto handed him the card.

"Here, I've cleaned the contacts. You wanna push it in, Winin? This is your baby, you know."

"If you think I wouldn't damage it, ma'am." Winin felt a thrill of accomplishment, silly for a man his age.

"Just be sure none of those components you welded on touch anything. Hey, Garrity, you got anything non-conducting we can slip in there to shield those components?"

Garrity handed Winin a fibrous sheet. "That can go in between."

Winin crawled back into the cramped passage, rounding his shoulders to fit. He guided the card into its slot, and slipped the sheet between his carefully constructed fix and the next card.

"Do I need to apply pressure to make sure it's seated?"

"Might be a good idea. Don't push too hard."

Winin did that, backed out of the passageway, and stood, suddenly feeling the tension in his shoulders, neck and back. He stretched, easily touching the ceiling, and rotated his shoulders.

Garrity ran through diagnostics again, and this time the tiny pictures on the screen showed the two aux enviro systems alternating as they should. "We did it! Now we can get some sleep!"

"But Winin, what about the navigation? You're pretty far gone, and Amy didn't look like she could take much more. Tevi's drugged to the eyebrows, and Sanchez. . . ?" Teramoto turned her drawn, tired face to him in dismay.

"Don't worry. I told you, in the Pacific I've navigated canoes for weeks at a stretch. I've learned to sleep on the bench, snatch an hour here and an hour there. The nav couch is more comfortable than my canoe's bench." Winin did not feel tired. Exhilaration buoyed him. It was as if he had been in prison, and the doors had opened to free him. "You sleep, ma'am, sir. Don't worry about the navigation—that's what I do."

Sanchez stirred in his couch and muttered something when Winin stepped back into the nav tank. Winin bent over him, noted that his color was better and his body no longer twitched. "Are you awake, Sanchez?" he asked. No response.

Amy looked terrible, her face gray, her hair sweat-soaked. But she was alert, holding the line to the sail taut and watching the waves and the horizon.

The canoe was running into trouble. Luminous gray clouds filled the sky, boiling across the ocean with alarming speed. He didn't have to ask if the whirlpool was still to the right; the choppy waves broke in a pattern that showed its presence.

"Have you had any trouble?"

"No, Winin. But had this storm got much worse, I would have called you." Amy bit her lip and shook her head. "I can't stay awake much longer."

"How long have we skirted the whirlpool?"

"Forty-two minutes."

"Rest now. I'll take over."

Amy saved her settings and dropped her cartridge into a coverall pocket. The corners of her mouth quirked in a smile as she slid out of the couch, and she saluted Winin from the doorway. He saluted back.

Winin had never taught wayfinding to women—not because he didn't think women could do it, but because it wasn't *traditional*. Maybe it was time for one old navigator to break with another tradition.

Winin turned his attention back to his surroundings. The *Sally Ride* sailed through unknown waters. Though he had memorized the hazards of the route south of the reef and the whirlpool, now they sailed on the northern side. His VR interpreted whatever lay ahead as a storm; it could be a real overspace "storm" or a permanent hazard that manifested in a similar way. No matter. He would note it, remember it—and deal with it.

"What hit me?" A slurred voice broke his concentration. Sanchez was awake.

"Enviro failed, and we spent some real time in overspace." Winin turned to look at the other navigator. Sanchez stared around, wide-eyed, at the waves and the clouds.

"Get me outta this mess. This crazy canoe bouncing around like this is gonna make me barf. Again." Sanchez started unfastening the couch restraints.

"I'll need your help. Go to the head, clean yourself up, take more meds if you need them, but return to the other couch."

"Hey, I'm sick. I need to lie down in my quarters. I can't help anyway —I never learned navigation in a canoe." He went to the sink in the head, splashed water on his face.

"If you ever want to navigate again, you'll return to your post once you've cleaned up."

Something in Winin's voice—the voice of a Master Navigator to a student—must have got through to Sanchez; he paused in his toweling of his hair and clothing to stare up at Winin. "Yes, sir." His tone was actually respectful.

Winin returned to his problem; finding out where they were, keeping on some kind of course, and weathering the storm. As long as the canoe came around the whirlpool and paralleled the reef, he could figure out where they were, but if the storm dashed them onto either of them. . . .

The canoe responded sluggishly to Winin's commands. "Teruo, more to the north, a little more, there." He could still sense the reef, a perturbation in the waves to one side, but it was less of a danger at this distance.

"How'n'hell can you tell where you are? Where's your star map?" Sanchez had returned to his seat in the canoe and swabbed it, and the deck, with a towel.

"The computer's down—damaged by the enviro failure."

"Then how do you know where to go?"

"I have the VR's output, converted from the raw overspace input by the nav computer. I have wind, and sea, and stars. I know roughly where we were before the AI was disabled, and I've seen the star map. What more do I need?"

Sanchez shook his head, mouthing, "Crazy wayfinder," and slid into his couch.

"Did your master never teach you to navigate without the star map?"

"Why should I? If the star map's there, use it. No reason to deprive myself of a tool."

Winin thought, for a long moment. The man was insolent, perhaps incompetent. But he was all Winin had. "I will teach you wayfinding."

Winin began as he did for his students, reciting the coordinates from Earth to the Maelstrom. "Under the rising of the Big Dipper to Beck's Star, follow the Eridani reef, keeping to the west side, under the rising of Cassiopeia to Epsilon Eridani. Then, still under the rising of Cassiopeia, keep to the east of Elliot's Pool until you sight Timani, then steer west of Timani, east of Little Blight, to Michuk. Then a long run under the rising of Cassiopeia to Kappa Reticuli, with Sarat Reef to the west halfway through the route. From Kappa, under the rising of Gamma Aquilae to the outskirts of the Maelstrom, then south of the Great Reef, well out so as to miss the Whirlpool. This is the route we have traveled thus far in this canoe. We have been thrown off our route, but we still have coordinates. This reef is an excellent landmark. Dangerous, but useful."

"Reef?" Sanchez seemed to be trying to understand Winin's explanation. "How can you tell we're near the reef?"

"Look to your right. The waves are choppy, there is a darkness beneath them."

"Is that what we hit? It happened so fast, I never saw anything." Sanchez sounded uneasy, but perhaps that was the pitching of the boat.

"One of the rocks in the reef, or perhaps a floaty. Flocks of them circled the ship as we crossed the reef to escape the whirlpool." Winin returned his attention from the other navigator to the waves and sky.

"*Crossed* the reef to escape the whirlpool? Oh, man, I'm glad I slept through it." His voice shook.

For the next two days Winin taught wayfinding to Sanchez. Teaching came naturally to him. As in his canoe in the Pacific, he ate when he was hungry, slept when he could, always feeling the waves beneath the canoe and watching the stars. Amy came to relieve him but he sent her away to watch Tevita.

Sanchez seemed content to lie in his couch, watching and listening. He slept, ate. Sometimes he asked questions, which Winin answered in detail. He seemed fascinated, no longer surly and belligerent.

"You can see how the storm behind us agitates the waves. But we don't need those waves. Look to the reef, how it spreads out here. It's dangerous, even though the rocks are farther apart, for there are more of them. We skirt it, head north until the dark places no longer show under the waves. Can you do that?" There comes a time when a student has to navigate for himself.

"I can, Winin."

And finally, sometime late in the second day, Winin said, "This is the end of the reef—can you tell? The waves come differently now. Here we skirt the end of the reef, head south, and find my old route."

Teramoto's voice said, "Winin, are you all right? Amy and Tevita are very anxious about you."

"Yes, ma'am. We're through the storm, coming to the end of the reef, and less than a day from the *Old Earth's Pride*."

"Great. I'll send a message to the *Pride* and tell them we're almost there. And how 'bout you, Pete? You holding up?"

"Ma'am, I've never been better. I've just spent two days with the best teacher of navigation I've ever known." Sanchez's voice rose, clear and confident, no trace of its old whine left.

"Keep it up, you two. As far as I'm concerned, you deserve medals."

"Thank you, ma'am." Winin clicked the intercom off.

"Winin, can I ask you a favor?" Sanchez sat up straight in his nav couch, looking straight into the older navigator's eyes.

"You may ask."

"When all this is over, could I study wayfinding with you? This . . . this is *real*. This isn't what they showed me in school. This is what I could never quite get, never quite understand, through all the trips I've navigated." His voice wavered, and he stopped.

Winin stared into the waves, silent for a long time. Then he turned and caught Sanchez's eyes again. "I will, but on one condition."

"What's that?"

"Do you know electronics? That's what I need to learn."

"It's a deal."

The setting sun turned the waves to molten gold beneath the outrigger float, under the canoe's hull. The tiny nav tank that was the Pacific Ocean shook with the laughter of two navigators.

## A Request

If you liked this anthology, please take the time to leave a review on the site where you purchased it and/or on one of the social media reading sites like Goodreads. Tell your friends that you enjoyed it. Suggest it as reading for your local book club. Request it at your local library (or more than one local library). This helps others learn more about the book and gets the word out. Please use the #hemeleinpubs and #tracethestars tags.

Thank you for your time, and thank you for reading this book!

Find more exciting books to read at hemelein.com.

**HEMELEIN PUBLICATIONS**

# Acknowledgments

I have a lot of people to thank for *Trace the Stars* being realized. One of the biggest is Marion K. "Doc" Smith, to whom this anthology is dedicated. You can read more about his influence in the Foreword.

Dave Butler, Jeffrey Creer, and Douglas Cootey were great sounding boards for all my crazy ideas. Dave Doering and Marny Parkin believed in this idea and helped with various political aspects in getting it going. Thanks to Steve Setzer, Dave Butler, and Sandi Monson for checking over some tricky legal stuff to make sure it was clear and worded correctly.

Thanks to Jaleta Clegg for being crazy enough to agree to co-edit this volume with me. I appreciate your experience, insight, suggestions, thoughts, and hard work. I hope someone with loads of money recognizes what a great editor and author you are.

Thanks to Rachel Heaps for guiding me through the perils of the L. Tom Perry Special Collections section of the Harold B. Lee Library at Brigham Young University. I wouldn't have made it without your help. I also appreciate the help of Cindy Brightenburg and Trevor Casper at Special Collections. I found some useful information there.

I really appreciate the overwhelming response when we put out the call for submissions. While we would have loved to do so, we couldn't include every story submitted. All of the authors who submitted stories believe in the symposium and its mission to help train current and up-and-coming writers, artists, editors, and other professionals in the many science fiction, fantasy, horror, and alternate history fields. Thank you for being willing to donate your story.

All the authors whose stories were selected were wonderful to work with. I'm still learning all the ropes as an editor, and all of you were very patient with me. Thank you, Kevin, Beth, Jaleta, David, Daniel, Nancy, Paul, Megan, Wulf, John, Emily, Eric, Eric (yes, there are two of them), Sandra, Brad, Julia, and James. You are a credit to writers everywhere.

Thank you to Kevin Wasden for donating your amazing painting for the cover art. It's everything cover art should be for a collection of space opera and hard science fiction. I hope to use your work again in the future.

If I missed anyone who should have been thanked, I apologize, ask for your forgiveness, and thank you.

Finally, I express appreciation to Heather, Ian, and Chiemi. Thank you for your patience, thanks for putting up with me, and thank you for your love and support. You are all wonderful.

—Joe Monson

I owe a big thanks to Joe Monson for inviting me to work on this anthology with him. It's been an honor and a privilege. I didn't know Doc Smith very well, but his legacy lives on in the people he touched and the stories he inspired. This anthology is for him.

Thank you to the authors who submitted stories. Without you, we wouldn't have an anthology. Your stories are full of wonder and angst and joy and pain and all the emotions that make us human.

Thank you to Kevin Wasden for the gorgeous cover art. It doesn't take much to make an awesome cover when you have such high quality art to work with.

And thank you to the fans and readers. Without you, our stories would be pointless.

—Jaleta Clegg

# About the Contributors

Kevin J. Anderson has published more than 140 books, 56 of which have been national or international bestsellers. He has written numerous novels in the *Star Wars, X-Files,* and *Dune* universes, as well as unique steampunk fantasy novels *Clockwork Angels* and *Clockwork Lives,* written with legendary rock drummer Neil Peart, based on the concept album by the band Rush.

His original works include the *Saga of Seven Suns* series, the *Terra Incognita* fantasy trilogy, the *Saga of Shadows* trilogy, and his humorous horror series featuring Dan Shamble, Zombie PI. He has edited numerous anthologies, written comics and games, and the lyrics to two rock CDs. Anderson and his wife Rebecca Moesta are the publishers of WordFire Press. Find him online at wordfirepress.com.

Beth Buck saw her first episode of *Star Trek* in second grade and has had stars in her eyes ever since. Her notebooks from middle school on are full of short stories and beginnings of novels set on space ships and alien planets, with time travel, intergalactic war, and adolescent inter-species romance.

Foolishly, she chose not to major in creative writing college because she wasn't sure she would be able to do something that fun in real life. She should have had an inkling that it was something she should be doing when she spent nearly all of her semester abroad in Egypt working on her (as yet unpublished) novel instead of doing her Arabic translation homework. When she realized her senior year that she loved writing and loathed translating Arabic newspapers, she began to suspect that she was in the wrong line of work but by then it was too late to switch majors.

It took another couple of years and a few kids before she had her Isaac-Newton-style epiphany that yes, writing is something she could do in real life. After that, she jumped in with both feet. Since then, she has published several short stories, a couple of personal essays, over 60 articles on emergency preparedness, and has a middle grade serial called "Faith and Patience" in progress. Maybe she might even get that novel published.

In addition to her writing pursuits, Beth is the acquisitions director for Immortal Works Press and presents at writing conferences around Utah. When she's not writing, she spins on her spinning wheel, practices Shaolin Kempo, and commands her small army of children. Visit her blog at bethbuckauthor.wordpress.com or follow her on twitter @ithilien19.

JALETA CLEGG was born some time ago and has filled the years since with plenty of make-believe. She writes science fiction adventure, fantasy of all flavors, and silly horror. When not writing, she enjoys playing with yarn, cooking weird vegetables, designing costumes and quilts, and generally messing around. You can find more about her at jaletac.com

DAVID FARLAND is a *New York Times* bestselling science fiction and fantasy writer with more than fifty novels to his credit. He works as the lead judge for one of the world's largest science fiction writing contests, the *L. Ron Hubbard Presents Writers and Illustrators of the Future*, and has helped mentor dozens of writers who have gone on to become *New York Times* best-sellers—people like Brandon Sanderson, Stephenie Meyer, and James Dashner. Dave lives in Saint George, Utah with his wife and family, where he is currently working on his next book. You can find out more about him at mystorydoctor.com.

DANIEL CRAIG FRIEND lives with his family in Provo, Utah, where he works as a freelance SF/F editor. He has edited stories for Dan Wells, Mary Robinette Kowal, Dave Butler, Frank Herbert, Robison Wells, Brian McClellan, and Writers of the Future winner Amy Hughes. Presenting at *LTUE* is a yearly professional highlight, and being included in this anthology is a great honor. You can engage his editing services at http://dcfeditor.wixsite.com/dcfeditor.

Nancy Fulda is a past Hugo and Nebula Nominee, a Phobos Award winner and a Vera Hinckley Mayhew Award recipient. She is also a recipient of the Jim Baen Memorial Award, which was created to honor the role played by science fiction in advancing real science. She has been a featured writer at *Apex Online* and a guest on the *Writing Excuses* podcast, and is a previous member of both SFWA and the Villa Diodati Writers' Workshop. She has written on request for David Brin, Tor Books, and MIT's *Technology Review*, as well as for the *Dark Expanse* space strategy game.

Her most influential work, "Movement", was a nominee for the BSFA, Hugo, and Nebula awards, and received the Asimov's Reader's Choice award in 2012. Other works of note include "Recollection", which tells the story of a recovering dementia patient struggling to reconnect with his family, and "Planetbound", which... well, that one you'd just better read for yourself. Her other fiction has appeared in *Asimov's Science Fiction Magazine, Analog Science Fiction and Fact, Daily Science Fiction,* and other venues. Reprints are available on Amazon.

Nancy earned both a Bachelor's and Master's Degree from Brigham Young University. She graduated with university honors, and her research on multi-agent systems and common-sense understanding for robotics has been presented at several IEEE conferences as well as the 2017 Conference on Robot Learning. From 2005 to 2010, she worked as an assistant editor of *Jim Baen's Universe,* one of the highest-paying speculative fiction markets of its time. From 2008 to 2009 she was the website content editor for the Science Fiction and Fantasy Writers of America, and until 2016 she was the owner, manager and chief web developer of Anthology-Builder.com. In 2018, she led a research team as part of Amazon's prestigious Alexa Prize challenge, a university competition to advance A.I.

Her approach to life includes a strong dose of optimism and a generous sprinkling of humor. During her graduate work at Brigham Young University she studied artificial intelligence, machine learning, and quantum computing. In the years since, she has grappled with the far more complex process of raising four small children. All these experiences sometimes infiltrate her writing. You can find Nancy online at nancyfulda.com.

PAUL GENESSE is the bestselling author of the *Iron Dragon* series, including *The Golden Cord*, *The Dragon Hunters*, and *The Secret Empire*. He has sold almost 20 short stories, and is the writer and producer of the *Star Wars* and *Steampunk Rock Operas*. He created and is the editor of the five volumes in the shared multiverse *Crimson Pact* anthology series featuring over half a million words and several *New York Times* bestselling authors.

He lives with his incredibly supportive wife Tammy and their collection of frogs. Find out more about him and download the first ten chapters of *The Golden Cord* for free, listen to podcasts, or watch videos about the *Iron Dragon* series at www.paulgenesse.com. Also, friend him on Facebook and send him pictures of dragons.

M.K. HUTCHINS regularly draws on her background in archaeology when writing fiction. Her YA fantasy novel, *Drift*, was both a Junior Library Guild Selection and a VOYA Top Shelf Honoree. Her short fiction appears in *Podcastle*, *Strange Horizons*, *Orson Scott Card's Intergalactic Medicine Show*, and elsewhere. A long-time Idahoan, she now lives in Utah with her husband and four children. Find her online at mkhutchins.com.

JOE MONSON has worked as a paperboy, hot dog vendor, soda jerk, ice cream maker, busboy, volunteer missionary, teller, notary public, web monkey, content writer and developer, collections manager, convention chair, guest liaison, art show director, newsletter editor, technical support analyst, team lead, website designer, customer service supervisor, network technician, satellite installer, and credit analyst. He currently translates and edits Engineer into English by day and expands the accessible knowledge of the world by night.

Because of his love of reading and books, he decided to get back into collecting amazing short works and sharing them with the world. His first anthology is *Trace the Stars* (co-edited with Jaleta Clegg), full of hard science fiction and space opera goodness. *A Dragon and Her Girl*, an adventure fantasy anthology also co-edited with Clegg, will come out in February 2020. A humorous military SF and space opera anthology, *Join the Space Force Now!*, is scheduled for June 2019.

Joe recently started writing short stories again, and the first appears in the Immortal Works anthology, *All Made of Hinges*. He also has a space opera adventure series in the works. He collects science fiction and fantasy art, but not as much as Paul (as if that was even possible). He lives in the top of the mountains with his wife, two children, and their pet library. Learn more about him at joemonson.com.

WULF MOON feasted on fantasy as a child when he lived with his Chippewa grandmother. He begged stories from her every night and usually got his wish—fireside tales that fired his imagination. If Moon had a time machine, those are the days he would go back to. Since he doesn't have a time machine, he tells his own stories.

His story, "The Last Ray of Light", won the Scholastic Art & Writing Awards national competition and became his first professional sale. It was subsequently published in the May 18, 1978 issue of *Science World*. He's had the privilege of being represented by Donald Maass, selling to a *Star Trek* anthology, writing the conclusion to one of Nora Roberts' romance novellas, and being published in numerous anthologies.

He recently won Second Place in the 2018 fourth quarter *L. Ron Hubbard Writers of the Future* contest. Learn more at driftweave.com.

Motivated by his lifelong love of reading, JOHN M. OLSEN writes about ordinary people doing extraordinary things and hopes to entertain and inspire others. His father's library started him on this journey as a teenager, and he now owns and expands that library to pass his passion on to the next generation of avid readers.

He loves to create things, whether writing novels or short stories or working in his secret lair equipped with dangerous power tools. In all cases, he applies engineering principles and processes to the task at hand, often in unpredictable ways with unusual results. He usually prefers "Renaissance Man" to "Mad Scientist" as a goal and aesthetic. It's a relief you don't have to be good at something to enjoy it, as witnessed by John's meager skills playing a ukulele he built just because he could.

You can often find him at writing events and comic conventions in and around Utah where he sometimes breaks out steampunk costuming. While there, he hawks a range of anthologies and novels spanning multiple genres. He is an award-winning author, having won first place in the Dragon Comet short story contest in 2018.

He lives in Utah with his lovely wife and a variable number of mostly grown children and a constantly changing subset of extended family. His website is johnmolsen.blogspot.com.

EMILY MARTHA SORENSEN writes clean fantasy adventures with clever characters, fun plots, and lots of humor. Her bestselling book is *Dragon's Egg*, about a baby dragon and his human parents; her second most popular book is *Black Magic Academy*, about a good witch who gets sent to a school for fairy tale wicked witches. Four of her other series are about a magical girl turned villain, a chatterbox who's trying not to become a child of prophecy, a Regency fantasy in which magic is forbidden and the main character has it anyway, and a teenage werevulture who clearly has to save the day. Basically, if it's clean, and it's fantasy, she probably wants to write it.

She runs a newsletter called *Clean Fantasy Reads*, which showcases three clean fantasy books every Monday. You can join the newsletter at emilymarthasorensen.com/cleanfantasyreads.html.

ERIC JAMES STONE is a Nebula Award winner, Hugo Award nominee, and winner in the Writers of the Future Contest. He has had stories published in *Year's Best SF 15*, *Analog*, *Nature*, and Kevin J. Anderson's *Blood Lite* anthologies, among other venues. His debut novel, a science fiction thriller titled *Unforgettable*, was published by Baen in January 2016.

One of Eric's earliest memories is of seeing an Apollo moon-shot launch on television. That might explain his fascination with space travel. His father's collection of old science fiction ensured that Eric grew up on a full diet of Asimov, Heinlein and Clarke.

While getting his political science degree at Brigham Young University, Eric took creative writing classes. He wrote several short stories, and even submitted one for publication, but after it was rejected he gave up on creative writing for a decade.

During those years Eric, graduated from Baylor Law School, worked on a congressional campaign, and took a job in Washington, D.C., with one of those special interest groups politicians always complain that other politicians are influenced by. He quit the political scene in 1999 to work as a web developer in Utah.

In 2002 he started writing fiction again, and in 2003 he attended Orson Scott Card's Literary Boot Camp. In 2007 Eric got laid off from his day job just in time to go to the Odyssey Writing Workshop. He has since found a new web development job.

Eric lives in Utah with his wife, Darci, and their children, Honor and Link. His website is ericjamesstone.com.

ERIC G. SWEDIN is a Professor of History at Weber State University. He has a doctorate in the history of science and technology. His publications include numerous articles, six history books, four science fiction novels, and a historical mystery novel. His novel, *When Angels Wept: A What-If History of the Cuban Missile Crisis*, won the 2010 Sidewise Award for Alternate History. Eric lives with his family in a house built in 1881. His website is swedin.org.

SANDRA TAYLER is a writer of essays, picture books, speculative fiction, and blog entries. Her short fiction has appeared in Daw anthologies and the Mormon Lit Blitz. He has released two picture books, *Hold on to Your Horses* and *Strength of Wild Horses*.

Sandra's day job is being the editor, publisher, and business manager for the *Schlock Mercenary* comic strip. This includes tasks ranging from weekly bookkeeping to sorting and shipping out hundreds of items at a time. Her most recent projects have been several short graphic stories that were featured in *Schlock Mercenary* books and the *Planet Mercenary* RPG book.

When she is not working, Sandra spends time with her house, her four kids, and her cartoonist husband, Howard Tayler. She also seems to have acquired three cats, which wasn't in the plan at all. She can be found online at onecobble.com or on Twitter @SandraTayler.

BRAD R. TORGERSEN'S award-winning, award-nominated science fiction has appeared in numerous magazines and anthologies. A veteran and Chief Warrant Officer in the United States Army Reserve, Brad has also served in half a dozen different countries.

His latest novel, *A Star-Wheeled Sky*, is a military space opera with hard SF leanings, was released by Baen in December 2018. His latest short work—a novella titled "Scrith"—was released in February 2019 in the fifteenth volume of bestseller Larry Niven's *Man-Kzin Wars* shared universe series.

Married for 25 years to his very first audio narrator, Brad lives with his family in the Intermountain West. He can be found most often at his Facebook page, and occasionally writes non-fiction for both his personal blog, and the *Mad Genius Club* group blog. A political Classical Liberal, Brad believes in having an open mind, so long as you don't let your brains fall out. Find him online at bradrtorgersen.com.

KEVIN WASDEN works as the director of professional development at Gibbs Smith Education. He was previously a teacher, the dean of culture, and the principal at Venture High School, where he used a unique blend of experiential education, community building, and character development in order to help students become moral scholars and community stewards. He received his master's of education in leadership and administrative development from Southern Utah University. He is also an advocate of creativity in education (and life!) and enjoys speaking to youth, writers, artists, and educators.

He is the co-creator and illustrator of the sci-fi adventure series, *Hazzardous Universe*. He also developed and illustrates the independent comic series, *Technosaurs*. His artwork graces this volume, as well as *Trace the Stars*, the first volume in the LTUE Benefit Anthology series.

Learn more at kevinwasden.blogspot.com.

As writers seem to do, JULIA H. WEST has held many arcane jobs. When she was a quality control technician for ultrasound heart machines, video recordings of cross sections of her heart were shipped all over the world with the machines. She's also been a genealogical researcher, an office manager, a secretary, a desktop publisher, a digger at an archaeological dig, a quality assurance tech, a webmaster, an aircraft electrician (and aircraft battle damage repair instructor) for the Air Force Reserves, and a keyer for the United States Post Office.

Julia loves music, and sings with the Utah Filk Organization (that's not a typo: filk is music of the science fiction and fantasy community). She was a founding member of the Salt Lake City, Utah chapter of the Society for Creative Anachronism and still enjoys researching medieval culture. She was active in the Science Fiction and Fantasy Writers of America for over ten years, and was awarded the Service to SFWA Award for work on the Nebula Award reports.

Julia graduated Magna Cum Laude from the University of Utah with a BA in Anthropology. When people asked her what she would do with the degree, she'd tell them, "Write science fiction." Many of her stories incorporate fascinating bits of culture she discovered while studying. She has had fantasy and science fiction stories published in a number of magazines—including *Realms of Fantasy, Oceans of the Mind, Spider,* and *The Friend*—and anthologies, including *Sword and Sorceress* and *Lace and Blade.* She also sold a fantasy poem to *Enchanted Conversation.* Many of her stories are now available as ebooks from Amazon and other distributors.

West Jordan, Utah has been Julia's home for over 30 years. She lives with her husband, two daughters, and far too many Cat Overlords. Her website is at juliahwest.com.

Born with the unfortunate talent of lying, JAMES WYMORE spent his youth explaining things he said before thinking. Gaining a kind of fame, people remembered him best for stretching the bounds of believability beyond breaking. His friends often benefitted from games or play time which incorporated these fantastic stories. However, family members usually just rolled their eyes and went on with what they were doing.

Taking the role of Charlatan to expert level, James pursued science and philosophy to better justify the ideas he created. Pushing theories and technology past their limits, he found plenty of safe space where nobody could contradict him. Or, if that didn't work, he'd just say, "It's magic." Eventually, he realized stories justify untruth with meaning. His efforts to become an astronaut, surgeon, dark wizard, and spy were all wasted. In the end, those credentials didn't have any significance. People will forgive any disbelief for a good ending.

In addition to having over thirty short stories published, James has edited six anthologies—*The Actuator: Borderlands Anthology, The Actuator 3: Chaos Chronicles, Windows into Hell, Choose Your Own Apocalypse, Mormon Steampunk: All Made of Hinges,* and *Backward Everything's*. He also acquired eighteen books for two different presses. His stand-alone novels represent the full spectrum of genres—*Theocracide, Exacting Essence, Salvation, Schism,* and *Thug #1*. Finally, the bestselling *Actuator* series includes work by 25 authors in every fiction genre and uniquely blends all the major tropes of genre fiction.

Find all the stories at jameswymore.wordpress.com.

# Additional Copyright Information

www.ingramcontent.com/pod-product-compliance
Lightning Source LLC
Chambersburg PA
CBHW050140120726
47903CB00002B/428